Secret Relations

ANNABEL DILKE

St. Martin's Griffin

New York

This is a work of fiction. All of the characters, organizations, and events portrayed in this novel are either products of the author's imagination or are used fictitiously.

www.stmartins.com

Library of Congress Cataloging-in-Publication Data

Dilke, Annabel.
 Secret relations / Annabel Dilke.
  p. cm.
 ISBN-13: 978-0-312-37866-0
 ISBN-10: 0-312-37866-1
 1. Upper class families—England—Fiction. 2. Cousins—Fiction.
3. Domestic fiction. 4. Psychological fiction. I. Title.

PR6054.I388 S43 2007
823'.914—dc22

           2006051215

First published in Great Britain by Pocket Books,
an imprint of Simon & Schuster UK Ltd

First St. Martin's Griffin Edition: March 2008

10 9 8 7 6 5 4 3 2 1

Praise for *The Inheritance*

"Marvellous novel . . . really first class. Authentic and sharp, every word rings true. And a terrific plot! A winner."
—Rosamunde Pilcher

"I loved this book. Exquisitely written and a lovely, absorbing story."
—Elizabeth Buchan

"A splendidly observed tale of love and infidelity in which each character reaches out for their own share of happiness."
—*Woman & Home*

"Charming, delicious, irresistible, Annabel Dilke's characters are wonderfully eccentric, beautifully drawn, and very real. When I finished the book I was sorry to leave them."   —Santa Montefiore

"If it's fiction you're really after, you could do no better than Annabel Dilke's *The Inheritance*. Anyone waiting for the new Penny Vincenzi should try this novel, as you won't be disappointed. The members of the self-destructive Chandler family are so well drawn that you wish you could jump in and steer them away from their inevitable downfall. It's not easy being rich, beautiful, and privileged. It *is* easy to read such a well-written book about it."   —*Bookseller*

"All the relationships in this novel are as painful as they are believable . . . a compelling psychological drama."
—*Times Literary Supplement*

"A cautionary tale of wealth and privilege taken for granted and suddenly taken away, leaving a family to reassess their values. Luxuriate in their wealth, sympathize with their loss. A very human story with a cast of likeable characters."   —*Telegraph & Argus*

Also by Annabel Dilke

The Inheritance

Acknowledgments

Thanks, as always, to my daughter Sasha for her terrific support and advice; to my friends John Crowley, John and Caroline Weeks and Lorna Vestey for help on various matters; to Bill Hamilton and Sara Fisher at A.M. Heath; Suzanne Baboneau and Melissa Weatherill at Simon & Schuster, and Rumi Ebert and Trader Faulkner for being so supportive.

For my mother,
Alice Mary, with love

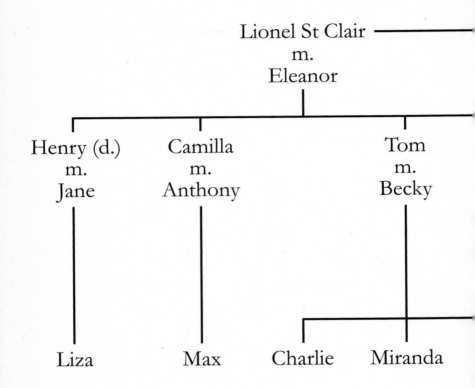

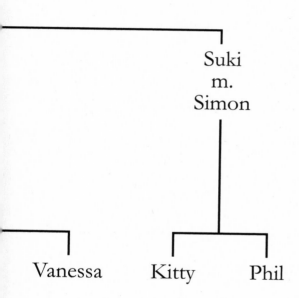

Hector St Clair

Suki
m.
Simon

Vanessa   Kitty   Phil

 Chapter One

Two first cousins were reclining in their best clothes on a high stack of dusty hay-bales and looking out through the open shutters of an old barn at a garden on the far side of a meadow. From their viewpoint, the lawn in the garden – backcloth to a swelling number of figures – appeared uniform emerald and the redbrick manor house set behind it diminutive like a toy.

The barn was still stuffed with heat and the sweet smell of hay. It had felt wonderful to fling open the stiff shutters to dazzling light. If it weren't for Max, they'd be in the garden now, fielding personal questions, pretending to be pleased to see distant family members. They'd been visiting this favourite place all of their lives, but it was only seven years since they'd been regarded as adult enough to join in the ritual of the summer party.

'Remember when you jumped on that pitchfork?' asked Kitty with a smile.

Charlie looked strangely happy, understanding that she was reminding him of a time when life had seemed simple, with even the bad bits bringing them closer. The accident had been thirteen years ago when they were ten. 'Jump!' Liza (of course!) had shrieked and, obediently, Charlie had leapt into six foot of space above a deep, innocent-looking mass of hay. All of them had turned ashen at the sight of his pain, and Liza had cried hardest. But it was Kitty who'd comforted him and messed up her favourite dress. Uncle Hector had the back seat of his new Daimler spoilt, too, and – once Charlie's knee was stitched and bandaged in hospital – became as fierce as he'd been tender. Charlie could have been killed, he'd told the cousins, and then nobody would ever have been allowed to come and stay with him again. Barns were for storing cattle food, and it ruined hay to be jumped on. One of the innumerable troubles about children, he complained – as usual ending up *con brio* – was that THEY NEVER LISTENED. 'And by the way,' he went on, still appearing stern but moving into joking mode because occasionally it was perfectly acceptable to swear, 'WHO'S GOING TO CLEAN UP MY BLOODY CAR FOR ME?'

'I love this,' said Charlie wistfully. In another seven years, in 1981, he'd be thirty and the prospect of all that he was expected to achieve before then filled him with panic. Kitty had confided that she dreaded the future, too. For her, the pressure was different, of course, though equally intense, she maintained – 'Because of Ma being married at eighteen.'

'What *does* she look like!' Kitty exclaimed suddenly, and they both watched as a third first cousin approached across the meadow. Why was she wearing a voluminous cardigan in blistering June? And, for some reason, both hands were clasped under her stomach.

'He will come, won't he?' said Charlie, as urgently as if they'd been discussing this all along.

'I think so.'

'What did he say exactly? Tell me again, Kit.'

It had been like talking to a helpless child, at first. She found she could still think of Max like that when deprived of the pleasure of seeing him. She'd telephoned late the night before as if — with the tender protectiveness he always brought out in her — she'd divined the exact moment when, finally, his mother had gone to bed.

'You can't not come!'

Silence from the other end.

'It's the party!'

Still no response.

'*We'll* be there, Max!'

She heard him sniff very faintly and dug the nails of her left hand into her palm in sympathy, striving to find the right words.

'We'll have a laugh! We always do!'

The spectre of merriment hovered for a moment before creeping away in shame.

'You don't even need to see anyone else,' Kitty rushed on, mortified with herself. 'We can just stay in the barn.'

'Uncle Hector . . .' Max began miserably.

Kitty had only an hour since given their great-uncle a promise ('I don't want Max told about this conversation,' he'd impressed on her). But now, without compunction, she said, 'Max, Uncle Hector has phoned me specially to say I must make sure you come! And you know what a state he gets into before his party.'

Was he touched? It seemed not. 'Didn't he tell you?' was all he muttered.

'Tell me what?'

'The thing is . . .' His voice tailed away miserably.

'*What*, Max?'

Max sounded desperate, also bewildered. 'He's written to Mummy saying *she* can't come.'

'Oh!' Kitty was really taken aback. This was so unlike Uncle Hector, to whom family was everything, whose kindness was legendary. What had got into him?

'Obviously my father won't be coming to the party now,' Max went on, with an odd new formality. 'But Mummy keeps saying how much she'd been looking forward to it and I don't know if I should . . .' His voice wavered.

'Max!' Kitty told him very firmly. 'Don't you see? What you need is a break from all that! And Uncle Hector's made it possible.'

Then Max had actually said, 'Thanks, Cuz,' in an uncharacteristically heartfelt sort of way. So there was no sense of unease, on her part, about encouraging him to defy his mother – only exhilaration.

'Is Max here?'

'Not yet,' said Kitty, looking down at her cousin Liza.

Liza pouted. She gave the impression that her trip across the meadow had been pointless. The sun gleamed on her naturally curly long pale hair, which had been ironed dead straight for this important family occasion. Rather surprisingly, in common with so many of the other young women at the party, she'd opted for Stepford Wife garb – with a high-necked ankle-length dress under her unsuitable cardigan. She looked a picture of the angelic young relative. 'He is coming, isn't he?'

'Aren't you boiling?'

'Who talked to him?'

'I did,' said Kitty.

Liza's raised eyebrows conveyed much. Now if it had been she who'd spoken to Max instead! Then she asked, 'Have you got any champagne up there?'

'How?' asked Charlie very reasonably, hoping to make Liza feel foolish. Uncle Hector's manservant, Merriweather, was the keeper of the champagne. If they wanted a drink, then obviously they must join the party.

'Can't believe this!' said Liza. In her turn, she could make Charlie and Kitty feel cautious to the point of dull. 'Hang on a sec.' She was about to retrace her path across the meadow then appeared to have a last-minute thought. She lifted up her cardigan and removed something. 'Look after this, will you?' she said very casually.

It was a black and white mongrel puppy, probably no more than three months old. Separated from Liza's warmth and the rhythm of her breathing, it immediately started whimpering.

Kitty put a hand to her mouth and glanced at Charlie.

Dogs were banned from the party. For some mysterious reason, Uncle Hector loathed them. If he got to hear about this, none of them would ever be invited again. In among the benevolence were flashes of alarming strictness. He'd maintain it was about standards. This time Liza had gone too far.

Kitty and Charlie descended the ladder at speed.

'You must be out of your mind!' Charlie told her.

'Isn't it the most darling thing you've ever seen in your whole life?'

'That's not the point!'

'Exactly!' Kitty agreed equally sternly. But when Liza thrust the puppy into her arms, her attitude softened just as Liza had anticipated.

Liza peeled off her cardigan and flung it on the grass and then she told a story of a rescue, with herself as heroine. She'd found the puppy chained to a beggar on Waterloo Bridge, apparently. 'You shouldn't make money out of animals,' she informed her cousins sanctimoniously, even though – torn between the desire to impress them and a profound knowledge of their reactions – she was about to reveal how much she'd paid to secure the dog's freedom.

Charlie was appalled. 'Five quid!' he kept repeating. Unlike Liza, he and Kitty were good with money. 'You're hopeless, Liza! Hopeless!'

Liza moved swiftly on. 'It's such a baby. I couldn't possibly have left it at home on its own.'

'What are you going to do with it when you go out to work?' asked Kitty.

Liza smiled enigmatically. Her mother would look after it, of course. More immediately, she'd not considered what would happen to the puppy when it was time for everyone to assemble for lunch. She hadn't even worked out if it was male or female, she told her cousins very innocently.

However, now that Kitty was taking care of it, she was going to steal a bottle of champagne for them all. After that, she'd be on far more solid ground.

Uncle Hector stood in a pool of noise on the edge of his lawn, welcoming his enormous family. Periodically, he'd let out his distinctive ecstatic roar – the laughter of a convivial very deaf person in some pain. 'HAA-HAA-HAAAA!' No wonder he was radiating such top-volume delight. The capricious barometer had told the truth, for once. His guests could stay in the garden all day, admiring its perfection (rather than seek refuge in his house and ruin his parquet with their stiletto heels). And, after lunch, the string quartet he'd hired would start playing in the gazebo.

But under the genial surface, anxieties nibbled. As usual, there'd been months of preparation and now, at the start of the party, the lawns were properly dense and green, free of dandelions and molehills. True, being pierced by a multitude of stilettos might aerate them, but would his precious grass survive the crush? Then, would the musicians he'd hired be up to scratch? (And how would he know if they weren't?) Most worrying of all, might this be the party that finally caused Merriweather to give in his notice?

And now there was a new concern to be added to the perennial ones – his great-nephew Max. When he thought of Max's parents (of whom, two weeks ago, he'd have maintained he was jolly fond), his nice pink face stiffened into lines of alarming harshness. Selfish was not the word, no! And to compound their crime, they'd GOT THE FAMILY INTO THE NEWSPAPERS – a filthy rag, to render it truly unforgivable.

Uncle Hector's ancient manservant, Merriweather, bound like a mummy in a spotless white apron reaching to his ankles, stood behind a long trestle table bearing ranks of gleaming glasses brimming with champagne. Behind him were barrels full of ice cooling dozens of bottles. He had a grumpy authoritative air, like the temperamental conductor of a super-professional orchestra. All round him hummed an intricate web of young staff brought in for the occasion: stacking silver trays with foaming goblets, scurrying through the crowds, appearing at elbows while adroitly dodging them.

After the guests had been welcomed by Uncle Hector, they made a point of greeting his servant effusively. Hadn't he murmured worriedly to each one, 'You will say hello to Merriweather, won't you?'

Max heard Uncle Hector's laughter in the distance once he'd switched off the engine of the prized green MG his father had given him for his twenty-first. 'HAA-HAA-HAAAA!' It triumphed above a twitter of birdsong and, nearer at hand, the muffled outrage of spaniels and Labradors confined to cars on a wonderful day. It even made him smile, for a change.

But as he prepared to leave the big field where guests were always directed to park, his sense of wellbeing fell away. What was he doing here? For a moment, he really considered driving back to London. But Partridge had seen him.

Uncle Hector's ruddy-faced head gardener was orchestrating the parking, as usual: beckoning on familiar drivers, lining up their expensive vehicles in neat rows, watching expressionlessly as they bade tender farewells. 'I know, it's *mean*. But we've left the windows open, and water. And kind Partridge will keep an eye on you. And when it's time for the Mozart we'll be back to take you for a w-a-l-k.'

'Morning, Partridge.'

'Morning, sir!'

It felt strange to be addressed like that by a much older person. Max thought, 'It's only here I call people by their surnames but it feels okay.' It hadn't happened to him since school (where, of course, it had been totally different). Here, it felt like dressing up: trying on a magnificent robe and gaudy crown that had once belonged to the family for real.

It seemed oddly natural too because, inexplicably and secretly, he'd always thought of this beautiful peaceful place as his. He watched, in very detached fashion, as a French bull terrier stood up in a front seat and started worrying at expensive-looking suede upholstery. He wondered if the other cousins felt the same.

As always, the house's grand rosy presence had come upon him suddenly, just as he believed that he was lost. Both prospect and refuge, it had held a strangely appealing mix of expectation and affection for as long as he could remember. Inside, thrift and generosity ruled in equal measure. Max thought wistfully of leaving the baking forecourt and ducking into the porch, cluttered with objects accorded respect quite incommensurate with their worth – the ancient trug overflowing with tangled twine, the rusty secateurs, the iron shoe-scraper clotted with mud which had once belonged to Uncle Hector's father. If he entered the house's cool stone-flagged interior, he could inhale one of the scents he identified with happiness – a mixture of beeswax from the furniture and the dried lavender heaped in the big blue and white porcelain bowl on the chest in the hall. Maybe he could briefly sit down at the mahogany table in the empty dining-room, or perhaps even run up the highly polished staircase and slide down its banister, pretending to be a child again. For all its bizarre rules – 'Monstrous boy! You've put the grape scissors into the corkscrew compartment *again*!' – this place was deeply soothing.

Always before, he'd looked forward to the family party. Besides the champagne and the salmon, it meant a shared laugh at the most ridiculous of the relatives: Crazy Claude with his stuffed Cullens bags, Droopy Julie with her multitudinous bra straps and thick make-up applied without skill or proper light, hairy-chinned Harriet, author of hilarious Christmas newsletters. ('And there's the dypso and the nympho,' Max's father would remind his family as he turned his Rolls-Royce into the drive leading to the house. 'What's dipso and nimfo?' Max the child had asked in his high-pitched voice. 'Who's the nympho?' his mother had inquired with an odd edge to hers.) There was usually the chance to meet a far-flung relative and be told solemnly (for family should never be mocked): 'THIS IS YOUR FOURTH COUSIN ONCE REMOVED WHO LIVES IN DAKOTA AND IS IN SHIPPING AND KNOWS ALL ABOUT BEGONIAS.' At the same time, there was a puzzling sense of reassurance at being part of an enormous clan (though there were remarkably few people he actually wanted to talk to), even a mystifying desire for approval. Best of all, it was a chance to relax in the company of his three favourite cousins, so close to him in age, who happened to be his very best friends.

But this year was different. Maybe, from now on, every social occasion would be. For the first time in his young life – to his absolute dismay – Max felt like a curiosity.

He took his place in the line of guests snaking across the lawn, waiting to be greeted by Uncle Hector. He told himself that those before and behind, all distant relatives, might not have heard the gossip yet – even though, just a couple of days ago, it had been served up in a waspish paragraph by Nigel Dempster. As he stared at his best black shoes pressing into the turf, he could hear the musicians tuning their instruments in the distant gazebo – raucous murmurings like the scary prelude to an argument.

'Just *look* at the herbaceous border!' sighed a cousin of his mother's, a woman in a homemade hat with a black veil like the netting used to protect soft fruit from birds. Max's father called her 'the fly-catcher', for some reason – he often gave the family names. Then she said: 'Tcch, hip's no better,' and Max followed her glance to his grandfather, hobbling across the grass in the distance.

'Hello Max,' said her husband (dubbed 'the button-manufacturer' by Max's father because his money derived from a majority shareholding in a London department store). 'Family not here?' (Which was a ridiculous way of inquiring about Max's parents, since there was nothing *but* family at this party.)

'Fuck you!' thought Max savagely. It didn't even occur to him that the question might have been well-intentioned.

He said politely, his face quite blank: 'Excuse me.' He'd go in search of his three cousins straight away and say hello to Uncle Hector later on.

But, somehow or other, out of the corner of his eye, Uncle Hector had absorbed this little drama. Immediately, but very courteously, he terminated his own conversation and, with real pleasure in his voice, called: 'Max!'

He didn't embrace his great-nephew – the older members of the family weren't tactile – but he radiated affection. As usual, he propped his huge bulk on a silver-topped stick, which bowed under the strain, and winced every so often as if caught unawares and then laughed even louder. He was never without pain, but didn't believe in complaining, though when guests stayed they could hear groans issuing from his bedroom in the early mornings – a crescendo of anguished mooing, Hector believing himself unheard, railing against fate (and probably galloping inflation, too). During active service in the last war, his right leg had been blown off below the knee by a mine. It was one of the reasons for his great popularity among children. It was a special treat to be allowed to compare the hard pink surface of his artificial leg with the mottled hairiness of the real thing.

'WHERE ARE MY PRUNING SHEARS?' he roared as he tweaked gently at a strand of Max's hair. 'HAA-HAA-HAAA!'

Max lifted his shoulders as if trying to sink into them, hung his head so his long black locks fell over his face like curtains.

'And I suppose that now you're just going to disappear for the whole day with those WRETCHED COUSINS OF YOURS?'

There was sudden panic in Max's dark eyes, which, a moment ago, had seemed quite blank.

'Do whatever you like, dear boy.' Uncle Hector beamed. He touched Max on the shoulder, only to remove his hand immediately as if he'd received an electric shock. 'As long as you DON'T INTERRUPT THE MOZART.'

Then his brow furrowed up with anxiety once more. 'Do remember to say hello to Merriweather, won't you?'

Max passed swiftly and gracefully across the lawn through knots of guests, looking neither to left nor right, hidden by wings of hair, greeting nobody. He knew what was there: tiers of relatives all dressed up and braying at each other, Merriweather being bolshy while a fleet of young waiters did all the work, deckchairs facing the gazebo for afterwards, and an enormous marquee where they'd very soon be summoned. 'I don't want lunch,' thought Max who, only a short time before, had believed himself to be starving.

He heard his name being called and, out of the corner of one eye, registered Kitty's parents.

'Max!' called Kitty's mother, more urgently. He'd have to stop.

He retraced his steps: stood looking down on Aunt Suki and Uncle Simon, sprawling on the grass. They were famously happy. Kitty's mother was wearing a long creamy dress and a straw hat with a garland of artificial pink roses. Kitty's father was stroking her back. Their sixteen-year-old son, Phil, was relaxing within their golden sphere.

'Max,' Aunt Suki repeated, smiling at him in a very friendly sort of way.

'Kitty's asked me to tell you they're waiting for you,' said Uncle Simon, with the same half-comforting, half-worrying mixture of affection and concern. He started tugging at his tie, more peevishly than seriously.

'Okay,' said Max curtly.

'Top secret location, though I have my suspicions. Wherever it is, Phil's banned . . .'

Max glanced at his young cousin, but he didn't look at all put out. Just sixteen, it was the first year he'd been admitted to the party, though he was taking the honour very casually. He lay on the grass in his suit and tie, eyes half slits through which he was observing the girls, a fuzz of dark hair shadowing his upper lip, a glass of champagne within reach. When had Max's life ever been that uncomplicated?

'Have a good time, darling,' said Aunt Suki. And then, as an afterthought, 'Don't forget to say hello to Grandma and Grandpa.'

*

When Max had gone, Simon said: 'Poor little sod.'

Suki sprang to her sister's defence: 'It's not Camilla's fault!'

Simon didn't respond but started stroking her back again. Her sister Camilla was moody and unpredictable, but this had become accepted within the family. Besides, wasn't that paradoxical mixture of coolness and volatility one of the secrets of her legendary appeal?

'Ant must have done *something . . .*'

More silence from Simon, who was very fond of his brother-in-law, Anthony. They all were.

'But . . .' She shook her head, bit her lip, quite unable to repeat the horror of the printed words. And, besides, they never knew when Phil was listening. 'I love Ant,' she said instead, sounding miserable.

'If you believe a word you read in that . . .!'

'There must be *something* in it.'

Simon shrugged.

'I can't understand how they got hold of it anyway.'

Simon didn't answer. In fact, his suspicions about who had alerted the newspaper almost certainly tallied with Suki's.

'You do think it's a . . .?' But again, she couldn't finish the sentence.

Simon smiled at her. In the course of their innumerable conversations about the matter, he'd already said there must be another woman, hadn't he?

But Suki wondered with new uneasiness, 'How can he just shrug it off like that?' She thought of her beautiful and very rich older sister, whose life had always until now seemed so uncomplicated. 'Anyway,' she continued, 'it's Uncle Hector who's outrageous.' But she said it like a momentarily petulant daughter criticizing an adored father.

'Yes, my love.'

'Camilla and I have been coming to this party since we were sixteen!'

'I know, I know . . .'

'If anyone deserves a nice day out, it's her.'

'If you say so . . .'

'What does *he* know about marriage?'

'Very true, my love.'

To be happily married was surely the greatest of good fortunes. '*Lucky old me!*' thought Suki (looking around in vain for wood to touch). '*Ordinary old thing that I am.*' It was this fortunate chance that made her such a favourite of Uncle Hector's. But now – suddenly – there was some secret her husband was not sharing with her. She could tell from his unseeing glances, the unusual restlessness of his body at night. She'd watched, appalled, as her sister's marriage disintegrated. And now suspicion had been ignited where none had ever before existed.

Suki's brother Tom approached across the grass, grave and pink-faced in an expensive but too tight suit: a successful QC specializing in criminal law and bent on enjoying himself with the same savage enthusiasm he applied to the working week, his wife, Becky, trailing behind with two mutinous teenage daughters.

'Good journey?' asked Simon perfunctorily.

'One hour and seventeen minutes door to door,' responded Tom immediately with a satisfied smile, and his daughters, Miranda and Vanessa, exchanged secret glances.

Suki tightened her lips. She and Simon had taken almost two hours to get to Uncle Hector's from Wandsworth – which was closer to the A3 than Bayswater, where Tom lived in some splendour with his family. True, Tom had a new Volvo, as opposed to their old banger; but it was typical of him to turn even a car journey into a competition.

However (she reminded herself) there were more important things to talk about. 'I've seen your Charlie.'

'Good,' said Tom. 'And Max?' He sounded genuinely concerned.

'You just missed him.'

'How is he?' asked Tom's wife, Becky, looking scared. It went with her look of a pale and pretty rabbit. Marriage splits were almost unknown in their family and the vicious nature of this one was affecting them all.

'They'll look after him.'

'Good,' said Tom, very relieved.

And now that major area of family concern was out of the way, they relapsed into normal mode.

'Have you heard about Kitty being accepted by the Bach Choir?' Suki asked her brother (whom she adored), with a fine display of nonchalance.

Tom raised his eyebrows, responded with another question: 'Did Becky tell you Charlie's favourite for the tenancy?' He exuded pride that his son had elected to follow his career path. He'd been able to help, too, through friendship with the head of the chambers where Charlie was serving his pupillage. The law was a real profession, being both solid and remunerative. The family was predominantly legal, with two high court judges – Second Cousin Once Removed James, and his father. He could see their pale panama hats gleaming in the sunlight in the distance. Even Hector had been in the business – running an enormous and very successful firm of solicitors before retiring two years earlier.

'Is that right?' asked Suki gently. Without actually saying so, she managed to convey the concerned message: '*Don't count your chickens just yet . . .*'

Then they brightened as Jane joined the group. They made room for her on the grass – their dear sister-in-law who, since the tragic and sudden death of their brother Henry, must attend family functions as a single and care for her daughter, Liza, on her own.

'You look nice,' said Suki. 'New dress?'

'Yes, it is, actually,' Jane agreed with a shy smile.

'And you've had your hair done, haven't you?' Becky pursued in an indulgent, curious tone.

'Mmm.'

They all studied her. Poor Jane who wasn't invited out so much now: for whom this grand family party was almost certainly *the* social occasion of the year. And yet, at the same time as they applauded any evidence that she was in better spirits, they secretly and guiltily begrudged it because Henry had been dead for barely twelve months. It was unjust, because they, too, were getting on with life though their hearts had been broken also.

'I s'pose your Liza's with the others,' said Becky.

'Oh yes!' Jane's face lit up. She couldn't contain her pride. 'Liza's just auditioned for Mimi in *La Bohème*!'

'Where?' asked Tom curtly.

'An excellent company. They go all over the place.'

'Oh, a *touring* company!' He managed to suggest a wealth of not being impressed. 'Still doing her little jobs on the side, I assume . . .' He went on smiling, seeming very jovial, but wiggling his eyebrows ironically. The unspoken question loomed: '*When is Liza going to sort out her life?*' Then, picking up his wife Becky's frantic eye messages, realizing – too late – that he'd been treating Jane with the same savage affection as his sister, he beamed alarmingly at her. Didn't she understand? He'd paid her a compliment! Jane was one of them: must realize that, beneath the scratchy sibling jostling, he'd do anything for her – anything.

In the barn, four reunited cousins looked at each other with delight and, forgotten for the moment, the puppy wobbled across an uneven bed of hay, wagging its stump of a tail so enthusiastically that it toppled over.

With ceremony, Charlie poured champagne into the four glasses Liza had managed to purloin, too, and they toasted each other.

'*Mimi?*' exclaimed Kitty. 'Wow! You're only a star!'

Liza bowed elaborately to imaginary applause. She'd gone up for the audition out of bravado: even she ruled out success. All the same, she'd long understood that she'd be famous. But while relishing her own ephemeral and fragile triumph, she could be genuinely thrilled for Kitty, who had a nice voice, too, but sang primarily for her own pleasure. 'Speak for yourself!'

'Oh well . . .' In turn, Kitty basked in cousinly congratulations while remaining properly humble. Being accepted by the Bach Choir was nothing, of course, compared to being a future diva. She shared Liza's disappointment that, until her career kicked off, she had to make ends meet working for an agency that specialized in providing home care for the elderly. ('Scurrying round after old biddies,' Uncle Tom called it disapprovingly.)

'As for Charlie!' said Liza.

'Oh, absolutely!' echoed Kitty breathlessly. 'Won't it be wonderful if the chambers let him stay?'

'My dad!' protested Charlie nervously. He wished his father would stop boasting on his account, nagging at him all the time to succeed. Nothing was promised, of course: he should have known better than to relay one casual (and rare) comment on a job well done.

'You know they will, Charlie!'

That left Max, who wasn't clever or talented or enjoying any sort of success; who wasn't pushed by his parents and didn't need to work at all because they were so rich, and was exceptional only on account of his beauty. But he didn't feel excluded or a failure. He felt cherished and safe. He always did, in the company of these favourite cousins.

The puppy started licking his hand and only then did he take in its significance. 'If Uncle Hector . . .' he began very anxiously. Then he caught sight of Liza's naughty face and, all of a sudden, began giggling. He shook with laughter so savage that he might have been crying as he lay on the hay looking up at the blackened bat-haunted beams of the barn roof. Finally he calmed down, though he still snorted occasionally. Then he gave a deep sigh. 'Mmm,' he murmured. He smiled at his cousins and shut his eyes.

Kitty and Charlie exchanged satisfied looks, like proud parents.

Liza was a shameless attention-seeker, and always had been. But she was also a life-enhancer. It was one of the reasons they loved her.

The eldest of the four and by far the most responsible, they'd been sharing a flat together for three months. It had been Kitty's secret plan to get Charlie away from his father. It was amazing, really, that his parents had agreed.

Like a real couple, they discussed the running of their household. More importantly, they shared heartbreak.

He was so comforting to confide in: a friendly voice from the enemy camp, a man with a sensitive soul. They were both too trusting, thought Kitty. Liza and Max played by a different set of rules.

What made a person attractive? She'd stare into the mirror at the sweet and vulnerable face that was so similar to her mother's and think of Max's mad smile that shattered the cold perfection of his features, his startling inky loveliness in the fair-skinned family. He was a man suddenly: the possessor of a physical presence so disturbing that it caused women to gasp and turn in the street. How would it feel to leave that confusion in one's wake? Kitty had to remind herself often that he was still Max: the little cousin she'd known and cherished for all of her life.

'They do have fun together, don't they?' Jane announced to nobody in particular, with an anxious smile. She knew about the puppy, of course. Liza used her charm like a weapon, trading on her position as treasured only child and reminder of a much-missed husband, enlisting her mother as reluctant accomplice. '*How could my daughter have brought a stray mongrel to the party?*' Jane remembered the first time she'd come as Henry's shy young fiancée, tongue-tied by the grandeur and order of the place, the confidence and sheer strength of this family, wondering for the first time, '*How much do I really know this man I love?*'

'In-deed,' said Tom. He managed to pack a wealth of sinister meaning into it. Liza had been ringleader in all sorts of naughtinesses when the cousins were children, like that dreadful business with the pitchfork, which might have injured his Charlie for life or even killed him. Oh, the poor kid had been through it what with her father's death, but once a troublemaker ... Thank goodness it wasn't Liza with whom his son was sharing a flat. In-deed.

At exactly one o'clock, one of Merriweather's minions brought out the beaten brass gong from India kept in the hall and set it up outside the front door. Bong-bong-bo-oong! The sound billowed in metallic waves across the verdant springy lawn and surrounding meadows, shoving at the warm air, bringing back memories of dull tasteless meals forgiven by excellent wine. It was predictably followed by Uncle Hector roaring, 'HURRY UP, HURRY UP! WE HAVEN'T GOT ALL DAY!' Punctuality was crucial in his world. Now his guests were required to head immediately in orderly formation for the marquee and study the enormous intricate place map pinned to one wall. It was like a family tree plotted by a dyslexic – the tiers of living generations all present and correct, but crazily jumbled up, in no order at all.

In fact, the map was the result of weeks of planning. This annual summer party wasn't only a social occasion. Uncle Hector took enormous pains to further burgeoning careers and even attempt to defuse long-standing family feuds.

He could have placed Charlie next to one of the established lawyers, or Kitty (for once) in the orbit of a suitable young man. But just this year – for Max's sake – he'd put all four young cousins together at the end of a long table.

It made it much easier for them not only to disguise the presence of the puppy (asleep once more inside Liza's cardigan) but also to avoid comment on the damp patch on the skirt of Kitty's new dress.

*

They'd not mentioned it once, just as he'd known they wouldn't. Merely by being themselves, his cousins had soothed him. He should relax and stop being so paranoid.

Sitting between Kitty and Charlie, Max observed the gathering surreptitiously through his curtains of hair. Yatter yatter yatter! The hubbub in the marquee was extraordinary, as if Uncle Hector's deafness had spread like an epidemic.

Thank goodness none of his family read papers like the *Daily Mail*. His grandmother – who took *The Times* – called it 'The Moron's Delight', just out of earshot of her cook who had it delivered each day, stacking old copies in the garden room for wrapping bunches of flowers picked for departing guests. How did his grandmother know the newspaper was for morons?, his grandfather would tease her with his poker face.

It was someone at the squash court who'd told Max about the item in Nigel Dempster. 'Any relation?' he'd asked with a disagreeable smile, thrusting the paper in his direction.

Max winced as he recalled reading it (though at the time he'd revealed no emotion whatever). 'A bitter divorce battle looms for property tycoon Anthony Newnham and his society beauty wife Camilla, who's from the influential St Clair family. A source close to Camilla confirms she'll be suing her husband for mental cruelty. No problem finding a suitable lawyer!'

'You mark my words, there'll be a woman involved!' . . . 'Is that mental cruelty, Maude? If that's mental cruelty, we'd all be suing for it!' . . . 'Doesn't do, different worlds' . . . 'She's a tricky girl, for all her looks and charm' . . . 'I pity that poor boy of theirs. Look at him, thin as a rail, white as a sheet' . . . 'Salmon's dry, as usual.

Can't understand why Hector hasn't pensioned off that manservant of his years ago . . .'

The old ones murmured enjoyably among themselves, worrying about fishbones, and the effect asparagus might have on their digestive systems. They prided themselves on not passing judgement, believing that age and experience had conferred wisdom and kindness. It didn't occur to them that the kindest, wisest way of behaving might be to ignore this scandal in the family. It was odd because – weathering their own inevitable patches of marital discord – it had come very naturally to behave as if none of it was happening.

Jane had been placed next to Cousin Claude. It was because she was recognized for her good heart and would make an effort.

Cousin Claude had squandered a sizeable inheritance on litigation, his final ruin precipitated by the decision to sue his own solicitor. Now, bereft of funds, but increasingly knowledgeable on finer points of the law, his pleasure lay in representing himself. He was not a man to cross. An insect in a bought cup of tea could provoke him, or even an overdue train. Hung with plastic bags full of papers, striking terror into the hearts of all those who must hire lawyers, he haunted the law courts, distributing leaflets to bemused passers-by with headings such as 'Update No. 16 on St Clair versus British Railways' or 'Update No. 32 on St Clair versus Lyons Corner House'.

Sitting next to Cousin Claude, trying to ignore his musty unwashed odour, Jane murmured: 'Mmm . . .' and 'How fascinating!' at regular intervals. But, at the same time, she was watching her daughter Liza in the distance.

She was getting over-excited. Jane could tell from her flushed cheeks, the way she tapped Max on the shoulder whenever his attention strayed. He was talking to Kitty now – or rather, listening as she spoke to him. '*Dear Kitty,*' thought Jane fondly.

Claude cut short a discourse on summary judgements, and – for the first time – studied her properly with his gooseberry-coloured eyes magnified by thick spectacles. 'I gather Camilla's not here today . . .'

Max's grandparents, Lionel and Eleanor, sat at the top table either side of Hector. They knew he wouldn't refer to Camilla's marriage problems – just as they'd affected to ignore his shocking and seemingly very uncharacteristic decision to ban their daughter from his party.

Hector disliked using his hearing-aid and often failed to insert it properly, so was unable to hear the murmurings of the old ones further down the table. But Lionel and Eleanor – who could hear them – made a fine show of disregard. They were, after all, Hector's closest kin and the true hub of the intricate wheel of family splayed out in the marquee. The rest – a panoply of graduated cousins – were offshoots from Lionel and Hector's numerous aunts and uncles: fourteen on their father's side, ten on their mother's.

They were mortified by this business with Camilla's marriage: appalled that, by some mysterious means, it had got into the newspapers. Even so, they felt very confident in the way they'd lived and brought up their children. They'd been right to foster competition, pitting one sibling against the next. After all, wasn't it a lifetime of racing neck and neck that had won the two old brothers their marvellous houses, their enviable lifestyles? (Though sometimes the dreadful thought would occur to Eleanor, especially: might their eldest child, Henry, still be alive if he hadn't worked quite so hard?) As for Max, the family would enfold him, providing the same support and comfort they'd shown another grandchild, Liza, in a time of need.

'Thinking of putting in an asparagus bed myself,' said Lionel, who'd been studiously ignoring the friendly glances of Claude, certain overture to the assault that must come. He was not looking forward to it. How could Claude have failed to pick up the family's cardinal rule, which was never under any circumstances to litigate?

Uncle Hector craned forward anxiously, fiddling with his right ear.

Lionel repeated his observation at top volume. He'd said it mostly to tease his brother. Why wouldn't he (a) invest in a hearing-aid that worked and (b) put it in properly? He was stubborn to the point of infuriating. It was like his leg. Why didn't he find a prosthesis that fitted? Spend some money on *himself* for a change?

'Ah!' Hector had managed to read his brother's lips, purple from pottering in his garden in the sun.

'Nice salmon!' shouted Eleanor, who had enjoyed the asparagus if not the fish.

'Takes seven years,' said Hector, shaking his head dolefully. If Lionel wished to compete on this score, too, he must understand the nurture and patience necessary before the first fragile green spears appeared. Such tender perseverance came naturally for him. Seeing his magnificent house and garden, nobody would guess at the ruin and wilderness they'd once been. It was a triumph, like the relationships he'd forged with his brother's children and grandchildren, creating an atmosphere where trust became natural and even the sternness was comforting.

This year, his party seemed more than ever like a patch of calm in the midst of chaos and madness: a celebration of family and all that mattered most. But the way the country was going, he wondered how much longer it would be possible to finance it – especially as, unlike Lionel, he was retired now. That fool Heath had made a pig's ear of things and now Labour was back, which would not be good for such as him. God only knew how they'd all got through the past months of strikes and blackouts and three-day weeks and even the threat of petrol rationing. 'The gravest situation by far since the end of the war,' the dying Conservative government had called it. Rich and poor alike had been forced to draw in their horns. But family was family and all the more precious when you were unmarried and childless yourself.

Once coffee had been served, the guests drifted out of the marquee and took up their places on the lawns once more. The sun beat down and those who'd brought parasols congratulated themselves.

'Thank you so much!' they told Merriweather very enthusiastically as they passed him by. He received it all in his taciturn fashion, while making it clear that – though he was actually two years older than his employer – he could hear every word.

It rankled that, for all his legendary generosity to family, his employer hadn't given him a rise for ten years now. Housekeeping money had become sadly impoverished, necessitating what Merriweather (who was ex-Army catering corps) mysteriously referred to as 'make and do'. To make matters worse, the tipping was inadequate. Most of these people appeared to believe it was demeaning. When they stayed the weekend, they offered the minimum, usually in an envelope so that each side could pretend it was something else ('Splendid weekend, Merriweather, erm, splendid . . .'). Occasionally – to his outrage – women guests offered pots of their homemade preserves instead.

The sun cast dappled shadows under the enormous cedar tree at the end of the garden as Uncle Hector took up his familiar position next to the gazebo, where four intense young musicians waited. An expectant hush fell, although everyone knew exactly what he was going to say and some had even started sloping off.

'NOT EVERYONE'S CIVILIZED,' boomed Uncle Hector, and delighted laughter fluttered round the prinked-up garden. 'IF YOU'RE THINKING ABOUT WALKING YOUR WRETCHED DOGS, PLEASE DO IT NOW!' The cousins heard him as they lay on the hay-bales in the barn and looked at each other and smiled.

The puppy had woken up during the strawberries and cream and urinated again – this time, with pleasing justice, over its new owner. It had started moving around inside Liza's cardigan and making increasingly noisy yapping sounds – though her response was to become even louder, as if trying to draw attention to herself.

'Gotta get out of here,' Max had said grimly. And, somehow or other, huddled together, they'd managed to escape from the marquee without detection.

They were comatose after the champagne, touched, despite themselves, by the beauty of the music floating across the meadow and finding amusement – as always – in the strange anachronism of the occasion.

'NOT EVERYONE'S CIVILIZED . . . DO REMEMBER
TO SAY HELLO TO MERRIWEATHER . . .' Max sounded
astonishingly like Uncle Hector. Then he mimicked the guests:
'Hello Merriweather. You must give me your recipe for treacle
sponge . . . Nettles and dock leaves! My word, how ingenious!'

'Your poor ma,' Charlie told Liza. 'I was watching her at
lunch.'

'She's always put next to Crazy Claude.' Liza went on,
sounding unconvinced: 'Maybe Grandpa'll manage to escape
him this year.'

The cousins could picture their grandfather as vividly as if
they were seated on the lawns in deckchairs with all the other
guests, instead of hidden away up here in the barn. His panama
hat would be tipped over his eyes as he tried to concentrate on
the music and block out the looming threat of Claude with his
drifting odour of personal neglect, his ridiculous accumulation
of papers. Because they'd seen it so many times before, they
could envisage Uncle Hector, too: sitting in pride of place in the
front row, moving his big bald head in perfect time to the
Mozart. But not the female violinist who was closing her eyes
in soppy ecstasy, making the young ones chew their lips and
study the grass intently.

For the sake of his family, Uncle Hector hoped the musician
was remarkable. For years now, he'd selected the same three
pieces – The Hunt, The Dissonance and The Hoffmeister –
and, thanks to a stopwatch (a thoughtful present from Camilla's
husband, Anthony), was able, from the first peremptory dart of
the leading bow, to identify the faint strains seeping through
layers of deafness. Once, as a very young man, he'd heard these
compositions performed by one of the world's finest quartets
in the most perfect of acoustic conditions, the Musikverein in

Vienna. Years later — far richer in one sense, maddeningly poorer in another — he comforted himself by conjuring up that matchless performance (and arguably enjoyed sweeter music than any of his guests).

Lying on her back with her eyes shut, Kitty experienced each floating strand of melody as powerfully as if it were being stroked on to her body. The notes coaxed from the distant instruments snipped at the velvet peace of the countryside and lingered, as fleeting and confusing as the day's happiness. '*I know who I am, when I'm here,*' thought Kitty. For wasn't that what this annual ritual, this gathering up of the clan, was all about? '*But as soon as I leave this place and these people, why am I perceived so differently?*'

When the party was over, all of them would have to return to real life.

 Chapter Two

Max opened his front door very quietly, thinking how much he hated London – and Belgravia especially. He'd noticed that the air definitely changed after Kingston, despite Richmond Park and its acres of woodland speckled with patches of deer.

His cousins had tried to persuade him to have supper with them. 'You can name the pup,' bribed Liza.

'Can't.' Mouth already dry at the prospect of going home, he'd sounded as if staying in their company was the very last thing he desired. Then he'd murmured almost inaudibly, 'Trigger.'

It was the housekeeper's evening off, so he could smell only polish and bleach overlaid with the stale fug of cigarettes. When Philomena had been cooking the English dishes his mother requested, there was always a whiff of spice, like a postcard from a homesick traveller.

The smell of fresh flowers was missing from the house, too: the heavy metallic scent of his mother's favourite white freesias dwarfing the subtle company of yellow roses that lasted just a few days. Usually there were big displays everywhere. But flower arranging required concentration and serenity.

'Is that you, Max?' his mother called. Who else did she think it might be? Not his father, surely, after the things she'd said. She was always in the softly lit drawing-room at this time of the evening, the drinks hour.

She was still cross, thought Max with dread, otherwise she'd have called him 'darling'. Well, what did he expect, after the way they'd parted that morning? Himself, for once in his life, shutting his ears to her, striding out of the house in tears, resolutely concentrating on the memory of Kitty's sweet concerned voice – '*What you need is a break from all that . . .*'

'Yes,' he agreed gruffly from the hall as he chucked his keys on to the tray offered up by the four-foot china blackamoor that had been there for as long as he could remember. The ritual was oddly comforting. Turbaned with minute white specks in his eyes where the varnish had cracked, the blackamoor guarded the thickly carpeted entrance, the secrets of this grand antiseptic house set in a square, metal grilles on its windows, far too big for three people (four with Philomena), artificially lit because the sun never reached it, with no garden except for a communal one to be entered with a key. They had a house in Gloucestershire, too, but it was even less to Max's taste. He knew how country houses should be: gently crumbling, guarded by ageing and increasingly autocratic servants, where it was considered feeble to notice the extreme cold or the saggy bony

furniture, and the wind howled down chimneys, ruffling deep
beds of wood ash, and twigs tapped like bossy ghosts on the
panes of your bedroom window at night. Interior designers
were regarded as charlatans there, and buying a new carpet seen
as an admission that the old one had been of inferior quality.

'Come and tell me about it,' he heard his mother say and, for
one crazy moment before he entered the drawing-room, he
believed everything would be all right.

She was arranged on one of the blue and white *toile de joie*
patterned sofas that always looked to him as if they'd been
inflated with a bicycle pump. At least she was dressed and made-
up (he'd had a lurking terror she might still be in her nightdress).
Max bent to kiss her. As he feared, she smelt of gin, too. He
asked coldly as if he couldn't care less, 'Haven't you been out?'
As he spoke, he kept his eyes fixed on the big photograph
leaning on the black mirror surface of the grand piano that was
never played: a dreamy creamy bare-shouldered portrait by
Lenare of a beauty in pearls even younger than he. It was his
favourite. There was a copy in his grandparents' house, as
prominently displayed as the cricketing and sailing cups
gathered up by his uncles.

There were no photographs of his father. His mother had
removed them all.

It was painful to remember his parents together at this
time: his mother freshly scented after her bath, pretty and
vivacious; his father like a machine in need of oil as he drank
one whisky fast, the second slow. There was always a mystery
ingredient – a frightening sense of the two of them hovering,
even as they joked and flirted, on the brink of something
perilous. Max would strive to please and, childishly, to
interrupt this disconcerting dialogue. And then the three of

them would eat in the dining-room with candles and mats and flowers and Philomena's roast chicken smelling of turmeric with onions in stodgy cheese sauce scented with nutmeg.

'I wasn't invited,' said his mother. She laughed without mirth. 'Don't say you've forgotten.'

Max put up a hand as if to protect himself. He could feel his guts contract with dread. 'Oh, Mummy!'

'*You've* been drinking champagne, having a whale of a time.'

'Oh, Mummy!'

'But I've had to stay here all day on my own.'

'Well, you could've . . .'

'What?' she demanded in the aggressive way that terrified him.

'I dunno,' he muttered, hanging his head.

'It's not my fault, darling.'

'I know, Mummy,' he agreed, sounding as miserably puzzled as she. Strangely, these glimpses of terror and softness affected him more than the sudden anger.

'I'm sorry, darling, I've had a lousy day. But who do I love best in the whole world?'

'Me,' said Max in a little voice like a child's.

'Who's the only man I ever want to be with?'

At these moments, he longed for a sibling to share in the confusion and guilt, make him feel less of a traitor for the odd critical thought.

It was a fortnight since his father had left the house. They should have eaten their usual Sunday supper of omelettes spiced with saffron. Instead, china had been broken. Max had heard his mother shriek like an animal as the first plate went and then he'd headed blindly for his bedroom at the top of the house. He'd contemplated putting on a record at top volume. He'd pretended not to hear when his father came knocking on his door.

'Max! Max! Let me in!'

There was a long scratch running down his father's cheek, beads of scarlet blood flowering from it. In a distressing way, it had suited his dark good looks. He didn't mention the wound, but neither did Max. He'd stared at him as if confident that, schooled in the ways of the family, Max would understand what was expected with nothing needing to be spelt out.

Finally, he said, 'Max, I have to go now.'

'Okay,' Max had muttered.

'I'll be at my club if you need me.'

'Okay.'

His father had scribbled a number on a piece of paper. 'Here. You can always leave a message.'

'Daddy?'

'Yes, Max?' his father had inquired very tenderly.

'Nothing,' said Max, like a sulky child snatching back a toy.

Then his father said softly: 'Look after your mother.'

But afterwards Max thought he must have imagined this. After all, he'd been left to cope alone, without apology. What sort of a father could do that?

As if reading his mind, his mother commented with bitter amusement: 'He's a shit, darling.' Her mood had shifted. Who knew how the evening might end?

Max often swore, but hated to hear her do the same. He stared at his shoes. Wisps of hay were caught in his turn-ups, he noticed. He thought of his cousins at their flat in Chepstow Place, laughing and playing with the puppy. At twenty-two, he shouldn't still be living at home. But, even before his father had left, his mother had protested with an edge to her laughter, 'Who would I talk to, Max?' and he'd been flattered at the same time as feeling increasingly suffocated.

'A bastard and a hypocrite.' She paused as if trying to control herself. 'I suppose everyone was talking about me . . .'

'Dunno,' muttered Max. Uncle Hector had given his hand a reassuring squeeze as he said goodbye. 'Lovely to see you, dear old chap. Come for a weekend very soon. We'll rustle up those cousins of yours.' Max loved the way Uncle Hector used the word 'rustle'. Now he played with the fancy of being a fox or badger on his great-uncle's estate: creeping over dark lawns, pushing through much-admired flowerbeds to the edge of the house and standing up on long hind legs to peep through the dining-room windows. It would be sparingly lit with the dim bulbs Uncle Hector was convinced saved on electricity (he was always on at the cousins to switch off lights), and he'd be eating leftovers served up by Merriweather, who'd be bad-tempered after the rigours of his day, voicing complaints with impunity. No wonder Uncle Hector had chosen never to marry, thought Max. He wished most fervently to be in his great-uncle's company, listening to his familiar stories, absorbing his kindness.

His mother had noticed the strange play of expressions across his face: alert and questing, strangely affectionate, finally disconsolate. But all she said was, 'A criminal.'

Max looked down at the pale blue carpet shampooed by Philomena on the first day of each month and noticed there was a burn mark on it. Although just a few hours ago he'd remembered the joy of being young and alive, he now felt burdened by anxiety as well as guilt. What was happening to his mother, who'd always been so fastidious? And what was his father's crime, anyway? So far as Max was concerned, it was leaving the family home – though he had to admit that trying to cope with his mother's moods had become like treading on eggshells. In a very private part of himself, Max mourned his father's departure and ached for his return. But '*Damn him!*' he'd think, because it was a lot less complicated. Besides, it was expected.

'Ask anyone, darling. He should be locked up!'

'Kitty was looking well, I thought,' said Simon – that soft expression, as always, when he talked about his daughter.

'Mmm, new dress. Maddening to spill something on it like that. I hope she can get it out.'

'Oh? Didn't notice.'

'You *must* have! All down the skirt. What did you think of the colour?'

'I thought she looked lovely.'

'Kitty'd look better in strong colours.'

'Well, *I* thought she looked *lovely*.' It delighted him that Kitty looked so much as Suki had done, at the same age. Suki had been married for five years by then. Next year, Kitty would be twenty-four. 'Almost on the shelf,' Suki would tell her daughter with a bright smile.

They'd been reviewing the day over supper, comparing notes on conversations, stressing the treat of it all for their son Phil's benefit because, typically, he'd seemed insufficiently impressed. 'Did you talk to Max?' they'd asked him, but there was nothing to be learnt there.

'You won't believe what Mark said to Linda!'

'Tell me, Pudding . . .'

Phil thought wearily, '*He is so embarrassing. And why does she*

*always tell him he's not going to believe something when she's going to tell him
anyway?'* He employed his usual way of registering disapproval,
which was a lengthy noisy gathering of phlegm from the depths
of his throat. But this time his parents didn't notice, which only
added to his irritation.

'He said, "You've got the flattest bosoms I've ever seen in my
entire life!"'

'No!'

'Then he said' – Suki giggled helplessly – '"No, no, come to
think of it, there's a fourth cousin once removed in Toronto
who's even flatter."'

Phil frowned as his parents shook and snorted with laughter.
Sometimes they called each other Stanislav, or Stan for short.
He'd no idea why and wouldn't dream of asking.

They ate in their kitchen, since a decision had been taken to
turn the dining-room into a study for Simon. It was a wistful
recreation of the country kitchen they'd never be able to afford
now – an enormous room with a long scrubbed pine table and
copper saucepans that were never used because they were a
nightmare to clean dangling among the dusty bunches of dried
herbs and strings of garlic bulbs. It was floored with linoleum
made to look like terracotta tiling. It had an Aga, which made
the kitchen too hot in summer and was ruinous to run, but Suki
had insisted on it. 'Since we can't afford another house . . .' she'd
said with that pleading look Simon found impossible to resist.
Tom and Becky had a second home in the country, of course,
very near the parents.

Suki had ordered a double stainless-steel sink, too, and
handsome solid oak cabinet doors and big angled spotlights to
beam on the Aga. But then the money ran out and the kitchen
became like the eldest son who has inherited everything. The

rest of the house lagged behind, reproachful and chipping. It would have to stay as it was now, including the stairwell, lined from top to bottom with Laura Ashley wallpaper and a crowded pattern of maroon dragonflies that had been a mistake.

'Ready for bed, Stanislav?' inquired Simon.

Suki glanced at the big clock. 'Bed,' she echoed with her tender docile smile.

'Bed?' echoed Phil, in utter disbelief. They could never tell when he was going to snap out of his day-dreaming and pay attention. 'It's only half-past nine!' Once – to his absolute horror and revulsion – his father had referred to their bedroom as 'the passion pit'.

'*You* didn't have to drive,' said his mother.

'Dad drove.'

'Exactly. And do stop making that ghastly noise, Phil darling. You're driving us mad.'

Sixteen-year-old Phil knew nothing of the deep comfort of marriage, the way his parents talked when there was only the two of them. Their big double bed was like a formerly bare and deserted island they'd landed on separately as scared castaways and transformed into a green and fertile land. But even as Suki laughed with her husband, she felt that troubling new uneasiness as if, under cover of darkness, an alien being had crept on to their territory. Had this disquiet been provoked by what had happened to Camilla and Anthony? Or was Simon really behaving like a man who was having an affair?

'How did you think Simon and Suki were?' Eleanor St Clair asked her husband, Lionel. They were sitting in their drawing-

room in their house in Hampshire, which was less than fifty
miles away from Hector's place but in a different county (a
superior one, they believed). They were tired, but would not
retire to bed until half-past ten. Discipline was the framework
of their world, enabling them to weather the unimaginable
agony of the death of a child. They'd already discussed the
party and garden – Hector's lupins weren't doing nearly so well
as their own, Lionel had observed over dinner – and watched
the news and now, for relaxation, were playing Scrabble.

'What do *you* think?' he replied. He hesitated before spelling
out SEXUAL. But, in the end, getting rid of his X more than
half-way through the game was more important than
momentarily offending his wife.

Eleanor raised her eyebrows and pursed her lips.

'Sorry, my dear.' His naturally stern expression softened as he
watched her. He loved the dreamy air that hid a complicated
mind. Eleanor who'd passed her crown of beauty to Camilla
and slipped into old age without his even noticing.

'I thought they were very well.'

Something was worrying her about their second daughter,
though – as always – she stated the opposite.

'Quartet wasn't up to standard,' she'd observed in the car,
though everyone at the party had agreed that, this year, the
music had been superb.

Lionel had learnt to trust her intuition and, though Camilla
was by far the more obvious focus for concern, he now started
to worry about Suki. Her husband had been unlucky, poor chap,
what with his parents losing all their money before he could be
launched into a proper career. But Simon was a nice man and
an excellent husband and father. Selling second-hand cars was
not a good field to be in at present, what with the price of petrol

soaring as well as everything else. All small businesses were struggling. Lionel frowned and shook his head slightly as he thought of the world they were living in. And, when they weren't worrying about galloping inflation and escalating interest rates, they had to be careful of IRA bombs, too. He took out his diary and scribbled a reminder in it. He would invite his son-in-law for lunch at the club once this case of his was over: do some discreet angling.

'Max looked all right,' Eleanor pronounced. For all its offensiveness, SEXUAL had opened up the board and she swiftly took advantage.

'LAMINA?'

'Something to do with rock,' she explained very confidently. She knew he wouldn't argue.

'You really thought Max was all right?' He couldn't help teasing her a little. Fond of his wife as he was, her contrariness offended his legal mind.

'Oh yes! And Camilla will pull herself together.' For a moment, she looked almost surprised by herself. It was she who kept the family up to standard, frowning on failure, commending success (though always holding something back, as if even the greatest of victories could be improved upon).

'Something must be done about Camilla,' said Lionel, for once taking a firm stand where their elder daughter was concerned. Unlike the rest of his family, he saw this marriage break-up as temporary. In his view no marriage was irreparable and it was clearly in both parties' interests to try harder. Camilla had always been a strong character, in much the same appealing manner as his wife, he reflected fondly: the steel hand concealed in the velvet glove. But, unlike Eleanor, Camilla was capricious. He smiled at some of the memories: a hunt ball and Camilla breathtakingly pretty in a white strapless dress but being cheeky to their grand neighbour Viscount Monkwell, who'd taken it very well, considering; Camilla a year later at seventeen, laying down the law at a formal dinner party. However, now she needed to be given a good talking to, told to swallow this shameful destructive rage of hers which was so very harmful for the child Max.

Suki would be the best candidate to approach her, sister to sister, he decided. And since – quite uncharacteristically – he'd now resolved to take a personal hand in sorting out family problems, it might be a good idea if another St Clair had a word with Anthony to find out how the land lay and ring a few alarm bells about Max. Tom was far too busy, of course. Lionel would never burden his son.

'Jane and Anthony get on all right, don't they?' he asked casually. He'd become increasingly fond of his son Henry's wife, long before the marriage ended so tragically. What on earth could one do with three O's and this damned Z? Was OZONIC a word? More to the point, would Eleanor know it was not?

'Oh, I don't think so especially!' his wife responded immediately with the smile that had caused him to fall at her feet and abandon all reason, more than forty years before.

The matter was settled.

Liza envied Charlie and Kitty. She loved the casual freedom from elegance they enjoyed: like being able to decide on long chintz curtains with wavy hems for their sitting-room that didn't actually go with anything. Kitty had bought the material in Barkers and run them up herself. Liza admired the oddness of the flat, too: its tall narrow slices of room dictated by bizarre partitioning that had turned one beautifully proportioned grand space into a recep., three bed., bath and kit. (as the ad in the *Evening Standard* had put it). And she liked the intriguing intimacy of it: her cousins' toothbrushes side by side on the glass shelf above the cracked basin in the minute bathroom.

'It is rather trendy, isn't it?' their grandmother had remarked on her only visit, bringing fragrant tea roses from her garden in the country to arrange with fabled talent in the only vase. It was strange to hear her use a word like 'trendy': stressing it slightly, as if enjoying a private joke. 'I believe I might have come to a party here once . . .' she'd told them with a faraway expression. Chepstow Place – always an impressive address. In pre-war days, one family – the Pargeters – had occupied the enormous house, confining their servants to the basement. It was even possible that, long before the slicing up took place, their grandmother had graced this very room: stood by a vanished mantelpiece, disseminating her cool and subtle charm. The classiness lingered in the ornate cornicing, now shared, the ceiling rose split between bathroom and kitchen.

Liza was the youngest of the four cousins at twenty-one but too old, in her view, to be living at home – especially since Charlie and Kitty had moved into this flat. She'd dropped hint after hint that she'd be only too delighted to appropriate the miniscule spare room. Why couldn't they pick it up? Soon she might ask them point blank.

She didn't know they'd already discussed it.

'She's so untidy,' Kitty had sighed. 'Oh dear, does that sound dreadful?'

'Of course not.' Charlie loved the order of their flat, too, which was exactly the right size for two people. Anyway, they could just about manage it financially between them – Charlie on the small sum he got from the chambers bolstered by an allowance from his father, Kitty (whose father couldn't afford to support her) on her salary as a secretary. 'Let's face it, she'd be a disaster.'

Kitty had been a little surprised by his vehemence. Charlie adored Liza. He sparkled in her presence.

'It's true she's not very good with money,' she'd conceded.

'Putting it mildly!' Then he'd smiled apologetically as he gave the real reason for not wanting Liza to move in: 'I need a study.'

Sitting in their tiny sitting-room equipped with a stained sofa that had come with the flat – now covered by a bright green Indian bedspread – and two armchairs from the grandparents (which meant the springs had gone), the puppy dozing in her lap, Liza said wistfully, 'You're *so* lucky!'

'We are,' confirmed Charlie, smiling at her pretty face. 'So are you, Mimi!'

But Liza wouldn't be distracted. 'It drives me mad, living with Jane,' she continued in the same soft moan. She'd occasionally call her mother by her Christian name when it was necessary to distance herself.

'You love your mum,' Charlie reminded her gently.

'Mmm,' Liza agreed. She would never question that. 'But she's always on at me to tidy my room. Nag nag nag! I'll *have* to move out soon.'

Charlie caught Kitty's eye, and both instantly looked away.

'It must be so amazing to be able to do exactly what you want.'

Charlie glanced at his watch and rose to his feet. 'Forgive me, girls. I've work to do.'

'It's Saturday evening!' exclaimed Liza.

'I know.' Charlie couldn't help sounding a little self-important.

'There's a not uncomplicated case I'm helping with that has to be prepared for next week.'

'He often works in the evenings,' Kitty explained proudly, like a wife. She didn't tell Liza Charlie was worried and she could tell from the tiny vertical line that had appeared between his eyebrows. He fretted a lot. Since starting at the chambers, he'd suffered from migraines, too.

When Charlie had gone off to his desk, also from the grandparents, which occupied a whole wall of the spare room, Liza poured herself another glass of wine and said, 'It must be funny, sharing with Charlie.'

'Not really.'

'*Nice* funny,' Liza amended immediately. She had an odd expression. 'What do you do about the bathroom?'

'What *do* you mean, Liza?'

'Oh, I don't know. Washing underclothes and stuff. I can't imagine sharing a bathroom with a man.' She corrected herself again: 'Actually I could, if it was Charlie.' She was starting to get cross. Kitty could be so obtuse. As for that awful pale pink dress she'd bought for the party! It made her feel less bad about what the puppy had done to it.

'Your mum looked nice today,' said Kitty, strategically changing the subject.

Liza stared at her mournfully. 'She's gone out with a man.'

'What? Now, you mean?'

Liza bowed her head as if at a funeral.

'Well, that's good, isn't it?' said Kitty briskly, once she'd absorbed this strange piece of news. There couldn't be anything in it, of course, because Aunt Jane was ancient. She said briskly, 'I'm sure whoever it is'll be a nice friend for her.'

Liza stared at her, feeling the irritation bubble up because

Kitty – of all people – would never understand because *she* still had a father. Soon Liza would start singing in her clear, pretty voice, distracting Charlie through the thin walls.

'Do you think Charlie's all right?' Becky asked Tom.

They'd been watching the news on television. It was no pleasure these days and Tom was predictably working himself into a lather.

'Have you any idea – any idea – how difficult it is for the ordinary man, striving his best to make an honourable living?'

'I don't mean work. I think he's coping all right, isn't he? What I mean is, he and Kitty seem so awfully comfortable together . . .' Becky had taken her shoes off and tucked her legs up on the sofa. Usually her husband stroked her feet. She let a toe brush his thigh but he was too incensed to notice.

'It means working for peanuts! I correct myself, working for the government!'

'. . . and it worries me sometimes.' Becky frowned. 'I wish he'd put the same effort into his relationships with his sisters.' Her pretty forehead crinkled up again. 'I don't really understand why he wanted to move out in the first place,' she said, though this was untrue.

'We might even have to think about emigrating,' said Tom. 'Why should one bother with patriotism or honesty when the country's being taken over by dictators?' He was going over the top now but Becky took it very calmly. 'We'd be better off financially, frankly, if I turned to crime. At least then I wouldn't have to pay all this income tax.'

'Don't get me wrong,' said Becky. 'I adore Kitty.'

'They're first cousins, woman!' Tom exploded, responding to his wife at last. It was amazing how he managed to listen acutely to what she was really saying (as opposed to what came out of her mouth), while engaging in one of his rants.

'I know, darling! But sometimes I worry that they hold each other back. It's so important for Charlie to find the right person.'

'In-deed!' Tom smiled at his wife, and took hold of one of her feet. He was an uxorious man, though outsiders sometimes pitied Becky for being married to such a boor. Nobody knew better than he that, with the right woman by his side, a man could touch the stars. But he should find that golden woman in his twenties. It was as crucial a part of a life plan as cementing the foundations of a proper career.

Merriweather's potted eggs were a family joke. Heaped in brine in an enormous stone urn in his pantry, they gave his cakes their unique musty flavour. Potting was a wartime habit he refused to break, even though, nowadays, there was an abundance of fresh eggs from the poultry run every day, most of which ended up at the market. Increasingly, Jane felt like one of those potted eggs – the same colour and shape as a fresh one, but wilfully preserved.

She'd wanted to consult Liza about her date but Liza had exclaimed 'Don't!' and clapped her hands over her ears. Her mother a sexual being? Impossible!

But Jane knew there was a deeper objection: Liza's father had been dead for only just over a year.

Becoming a widow had been a revelation. Married men (family friends she'd known for ages) had asked her out to lunch and, at first, she'd taken this for simple kindness, only to find herself being propositioned over the coffee (though usually in an oblique way that left her too confused to feel able to be cross, especially if the man was attractive). A girl she'd been to school with had lost her youth and prospects to a married lover. '*Never!*' thought Jane. Floundering in a futureless world, it was the one thing she could prophesy for herself with conviction.

This was her first real date since Henry's death: an invitation to dinner from a man who was not married or otherwise engaged, who was the right sort of age (hers) with a profession (accountancy) the St Clair family would approve. She found she craved their sanction more than ever now that Henry was gone.

She'd met the accountant at a drinks party given by married friends, and some ten days later he'd telephoned. She hadn't remembered warming to him, but – once he'd asked her out – reviewed the situation. So she bought herself a new dress and had her hair done, and found these efforts favourably commented on at the family party.

The trouble was, he was all wrong. It was plain from the moment she opened her front door, bang on half-past seven, to find him wearing a thick olive pullover (presumably signifying this was a day off). She'd forgotten the way he brushed his hair over his forehead. And he hadn't booked anywhere – though, after he'd accepted two large gin and tonics, he asked if she knew of a little place locally.

'Big lunch,' he announced in the bistro round the corner, patting the olive pullover. 'I'll have the Spanish omelette,' he told the waiter, 'and a carafe of house red.'

Jane's sister-in-law Camilla had once informed her that if a man was interested, he revealed his true self on the first date. She'd added with her ravishing smile, 'I'm not talking about what he actually says.' It had been typically puzzling and also annoying.

The accountant told Jane about divorced parents, an

authoritarian stepfather, boarding-school misery and the consuming nature of his work. Was she any the wiser? Unlike the married men who'd invited her for lunch, he didn't appear to find her attractive or interesting and, at the end of the evening, gave no indication that he ever wanted to see her again.

'Disaster,' she said, as she shut her front door behind her. 'Finito. Don't you agree?' She often talked to her husband Henry like this. He was still here, in the house, of course – for how could he have borne to leave them? It was bliss to be alone again, she assured him. But Liza was still out with her cousins and the silence gathered force, became deafening.

'*Why?*' thought Jane, bemused by the unfairness of everything. But after she'd poured herself a large whisky, she rewrote the evening. '*Perhaps I didn't listen enough. Maybe he's shy. I mustn't become too choosy. I am forty-two and Liza will be off soon. Perhaps, if he does ask me out again, I should give it one more chance. Or maybe I should take the initiative and arrange a dinner party – it's high time I started doing that.*' And she said out loud, the words vanishing into the void: 'Tell me I'm right, my darling.'

Uncle Hector communed with the dead on the evening of his party, too, and that was also a private matter.

Being left on his own was far less desolate than his guests imagined as they returned to lives crammed with spouses and children and pets. He could be very lonely at times, but this massive annual shot of family would sustain him for weeks. Besides, as they'd noticed, in spite of his loving and generous nature, he seemed to have an aversion to real intimacy. Why else had he never found himself a wife?

It was true what Suki had said to her husband: Uncle Hector knew nothing about marriage. Neither had he been a parent, of course. But it didn't prevent this usually surprisingly un-judgemental man from holding strong views on marriage and parenthood. It was his profound love of children, his fierce desire to protect them, which governed his rigid and blinkered stance that – if children were involved – separation and divorce must be out of the question. So what if couples made each other miserable? To Uncle Hector's way of thinking, it was pure selfishness for them to consider their own feelings. Furthermore, he believed that it was mothers who bore the greatest responsibility for their children's security and happiness. This was why he'd forbidden his niece Camilla to attend his party. She'd angered and disappointed him. For Max's sake, she must come to her senses and make peace with Anthony (even if it was he who'd caused the trouble in the first place). Then – and only then – would he welcome her back into the fold.

'Bang their heads together,' thought Hector with a mixture of distaste and impatience. He'd heard the rumours, of course, but had no desire to be told lurid details. He pressed the bell hidden under the dining-room table so Merriweather could clear away dinner and then – oblivious to his servant's noisy grumblings – carried his glass of port into his big drawing-room, where the fire was only lit for visitors and there was no television set. Uncle Hector disapproved of television, even though he'd never once watched it. In his opinion, it required far too little effort.

As usual, on the night of his party, he would use the port (so bad for the gout in his remaining ankle) to drink a private toast to an absent and much missed guest. Nobody had spoken of her, of course. They hadn't for years and years. It was as if she'd never existed. 'Heart' was what had always been said. 'Yes . . .'

muttered Hector, the family's archivist and conscience, 'and too much soul and intellect, too.' He was not a whimsical or even particularly religious man and yet, as he sat in his hard armchair with a lumpy cushion at his back, he fancied her vibrant spirit shimmered past. It even seemed to him that he could catch the scent of the Egyptian cigarettes she'd smoked in secret, discern drifting skeins of blue-grey smoke in the still air.

He raised his glass, his expression very soft. 'Are you there, my dearest?' he whispered. But there was only silence.

Abruptly he set the glass down and put his head in his hands and his shoulders shook with grief. 'Fool!' he muttered.

A moment later, he'd composed himself. He blew his nose very thoroughly on an enormous well-ironed white handkerchief and then he fitted on his spectacles and picked up a legal journal.

Chapter Three

'We've been set up,' said Anthony, showing off his excellent teeth, brilliant white against the dark and lustrous looks Max had inherited. It was typical of him to joke about something serious. 'All right for you?' he'd asked, as if genuinely concerned.

'*I'm being disarmed*,' thought Jane, even as she found herself smiling back, allowing a waiter to smooth her napkin on her lap for her, wondering how she could explain all this to her father-in-law. What would have happened if she'd said no? Would Anthony have swept her out of this fabulously expensive restaurant and arranged for them to be chauffeured off to another?

'You'll have some champagne with me.' It sounded more of an order than a suggestion.

Perhaps he was nervous about this meeting, too, she told herself without conviction, studying his thick glossy hair as he perused the wine list. He knew what it was about, of course, because – by now, painfully wary – she'd felt obliged to explain on the telephone. She'd pointed out that it had been Lionel's idea they meet. Anthony would understand the pressure she'd been under – might even guess that Lionel's call had immediately been followed up by Eleanor who, as everyone knew, was the real power in the family. 'I understand Lionel has talked to you . . . We're all very worried about Max . . .' After the gentle coercion, came the reward: 'It's occurred to me that it's high time you came for the weekend, Jane dear . . . Let me consult my book.' Jane had been flattered to be involved. Sometimes, when feeling particularly lost, she'd think of the confident massive St Clair presence at her back – her family now.

Anthony's attitude to money made him very different from them, as did the way his wealth had been created; for it had sprung from a youthful gamble that had paid off astonishingly quickly. Jane fancied that she, too, believed in dreams and risk. After all, didn't she support Liza's very un-St-Clair-like ambition to become a singer? And she and Anthony had something else in common. Though their children carried St Clair genes, they had none. They were outsiders, the formerly disapproved-of ones: Anthony because his whole approach to life was so foreign, Jane because she'd brought neither money nor the right kind of background to her marriage.

The St Clairs, of course, believed in reliable professions like the law, and a discreet patina of wealth built up through generations by prudent investment. Their desire to play safe extended to marriage, where there was a general mistrust of passion, which was the greatest gamble of all.

The story of Anthony and Camilla's courtship had always

appealed to Jane. It put a romantic gloss on what she saw for herself: an uneasy relationship between a cool spoilt beauty and a charming but unreadable man. She knew that Anthony had started dabbling in the property business in his early twenties and, within five years, had become seriously rich. He'd cut a swathe through the men nineteen-year-old Camilla was meeting then: scions of good English families but lacking comparable ambition or glamour. Nevertheless, Lionel and Eleanor were opposed to the match, though Henry had told her they never really explained why. After all, wasn't Anthony clever, good-looking, rich and charming – besides being besotted with Camilla? It was Hector who'd persuaded them to give in. 'Seems solid enough on balance,' he'd pronounced, as if he'd weighed Anthony on the family scales.

It was a running private joke between Suki and Tom that their mother – who would have been horrified to be described as racist or snobbish – had never been heard to refer either to Anthony's Jewish blood or the fact that his parents had run a successful clothing business. The truth dawned on them only once they'd grown up.

'I'm afraid he comes from a very different background,' Suki would tell Tom, shaking her head worriedly, mimicking Eleanor's precise way of speaking and her habit of pronouncing 'very' as 'vay'.

'He went to Eton and Oxford, didn't he?' Tom would respond robustly, sounding completely mystified, 'and I believe his father's a mercer, isn't he?'

'Vay vay different,' Suki would confirm in the definite shutting-down way the family had learnt to accept.

When Jane first met Anthony, the marriage had been going for a year and Camilla was newly pregnant.

The family was to become very fond of this clever, genial, generous man. Besides, Suki had once commented with a sly glance at her mother, he'd added interest to the gene pool – though Tom had immediately pointed out that Anthony didn't seem to have passed on any of his brains or ambition to Max.

'What about his beauty?' Suki had retaliated.

'His *what*?' Tom had snorted.

And now, of course, Anthony could play this lunch as he wished. He certainly didn't seem in any hurry to be brought to the point.

'Little Jane,' he said, sounding genuinely tender as he looked at her across the table and Jane fiddled with her hair, felt glad it was nicely cut and also embarrassed – which was silly, really, as he often talked to women like this. He'd make them feel special. It was part of his charm – though, once, at a family gathering, Camilla had accused him of being patronizing.

'You're looking well,' he went on with the same unnerving intimacy. '*Are* you?'

'I'm fine,' said Jane abruptly, to counteract the emotion she felt welling up. It happened all the time now. Since Henry's death, it was as if she'd lost a skin: the new vulnerability provoking a puzzlingly familiar mixture of anxiety and longing.

'I'm glad. And your Liza? How's she doing?'

Jane thought about Liza's reaction on failing to win the singing role she'd auditioned for: the storms of over-the-top grief. This (not unexpected) blow had come very soon after Uncle Hector's party, which had been nearly two weeks ago now, but Liza's mood hadn't improved. ('I don't *want* an ordinary life!' she'd cried that very morning as if it was the worst that could happen to anyone.) However, to Anthony, Jane revealed only the bare facts.

'I expect she was very disappointed.'

'A bit,' she admitted, and couldn't resist adding, 'but it was a compliment to be auditioned, wasn't it?'

'Oh definitely!' he agreed. 'She should be at music school.'

'Well, she has lessons. The teacher was highly recommended.'

'Did nobody suggest trying for the Guildhall or somewhere like that?'

'Well, no . . .' Liza's ambition was not taken seriously within the family, and therefore tacitly discouraged. Even Jane secretly hoped it would be overtaken by marriage.

'They should have,' pronounced Anthony.

She noticed him nod to someone across the room and, turning, saw a couple at another table subjecting her to a curious unsmiling scrutiny. They must have read the newspaper item, she realized with an uncomfortable feeling.

When she turned back to him, he was smiling faintly as if to confirm that, by being in his company, she was indeed compromising her reputation; and she was made aware that this was the first time they'd ever been alone together.

Their last encounter had been two months ago when Camilla had invited her for dinner. 'Nothing grand,' she'd said, 'just us.' Jane had found herself mourning the loss of a dinner party. Why didn't Camilla understand that she longed to meet new people, enjoy the illusion she could start her life afresh? She couldn't tell her so, of course. She'd always been a little afraid of this particular sister-in-law. It was because, despite the charm, she never quite knew what to expect. Camilla had been alone when she got there and already surprisingly drunk and Anthony hadn't turned up until nine. Though he'd apologized most charmingly, blaming pressure of work, Camilla had been very obviously angry in a controlled sort of way and Jane had left as soon as she decently could.

Suddenly she felt mortified with herself for enjoying Anthony's company. But she managed to ask coolly, 'How are *you*?'

'Oh,' he said, 'surviving' – and he wriggled his black eyebrows at her as if privately amused.

'The party was fun,' she went on primly, trying to rein in the lunch and set it back on track.

'Good,' he responded, sounding absolutely uninterested. But perhaps that was because his invitation had also been withdrawn. Then, as a waiter materialized at their table, pad in hand, he inquired: 'Any luck with deciding?'

'I'm not sure.' The menu was enormous and the evening with the accountant was still painfully fresh in her mind.

'What about caviar?' He sounded as casual and bored as if he ate it every day. He asked the waiter, 'And how's the saddle of lamb?'

'Very nice, sir.'

'Caviar and lamb suit you?'

He asked the waiter to bring them a bottle of Château Latour and then he spoke at length about the long boom in property. And as she politely listened, she realized that it was quite possible he'd go on talking about it until the lunch was over.

He tasted the lamb with exactly the same expression he wore when listening to music – alert yet totally absorbed – then asked abruptly, 'How do you think Max is?'

So there they were at last. Jane thought of the young man briefly glimpsed at the party – even more exotic when set against the sandy ranks of St Clairs but uncommunicative to the point of rudeness. 'Hard to tell,' she said diplomatically.

('Something needs to be done about Max,' her father-in-law had informed her in a voice heavy with disappointment. This particular grandchild had been a worry even before the marriage split: spoilt by his socialite mother, neglected by his workaholic father, allowed to drift on looks and charm.)

'His grandparents are very concerned,' she offered.

Anthony sighed, as if this was only to be expected. His usual flippancy had fallen away and, for the first time, Jane appreciated the depth of pain he must be suffering at the end of his marriage, besides his great anxiety about his son.

'If only he had a burning ambition, like your Liza.'

'Isn't there anything he really wants to do?'

He shrugged unhappily, as if he'd tried and failed so many times to ignite the competitiveness that came naturally to the St Clairs.

'You probably think I was brought up to all this,' he said suddenly, gesturing at their surroundings – the ornate décor, the plush seats, the fleet of waiters.

'I know how you were brought up,' Jane told him.

'I wonder,' he responded. 'My parents were very hard on me. I had to earn every toy, every treat and, more crucially, every single bit of education, so I wouldn't take it for granted. I won scholarships to Eton and Oxford – did you know? I was led to believe I wouldn't have a proper education otherwise. Oh, I loved my parents just as much as I knew they loved me, and I didn't let them down. But it was hard.' He sighed. 'And I didn't want that hardship and struggle for Max – not when it was unnecessary. And anyway . . .' There was no need to finish the sentence. Camilla would never have allowed it – they both knew that. 'For my Max,' Anthony went on, 'I wanted the perfect childhood . . .'

Silence fell and Jane thought about the attractive little boy who'd been showered with expensive toys and treats. She considered the chimera of the perfect childhood. What would Liza – who'd idolized her father only to lose him – say about hers? Or Charlie, who'd been pressured to achieve since infancy? Or Kitty, whose parents doted on each other to the exclusion of all others?

'The trouble was . . .' He sighed. 'I was hardly ever there. But now' – he shrugged helplessly as if all this was very painful to admit – 'my son refuses to see me.' He stared at Jane with his very dark eyes, which seemed even brighter than usual, and said softly, 'It's not as if I *wanted* to leave him . . .'

Afterwards, Jane cursed herself for not following this up. After all, wasn't the whole point of this meeting to find out about Anthony's relationship with his son? She must have given the impression of shivering away from further, possibly unpleasant revelations. In fact, it had been simple shyness that stopped her, a natural awe of Anthony's glamour and wealth – and then the moment passed.

'Well, I wish I could tell you about Max,' she said, when he failed to elaborate. 'But we didn't talk at the party. Nobody saw him really.'

'Nobody?'

'Only his cousins, of course.'

'Ah yes,' he said with a sigh, as if acknowledging that nobody on earth could compete with the cousins for Max's affections. 'And what did your Liza say afterwards?'

Jane thought of Liza's robust (and suspiciously personal) condemnation of all parents who didn't live their lives solely for their children. 'You know how they are,' she answered. 'They're very protective of each other.'

'So I'm the villain of the piece for them, too?'

Jane gave him a helpless look.

'I see.' Then, with a twisted smile, he said: 'I assume everyone at the party had read the *Daily Mail*?'

'Nobody reads the *Mail* in our family,' Jane replied, poker-faced, and they both laughed and the mood lightened.

'Pack of lies.'

'Really?' she asked rather daringly.

'Who do you think planted it?' He smiled at her shocked expression. 'Come on! It had the hand of Camilla in every line. I can't believe I'm the first person to point that out!'

'But why?' Jane felt disloyal to the family, even asking.

'To make me look bad,' he said with a shrug.

'It's a bit extreme!'

'There you go,' he said, as if excessiveness was only to be expected of Camilla. He even sounded a little proud, she thought – as if, quite objectively, he could appreciate this quality in her.

'Is it really over?' Straight afterwards she thought, '*I must be getting drunk to have asked him that!*'

'I believe so.' He looked very sad.

'I'm sorry.'

'Don't be.' Then he said suddenly, as if making a real effort to pull himself together, 'I wasn't expecting to enjoy this lunch.'

'*Nor me*,' thought Jane but, typically, she only smiled a little awkwardly at him before looking down at the tablecloth.

'I thought I was in for a ticking off.'

'I'm sorry.' She meant that she was sorry for allowing Lionel and Eleanor to manipulate her into believing she could make any sort of a difference.

Then, to her astonishment, she heard him say: 'You've been lucky.'

'Lucky?' she echoed. Could he really have said it?

'My parents were, too,' he mused, seemingly quite unaware of his tactlessness. Then he put a warm hand on hers and said, 'You *were* lucky, you know. You must hold on to it.'

The situation was exactly what she'd come to dread. Sympathy and kindness were enemies now. She thought of the dreadful day of Henry's funeral and everyone behaving like soldiers and managing, because she was in shock, not to cry and how, one by one, the family had murmured stiffly, 'Well done, Jane.' And then she remembered Tom paying her a visit soon afterwards with a set businesslike expression and a briefcase of papers concerning insurance and a trust for Liza. He'd come to offer practical advice, as he'd immediately made clear – 'I'm not going to talk about what's happened, Jane.' None of them had spoken of the terrible pain of losing Henry (not even warm-hearted Suki, whose eyes still filled with tears at the very mention of him. 'Mustn't, mustn't, mustn't!' she'd mutter, in a panic – and never did).

'People change,' was all Jane was capable of murmuring to Anthony for the moment.

He frowned. He didn't understand, of course. Nobody did. '*Ah*,' thought Jane with pain in her heart, '*if only I could meet a man who understands about grief.*'

As Anthony leant across the table, she caught a whiff of delicious and expensive perfume. None of the St Clairs used aftershave. They didn't believe in deodorants, either. Tom, who sometimes smelt quite strongly of sweat, called it 'poof juice'.

She tried again. 'You know what Henry was like . . .'

Anthony nodded. Intense strawberry-blond Henry, once a classics scholar, with skin so pale from lack of exposure to the sun that it was almost purple; who'd been a less vivid version of Tom in looks (as if the stamp on his entrance visa to the world had started to run out of ink) – and who'd collapsed aged forty-five on the floor of his office at the bank one Thursday morning when he should have been discussing gilts. His secretary had found him like a felled tree when she took in a cup of milky coffee with one sugar at half past ten.

'He could be really funny, in his silly old way.'

Anthony raised his dark eyebrows as if surprised and she was made painfully aware that the family had sometimes laughed at Henry for his seriousness.

'He liked playing practical jokes. I don't think even his own parents knew that . . .' Henry had once made Liza an apple-pie bed, just as he'd had to suffer on his first night at his prep boarding-school. 'And he could be very romantic . . .' Inspired by the summery look of her, Henry had once stopped on the way to Uncle Hector's party to make love in a field of long grass entwined with scarlet poppies. He'd got a smear of cowpat on the right sleeve of his best suit and, when they arrived at Cedar Manor, had to head straight for the icy men's lavatory on the ground floor to sponge it off. 'But now, suddenly, he's got to be a saint – for Liza's sake, for all their sakes. Oh yes, people change. And – I wonder – does that always happen to them when they die?'

A silence fell, and then she saw Anthony nod almost imperceptibly at a waiter for the bill. 'What are your plans?' he asked and she saw him glance at his watch.

Jane felt as if a stone had settled on her fluttery unfamiliar heart. How idiotic she'd been. It was always like this with the family: you believed you'd made an advance, only, at the very next turn, to meet an impenetrable wall. They hated self-pity or any sort of weakness. How could she have forgotten? And now, for all his apparent difference, Anthony had just demonstrated he was the same.

'We're okay for money,' she replied, pulling herself together and thinking this was the kind of talk he would appreciate. 'I mean, not so we have to worry too much. Henry saw to that, and Tom's been helpful, too. But I'm going to try and get myself a job soon. Not sure quite what. Something to keep me occupied.'

'No,' he said, smiling, 'I meant now.'

'Now?'

'I've – decided to play truant for the rest of the afternoon. I was wondering if you'd care to join me.'

'Jane?' Eleanor's tone was warm, masking the irritation provoked by a previous call. Suki had just told her that she'd tried to telephone Camilla – 'but that foreign housekeeper of hers always says she's out.' 'Well, go round there, then,' Eleanor had suggested quite vigorously and had been most irritated when Suki responded, 'You *know* what Camilla's like. I can't *force* her to see me.' It had all reinforced Eleanor's suspicion that something was troubling Suki. It was unlike her to be unhelpful.

Jane was a different matter . . . Darling Henry's wife, so gentle and malleable, a most satisfactory daughter-in-law, as it had turned out. Now that she'd finally tracked her down, she could count on discovering how the lunch with Anthony had really gone.

'Hello, Mama,' said Jane docilely, using the same name her husband had used.

'I've been trying to telephone you all afternoon, Jane.'

There was a tiny hesitation before Jane explained, 'I went shopping.'

'Oh ...' Eleanor considered for a moment what her daughter-in-law might need in the way of shopping and, without uttering a word of criticism, somehow managed to convey disapproval. 'I thought you were having lunch with Anthony.'

'I was.'

'You had lunch together, did you?'

'Yes, Mama,' she heard her daughter-in-law agree meekly.

'Anywhere particular?'

'Not really.'

'Where?'

'Oh, only the Mirabelle.'

'Did you say the Mirabelle, Jane?'

'Mmm, I did, actually.'

'*I* see. And after that, you did your shopping, did you?'

'Mmm.'

'How did you get on?'

'I didn't buy anything.'

'Oh, you didn't buy anything.' There was a long pause. 'So how did you get on with Anthony? ... Jane?'

'Fine,' she heard Jane say very definitely. 'Absolutely fine.'

'What did he say about Max?'

'Of course he's worried about him.'

'Has he seen him?'

'No, no, he hasn't.'

Then Eleanor heard a door slam in the background and Jane

said, with the usual lift in her voice (she adored that naughty daughter of hers): 'Here's Liza.'

'Liza?'

'Yes.'

'Is Liza still doing her little jobs?' Eleanor inquired.

'For the time being,' Jane responded equally pleasantly. Then: 'Mama, I have to go and do something about supper.'

'Supper?' Eleanor reacted as if Jane had used a foreign word. She and Lionel had already had dinner. They ate at half past seven on the dot because their cook would not have tolerated anything less. And then they watched the news at nine.

'Liza's starving, as usual.'

'Well, we must talk more,' said Eleanor, sounding very cool.

'Definitely,' Jane agreed. But there was a certain note in her voice that suggested she might not welcome any more conversations with her mother-in-law for the time being.

Chapter Four

'The trouble with you, Kitty, is you're too nice.'

'So are you, Charlie.'

'Why can't any of them see it, then? Why are they all so pathologically terminally chronically moronic?'

It was almost midnight on a Friday night and rain lashed the high windows of the flat in Chepstow Place in vicious uneven waves. Charlie was lying on his back on the kitchen floor, staring up at the innards of the sink. His body was too long for the little room and his big feet poked through the door in the polished black shoes he was obliged to wear for work.

He'd been very silent at supper and straight afterwards had disappeared into the spare room with a hunted expression. 'Leave the washing-up, Kitty – I'll do it later.'

But when, after failing to do the washing-up herself, she tentatively put her head round the door, he told her in a panic, 'I've been reading this over and over again, and I can't make any sense of it.'

'What's it about?' she asked, looking with interest at the brief on his desk. She'd always liked the look of these documents bound up with pink or red ribbon, like presents.

'You don't want to know,' he said wearily.

'Tell me.'

'Something about a boundary line . . . I don't understand how anyone can possibly get worked up about six inches. My pupilmaster . . .' His voice dwindled helplessly away. Kitty knew all about it. The barrister he was meant to be shadowing hardly ever spoke to him and, when he did, seemed at boiling point of exasperation. The other pupil, Charlie's rival, was faring much better. 'He just expects me to know,' he ended miserably.

'Sounds interesting to me,' said Kitty, who'd spent the afternoon taking dictation about capital gains tax. Could anything be more boring?

'You *are* joking!'

'Honestly not! Tell me what it's about.'

'You don't want to know!'

'I do! I really do!'

'It's these neighbours,' said Charlie in a tired voice. 'Two couples. They're both retired. Oh look, this is *so* boring!'

'No, it's not!'

Charlie rolled his eyes. 'About eighteen months ago one lot cut down a hedge, and the other lot said it was theirs . . .'

'Go on.'

'They went to a solicitor.'

'About six inches?'

'They won't settle. They say it's a matter of principle.'

'I can understand that.'

'It's cost thousands already. It's probably going to take all their money. Imagine Grandpa and Grandma being so ridiculous.'

They both thought of their grandparents, who lived in spacious splendour and didn't have any neighbours encroaching on them. Besides, their grandfather, who'd been a lawyer all his life, would never countenance litigation.

'So how do you find out whose hedge it really is?'

Charlie frowned even more. Why was Kitty showing such interest? She must be winding him up.

'We'll have to trace the deeds. Go back hundreds of years, if necessary.'

'Fascinating!'

'Anyway,' said Charlie, who'd had quite enough of this, 'did you want to ask me something?'

'Sorry, Charlie, the sink's blocked again.'

The job was taking forever. But she knew the furrow between his eyebrows would have vanished. He enjoyed fixing things. Before he'd started working for the chambers, he'd done carpentry in his spare time.

Now he was talking to her as he worked in the way they so often did – spilling out tales like Scheherazade's, but woeful, without romance.

Kitty's role model for a happy marriage was, unsurprisingly, her parents', and times like this had the same flavour of easy intimacy. Her experience of men as lovers was making her fear emotional involvement. Just for now, though, sharing with

Charlie felt like enjoying the best bits of being a couple with none of the anguish. It was all the sweeter because quite soon one of them – Charlie, for sure – would get married and then this happy period would be over.

'I didn't even like her that much,' he said, as – with a surge of effort – he unscrewed the trap and let loose a flood of greasy water into the pudding basin she handed him. It was very satisfactory to be able to identify a problem and go straight to the heart of it. She'd sort out the mess after he'd finished his story – she commenting at regular intervals, like lending her surprisingly powerful and rich contralto to a chorus.

'Now that's not true!'

'All right, I was besotted.'

'You were.'

'Oh God, I must have bored you!'

'Charlie!'

'But when you ask a woman six weeks ahead if she'd like to come to the theatre, when you fix a date, when you pay a *fortune* for the tickets . . .'

'So nice of you!'

'And then – at the very last minute – she blows you out . . .'

'Bitch.'

A little surprised, he pulled his head from under the sink to look at her. 'And it was too late even for *you* to come, because of your choir night . . .'

'I'd have been so flattered, Charlie,' she told him earnestly, 'if someone had taken all that trouble for me.'

'And then – to cap it all – the woman doesn't even say sorry.'

'Bitch,' said Kitty again, very uncharacteristically.

'Just told me something had come up, and as I seemed so upset it was best to call it a day.'

'Well, I'm glad you found out about her now, before you got more hurt. Honestly.'

'Silly me,' he said sadly. He sighed deeply. 'It's probably just as well. At least I got some work done. Anyway, I'm giving up on women now.'

There was no doubt that swapping sagas of misery and betrayal was becoming strangely addictive. Last week, a boyfriend had dumped Kitty during the fifteen-minute interval of a concert she'd invited him to at the Festival Hall.

'Bastard!' Charlie had pronounced when she arrived home. 'Why did he have to do it in public?'

'It was so awful, Charlie! I love those Schubert Impromptus.'

'You should have got up and left.'

'The only thing that got me through it was the thought of the F Minor.'

But she was not being entirely honest. All the way back on the tube, trembling with humiliation and misery, she'd anticipated telling Charlie.

Now, he reappeared from beneath the sink to take a swig from the bottle of red wine they were sharing. Kitty's mouth had been round its neck a moment ago but he didn't wipe it with his hand, just as Kitty hadn't a moment earlier.

'Silly her,' said Kitty firmly. Then: 'We all make mistakes.'

'Not everyone.'

Charlie had a point. Other people their sort of age – most particularly young members of their family – seemed to have no problem at all in meeting Mr or Miss Right. The point had been forcibly made at Uncle Hector's party. Cousin Esther, aged twenty-three – carrot-haired, lisping, known as 'Lickle Me' because it was how she habitually referred to herself – was suddenly less irritating and even attractive for the first time, with a decent-sized diamond on the third finger of her left hand and a perfectly okay fiancé with a good job in commerce on her arm.

'What'th wrong with Lickle Ole Me?' Charlie asked, but there was real despair in his tone, issuing sepulchral-like from under the sink.

Kitty seized the bottle. 'There's nothing wrong with you, Charlie.' It was true. He was perfectly nice-looking in a big gingery way, even when covered in muck. He was clever and hard-working. He could be very funny when he wasn't taking himself seriously. Most important of all, thought Kitty, he was decent and kind.

'You just haven't met the right person yet.'

'No.' He sounded utterly doleful.

'Nor have I,' Kitty reminded him with grim chirpiness.

'Well, I don't know about that!' He assumed a ponderous reproachful tone very reminiscent of Uncle Hector: 'You could have been Mrs Dave Rigsby by now and SAVED EVERYONE A LOT OF GRIEF!'

It was a familiar tease. Third Cousin Dave Rigsby (whose St Clair mother had married late and beneath her) had once asked Kitty out and been politely turned down. It so happened that not long afterwards – according to the family grapevine – he'd tried to set fire to his parents' house with them in it. Seeing him so subdued and polite at the party, handing round cake to the older relatives once the music was over, made it difficult to believe the story.

'You're driving me cra-azy!' sang Charlie as he screwed the trap back on. 'You're going to have to stop pouring fat down here, Lickle Miss Heartless.'

'If only I could meet a man like you, Charlie.'

He rolled over and got to his feet. He was making a pained face.

'I mean it!'

She said it to cheer him up, of course. It was true that she believed she craved someone with his qualities but, for some reason, she never seemed to end up with men like that.

It was to her absolute astonishment that Charlie responded, sounding very casual yet at the same time overcome by weariness, 'Well, if neither of us is married by the time we're thirty . . .'

Kitty blinked rapidly, as she always did when taken aback. Then, to her horror, she felt a blush starting. They were first cousins, but closer than brother and sister. They even looked similar, with their vulnerable brown eyes and uncoordinated movements. Their relationship was far more intimate than hers and Phil's. It was Charlie who incompetently snipped off her split ends with a pair of unsuitably curved nail-scissors when she couldn't afford to go to the hairdresser's and clasped her in a bear hug when she was really upset, whacking her on the back like beating the dust from a carpet. She was so overcome that she dropped the pudding basin full of water that she'd been about to empty. It shattered, adding to the chaos, and Charlie looked at her with sudden alarm even though she broke things all the time.

He hadn't been serious, thought Kitty. Of course not. He was as embarrassed as she.

They were still staring at each other, seemingly in shock, when the doorbell rang.

It was perfect timing. But then, all four cousins were telepathically close. It was a long-standing joke that very often, just after a bottle had been uncorked, Liza would arrive unannounced.

*

'What are you doing?' asked Max, wide-eyed. He'd driven through the rain in his MG, clearly with the roof down, almost certainly too fast.

'This *is* a nice surprise,' said Kitty in the usual tender motherly way, eyes fixed on his exquisite face with the long hair falling round it in wet rats' tails. He shaved now, of course, but the hair was fine and weak – not like Uncle Ant's, which pushed vigorously through his skin in blue-black shadows. When she kissed Max, his damp cheek felt as smooth as hers.

'Sink was blocked,' Charlie explained tersely.

'Why didn't you get someone in?'

'Only money, Max!'

'Money?' he echoed wonderingly, lips in a perfect pout. Then, as he took in the flooded kitchen floor: 'It looks awful.'

They were both staring at him, not wanting to ask for explanations though naturally curious and, of course, concerned. There was a strange delicacy in the way they approached relationships with parents. They were conscious of their separate problems: it had made them even closer.

'Can I stay the night?' asked Max, his voice trembling a little as if he feared rejection. To anyone else, it might have sounded strange coming from a fully-grown man.

Kitty glanced a little anxiously at Charlie but, to his credit, he responded immediately: 'Of course!'

'Can I really?'

'I've said so, Max. You can sleep in the study.'

It turned out that Max had brought a hastily packed bag, but left it in the boot of his car, just in case. Kitty found that touching and also encouraging. They'd always appreciated that his upbringing had been of a different order from theirs. After all, would they have been quite so considerate without steady watchful parenting? But Max did think of others and here was the proof.

While he went off to retrieve his bag, she and Charlie mopped up the water on the floor and discussed the situation.

'That was so nice of you, Charlie!'

'Not at all.' Charlie's face was very close to hers and his breath smelt fresh and male, like Oxo cubes.

'I'm glad he felt he could come here.'

'Me too.'

'Poor little chap looks terrible.'

'What d'you think could've happened?'

But they'd guessed, of course. Max wouldn't need to say a word.

The drama had expunged any awkwardness between them: restored their relationship to its usual easy affectionate state.

'You *are* an angel!' (Sometimes Kitty sounded astonishingly like her mother.) 'Are you sure you don't mind if he sleeps in your study?'

'Not at all.'

'It'll probably only be for one night.'

'No problem.' But he was deeply worried. Tomorrow was a Saturday so Max was bound to sleep late and therefore he'd be unable to use the study until at least noon. His brain felt cottonwool-like under the strain of pushing it so hard and now that the enjoyable task of fixing the sink was over, the panic had returned, worse than ever. He should go to bed – but he knew he'd worry about work even more, and probably not manage to sleep at all.

The doorbell trilled again. It seemed Max had brought a

squash racket, also, and a transistor radio. This worried Charlie, but he didn't comment and neither did Kitty, who had surely noticed them, too.

'Would you like a hot drink?' she asked Max gently. 'Charlie and I usually have one.'

'Indeed we do.'

'Horlicks is so nice and soothing, isn't it?'

'Definitely!' Charlie sounded as if he hadn't a care in the world.

'You are funny!' said Max.

'And then I'll get a towel and dry your hair for you if you like, Max.'

'Okay,' he agreed casually, as if he really had no idea how much pleasure this would give Kitty.

As she measured out Horlicks with one of the badly tarnished Apostle spoons from a bunch of old cutlery her mother had given them, she thought of how greatly she appreciated Charlie's goodness and made a mental note to give Max an early wake-up call next morning and turf him out of the study in good time.

'*If neither of us is married by the time we're thirty . . .*'

The shock of it had worn off a little by now. She smiled shyly at Charlie and saw him beam back, obviously relieved.

Quite likely, they'd never speak of it again. But with each minute that passed, the idea of being able to settle for him if all else failed became fractionally less bizarre. She even began to find it comforting: as if they'd taken out a mutual insurance policy against loneliness.

She wouldn't tell Liza or Max about the conversation, of course. Liza would be sure to tease and, if Max joined in, she didn't think she'd like that at all. It was absurd, of course: could never happen. Even so, she acknowledged for the first time that she often compared other men with Charlie and found them wanting.

Chapter Five

Camilla telephoned Tom at midnight.

It was typical, he thought, bloody typical, once he'd woken up sufficiently to demand who'd had the audacity to break into his precious sleep. It was just like his elder sister to phone on the eve of an important day in court; ditto for her to be imperious rather than apologetic.

Becky would quite happily have dealt with the call – protectiveness was one of her great qualities as a wife – but he insisted in taking it himself.

'Have you *any idea* what time this is?'

'I've lost Charlie's number,' came Camilla's reply.

'Oh really?' But sarcasm was wasted in this case.

'Suki won't give it to me,' she went on so loudly that Becky, cosily cuddled up against his back, could make out every word.

'What?'

'And Jane's not at home . . .'

'What?'

'And I can hardly wake up Mama and Pa, can I?'

'What?'

'Why do you keep on saying that?' asked Camilla, sounding really irritated, not appreciating that – like one of those Japanese words that possess a multitude of separate meanings – each 'what?' had conveyed something different. There was a lot for Tom to take in. Suki and Camilla had apparently fallen out. Then, Jane was very surprisingly not to be found at her home late at night. And why did Camilla deem it unacceptable to wake up their aged though still active father (who, as a judge, could shortly look forward to a substantial index-linked pension) and yet think it perfectly okay to wreck an important day in court for him, who was well-paid, certainly, but freelance?

'Why do you want it?'

'Just give it to me, Tom,' said Camilla wearily.

'Why?'

They'd never got on. It was he and Suki who'd been friends – perhaps in response to the stunning success, in different ways, of gorgeous Camilla and Henry the swot (though Tom had caught up with his brother later in a deadly surge of competitiveness). Camilla was an attention-seeker, pronounced Tom, without any conception of the real world. Maturity and distance lent uneasy peace, but when one of them was unhappy all the old irritation flared up.

'If you must know,' said Camilla, and he could hear the anger in her voice, 'Max has walked out.'

'Ah!'

'Why do you say it like that?'

'No reason,' said Tom very genially, 'no reason at all.' Actually it was because he'd been proved right, which was always most satisfactory. 'You mark my words, that boy's going to leave,' he'd told Becky that very evening as he'd sipped his wine and watched her drying glasses.

'I think he's gone to Charlie and Kitty.'

'Very probably,' Tom agreed in the same jovial way. Then he inquired, 'Would you like me to give Charlie a bell for you tomorrow?'

'No I would not, Tom.' Camilla enunciated each word slowly, like speaking to an imbecile. 'I would like you to give me the number now so I can telephone my son myself.'

'*Not* a good idea,' said Tom. 'Charlie needs his sleep.'

Then he had to hold the phone at arm's length because Camilla lost her temper in spectacular fashion.

By the following morning, the senior layer of family had learnt about Max's flight from his mother.

Becky informed Eleanor, sounding very anxious: 'Charlie says Max has already asked if he can stay on.'

There was a silence on the other end of the phone while this was absorbed.

'It's not a good idea,' said Becky.

Her mother-in-law might even have agreed with her. But in typical fashion she responded robustly, 'Oh I think it's a very good idea.'

'Charlie's pupillage . . .' Becky began anxiously. As he'd left the house, Tom had said fiercely, 'I will *not* have my son's chances ruined by that useless child of Camilla's.'

'*Kitty* can look after Max,' Eleanor told Becky, sounding delighted with herself.

The fact was that, whatever misgivings she now had about

Charlie sharing a flat with Kitty, Becky had encouraged it and secretly worked on Tom to get him to agree. She knew it was no good for Charlie to be too near his father. She said miserably: 'If the worst comes to the worst, I suppose he'll have to come home.'

'Oh, nonsense!' said Eleanor. 'It'll be good for him, being with the others.' She meant Max, of course. She was thinking that now she and Lionel could keep tabs on the boy, which had been difficult when he was living in the house in Eaton Square – try and give him some sort of direction at last. So could Hector, who was apparently planning a weekend very soon for all four cousins.

'Camilla will be all right,' Eleanor told her husband confidently.

'Indeed,' Lionel agreed with his sweet smile. Secretly, though, he was as worried as she.

His plan to take a personal hand in sorting out family problems had not up to now yielded much success. Jane had been extraordinarily vague about her meeting with Anthony (so far as he could gather, the subject of Max had hardly been mentioned) and nobody in the family had managed to talk to Camilla. He thought of the spoilt and pretty girl he'd always doted on. Without his knowing quite how it had happened, she'd become distanced from the family. He couldn't even recall the last time she'd come to stay; and as for having a proper conversation . . . Her husband's great wealth was probably to blame. Though thankful that, unlike his other daughter, Camilla had no money worries, he disapproved of so vapid and idle a life. But now even that had turned sour. He suspected that being abandoned by both husband and son would not go down well in her world, where appearance was everything.

'Highly strung,' pronounced Eleanor.

'A handful,' Lionel agreed, turning over a page of his *Times*.

'St Clair women have always been strong.'

'Indeed.' He beamed at her. Wasn't he married to the strongest of them all?

Chapter Six

Uncle Hector didn't hear the sound of Max's noisy car pulling up in the distance and his head gardener, Partridge, decided to say nothing since his employer would learn soon enough about the arrival of his visitors and, anyway, his throat was quite sore from the usual bellowing.

A stranger coming upon the scene might easily have assumed that both men were paid employees of this imposing estate. After all, they were dressed in similar old blue gardening overalls (though Uncle Hector's were dirtier and older) and sharing a job equally: Partridge pumping away with his foot at an ancient complicated contraption while Uncle Hector aimed the fine erratic spray it emitted at the glorious display of gold and crimson blooms that adorned the southern wall of the rose garden.

When Kitty touched her great-uncle on the shoulder, he

produced a beaming face like a magician. 'Ah!' It was such
pleasure to see them all, especially Max, for whom he'd planned
the weekend. The boy seemed very pale and awkward but he
noticed that Kitty was being even more protective than usual.
Dear Kitty! So like her darling mother.

'Good journey?'

'Fine,' shouted Charlie, stretching his mouth into a
letterbox shape, so Uncle Hector could lip-read, if he felt like
having a shot. It wasn't true. Overtaking as they approached
the brow of a hill, Max had only just missed a truck coming
the other way. Afterwards, still trembling with the horror of
what had nearly happened, they'd invented suitably dramatic
headlines. 'Cousins in carnage,' said Charlie grimly, and
couldn't help thinking of never having to worry about work
again. 'Friends forever,' said Kitty, and found peculiar comfort
in the idea of dying with Max. 'Future star scraped off road,'
giggled Liza. But it hadn't really been funny at all, though Max
had let out a strange crowing laugh as they shot past the truck
in a wake of blaring horns, so close that the car seemed to
shiver, too.

'Splendid,' said Uncle Hector, as if this was only to be
expected. 'Now, I expect you'd all like some tea.' Then,
worriedly, because the terror of his ancient manservant giving
in his notice was ever-present, 'Have you all said hello to
Merriweather?'

They hadn't, of course, though they'd just greeted Partridge
fondly. 'Only arrived this second,' Charlie yelled.

On the way back to the house, wincing discreetly with pain,
Hector leant heavily on Charlie, who was the tallest and
strongest. 'I won't be able to do this when you're a member of
your smart chambers,' he boomed, and a small procession of

rooks flapped in a stately way out of a chestnut tree. 'You'll be far too grand.'

Charlie made a helpless face, which no one noticed. He knew he shouldn't have come away but the others hadn't allowed it. He should have taken advantage of the empty flat. Max's presence was very disruptive and, to make matters worse, Liza had started turning up most evenings like a living reproach. He was becoming seriously anxious about work but all Kitty's concern seemed to be for Max now. He missed their old times.

Liza was humming softly. She'd found herself an extra job singing in a pub. They hadn't been to see her yet. She was making them feel guilty about that, too.

'Seen my abutilon?' said Uncle Hector with enormous pride, and they all stared at a spindly shrub with fragile yellow blossoms, preoccupied by their separate thoughts.

Merriweather was preparing tea for them in his cavernous shabby kitchen, the pattern in the linoleum long shuffled off between the ancient range and the table, an enormous heavy kettle coming very slowly and noisily to the boil like an old dog chasing rabbits in its dreams. He'd made a dozen bullet-like cakes in one of his tins hours ago so they'd be cold by now, and there was also a quantity of brown liquid with a skein of orange fat laced across it in a big saucepan on the range. Their spirits fell a little. Merriweather's soup for dinner, obviously, to be followed by another of his specials – pray God not his liver fricassee.

He didn't seem particularly pleased to see them, even after Liza had handed him a box of Rose's chocolates. Jane had given her enough money for a decent tip, but most of it had been spent on cigarettes and drinks on the way down. 'I was expecting you for lunch,' he told them.

'Oh no,' protested Kitty earnestly. 'We were always going to arrive at teatime.'

'He told me lunchtime,' said Merriweather in a voice that brooked no disagreement. 'Course I couldn't raise it with him – didn't want him to get himself in one of his states.' He added accusingly, 'Had to eat his leek and ham rissole on his own, didn't he?' He let them stew in the guilt of imagining four more painstakingly prepared rissoles, all of which had had to be thrown away.

'I spoke to him last night,' said Liza, who was naturally confrontational, 'and he definitely said four o'clock.'

It was a bad start to the weekend. Trying to make Uncle Hector appear as if he was losing his mind was one of Merriweather's few pleasures.

The years were falling away and being treated like children again was as strangely comforting as it was irritating.

They were always given the same rooms. It was a question of seniority. Charlie, the eldest man, was given the Green Room, which was actually blue, and had a much envied four-poster in it (though a very lumpy mattress) and an antique armchair with string bound tightly round one arm and a label attached to it inscribed in Uncle Hector's distinctive spidery writing – '*This chair has had to be mended five times!!!*'

Kitty could expect the Wisteria Room, where fragile mauve blooms had once framed the exquisite view of the rose garden. There was a small jade tree on the dressing-table, so placed that, almost inevitably, guests swept it to the floor as they brushed past. Their hearts contracted with terror until they noticed that all the jade leaves were chipped: it had happened many times before. The tree had been as provocatively arranged as the precious plates set, in upstanding fashion, on a polished table at the end of a corridor. The slightest movement set them trembling and once Charlie, with his heavy tread, had had to make a flying tackle for a piece of second-dynasty Ming. The house was full of hazards: even descending the highly polished wooden staircase was perilous. It was as if it had been deliberately set up as a specialized assault course for guests.

'It's not fair,' said Liza, like a child. As the youngest, she got the Box Room, which didn't have a single box, though she was sure it possessed a ghost. She said so without much hope. Uncle Hector had always told them he didn't believe in ghosts and, anyway, would never allow her to move. She'd be sharing the bathroom situated opposite with Max, who got the End Room, so-called because it was the last room at the bottom of a corridor. None of the bathrooms were at all warm or comfortable but this was the worst – painted stark white, freezing even in summer, with deep brown stains on the ancient enamel and a hollow cylindrical plug that was impossible to insert so you couldn't even fill the bath properly; and a hot tap that set up a vibrating moan and only delivered water in a brown trickle when the noise had almost driven you mad; and a strange slatted wooden affair like a breakfast tray, which fitted across the bath and held a pumice stone and a slimy natural sponge. To cap it all, there was a long mirror that made the slimmest of naked bodies appear fat. She was already in a bad mood. Her cousins had forbidden her to bring the puppy, even though she'd argued fiercely that hiding it would pose no problem in so large a house. It was deeply unfair that Max had been allowed to move into the spare room at Chepstow Place.

On top of everything, her mother had been in a funny mood for ages now. Something had happened to her but, most irritatingly, she was keeping it to herself.

'What's the matter with you?' Liza had asked only the day before.

'Nothing!'

'Yes there is, Jane. Why won't you tell me?'

'Darling, I don't tell you everything!' her mother had exclaimed in a maddeningly amused indulgent way.

'Yes you do!' Liza had exclaimed, honestly astonished. Since her father's death, her mother had treated her more like a sister, as if this was the only way to endure the tragedy. A deeply childish part of Liza had been punishing her by spending so much time at Charlie and Kitty's but infuriatingly, her mother didn't seem to notice. She'd sit at the breakfast table with a dreamy look on her face, not concentrating when Liza spoke to her. She'd even stopped asking if she'd be home for dinner. And Liza – who never noticed anything – had observed that the awful strained look her mother had worn for months had vanished.

Tea was served in the drawing-room – watery Earl Grey and Merriweather's bullet buns, but only after they'd ploughed through bread and butter (which tasted suspiciously like margarine). Uncle Hector had adjusted his hearing-aid properly now, so he could go through the ritual of catching up.

This involved each cousin in turn telling him about any new developments in his or her life while nervously balancing Spode cups and saucers considered so precious that – rather than trust them to Merriweather – Uncle Hector would wash and dry them himself. (Not long ago a cup had slipped from his arthritic fingers and smashed on the stone sink in the scullery and Uncle Hector had set up the same anguished mooing sound guests sometimes heard issuing from his bedroom in the early mornings.)

Uncle Hector would look impressed, worried or amused as meaning percolated.

He was very gentle and forbearing as he talked to Max. 'Any news on the job front, dear chap?'

'No, thank goodness,' muttered Max.

'What's that?' As Uncle Hector articulated the familiar question, a big gob of half-masticated bun landed on Charlie's lapel, but – with his characteristic courtesy and amiability – Charlie ignored it till later.

'Max has decided to take up real tennis,' he informed his uncle, coming to the rescue.

'Ah!'

Uncle Hector patted Max on the knee, and removed his hand almost immediately. What a worry the boy was: no ambition, never any proper direction from his parents. What a curse all that wealth had turned out to be. And Anthony and Camilla were still warring, it seemed. Like his brother, Lionel, Hector had been hoping this awful business would be resolved by now. He was furious with his niece for being so obdurate. But, in typical family fashion, he avoided confrontation, letting silence (and his formal letter cancelling the invitation to his party) speak for itself.

'So you've become A LODGER . . .' Uncle Hector made it sound like a joke. At last Max had become something! It was the closest he'd get to referring to the trouble between the boy and his mother.

Max nodded, hiding behind his wings of hair, and his cup and saucer clattered musically on his knee.

'Splendid!' Like Lionel and Eleanor, Hector could only see the advantages of Max moving in with Charlie and Kitty. They were both so eminently sane – bless them! Just what the poor boy needed.

It worried him that Liza was still set on a singing career. The idea of a girl from her background harbouring such an ambition was novel, in the early seventies. Did she have any idea how hard one had to work to achieve even the first rung on the ladder of success? Jane had assured him she practised a great deal. But was it enough? Looking at Liza's flushed and pretty face, the extraordinary patchwork waistcoat she'd chosen to wear, he doubted it. Of course, she should be commended for going out and earning money for her keep – albeit in a menial capacity with no prospects. 'Well, I think it's JOLLY ADMIRABLE that you're paying your OWN BILLS.' However, he was not amused by her habit of turning her experiences of looking after distressed gentlewomen into stories (she'd just told an upsetting one about a meal of curried catfood, shrieking into his ear in between wild bursts of laughter, biting her lip in saucer-eyed horror as, too late, she clocked his reaction). Naughty since infancy but so endearing – and forgiven for everything because the earth had only recently settled on her father's grave. Poor, dear Henry. What a tragic day that had been. He pretended to scowl at her. Thank goodness he didn't hear her say softly: 'I've decided I'm going to advertise for a sugar daddy.'

But Kitty never disappointed. *Such* a sensible girl, thought Uncle Hector, who was kept in happy ignorance about her love life. She'd get married soon. Dear Kitty. Almost twenty-four. It was high time. Then, just like her mother, she could pour all her energy into a family.

As for Charlie, he was the golden boy, though as a child he'd been more conscientious and diligent than brilliant. It was immensely gratifying that, after some hesitation, he'd agreed to take up the family baton and go into law. And it was a fine idea to have chosen chancery because, though he'd confessed to finding it less interesting than criminal law, he would not be in competition with his father.

But Uncle Hector, who was highly sensitive to the young, noticed how tired Charlie looked. Those bar exams had been tough, and pupillage terms could all too often lead nowhere. For all Tom's deep pride in his son, he pushed him to the limit. Uncle Hector shivered with anxiety, as always, when considering the frailty of the flesh.

Young guests were expected to earn their keep at Cedar Manor. It was part of the discipline of the place. So after tea, the cousins were allotted tasks that could just as easily (and without doubt more efficiently) have been carried out by Partridge or even Merriweather. In a spirit of fairness, Uncle Hector gave himself the dangerous job of smoking out a hornets' nest. He prepared for it by dressing up in an ancient head-protector like a linen lantern with flaps and enormous padded gloves. It would have been more sensible, of course, to leave the job for Partridge, who'd gone home for the day.

Charlie touched his great-uncle on the arm and, as tactfully as he could, bellowed words to this effect.

The flaps shook violently. Out of the question!

Charlie's task was to collect mounds of dark earth desecrating an emerald lawn and convey them to a much bigger heap by the greenhouses (though the reason was not explained to him, nor the use that would be made of all this soil). Max was detailed to tie drooping dahlias to stakes – 'not too tight, dear boy!' – even though the blooms were almost over. Kitty had been asked to put up the mah-jong table – 'so I can watch the four of you enjoy yourselves after dinner'. And Liza – what could she be trusted with? Uncle Hector set her to sorting out packs of playing cards jumbled up by a previous party of young houseguests.

She did it very rapidly and efficiently, shivering in the cold drawing-room, where the fire would not be lit until six o'clock, and afterwards amused herself by reading the visitors' book, which was kept on a polished round table by the window and went back for decades.

'22nd–24th September 1945 Chute Chute' was one entry, which Liza correctly interpreted as meaning that, following the end of the last war, Lord Chute of Chute had graced Cedar Manor with his presence for a weekend. Had he enjoyed himself? Been an interesting sort of guest? There was no way of telling. Uncle Tom's visitors' book in the country – where people were encouraged to insert comments – was far more enlightening and entertaining.

Frustrated, Liza turned to Uncle Hector's photograph albums, which were also kept on the table. She was curious about what he'd looked like as a child, or even a young man. But, again, there was no information. The albums started in 1926. He must have stored the early ones elsewhere – presumably for reasons of space. Perhaps, if she asked sweetly enough, he'd let her take a look.

'Finished?' asked Kitty.

But Max hadn't even started. He was standing by the dahlia bed, smoking a cigarette (which was forbidden in the house) and staring into a private abyss.

'Max?'

Still he didn't answer and Kitty felt the now familiar mixture of terror and concern.

'Max,' she repeated, laying a hand on his arm. She often touched the people she loved, as Charlie knew better than anyone. 'Look!' she'd direct, patting him on the shoulder; or she'd shove him affectionately – 'Get on with you!' After his astonishing suggestion the night Max had arrived, they were thoroughly back to their old easy brother-and-sister-like relationship.

But touching Max was, all of a sudden, loaded and scary. 'Why?' Kitty wondered, dismayed and fearful of stumbling on the answer. Since his arrival at the flat, being in his familiar company had become like straying into a secret room. She was painfully conscious of his presence all the time. She'd find herself fingering his things, as dazed and foolish as a sleepwalker: holding his just-used toothbrush to the corners of her lips, brushing his damp towel against her cheeks. It was shameful and bewildering, coming to.

Max turned obediently and looked at her, but without comprehension. He reminded her of the beautiful white marble statue by the bench in the rose garden. It was Narcissus, Uncle Hector had informed them as children, and proceeded to tell the story of the myth.

'Come on!' said Kitty in the cheery, encouraging fashion that was becoming more and more natural (and probably more irritating, too, she told herself), and started briskly tying up the dahlias.

Only then did Max snap out of it, like a person awakening from a trance. He looked flustered and very young. 'Sorry,' he muttered and smiled at her – his crazily inappropriate grin that gave the impression that, really, he was still full of joy and optimism – and, for the second time, Kitty's confused heart did a flip.

After dinner, Uncle Hector asked them if they'd mind conveying the dirty dishes to the scullery.

Merriweather had been very truculent as he served the food – fishcakes made mostly out of potato to follow his soup, and tinned pineapple chunks accompanied by single cream with an unpleasant aftertaste. But there'd been two bottles of marvellous Moselle to go with the meal and Amontillado sherry beforehand. The drink was always first-class and plentiful at Cedar Manor.

'His back's playing up,' Uncle Hector told them, looking very worried. He was in a sorry way, too, with a crimson swollen nose like a clown's, but had rejected all expressions of sympathy.

Merriweather had asked his employer for a washing-up machine some time ago. It had been a reasonable request, what with all the entertaining, but it had taken more than a year of dark threats and sulking to get Uncle Hector to agree. The gleaming white appliance looked odd in the ancient flaking scullery, where stiff incontinent taps left limestone trails on the deep square stone sink. When it first arrived, Uncle Hector and Merriweather had pored over the instructions like a long-married couple: Uncle Hector penetrating Merriweather's territory as a right because serious money had been spent and therefore mistakes must not be made. Pre-wash? Intensive programme? Technology was astonishing!

'Tell him to be sure to wash the dishes properly first,' Uncle Hector reminded the cousins, as always. 'And he mustn't put in my bone-handled knives, or my crystal glasses.'

*

After the mah-jong, the cousins went for a night walk. It was a ritual. Besides, Uncle Hector went to bed promptly at half-past ten and they were tired of mah-jong, which they never played anywhere else. Yes, they agreed meekly, when he asked them to be sure to lock up properly when they returned (two big bolts on the front door) and turn the lights out. He'd never had a burglary, but lived in constant fear of losing the precious oil landscapes in the dining-room that crouched in the grime of years and the gloom of low-wattage light bulbs and might not even be noticed by intruders.

The sky was dense black, traced by the milky markings of stars. On a night like this, thought Kitty, you could believe in magic.

'What do I wish for?' she wondered, very conscious of Max beside her in the dark though it was Charlie who thought to put a hand under her elbow in case she slipped on the shallow stone steps leading to the rose garden.

A full moon sailed out from behind a lone cloud and the trees and grass assumed an eerie shade of blue and Liza shrieked, 'I'm a werewolf!' and started galloping with wild abandon over the lawn and Kitty felt Max shiver for some reason.

His mother rang him several times a day. His father called often, as well, but Max refused to speak to him. Letters arrived regularly – stiff cream envelopes adorned with Anthony's brisk blue handwriting – and lay unopened on the rickety table in the tiny hall. Other members of the family tried to find out what was going on, seeming to believe it was their right.

Max would answer all of them with monosyllables or silences.

Unlike the rest of the family, the cousins never asked him

about the break-up or his own jagged feelings, but he didn't volunteer any information to them either. They were sympathetic though secretly a little hurt. Who could possibly love or care for him more? 'Should I say something?' Liza once whispered when he'd momentarily left the room where she and Kitty had soothed and spoilt him all evening. 'He'd hate that,' Kitty found herself objecting. But was it she who'd have hated it if Liza got in first?

Max was very selfish to live with. He never cleaned the bath or helped with the washing-up, and the spare room had almost immediately become a tip, dirty underwear and shirts festooning the once grand desk where Charlie should by rights have been working. They were like indulgent parents clearing up after him, protecting him. Kitty worried about Charlie, too; but that concern had been overtaken, like one mound of finely sieved dark earth buried by another.

All together in the darkness, the cousins communicated, nevertheless. They could feel the threads of blood and time connecting them and the odd new tensions seemed to fade away as they delighted in each other's company in their favourite place. After a moment, every one of them followed Liza on to the dark lawn, prancing around in crazy whirling gallops.

But it seemed to vulnerable imaginative Kitty that something else was out there, too: a watcher in the darkness, a spectre who hesitated to join in.

Then Liza threw herself on Max, rolling over and over with him on the dewy grass and the fancy vanished – to be replaced by jealousy, as unmistakable and black and destructive as the hidden rhizomorphs even now eating away at the roots of the old cedar tree looming in the background.

 *Chapter Seven*

All houses steal something from their inhabitants, adding to the mysterious distillations of happiness and betrayal and sorrow: those ghosts of past emotions that flavour bricks and mortar far more permanently than the aroma of frying onions that Kitty could smell as she opened her parents' front door.

In the grandparents' house in Hampshire – and Hector's, too – it was restraint and formality that met visitors like a long-serving butler. As they stepped into the imposing hall scented with dried rose petals and overlooked by a stuffed buffalo head, the stealthy pendulum tick of the grandfather clock passed through the family for generations reminded them of the inevitability of death and, consequently, the all-importance of structure.

In Tom and Becky's smart house in Bayswater, where the

girls' stringed instruments and tennis racquets were laid on the wooden pew in the hall in readiness for the next lessons, it was tension and impatience that struck the first note even if Tom couldn't be heard bellowing somewhere in the background, chivvying his family on, determined they should excel.

Jane's house seemed confused. One moment, it had been peaceful and forward-looking; the next, it felt as if a passing murderer had broken in. Only yesterday Henry, returning exhausted with his briefcase, had invigorated the house. Today the absolute lack of him was reflected in the blank dark windowpanes and dead silence when his family came home at night. No wonder Liza longed to escape.

But Kitty's parents' house had always been simply and unmistakably happy, stamped with years of loving and teasing and sharing. She couldn't remember a time when she'd heard her parents' voices raised, or seen them find anybody more interesting than each other. 'Always knock on our bedroom door,' she and Phil had been warned when young. It had been hard, sometimes, to be the child of such a couple. 'Ah!' Uncle Hector would beam on his visits; but, after a while, he'd fall silent and sigh, as if remembering his own bleak upbringing and reflecting on all that he'd missed. It would be good for Max, thought Kitty a little smugly, to see how real families worked.

'Is that you, Kitty?' came her mother's musical voice from the kitchen in the basement.

'Yes, Ma!' Kitty turned to smile encouragingly at Max as she shut the front door behind them. She went round to her parents for supper once a week. She'd told Max it would be good if he came too.

'Good?' he'd echoed with a puzzled frown.

'It'll be fun, Max. And Ma's a wonderful cook.' Proper food, thought Kitty, not the stuff his mother's housekeeper produced which always tasted so weirdly unlike it looked. 'And you'll see Phil.' Her brother might be maddening, but at least she had one. How lucky she was, compared to Max.

She'd enjoyed the journey there: having Max to herself and the assumption people must have made when they saw the two of them packed into the MG that flashed by far too fast. Max attracted such attention these days. Meanwhile, back at Chepstow Place, Charlie could work without distraction, which was another benefit of the exercise.

'Is Max with you?'

'Yes, Ma!' Kitty thought how comforting it was to come home, though she treasured her independence.

'Oh, good!'

Kitty turned to Max and silently reassured him with a glance.

As Suki and Simon's kitchen was in the basement, those already installed could watch visitors descend the open stairs step by step, until finally the whole person was revealed. But those descending had no idea, until they neared the bottom, exactly who they would find sitting round the long pine table with its wax-encrusted china candlesticks, its omnipresent piles of letters and newspapers, its roses gathered from the garden, always when slightly past their best.

Max's wariness was unjustified. The only person in the kitchen was his aunt, the creator of the delicious smell that had hit him as soon as they entered the house. She was wearing a rather stained blue apron over one of her familiar drooping flowery dresses and, as they watched, she tipped mince into her pan of onions and started to chop at the meat with a wooden spoon, her long hair hanging over her flushed face. On another hob, liquid was bubbling away in a saucepan, every so often hurling up greasy red blobs to spatter the Aga. The room was stiflingly hot in spite of the French windows open to the long and narrow strip of garden that Max could see was overgrown and untidy.

'Max! I'm so glad!'

Max let himself be kissed. His aunt felt much softer than his mother did, with a very wholesome natural scent rather than the cloud of Chanel No. 5 his mother moved around in.

'How are you, darlings?' She glanced at the big round wooden clock on the wall. 'Oh God, is that the time? Dad'll be home soon. Kitty, can you watch this pan for me?'

Kitty smiled knowingly at Max as she took over the stirring. For as long as she could remember, her mother had removed her apron and combed her hair and put on lipstick for her father. It was one of her rules.

She saw Max look round the warm untidy room and drew an imaginary balloon for him: '*This is how real homes are. This is how proper mothers behave.*'

The front door banged up above. 'Anyone ho-ome?' called Simon, and Kitty beamed at Max once more. In that house, the joyous expectant noise of her father returning was as punctual as birdsong.

Then there was the thump thump thump of his feet on the stairs to the kitchen.

His legs in dark trousers were revealed, and a shirt (he'd flung off his jacket on entering the house), hands already tugging at his tie, and finally his delighted face as he saw Kitty.

'What a treat!' Though she always came to supper on

Thursday evenings. After he'd kissed her and patted her cheek, he pronounced: 'You're looking well, my sweet.'

Max was made to feel almost as welcome. Simon shook his hand vigorously and clapped him on the back. 'How are you, my dear old chap? Now – let's get you both a drink.' He pulled a bottle of already opened white wine from the fridge, examined it with a frown – 'Hope this isn't *too* poisonous' – and filled glasses.

After a moment, he said: 'Well, let's get this table laid, shall we?' He gave a token bellow: 'Phil!' But predictably there was no reply. If Phil was to be made to help, somebody would have to climb the stairs to his room and knock sharply on the door. Even then, he might not hear. He lived in a world of dreams, his grandmother said.

Then Simon asked: 'Where's Mum?' And Kitty knew that, for him, the room might as well have been empty. As always, it was a desolate realization that she, his beloved daughter, unseen for a week, wasn't enough. He was lost without his Pudding, his Stanislav; wouldn't want to miss out on one second of the unique and precious comfort of her presence. In a moment, like always, he'd race eagerly up the stairs, balancing two glasses of wine, and Kitty would hear their joyous intimate laughter in the distance.

'Upstairs, getting ready.'

'Oh well . . .' he said a little helplessly, almost as if afraid of being a disappointment. And for once, to Kitty's astonishment and pleasure, he stayed put.

Max grasped the bundle of cutlery Kitty handed him but didn't appear to know how the separate utensils should be arranged (which was absurd since he'd seen formal place settings enough times). He seemed amused by his own incompetence. 'Here?' he asked, waving a spoon around with his sudden, almost ugly smile.

Then the doorbell rang.

Max glanced at Kitty inquiringly, but without anxiety. He was thoroughly relaxed by then.

Kitty shrugged. 'Probably someone trying to sell something,' she suggested. 'Or Jehovah's Witnesses?'

'What's that?' Max was astonishingly ignorant about the world.

'We're not expecting anyone,' said Simon very definitely as he set off up the stairs (and Max remembered that later and put his own spin on it).

Kitty and Max heard the front door being opened and then they froze.

They were trapped in the bowels of the house, cut off by the staircase that led to the hall, though Kitty saw Max glance in the direction of the garden penned by wooden fences, as if he were actually calculating the odds of making a last-minute escape.

When his eyes met hers again, they were quite blank: as if a shutter had come down in his mind and she was no longer a person who mattered; as if all her kindness to him and the relaxing and joking just now had never happened.

Simon and Suki set great store by hospitality. Therefore when Camilla turned up so unexpectedly, they appeared delighted. Hadn't Suki been trying to talk to her without success for weeks? There was plenty to eat, of course – there always was in that house. And by a lucky chance Max was visiting! Lovely for them both!

Kitty and Max heard it all: Simon's welcome as he opened the

door and then his 'Excellent! You'll never guess who's here!';
that familiar cool and lazy voice, though a little louder than
usual, heels clipping the tessellated hall floor (she always wore
high heels); Suki trilling faintly from her bedroom at the top of
the house, 'Who is it?'

They assumed it was sheer coincidence that Camilla had
chosen tonight to drop in. They weren't to know that she'd
phoned the flat in Chepstow Place in an attempt to talk to Max
and caught Charlie at a weak moment. Kitty seldom allowed
him to cook, so he'd enjoyed creating an omelette stuffed with
Gruyère cheese and grated celery. But after that, with the place
to himself at last, he'd found it impossible to get down to work.
So he'd seized on the chance to chat to his aunt, who was being
charming. He told her he didn't know where Max was (though
he disliked telling lies), but believed Kitty had gone to her
parents. So Camilla put two and two together – making a
triumphant four when she found Max's distinctive little green
MG parked outside the house.

It was Kitty's fault, really, that Suki and Simon didn't appreciate
quite how unfortunate the situation was. They were always
trying to pump her about Max's relationship with his parents.

'Does he see them at all, darling?'

'Dunno really.'

'Do they at least talk on the phone?'

'No idea, actually.' Kitty would give them her sweet
apologetic smile that was so like her mother's and made it
impossible for them to be cross with her. The loyalty those
cousins showed each other was touching and admirable,
really.

However, it was obvious to Simon now that Max hadn't seen

his mother for some time. Why else had he turned so pale and quiet? And why did she crow, 'Darling!' in that triumphant way?

Then Suki ran down the kitchen stairs to greet Camilla.

'Oh, are you sisters?' people meeting them for the first time would often exclaim. But Suki was used to this by now, could even forestall it with a smiling, 'My sister's beautiful, isn't she?' It never occurred to her that it was their difference in character which made the greatest impression.

'You look lovely,' she said now, responding, as always, to the expectation in Camilla's eyes.

'Lovely,' echoed Simon just as automatically, but he and Suki had already exchanged troubled glances.

Of course Camilla was good-looking in a very English fine-featured blonde fashion, but far more remarkable than her looks was her self-possession. People stared at Camilla mostly because she willed them to. It was as if she'd absorbed all the discipline and competitiveness of her upbringing for her own purposes. If you behaved like a beauty, she'd once told Suki, the younger sister, with that flashing determined smile so like Tom's, then people believed it.

But tonight something about her was fractionally off kilter. She was exquisitely dressed, as usual, in an elegant black suit, and she wore diamonds in her ears. She looked as if she'd intended to go to a cocktail party rather than drop in, uninvited, on kitchen supper with her far less fashionable sister. But when Suki kissed her, she was astonished to discover that, under the Chanel No. 5, Camilla smelt of sweat.

In the tradition of the house, she was straightaway provided with a brimming glass. As she sipped at it, she looked round the cosy cluttered kitchen, seemingly curious and a little amused (and, for the first time, Suki saw her fake rustic decor as more absurd than enviable).

Then Phil lounged down the stairs, his internal radar having informed him to the minute when food was about to be served.

'Well done!' said Suki sarcastically, as usual. She turned to her sister. 'You're just in time for supper, too, Camilla.'

But Camilla started scrabbling in her handbag and pulled out a packet of cigarettes. Then she searched for a lighter.

'You're not going to smoke, are you?'

Camilla came very close to Suki. 'Do you object?' It was said with a smile, but Max abruptly went to the French windows to stare out at the garden with its narrow bumpy lawn and lengthening shadows.

'Not at all,' said Simon. 'It's only eight. Supper'll keep, won't it, Pud?'

'Of course,' Suki agreed even more pleasantly and Max returned from the windows as if tugged by an invisible string.

The cigarette seemed to calm Camilla and afterwards she obediently sat down at the table.

She accepted a plate of food from Suki. 'This is a treat.'

'It's only spag bol, Camilla!'

'It looks delicious,' said Camilla, smiling. 'But actually, I meant seeing my son at last.'

Sitting opposite Max, Kitty saw him make a movement she'd almost forgotten – hunching his shoulders as if he wanted to bury his head between them like a sleeping bird.

'So how are you, darling?' Camilla asked.

'Okay.' Max sounded as gruff as Phil. He didn't raise his head. As usual, his hair concealed any reaction.

'Is that all you can say?' She smiled indulgently at the others. 'It's been weeks now. And I've missed him, you know.'

Max made a noise in his throat that might have signified either contrition or embarrassment.

'So tell me – what have you been doing with yourself?'

Max shrugged. 'Just – things,' he mumbled.

He could be deeply irritating, thought Kitty fondly. Why didn't he just make an effort and give his mother what she wanted? It would be so easy to tell her about the squash and the real tennis – his whole idle complicated programme for filling his days.

'I see!' Once again, Camilla glanced round at the others as if to check they were taking this as humorously as she. Then her smile vanished. She gave a deep sigh. 'It must be jolly being with the others. Not like staying with your poor old mum. I rattle around Eaton Square now. I haven't even got Philomena. She's taken the week off.' She laid down her knife and fork with a clatter and lit another cigarette.

Kitty watched her mother start to say something – everyone knew she hated people smoking in the kitchen and, besides, they were still eating – and saw her father shake his head slightly at her as if indicating, 'I'll deal with this.'

It was one of Simon's talents to inject calm and humour into tricky situations. It proved invaluable when a car he'd just sold turned out to have a malfunctioning alternator or a fanbelt that broke the first time it was taken on the motorway. It came from Harrow, he recognized in maturity: the school he'd hated at the time but now felt such nostalgia for. It was one of his many regrets that he'd been unable to buy Phil the same brand of confidence to carry him through life.

'I say, Camilla, out of interest – how many of those things are you on a day now?'

Camilla shrugged, put two fingers up – presumably to

indicate two packets – and inhaled deeply. Smoke poured over the laden table.

Suki abruptly rose and opened the back door even wider. Then, as if a little ashamed to have shown her irritation, she announced: 'I've made chocolate mousse.' She directed a warm smile at Max. 'I seem to remember someone loves it.'

'Chocolate mousse!' exclaimed Simon. 'I always knew you were a clever old Pud!'

Phil cleared his throat elaborately like he always did when embarrassed and Kitty tried to smile at Max – '*Just listen to them!*' – but it was no good. He wouldn't even look at her now.

Her parents *were* embarrassing the way they broadcast their happiness. It was as if everyone else was an interruption. She could imagine that someone less contentedly married might find them smug and even hurtful – not that they ever meant it like that, of course.

Simon said with great interest and enthusiasm, 'How are the Cotswolds?'

'Haven't been,' said Camilla shortly. She stubbed out her cigarette, immediately lit up another.

Simon continued undaunted. 'Met a woman the other day who said she hunted up there. Now, what was her name?' He beat his forehead. 'Smithson? . . . Sanderson?'

'You never told me,' said Suki.

'Didn't I, Puddy? Thought I told you everything.'

'Sampson,' said Camilla. 'Mariella Sampson.'

'That's it!' Simon beamed, seemingly delighted that now he could file away the correct name.

'Anthony fucked her,' Camilla announced.

Straight afterwards, it seemed impossible that she'd said it. Elegant Camilla in her suit and diamonds? Not a chance!

Especially as she still had a pleasant little smile playing over her lips.

But Phil had certainly registered that something very different and extraordinary had happened. It had cut right into his daydreaming and he wore a cautious but incredulous grin as if, suddenly, this tedious evening was starting to look up.

Suki frowned and said: 'Kitty, darling, why don't all you children go upstairs and . . .'

'What a good idea!' said Simon energetically. 'You can watch the news for us. Tell us what's happening in Northern Ireland. I tell you, I hate feeling so unsafe. I don't know about anyone else?'

'Her and half the Beaufort,' Camilla observed in exactly the same coolly amused tone.

Simon removed the bottle from Camilla's reach. '*Oh Lord!*' he thought. Must have tanked up before getting there. Funny she wasn't slurring her words, though. She was behaving as if a switch had failed to trip – like the relentlessly overheating engine of an elegant Rolls-Royce.

'Yes, why don't you go upstairs, kids?' said Suki, sounding very anxious.

'No,' said Camilla, 'I'd like them to stay. I think it's high time Max knew what sort of man his father is. And it'll be – instructive for Kitty.'

Kitty stared at the tablecloth, her whole body rigid with sympathy for Max. On impulse, she reached under the table for his knee and pressed it. But his response was dismaying. His eyes widened with shock; he moved his leg sharply away.

'Can't keep his trousers on,' Camilla announced to the company. Her hand shook a little as she stubbed out her cigarette, as if, after the admission, her composure was beginning to crack.

Kitty froze. Uncle Ant always looked as if he had a secret – it was part of his gleaming smiley attraction. But this couldn't be right! The very thought was repulsive. Anyway, he worked too hard to be unfaithful. Even in a naturally industrious family, he was famous for it. 'My Dad's always in his office,' Max had moaned to her once and she'd countered briskly, 'Well, who else is he doing it for but you?' Uncle Ant, who gave wonderful expensive Christmas presents (which the St Clairs didn't) and was forever popping open champagne and laughing and, after Hector, was the most popular relative. Could Aunt Camilla possibly be making it up? But she seemed so deeply and genuinely angry: Kitty could tell from her glittering eyes and flushed cheeks. And why would she say such dreadful things unless they were true?

Suki was remembering being a sixteen-year-old bridesmaid, round-faced in bunchy magnolia, and following a beautiful couple out of a church and intercepting an exchange of looks as intense as the beating of wings and vowing, 'I'll never ever marry unless it's like this.'

She knew very well that someone should be stopping Camilla most forcefully, especially for Max's sake. But instead she found herself transfixed: listening with appalled fascination as her sister began to open one hidden compartment after another.

'It's a compulsion.' Camilla's voice was starting to rise. 'No. A sickness. He thinks he loves women, but he despises them really. He's – incapable of passing up an opportunity.'

Suki became aware that Max's leg, next to hers, had started jiggling frantically and finally – far too late – moved in to protect him. 'That's quite enough now, Camilla!' At the same time, she wondered why Simon hadn't done it first. But it wasn't his way, she acknowledged a little sadly. He slid away from confrontation. His style would have been to divert Camilla with a story or a joke – but perhaps, for once, his composure had deserted him. It wasn't so surprising, really, in the circumstances.

'No,' Camilla corrected her. 'It's never ever been enough.'

It was quite useless for anyone to try and stop her. She wasn't finished. In fact, as it turned out, she'd only just begun.

Chapter Eight

Suddenly, it seemed, Liza hated the country. She resented the lack of shops and general entertainment, she told her mother, and failed to see the point of nature. For this reason, she explained – abruptly on the edge of tears – going to stay with the grandparents would be duller than dull.

'But you couldn't wait to get to Hector's the other weekend.'

'That's because the others were going. Anyway . . . it's different there.'

'The grandparents would love to see you, darling. And Tom and Becky and the girls are coming for lunch on Sunday . . .'

'Not Charlie, though.'

'I'm sure they wouldn't mind if you brought the puppy.'

'There's *no* way I'm leaving him behind again.'

'And you can put flowers on Pa's grave. It's time we did that, darling.'

There. Jane had finally brought out the real reason why Liza didn't want to go anywhere near her grandparents' house now.

Henry was buried in the churchyard of the chapel that was part of their property. It had been generally assumed there was no other option and Jane had been too broken to protest. But she would have liked to be consulted. It meant that visiting his grave required planning. And it became a performance. Even though the churchyard couldn't be seen from the house, you felt your grief was measured and perhaps even found wanting.

'Would you like to help me feed the chickens?' Eleanor asked Liza once they'd had tea in the drawing-room and recovered from their journey.

It was one of the duties of Blackstock, the gardener, to clean out the run and wring birds' necks when their time came. But it was Eleanor who dispensed grain in the morning and evening, calling to the chickens by the special names she'd given them.

'Yes, Grandma,' Liza agreed meekly as if still a dutiful child. She guessed why her grandmother wanted to be alone with her.

'How's Max?' Eleanor asked very casually as she oversaw Liza measuring out grain from the big sack kept in the shed near the chicken-run.

'Okay.'

'I heard there was a family supper at Suki's.' She added the faintest of question marks.

'Mmm.'

'How nice.'

Liza said nothing.

'But I know you weren't there, darling,' said Eleanor, implying that she knew all about the evening anyway. She asked very casually, 'Did Kitty mention anything about it?'

'Not to me, Grandma.'

Eleanor let it go for now. 'Remember,' she said, as if talking to her poultry, 'one small scoop each and one for luck.' But there was an edge to her voice that should have warned Liza. 'How's the singing going?' she went on in a bright tone.

'I've got a job,' Liza told her proudly, hurling a handful of grain across the chicken-run in a grand gesture, like throwing her talent at the world.

'I thought you had lots of little jobs . . . Not like that, darling. Gently, scatter it gently. And give Blackie a smidgeon more, she's chicks to care for.'

'No, I mean a real job, Grandma.'

'Oh, a real job . . . Isn't looking after your old people a real job? Look at Speckledy! I always call that her "Oliver Twist" expression.'

'It's for an hour and a half every Tuesday and Thursday evening, and I can sing what I want. And afterwards they pass round a hat.'

'Whatever for, darling?' asked Eleanor, crinkling her brows under the pull-on felt affair she wore for the garden.

'So people can put money in it,' Liza explained blithely. 'Last week, I did "Summertime" and everyone stood up and clapped. I made ten quid!'

Her grandmother's frown deepened. 'And where is this exactly?'

'Actually it's called the King's Head,' muttered Liza, realizing – too late – that she should have explained it all differently.

'What an odd name. What kind of a place is that, darling?'

There was no way out. 'Actually it's a pub, Grandma.'

'A pub.' Eleanor stopped what she was doing and the birds clustered around her feet, clucking fretfully while continuing to peck in a dim mystified way at the ground. She looked very troubled. 'Is that really a good idea?'

Liza thought of her night of triumph: of trembling with relief that she'd executed the songs so well and being astonished by the strength of the applause and afterwards being bought drinks and assured that she had a shining future. But now all of this seemed to fall away because it meant so little in terms of accomplishment here.

Liza was very silent as she and her mother set off for the churchyard, Trigger ambling alongside and falling behind every so often to relish the smells and sounds of the countryside. He'd thoroughly settled into his new life. He couldn't even remember his first owner, though he still cringed at sudden movements.

'You didn't *buy* flowers!' Eleanor had exclaimed disbelievingly, looking at their enormous bunch brought from London. 'Red roses, too! Where *did* you find them? There's a mass of chrysanthemums in the garden. *So* pretty. I put some on the grave only a few days ago.'

Jane glanced anxiously at Liza as she pushed open the wooden gate. It was a year since they'd watched Henry being lowered into a narrow deep space cut in the earth, like the shaft of a lift only carrying passengers down. After clods had rattled on to his coffin, he'd been left to the mercy of the weather: Henry, who felt the cold keenly and had been sociable. Liza must be experiencing the same pull between unchanging love and a growing and shameful impatience to escape from all things dead. They should continue to pay their respects to everything he'd been and given them and yet, at the same time, remember their duty towards themselves. '*I never thought I'd get to this point,*' thought Jane. '*I remember visiting his grave and whispering into it. I said, "I promise I'll never love anyone else."*'

'Mum,' said Liza, sounding a little outraged.

'Mmm . . .'

'Why did you smile just now?'

'Did I, darling?'

The little churchyard was dark and dank, as if the sun never reached it. It was crowded with tombstones commemorating forgotten members of other families, sour from the scent of withered bouquets tossed on a compost heap. Liza knelt next to her father's grave with an expressionless face, removed white chrysanthemum sprays from the stone vase and laid them aside to be put on the compost heap, too, though they were still quite fresh and could have mixed attractively with the roses. She refilled the vase with water from the tap by the gate and began to arrange the flowers she'd chosen, which now struck her as shockingly vivid and alive.

'Mum, *you* don't think I should give up my career, do you?'

'Of course not! You know I don't. Who on earth's been telling you so?'

'I don't think I have any talent,' said Liza and, as she bent over the roses, a tear trickled down her cheek. 'I think I'm an idiot for going on with it and I ought to get a proper job like Kitty.'

'Pa wouldn't want you to give it up,' said Jane very definitely. 'I know it.'

Trigger was sitting quite still on the grass nearby, his ears pricked, turning his head this way and that as if tuned in to a multitude of soft whisperings. Jane's skin tingled and she felt more than ever convinced of her dead husband's presence. But what would he say to her now? For the first time, she wasn't sure if she wanted to know.

'We must discuss what to put on Henry's stone,' said Lionel, after dinner, and Jane understood that this was one of the reasons for the weekend invitation. As Henry's widow and only child, she and Liza were entitled to a major say, even though it seemed Lionel and Eleanor had already found a suitable engraver and more or less decided on Portland, which would blend well with the other memorials in the churchyard.

The four of them were in the drawing-room, where a pile of logs glowed and crackled on a deep bed of ash but a line of ancient overweight spaniels had efficiently taken up position, blocking the heat. Lionel and Eleanor, both brought up in enormous freezing houses, never seemed to notice the cold or the shivering of their guests. Trigger was on Liza's lap, his nose wedged in her armpit as if he were trying to burrow into her body. He had not responded well to being shut in the garden room during dinner – they'd heard his querulous outraged yapping in the distance – and nor was he going to take kindly to being returned there for the night with the house dogs (though Liza was secretly planning a rescue mission once the grandparents had gone to bed).

'I want "beloved",' thought Jane. *'I want "beloved by his wife Jane and his daughter Liza".'*

'We thought a quotation from Psalm 25 would be nice,' said Eleanor brightly.

'Oh,' said Jane faintly.

'Vay simple. "I have put my trust in the Lord" – and his dates.
But of course it's really up to you two, isn't it?'

The first time Jane had come to stay in this house, she'd been
nineteen and Eleanor had been only a decade or so older than
she herself was now.

She'd seemed old to Jane, then: a very confident and good-
looking woman with a distinguished adoring husband, two
successful sons and both daughters already married. That
weekend Camilla and Anthony had also stayed. They were
frighteningly glamorous: as impossible to relate to as film stars.

Smooth was her first impression of Anthony. Handsome and
clever, too – but overly charming, with manners so perfect that
he might have been wearing a mask.

As for Camilla, she was a languid blonde with beautiful
clothes and the same unshakeable confidence as her mother.
But the picture was marred by a strange discontent. Jane
couldn't understand why Camilla was so aggressive towards
Anthony, who appeared only solicitous.

'You'd better not play tennis, darling,' he'd suggested.

'It's only because you don't want to lose,' said Camilla, who
didn't seem particularly happy to be pregnant.

'I've just had a tennis court made for her in Gloucestershire,'
he told the others with an indulgent smile.

'No you didn't,' she corrected him sharply. 'You know
perfectly well you had it made for yourself.'

Jane had perceived tension in Camilla's relationship with her
mother, too. The only member of the family she seemed
relaxed with was her father, and – in return – was most
obviously adored. (When Jane looked at the photographs of
Eleanor as a young woman, she could understand why.)

'*I didn't trust him*,' thought Jane. And, this time, it was her mother-in-law who noticed a dreamy inappropriate smile and was puzzled.

In theory, there was plenty to do in the country. After all, there was an enormous choice of picturesque walks and old dogs that rose gamely to their feet with alert expressions each time someone made a move towards the front door; there was a tennis court and even a semi-retired horse with a flickering temper for the foolhardy.

But, in practice, boredom descended very soon. There was no point in starting a book (every one of which had an elaborate inscription pasted inside proclaiming 'ex libris L.L.W. St Clair') because one wouldn't have time to finish it. Stodgy, plentiful meals punctuated the day but there seemed acres of time in between and nowhere comfortable or warm to sit and wait. Although no demands were made, one was somehow made to feel idle: especially when Eleanor entered with a distracted look and a basket full of cut hydrangeas on her way to the garden room or Lionel put his bespectacled head round the door to search for some crucial bit of paper on his desk. One felt the necessity to appear busy.

'Interesting,' Lionel had commented to Jane, the last time he'd come in, noticing a thin volume lying on her lap. It was a monograph on the family and the author was Hector. He'd had it privately printed, circulating it to all the family with last year's Christmas cards. There was a copy somewhere in her house, too, though she'd not got round to reading it.

'Oh, very!'

'Fascinating lot,' he went on. 'Where have you got up to?'

'Oh . . . somewhere in the eighteenth century.'

'Ah!' he said, 'Rufus St Clair and the terrible twins? Or Ethel Valance, who married Rupert and wrote tolerable poetry? I believe I've a slim volume somewhere.'

'Both,' Jane muttered.

He wasn't fooled. But he was the most courteous of men, invariably prefacing any parcel of information he was about to share with: 'Of course, my dear, as you would know . . .'

On balance, thought Jane, the weekend was going well. Last night, after the discussion about Henry's gravestone, her mother-in-law had announced: 'Jane, dear, I'd like to leave you my pearl and garnet necklace.' However, when she'd unearthed the black exercise book where all such decisions were recorded, it was discovered she'd already bequeathed it to Becky. 'What a pity,' she'd said, sounding sincerely regretful. And Jane had been more flattered than disappointed, having been made to feel very much one of the family.

When Lionel had left the room, Liza informed her mother: 'I'm so bored I could die!'

'Why don't you practise your singing? I'm sure Grandma wouldn't mind if you used her piano, too.'

'No point,' said Liza, with a miserable expression.

'Oh, darling,' said Jane helplessly. 'You mustn't take things so hard. I'm sure they're not meant.'

Tom arrived for lunch on Sunday with Becky and the girls.

As usual, he galvanized the household and Jane was struck once more by his great difference from Henry. Tom complained loudly about the bad behaviour of his parents' dogs, which were milling around him in an elderly decorous sort of way – even though his own Labrador, Boomerang, had just peed on the doormat as was his invariable practice when visiting this place.

'It's not his fault he thinks he's still outside,' said Tom by way of an apology as he rubbed his hands briskly together and stamped his feet in the hall. 'Christ, it's cold in here!'

Then he went to find Mrs Percival, who was toiling over her Yorkshire puddings, and demanded a cup of coffee, though lunch was in less than half an hour. 'Why do they *never* have real coffee in this house? Good God, they can afford it!'

'So you won't be wanting the Nescafé, sir?' asked Mrs Percival, flushing with suppressed annoyance in her old apron, all hot and greasy and dusted with flour like her waiting Yorkshire pudding tin. She hated her kitchen to be invaded. She couldn't bear seeing her cupboards flung open and rifled through, her bicarbonate of soda and gravy essence made all higgledy-piggledy.

'Did I say so, Mrs P.?'

He roared at the girls. 'Lazy little tykes! What are you?'

Liza looked at her teenage cousins, somehow managing to appear both embarrassed by their father and distanced from him, and felt grateful that she was grown up – and then remembered her own pale overworked father and was no longer so sure. Uncle Tom was completely exhausting, but it was hard to imagine anyone more alive.

'Christ, it's cold in here!' he repeated as they went into the dining-room, even though both bars of the electric fire had been switched on for him since noon. It was a measure of his mother's love. The rest of the country might need to be exhorted to conserve energy. Not Eleanor. When, last winter, the government had urged the nation to heat only one room at a time, she'd been genuinely puzzled. What did everyone else do?

Tom frowned. 'What on earth's that appalling whining sound?'

'That's Liza's little dog,' said Eleanor with a smile.

'Aha!' he said. 'The gatecrasher.' He tapped his nose, nodded meaningfully at Liza. The girls had told him about their naughty cousin smuggling the puppy into the family party. They'd spotted an odd shape moving around under Liza's cardigan and heard muffled yapping and followed her and Kitty and Charlie and Max to the barn and spied on them. 'I thought you said Hector wasn't coming.' (For, due to Hector's strange aversion to dogs, they had to be shut away whenever he visited.)

'It has a nasty habit of begging,' Eleanor told him. Her own dogs would never dare do such a thing, of course. They were behaving perfectly: crouching under the table, hoping for accidents.

'Who's been gatecrashing?' Lionel inquired mildly.

'Do stop it, darling,' Becky told her husband very calmly with a smile.

'What?'

'You know perfectly well what.'

Eleanor viewed all of this upheaval very indulgently. She loved having Tom around.

Tom had had a hard week, as usual, he told them over roast beef and roast potatoes and cabbage, all overdone and served on cold plates. ('Isn't it extraordinary,' he observed very genially, 'the way Mrs P. can never warm them properly?') He'd just wound up a murder case and he and Lionel discussed intricacies, as they loved to do: Lionel displaying his vast knowledge of the law, Tom reliving his triumph in court.

'Wretched lives some people lead!' Tom would often say this, shaking his head as if puzzled by the pain he felt to witness such misery. It seemed that, for all his fierce ambition, there was a delicacy mixed in there, too. He was very sought after: it was no wonder he'd taken silk early.

Jane had once asked Henry why *he* hadn't followed the family profession. 'Oh, I don't know,' he'd replied after a moment's reflection, 'maybe I'm better with figures than people.' He'd smiled at her because she, of all people, should discount the modesty. But perhaps he'd recognized early on that, in this field, there could be no competing with Tom.

'Any more thoughts about moving?' Tom asked his parents very innocently, over glutinous bread-and-butter pudding and cream.

'No,' responded Lionel as warily as if in court, 'but that's because I never had them in the first place.' He wore a faint smile as if he'd been expecting this from his son and was now settling in to enjoy himself.

'Vay happy here,' confirmed Eleanor. She added quickly, like someone touching wood: 'So long as we have our dear Mrs Percival and Blackstock.'

'Well, they won't be up and running for much longer,' Tom reminded her, looking very concerned. 'Blackstock was only telling me how bad his rheumatism's getting.' He sighed. 'And we all know about Mrs Percival's dicky heart.'

Eleanor looked thoroughly alarmed for a moment, but then she caught Lionel's eye. 'You know we love this house,' she protested, but comfortably, as if her husband had laid a soothing hand on her.

'You're rattling around here! You don't need all these rooms!'

'Oh yes we do,' said Lionel. 'Where would I put my books?'

'What *you* need,' said Tom indulgently, 'is a thorough clear-out.

Then you'd think again! Now' – he assumed a businesslike expression – 'Becky and I are prepared to give up a whole weekend to come and help you.' He paused for a second so they could absorb the generosity of this offer. Then he looked round the old dining-room with its flocked crimson wallpaper interspersed with enormous portraits, its sideboard loaded with decanters of every size, many wearing tarnished labels like medals, its abundance of grand uncomfortable chairs. 'Beats me where you collect all this rubbish . . . You'd be amazed what you can manage without.'

'Oh, do shut up, darling,' said Eleanor affectionately.

'I'm only thinking of you!' Tom complained indignantly, but, for the time being, his mother had had the last word.

For months now, he'd felt aggrieved about his father's sudden decision to change his will and split his estate equally between his remaining three children. As the only son, Tom might quite reasonably have expected that the house would be his, with his sisters getting the furniture and jewellery and so on. After all, hadn't the right of primogeniture operated among St Clairs for generations? But conventional Hector (who prided himself on guarding the interests of every member of the family) had pointed out to his brother that, whereas Camilla had become rich through marriage, Suki needed protection. (It was quite immaterial, Hector told himself in all sincerity, that Suki was his favourite.) One should adapt to changing times, he'd advised his brother, but also be fair. After all, he'd stressed, it wasn't as if Lionel and Eleanor had any sort of obligation to keep their house in the family.

It was an excellent and much-envied Queen Anne mansion with a big well-established garden, a trout stream running through it, and the added bonus, as it had sadly turned out, of a chapel. But it wasn't Lavenham, the Gothic pile in the West Country where generations of St Clairs had lived since the seventeenth century.

When Lionel had inherited Lavenham a little earlier than expected, he was a barrister with a young family, ruled by death duties, who couldn't even afford to pay for the roof to be repaired. He and Eleanor played at being owners for a while, chasing their children through the echoing procession of imposing rooms and spinning unrealistic plans. But there was no choice really. So he sold the house where his childhood had been spent, took the grand furniture (much of which had to be put in store) and abandoned a host of mouldering ancestors in the graveyard. He claimed he'd never regretted it. But sometimes, even now, he dreamed of walking the freezing corridors at Lavenham, searching for his old uncomfortable room. He'd hear the peacocks miaowing mournfully in the maze, too; and nightingales, as elusive and fabled as ghosts.

Henry was the only St Clair to be buried in the graveyard attached to this house where Lionel and Eleanor had happily spent most of their marriage.

'Dear old Henry,' Tom would say mournfully. 'God bless him.' Then, after the briefest of pauses: 'But one shouldn't let sentiment rule one's life.'

The sooner his parents were persuaded to sell up, the sooner they could all benefit – now, when they had young families and really needed the money.

Tom was incapable of relaxing, and nor could he bear his family looking as if they were doing nothing. So, once lunch was finished, he suggested a walk.

'Do we have to?' pleaded his daughters.

The grandparents had settled, as usual, in the drawing-room. They were not expected to take any exercise. It was one of the privileges of being old. Lionel could doze off reading the Sunday paper while Eleanor occupied herself with sewing or, more likely, stared into the fire, as she'd been doing more and more of late.

'I think, just this once, they could stay with Grandma and Grandpa,' Becky began persuasively. 'It is the weekend.' And – crouching in front of the heat, looking pale and tired and vulnerable – Miranda and Vanessa nodded vigorously.

'Oh, no you don't, you idle little tykes! Look at their pasty mugs!'

'They *have* had a hard week, darling.'

'They'll only get fat. Then who's going to take them off my hands?'

Jane caught sight of her own daughter's expression: half amused, half wistful.

Liza could have got out of the walk: Tom had no control over her, after all. But she searched for the pair of house gumboots that fitted her and struggled into one of the ancient muddy coats hanging on the pegs in the hall. She could feel a whistle in one pocket, a withered carrot and a couple of misshapen sugar lumps in the other. She blew the whistle, which emitted a silvery high-pitched whisper, and Trigger started up in her arms, echoing the sudden alertness of the three ancient spaniels and Boomerang.

Tom laid a heavy arm on her shoulders and she bumped against him briefly in return.

'How's the singing?' he asked with a half-smile as if it were hardly a serious question. He was thinking that if Liza was *his* daughter, he'd soon sort out her life for her. She should give up on this ridiculous dream of hers and look for a proper job. Better yet, she should find herself a suitable young man and get married. Singing was a nice little accomplishment, but hardly a means of earning a living. It made him cross, too, to think of Liza playing servant to people like his mother.

But at least she *did* something, unlike Max. It made Tom really angry to think of Max idling away this crucial time of his life – especially as he was threatening Charlie's chances. He was like some gilded cuckoo, the way he'd moved into Chepstow Place, disrupting everything. Tom was damned if he could understand why such a successful self-made man as Anthony hadn't pushed his son more. '*But come to think of it,*' thought Tom with a frown. Come to think of it, it seemed his brother-in-law had been pretty distracted, what with one thing and another . . .

He hastened to catch up with Becky and Jane and left Liza chatting with his two young daughters, who admired her for her difference.

He put an arm round Becky and dropped a kiss on her head and Jane felt the usual pang that she was no longer part of a couple. Tom was exhausting – she couldn't imagine being married to such a man – but there was no doubt he was a loving and protective husband.

'I say,' he said with relish, 'heard about old Ant, Jane?'

'You're not supposed to talk about it,' Becky reproved him. 'Suki made you promise! Remember?'

'Jane's family, darling! Anyway, she's hardly going to blab to the parents. Are you, Jane?'

Jane shook her head. She could feel her body dictating the

movement, making it happen, even as she watched her gum-booted legs move stiffly, one after the other, along the rough path they were following. They were skirting a field of kale, the fleet of accompanying dogs bustling noisily in and out of it, the old ones briefly rejuvenated as they savoured smells magnified beyond human endurance, fancying rabbits in every crisp rustle.

'He's been a bad boy.'

'I couldn't believe it when Tom told me,' said Becky, shaking her head in shocked disapproval.

'Oh, it's true all right! I know Camilla can go off the deep end sometimes but she's hardly going to invent something like this! Besides, how well do any of us *really* know Ant?'

'Poor Camilla. It explains everything, really.' Becky mimed someone raising a bottle to their lips. 'Problem!'

'A very very bad boy.'

Loitering with her young cousins, regaling them with her pub triumph – even singing a few bars of 'Summertime' – Liza saw her mother, some way ahead, turn suddenly and look at her. Her face was pale and anxious. It was almost as if she were checking that Liza still existed, just as she'd done when she was tiny and in real need of supervision.

 Chapter Nine

'Apple crumble slathered in Bolognese sauce and thickly sprinkled with parmesan cheese,' said Kitty, glancing covertly at Max.

The others shuddered gratifyingly but Max acted as if he hadn't heard. When concentrating, he would stroke his bare chin like an old man fondling his beard. It was the only time he ever appeared wise. 'Beluga caviar with profiteroles,' he offered eventually. 'The ones with custard.'

'Brilliant!' said Liza before Kitty could. 'Charlie?'

'Um . . .' Charlie considered, the familiar vertical crinkle between his brows, 'tripe with . . . um . . . strawberry jam . . .'

It had to be a close contest.

'Merriweather's sweetbreads,' Liza brought out in a sinister teasing tone, 'boiled in his lemon curd!'

The others groaned in unison. She'd won again.

They'd not played vomiting meals for years now. It had been Kitty's desperate idea to re-enact a childhood ritual, always before played on the train on the way back from Uncle Hector's. They felt self-conscious, as young adults; and, anyway, it hadn't worked. In the flat at Chepstow Place, it only emphasized the new tensions between them. She caught herself wondering what other dramas had been played out in that grand sliced-up room. Had other young people – now old and grey – been most terribly misunderstood? Endured the visceral pain of jealousy?

As they'd left Aunt Suki and Uncle Simon's house that dreadful evening, Camilla had shrieked at Max that if he wouldn't come home with her that very minute, she wanted nothing more to do with him. All her legendary control had vanished. He could forget being her son, she'd screamed as Suki and Simon watched, appalled, from their front door and a sash window shot up somewhere on the street. 'Don't take any notice,' Kitty had told Max, wanting to protect and comfort him but thereby making her situation even worse. How could she have forgotten a crucial tenet of the relationship between all four of them? Discussion of parents was off limits.

What happened next had been horrifying. He'd driven too fast – he always did – overtaking in narrow streets, roaring up to traffic lights, speeding through red. And then, along with the terror, she became aware of the disgusting things he was saying.

'Fucking bitch! Fucking ugly stupid bitch!'

Kitty had flinched at the savagery in his voice. Poor poor Max! But at least he was releasing the anger at his mother, rather than denying it and letting it fester.

Then he'd snarled, 'You've ruined everything now! You

fucking hateful bitch!' And he'd turned his cold beautiful profile
to her all the way back.

He'd not relented since, even though his mother was on the
phone first thing the following morning. Nor did it help when,
prompted by Kitty's tearful pleas, Charlie muttered an
embarrassed apology: 'Sorry about all that, Max. My fault
entirely. Wasn't thinking, as per usual . . .'

Charlie had been horrified by Kitty's account of what he'd set
in motion. But Max appeared to blame him as little as his
mother. It was Kitty, for so long his loving protector, who, for
some perverse reason, became the villain in his mind.

He avoided looking at her at all now. If communication was
really necessary, he'd do it through the others; and if, by mistake,
his gaze met hers, it would become as bland and incurious as if
passing over a piece of furniture.

It was Liza he talked to most of the time and, being Liza, she
played up to the attention. It had always been part of her nature
to flirt but now it seemed to suffering Kitty that, each time Liza
touched Max on the shoulder or laughed into his face, it was
done to discomfort her.

Yesterday evening, Liza had shown her very worst side.

Kitty appreciated that Charlie must have sensed her
unhappiness because, despite his obvious exhaustion, he made
a point of drawing her out as they all sat at supper.

'What are you singing at the moment, Kit?' he inquired. It
was the first time for ages that he'd asked about her work
with the Bach Choir. People tended to forget what a nice
voice Kitty had. It was because she was so discreet about it
herself.

'Me?' asked Kitty, as if she found it hard to believe that anyone could be interested in her.

'You!'

'Oh, actually it's Beethoven's *Missa Solemnis*.'

'Do I know it?'

'It's wonderful!' Kitty enthused, and her eyes started to shine as she thought of the pleasure of being involved in such an enterprise. 'A masterpiece. Maybe his greatest work. It's unbelievable that he only ever heard it in his head.'

'Oh yes, he was deaf!' commented Liza in a superior sort of way. And she made a face at Max as if to say, '*Boring!*'

'Sing us a bit,' Charlie urged with a smile, though not before Kitty had seen him glance swiftly at his watch. But, even as she smiled back and obediently sat up straight to prepare herself, even as she started to draw breath, Liza darted in with her sweet high voice. '*Vissi d'arte*,' she trilled, as if she'd never heard Charlie, never seen Kitty gather up the shreds of her confidence because she knew there was one special gift at least that nobody could take away from her.

Charlie worried about work more than ever. He'd joined in the vomiting meals game because they were still sitting over supper but now he was preparing to leave. He frowned as he folded his napkin and replaced it in the silver ring he'd been given at his christening by Suki, who was one of his godmothers.

When Liza had finished her song and Max had applauded it far more than it deserved, Charlie started to rise from his chair – but Liza had more excitement for them. 'Guess what? I've found myself a sugar daddy.'

'You haven't!' Kitty exclaimed dully.

'Excuse me,' said Charlie.

Liza plucked at his sleeve as she laughed up at him. 'Don't you want to hear about it?'

'Sorry, Liza. Got to work. Kitty can tell me later.'

Liza pouted. '*I* wanted to tell you!'

She'd placed an advertisement in *The Times* personal column, rather enjoying the possibility that her grandparents might see it, too. After all, now they were over seventy, they followed the deaths notices closely. They'd never make the connection, of course. 'Talented young soprano seeks patron.' She'd had six replies, one of which had sounded genuine.

His name was Felix Munro, she told Kitty and Max, and they'd arranged to meet in the American Bar at the Savoy the following evening. He'd promised to identify himself with a red carnation in his buttonhole. 'I'm a blonde,' Liza had informed him gaily, 'and I'll be dressed in white.' But she'd be no such person, she assured her cousins, laughing. She'd cover her hair and wear black and, if she didn't like the look of him, she'd scarper.

'Does your mother know?' asked Kitty.

'You're not going to tell her,' said Max, appearing to address Liza's flushed and pretty face. He sounded disdainful, as if stating the opposite: making the point that Kitty was no longer a person to be trusted, let alone forgiven.

'No,' Liza told Kitty with another pout, '*she* never tells me anything any more.' Tit for tat. Her mother's sudden and mysterious bloom had vanished – the smiling at secret thoughts, the new softness. Now, caught unawares, she looked drawn and almost tearful, and sometimes her lips moved and her eyebrows soared and swooped like seagulls, as if she were taxing some invisible person. Nothing was the matter, she'd insist to Liza. Nothing. But she jumped when the telephone rang and made sure she got there first.

'Do you want me to come along?' Max suggested, to Kitty's astonishment.

Liza looked delighted. 'Would you?'

'I like the American Bar.' Max gave his crazy grin. 'I could be someone having a drink. A whisky sour.'

'Shall I come too?' asked Kitty.

The smile faded. He shrugged, not looking at her.

It was Liza who said lightly, 'You don't have to, Kitty. He'll protect me — won't you, Max?'

Two hours later, when she and Max were left alone together, Kitty thought of having known him for as long as she could remember — of all the weekends and holidays they'd enjoyed as children and the trust that had built up. There'd been no competition between any of them ever and, witnessing the intermittent fractious interplay between their various parents, they understood this had to be one of the best things about their relationship. But now Kitty found herself thinking, with a quite new resentment: 'It wasn't *her* who held the basin for him that time.' Staying with Uncle Hector, nine-year-old Max had been revoltingly, copiously sick and Liza had fled screaming. Even Max had admitted, 'I wouldn't do that for *you*, Kitty.' He'd sounded thoughtful rather than unkind, as if acknowledging that his parents had given him everything except the example of tender consideration.

'Would you like a hot drink?' she asked him now.

It was impossible for him to go on pretending she didn't exist when there were only two of them.

'Charlie having one?' he muttered, looking at a point somewhere above her left shoulder.

'I don't want to disturb him.' Kitty swallowed. 'Do you mind if we talk?'

Max nodded curtly. Perhaps he was secretly apprehensive, but there was no way he could refuse, as a guest. 'I'll have some more wine,' he said ungraciously. Kitty had seen his stuffed wallet many times – it was often left lying around – but he'd never yet bought groceries or drink. It was as if he required proof that he was loved – more and more of it – and, because he was safely snagged within the net of the family, understood there could be no limits.

Two bottles had already been consumed between three of them (Charlie drank water when he was planning to work) and Liza had left singing loudly. Tosca's emotional lament had seemed even more inappropriate the second time around. On Liza, it sounded as if she was complaining about having to go home.

Kitty opened more wine in the tall wedge of a kitchen, and after that they sat down with mismatched glasses in the lofty mini-oblong of a sitting-room.

Unlike Max, she was the child of a supremely happy marriage, but its recipe had been kept secret. How could she know about her parents' absolute determination to sort out differences, the mutual sacrifices they agreed on in the privacy of their bedroom? So far as she and Phil were concerned, they were just lucky.

But Max had come from a marriage where the guns were always pointed, though seldom fired. He'd learnt to judge the exact strength of his mother's anger from a look, a minute variation in her cool voice – wincing with fearful apprehension when his father blithely (or so it seemed) failed to take note. For years, they'd quarrelled in silence; when his mother finally burst through her shell of good behaviour, the shock had been awful.

Kitty felt dizzy from all the cheap alcohol, but she finished her glass and poured herself another for courage and began to speak in a way that was very hard for her because it invited more hurt. 'Oh Max, all this is making me so miserable.'

Instantly, his face stiffened.

'Not talking to me,' Kitty went on, her voice trembling, 'pretending I don't exist . . . It wasn't my fault that evening – you know it wasn't.' She added quickly: 'Charlie didn't *mean* to say anything, either.' She took a deep breath. 'I can't tell you how sorry I am. Couldn't we go back to how we were?'

He shrugged, giving the impression he'd no idea what she was referring to.

'I'm Kitty, remember?'

Max smiled a little unpleasantly, and she should have been warned.

'I love you, Max. I'd do anything for you.'

His mother used the word 'love' all the time. She'd told him she loved him on the telephone the morning after that excruciating evening, as if it made everything okay.

But for Kitty, 'I love you' meant only tenderness and commitment. Didn't her parents say it to each other every single day? 'I do love you so, Stan' . . . 'I adore you, Pudding.'

Next door, in his sliver of a bedroom with its flimsy partition walls, crouching over a formidable jumble of papers, Charlie put his head in his hands. He'd heard the whole prelude to this – Liza's over-excitement, Max playing up to it, Kitty's increasing silences – and knew he should have stayed. '*Just for once,*' he told himself miserably, '*I should have put her before my wretched bloody work.*'

Kitty continued to talk to Max, forgetting that – if the house were still in its grand and undivided prime – Charlie might just as well have been lying on a chaise-longue only a few yards away.

'Say something, Max!'

Charlie guessed that Max shrugged, hunching in his leather jacket, his beautiful face stony as he stared down at his elastic-sided boots.

'All *I'm* saying is that I care about you.'

Charlie made a sudden movement as if to stop Kitty, and the bed creaked.

'Please don't ever forget that, Max. I really really care about you.'

Max spoke at last with real savagery: 'I don't *want* you to care about me.'

Charlie thought he heard an involuntary gasp. Then there was the scrape of chair legs against parquet and Max's voice: 'I'm going to bed.' A glass was set down with a crack on a surface, a door slammed.

Now Kitty was alone. As if the wall between them had melted away, Charlie saw her humped in a chair, tears starting to well up and trickle down her cheeks. He made another spontaneous move and the bed creaked again. Then he understood that he must allow Kitty the illusion that her humiliation had been unwitnessed.

As he stared at the blank partition wall, Charlie realized that he'd never taken any of Kitty's men seriously: those cold-hearted bastards some masochism in her seemed to seek out. After all, he'd been the one she came home to: her family and the closest friend of all.

But Max was blood, too, in every sense.

Chapter Ten

'Are you okay?'

'Mmm . . .'

He sounded content and everything that had led up to Jane's question indicated he should be. But that rich sleepy murmur might mean anything, she reminded herself. What it probably signified was, 'Don't bother me. Talking's the last thing I want.'

She was always bringing herself up short now, snipping off hope and sentiment in the bud, even though some part of her still longed to believe that the passion – and even the tenderness – he demonstrated could not be disembodied.

'Are you asleep?'

He didn't answer.

As usual, she prayed for him to oversleep. But he seemed to possess some internal clock that allowed for exactly twenty minutes' dozing.

'*Anthony's next to me – in Henry's bed!*'

Her sister-in-law's husband lay naked beside her. Glamorous wealthy Ant, whose sleek black hair and shiny eyes and wonderful suits she'd admired from a distance; who'd always been kind to her. Of whom Henry had once said, with a slight frown, sounding just like his mother, 'Of course, Anthony is very different from the rest of us. Very.'

How could it have happened? The blush of the reality had begun to fade after the first few times but since Tom's shocking revelations it had returned, stronger than ever.

'Hundreds of them!' Tom had announced with some pleasure, that Sunday after lunch with his parents, when they'd all gone walking. He'd been expecting Jane to enjoy this ripe piece of gossip as much as he had. When one was a model of fidelity, others' transgressions couldn't help but be thrilling. He'd become increasingly fond of Ant, who was so absurdly generous: whose industry and cleverness in a successful, hard-working family were admirable. Like the rest of them, he'd been hoping the marriage would mend itself. But this . . . this was unforgivable. No wonder it had all gone wrong.

'Dirty dog!' he'd commented as they'd watched the kale shiver and divide with the pack of hidden excited animals bounding through it. There'd been a whole catalogue of infidelities, apparently, starting on the honeymoon – 'Can you credit it? He even made a pass at the maid!' Oh, Camilla had dished the dirt all right, that evening at Suki and Simon's, said Tom. Chapter and verse. She must have kept her eyes peeled for years.

'But you would, wouldn't you?' Becky had interrupted a little plaintively, 'once you'd stopped trusting your husband.'

There'd been no stopping Camilla, apparently, said Tom, until

Max – poor little sod – had shot up from the table like a cork and rushed out into the night and Kitty had gone tagging after him, looking almost as distressed. Poor old Camilla! Tom had sounded properly concerned about his sister now the shocking details had been passed on. Not that he was condoning her insensitivity where her son had been concerned, of course, but all the same, all the same . . .

Oh, Jane might agonize now to think of being involved with such a philanderer, but she knew how it had happened all right. It started the moment he put his hand over hers in the restaurant. He'd felt so shockingly warm and alive. He must have gauged her vulnerability very precisely from the way her own hand trembled and her eyes fluttered away from his. He was an expert on women, after all.

In his Rolls-Royce, separated from his driver by a glass window, he'd said, staring at her, 'I know what I'd really like to do now.'

She could have pretended ignorance, of course: inquired in a cool uninterested way, 'What?' as if he might be talking about visiting an exhibition or an art gallery. More crucially, she should have remembered that he was married to Camilla. But instead, she'd simply looked at him and nodded.

'Nice,' he'd commented, that first time he entered her bedroom. It was he who'd led the way – Anthony the adulterer – still holding on to her hand as if genuinely afraid that, even then, she might change her mind. '*You should have!*' said a voice in Jane's head. Instead, of course, she'd left her old self outside the door: surrendered to this passion that was so unexpected, allowed all the feeling crushed down since Henry's death to come flooding back.

'You're crying,' he'd observed, sounding concerned. (But the compassion had been nothing more than a reflex action, of course, she told herself now.)

'Sorry.'

'Don't be.' And he'd actually kissed away the tears.

Later, as he put his clothes back on, he'd wandered over to her dressing-table and touched the purple and green and yellow pottery crocodile holding hairpins, which Liza had made for her aged six at school, and – very lightly like a benediction – the photograph of Henry, looking young and earnest in a cricketing sweater. Family.

By that time, of course, she was already searching for explanations. And a damped-down memory returned: of once brushing past Anthony at a family gathering when Henry was only a few yards away and feeling all of a sudden as confused and powerless as if she'd stumbled into a magnetic force. Henry had noticed nothing, of course: not even her silence on the way home.

Henry had been kind and thoughtful as a husband. He should have pity now and understand how impossibly susceptible she'd been to such a man.

So why did his spectral voice tremble so with disapproval?

'You cannot possibly carry on with this, Jane!'

As Jane lay next to her sleeping lover in her bedroom, until recently associated with the bitterest of losses, she thought of the world outside. As she stared at her familiar white ceiling and magnolia walls, watching bars of sunlight travel across and down them, she registered the brisk light clatter of a baby buggy being trundled along the pavement outside. She pictured nosy old Mrs Murphy, the sitting tenant in the house opposite, who'd no doubt observed Anthony's arrival in his Rolls clutching tissue-wrapped champagne (and perhaps even overheard his instructions to his chauffeur to pick him up in a couple of hours); and the old man a few doors away who spent his life leaning on a gate. After that, of course, the street had witnessed the unambiguous sight of her bedroom curtains being pulled shut.

Love in the early afternoon. There were two half-full champagne glasses on the table his side (the right, like Henry), and the bottle rested in a bucket of ice on the floor nearby. There was also the debris of lunch – plates with pale smears of *pâté de foie gras* (also brought by him) and toast crumbs, and a few fresh strawberries in a bowl. 'Nothing heavy,' he'd say, crinkling his black brows, when she suggested cooking for him. 'Tell you what, let *me* deal with it.' It seemed that eating was not a priority.

If she didn't know better by now, she'd have said his objective was her happiness. He was extraordinarily tender as a lover. It was terrible, thought Jane, not to be able to accept their relationship for what it seemed: to have to remind herself of the legions of other women who had flowered under his hands. It was amazing, really, that he'd found time for them all.

'*Don't tell me I should end this,*' she protested to the dwindling shade of her husband, '*because I can't. I can't even bring myself to ask questions because it might provoke the end – and that would feel like shutting myself up in the same dark room I've escaped from.*'

There was a candle burning on the mantelpiece, its flame invisible, disseminating the sweet and musty scent of sandalwood. It had never occurred to her to burn candles in her bedroom when she was a wife. 'It's not very safe, Jane,' Henry would very probably have warned. Besides, he might have added with a frown, candles could leave smoky marks on the ceiling, which had only recently been painted, and – when it came down to it – what was really the point?

'*I like being a mistress*,' Jane thought with fresh determination. '*I like preparing my body with such care and reverence – making it all smooth and deliciously scented and dressing it in new underwear I have to hide most carefully from Liza. I like the fact that he can't wait to get me into bed. I like the fact that, as soon as we're there, it all feels so entirely right. I like the jokes, too – it should be fun. And even if he's going straight off to make love to someone else, I intend to be glad for the rest of my life that this has happened. So there!*

'*I should line my curtains*,' she was musing, with a picture in her mind of a dark room instead of a bright one; a summer affair moving into the autumn and beyond, and forgiving shadows cast by candlelight. '*And maybe I should move the record player up here so we could have music, too.*' And then – before his twenty minutes were up – the telephone rang.

It was bound to be either Liza or Eleanor, she thought a little resentfully, as she stretched out a hand for the telephone beside the bed. It was uncanny how – nearly every time Anthony was there – one or other of them happened to ring.

'Mum?'

'Yes, darling.' Jane sighed a little as she felt Anthony, curled next to her, stir. But she was glad it was Liza, even though her intuition was far more focused than Eleanor's.

'Where are you?'

'In the kitchen.' Jane hated telling fibs. 'What is it?'

'The most dreadful thing's just happened.' As usual, she sounded as if it was her mother's problem.

'What?' Immediately Jane was filled with apprehension, even dark thoughts of retribution.

'It wasn't my fault!'

'Tell me . . .' Jane urged with the usual tenderness. She felt the bedsprings shift as Anthony rolled over and got up.

She shook her head at him – '*Stay!*' she mouthed – but he smiled as he continued to head for her bathroom. He looked wonderful, nude. He made her feel so comfortable with her own nakedness. Suddenly she felt very cross with Liza, thinking, '*Why does she always do this to me?*' It would be unimportant, of course. It always was.

As Liza told a story involving a fractured ankle incurred when one of her clients had slipped on a plastic shopping bag inadvertently left on a floor, Jane cut in with: 'Where are you?'

'Why?' asked Liza immediately.

'Only wondering.'

'You're afraid I'm going to come back suddenly, aren't you?'

'Don't be ridiculous, darling.' She could hear water pattering into the shower tray in the adjoining bathroom and wondered if Liza could pick it up, too.

'Is someone there?'

'Who on earth would be here?' asked Jane, trying to sound incredulous and amused.

'You tell me . . .'

Why did she behave like this? 'You're hiding something, Jane,' she'd accused a couple of evenings ago. 'Why won't you tell me?'

'How's Liza?' asked Anthony with a smile, when he returned from the bathroom with one of her best pink towels folded round his waist. She only put them out when he was coming. They were far too good for every day.

'I wish she didn't have to do that awful job. It's so depressing.'

He sat down on the bed and stroked her hair and then he kissed her and, if she hadn't known better, she might have believed he was genuinely sad to leave. 'Well, *does* she have to do it?'

'She has to learn about the real world,' said Jane, just as her late husband Henry had done.

'Still singing in the pub?'

'Oh yes!'

'Well, that's good, isn't it? It could easily lead on to something.'

'Actually, there might be another audition coming up later this week.'

'Excellent!' He started searching for his socks and found one tossed into a corner.

Jane beamed with pride. 'It is, isn't it?'

'And Max?' But he sounded very casual, as if making the point that he hadn't spent the past two hours with her in order to find out about his son.

'I haven't actually seen him.'

'Ah.' His shirt still looked very fresh and crisp. There was a laundry service at the club where he was living, naturally.

'But Liza does all the time, of course.'

'Ah?' He was knotting his tie now. He had the familiar concentrated expression Henry had worn and, just for a second, it seemed to Jane that her husband's pale worried face became superimposed on his – here in the same bedroom where Henry had knotted his tie so many thousands of times.

'She says he's really settled in,' she went on. 'You know how Charlie and Kitty are.'

'Mmm.' Now he was repackaged in the beautifully cut navy

pinstriped suit he'd arrived in. 'Well, that's good, isn't it?' he went on very tenderly, as if only thinking of Max's welfare. 'Good for them all to be together.'

He picked up her hairbrush and smoothed his hair at the mirror and Jane found herself wondering bleakly how many brushes his glossy black hairs were entwined in, all over London. His expression was oddly blank, as if he gained no real pleasure from his reflection.

'How is everyone, anyway? I haven't heard from any of them for ages.' He sounded bewildered and a little hurt. But, of course, he was ignorant of the evening Camilla had turned up at Simon and Suki's and the gossip that ricocheted around the family. For all he knew, Suki and Tom and the rest of them were keeping away out of awkwardness – they hated messiness, after all – and this was a mere hiatus. He was unaware that he'd been charged and found guilty: his punishment removal from the network for good. As the family saw it, he'd displayed contempt for the rules. How could their sentence possibly have been otherwise?

'Busy,' she replied, apologizing for them all, even though she was just as much of an outsider as he. But how could she enlighten him? Her position was impossible. Even so, she'd get the odd feeling sometimes that he, too, was withholding some crucial piece of information. '*He wants to warn you not to get serious,*' she'd remind herself sharply.

She knew from Liza that Max no longer talked about his father. He never wanted to see him again, Liza had informed her. Not that he'd said so, she'd added quickly with a stern look, even though she was talking to her mother.

'Oh well . . .' he said helplessly. It was how he usually ended up saying goodbye.

After he'd gone, Jane would put the most positive of spins on that, too.

And probably hear a voice saying faintly: '*You're mad, my love. Quite quite mad.*'

 Chapter Eleven

In old age, it suited Lionel to live in Hampshire and work in London. He didn't mind spending at least four hours a day in a train because he could afford to travel first class and there was always a seat for him, usually in an empty compartment, and plenty of space to work. He liked the illusion that he could separate off the filth and despair he encountered each day at the law courts. At nearly seventy-two and finally about to retire, he'd try not to bring work home – or at least confine it to his car. He'd fancy that material describing the awful careers of murderers or paedophiles might leave some horrible permanent residue in his beloved study stacked with books and memorabilia, with its sublime view of lawns sloping down to his trout stream and, when the sun shone, the extra pleasure of Eleanor pottering among the shrubs in the hat that reminded him of the day he'd made the most important decision of his life.

Each time he found it more painful to leave the country. After driving himself to the station and parking his Bentley in the mostly empty car park, he'd greet the stationmaster – 'Morning, Andrews!' 'Morning, Sir Lionel! Lovely weather for you!' – and think gloomily (and quite unfairly) that these might be the last positive friendly words he'd hear for the rest of the day. Then he'd stand on the quiet station platform, listening to the distant plaintive toot of his train coming ever closer as it snaked through fields and woods, and imagine he was about to be borne towards the gates of hell.

Simon was looking forward to lunch with his father-in-law at the Reform Club.

As he ran lightly up the short flight of steps from Pall Mall and passed through the pillared portico, he felt as if he were re-entering the world of his youth when all options had seemed open. If things had been different then he, too, could have been one of the lawyers thronging this vaulted space, managing the dodgy acoustics, tolerating the bland food. But it wasn't in his nature to agonize over what might have been. He appreciated that, where it truly mattered, he was a lucky man.

'Can I help you, sir?' asked the doorman.

'I'm meeting Sir Lionel St Clair.'

'Sir Lionel is waiting for you in the morning-room.'

Just like his father-in-law earlier that day at his country station, Simon felt warmed by the affable, though unequal, exchange – but for a different reason. It gave him back a sense of self-worth, exactly like he knew being waited on at lunch would do. He'd tip the doorman a little too much on the way out, let him believe the benefit was one-sided.

He was only five minutes late, but guessed correctly that his father-in-law had been there for some time. His generation had an obsession with punctuality. As Lionel glanced up from his *Times* with his naturally stern expression, appearing for one brief scary moment not to recognize him, Simon was struck by terrible premonition. Then Lionel smiled – that sweet shy beam that always came as a surprise and a delight – and rose to his feet a little creakily and they shook hands and Simon relaxed.

Simon's grandfather had made millions from building a railway across wilderness in the New World. But his father had frittered away his inheritance, mostly in casinos, and by the time Simon was a young adult, he was left with nothing but an expensive education. 'Clogs to clogs in three generations,' he would remind Suki when money was short and she bemoaned their inability to do more for their children. Phil should have been sent to Harrow, too, she'd say with that note in her voice which always upset him: he was bright but needed pushing, like all boys. And Kitty should have had a grand party. If they'd been able to launch Kitty properly, she'd tell him mournfully, she'd almost certainly be married by now.

Lionel was thinking what a charming man Simon was. He was exceptionally nice-looking, too, with his thick blond hair and neat features and athlete's body. It was astonishing how youthful he'd remained. It seemed to Lionel that he looked exactly the same as when Suki had first brought him back to meet them, nearly a quarter of a century before. She'd been unusually silent (only later confessing to extreme nervousness). It was Simon who'd done the talking – easily and naturally – as if in no doubt whatsoever that he'd be welcomed as a son-in-law. He was right. By the end of the evening, his lack of money and significant employment seemed to matter far less than his magical effect on Suki.

But at the same time as admiring Simon, Lionel was wondering what could be wrong. He'd found that Eleanor's intuition was almost invariably accurate. While appearing aloof, she could tune into hidden anxieties and private dreams to a quite uncanny degree. 'Mama's a witch,' Camilla had once complained as a teenager when trying unsuccessfully to keep a boyfriend secret. It must be why Eleanor was generally regarded as so intimidating, thought Lionel – though, for him, this was absurd.

As he and Simon ate steak and kidney pie with English mustard and discussed the steeply rising cost of living, he found himself wondering if infidelity might be the problem. It was on his mind.

The other day, Tom had let drop a most shocking piece of information about Anthony. 'Shouldn't have said that, Pa,' he'd apologized straight afterwards (though Tom never said anything by mistake). 'Forget it, will you?'

As if he could! Beneath his urbane exterior, Lionel boiled with rage on behalf of his daughter, who'd been put through such humiliation and had apparently valiantly concealed it for years. He knew his proud Camilla, he told himself: understood that she'd never make herself appear pitiable without sound reason. With no word of explanation to Anthony, Lionel had severed their long and happy association for good. But he hadn't shared with Eleanor the real reason for his disaffection and probably never would. After almost fifty years, there was a profound connection between them but also delicacy and restraint. When he was younger, an earthy uncomplicated woman had occasionally visited him in dreams and he'd awaken to a mood both mournful and ashamed. But he'd never been unfaithful to

Eleanor, partly (it had to be admitted) because he was too afraid of being caught. Besides, you could ignore the itches of the flesh, like so much else, and in the end they went away. It was one of the few advantages of getting old.

It would be shattering for Suki, thought Lionel, if infidelity was the nature of the problem. Simon had turned her from a shy and under-confident girl, in the shadow of her older sister, into a calm and very contented wife (not to mention a beauty in her own special right, he thought fondly).

'Price of petrol's set to go up even more,' said Simon gloomily. 'Can you believe it was forty-two pence a gallon at the start of the year? They're saying that'll double by 1975.'

It was the natural cue to ask about Simon's business, but a waiter was hovering and Lionel decided to bide his time.

'Everything all right, sir?' Because Simon had left half his red cabbage uneaten.

'Delicious! Just ... you know ...' Simon patted his flat stomach and smiled charmingly at the waiter.

'Still playing cricket?' asked Lionel.

'Oh yes!' Simon's annual fixtures with his old university cricket team were like visits to this club: excursions into what might have been. After all, the settings didn't change – country greens where the peace was ruffled only by the thwack of balls on willow bats, the drowsy buzz of bees and languid smatterings of applause from wives and children relaxing on the grass. The other players in his team included a captain of industry, a top civil servant, a consultant. Nobody else sold second-hand cars for a living.

'You'll have some pudding with me.'

'Oh yes! Can always make room for pudding!' Simon smiled

at the private joke. He'd tell Suki about it later, he thought with the usual tenderness.

When two portions of plum crumble and custard had been brought, Lionel remarked very casually, 'Bad times for everyone.'

'Not you,' observed Simon pleasantly.

'Well, no,' Lionel agreed with a wintry smile, 'so long as people go on wanting what they can't have, there'll always be work for people like me.'

At the same time, he noticed that his son-in-law had deflected what had really been a question. He decided to rephrase it more frankly, though very gently: 'What you were saying about the price of petrol . . . Your business must have been affected. Are people still buying cars?'

'People always want cars,' replied Simon with an easy laugh.

It was then that Lionel realized not only that his son-in-law was by no means as transparent as he seemed, but also that Eleanor had been right. There was something very wrong here. Moreover, he feared that his daughter probably knew as little as he did.

Nothing more would have come out of the lunch if Simon hadn't all of a sudden felt guilty for taking his father-in-law's generous hospitality and giving so little back. It was a question of good manners. He momentarily forgot that he was talking to someone whose special subjects were temptation and deception.

'As a matter of fact,' he went on chattily, with another sweet and open smile, 'somebody broke into the garage a few weeks ago and stole two.'

'Oh?' Instantly Lionel assumed his stern face — bushy

eyebrows drawn together in a thick bar, mouth compressed into a thin line – and, though he always looked like this when he was concentrating, Simon suddenly found himself very nervous. 'A few weeks ago, you say?'

'Mmm.' Simon gazed ingenuously at his father-in-law while his heart secretly pounded. 'I thought I mentioned it at the time.'

'No.' Lionel's memory was one of the reasons why he'd made such an excellent lawyer. 'No, you certainly didn't do that.'

'A pain,' said Simon and even managed to eat another spoonful of plum crumble.

'A little more than that, surely?'

'Oh, well!'

'Expensive cars?'

'A Mercedes and a Jaguar, actually.'

'Ah!'

'Yes,' said Simon as if making another joke, 'they had good taste.'

'Anybody see anything?'

'Not a soul.'

'I see . . .' Minutes seem to tick past. 'Police on the case?'

'Oh yes!' Simon assented with rather too much enthusiasm.

'Good, good.' There was a long pause while Lionel appeared to be working something out. 'Insurance will probably pay up, then?'

'Oh, I hope so,' Simon agreed very innocently and heartily, but inside he was cursing himself. 'Fool! Total and complete blithering idiot! Now I'll have to tell Suki, after all.'

 Chapter Twelve

'Marriage is like a farmyard,' Eleanor had been warned the
night before her grand wedding. Her mother had looked agitated
but determined, rather like a frightened hen herself, but refused
to go into more detail, having said quite enough. It was puzzling
and a little alarming when she hissed as an afterthought, 'But
whatever you do, dearest, never say no to your husband!'

Marriage had definitely been a shock to that sheltered girl. The
first night of her honeymoon, Eleanor truly believed Lionel had
gone mad, especially as he never explained and the whole painful
(though thankfully brief) episode took place in silence. But she
heeded her mother's words and once she got used to his strange
ways (and discovered to her astonishment and delight that they
produced children), found there was much in common. They
would come to enjoy a great contentment in each other's
company, a profound appreciation of their good fortune.

His upbringing had taught obedience and stoicism, too. She appreciated it the first time he took her to stay at Lavenham where, despite the flaking splendour, there was a palpable feeling of sadness in the air, a distance between Lionel's parents as marked and unbridgeable as a wall. They'd suffered a great tragedy, of course, a few years before.

Lionel told her about it as, simultaneously, his car emerged from a long avenue lined with ancient beech trees. And there, suddenly, was the house – a Gothic confection of soaring buttresses and lacy turrets and carved angels – like an enormous grand but very worn tapestry being unrolled for her delectation. He must have heard her gasp in her seat beside him. He might even have smiled faintly because Lavenham invariably had that effect on guests visiting for the first time. It was only later that they learnt about the absolute inefficacy of any sort of heating: the deadly chill intensified by draughts that whistled down the long corridors, lifting the precious but threadbare rugs and knifing through countless cracks in the ancient windows. The beds were appallingly uncomfortable, too, and the food was awful. But none of this would come as any real surprise to Eleanor, which was another reason for their compatibility.

'I should tell you about my sister, Eleanor.'

'I didn't know you had a sister.' She smiled under her cloche hat as she said it (causing Lionel to make a difficult but momentous decision). It was because she was watching the three fountains out of four that worked, playing in the forecourt. She hadn't known there was a house like this, either, though it was clear from everything about him that he came from an aristocratic background similar to hers where the money was dwindling away now. Unlike her, though, he seemed to know about the world. He had not, at that point, been through a war but was far more mature than most of the young men she met, as if his growing up had been forced. She'd met his younger brother, Hector, in London but this was to be her first proper introduction to his parents. She was a little nervous in case they were as oddly unfriendly as Hector had been — rather as if, she'd reflected afterwards, he was afraid of getting to know her too well.

'Well, I don't any more,' he said. 'Nancy died two years ago.'

'I'm sorry,' said Eleanor with real sincerity. She was puzzled. '*Why has he told me now? This was something he should have confided right from the beginning, at one of our private dinners when we were getting to know each other.*' But it was too late for proper consideration.

'Her heart,' said Lionel. 'The thing is, my dear . . .'

'*He called me my dear!*' The niggling worry had been overtaken by delight. It was the first time he'd used an endearment, though of course being invited to Lavenham had to be even more significant than the introduction to his brother.

'. . . they don't like talking about it.'

So he was warning her. She should know about his sister so as to understand that it was grief not anger that divided his parents, but she must never mention her. Of course she would take note! But it struck her as unusual, then, that time had done nothing to ease the suffering.

And suddenly it was too late for more discussion — and maybe Lionel had planned this to the minute also — because already they'd drawn up on a wide sweep of gravel and an elderly butler was stepping forward to open the car door and usher them into the house and, even then, his as yet unseen parents were moving like chess pieces under the chandelier and across the stone-flagged floor of the vast and gloomy hall to greet them.

'They'll love you,' said Lionel with a smile and once more she secretly hugged her happiness.

She never really asked about Nancy again because she'd gained the very strong impression that Lionel didn't like talking about it either. It was only when, much later, her own first-born died that she deplored the insensitivity of her younger self. She understood, finally, that it was impossible to surmount such loss.

Henry, a good and dutiful son, had telephoned her the day that he died. She wished afterwards not only that she'd been more vigilant but also that this last conversation had been more memorable.

'Mama, is this a good time?'

She'd glanced at the watch Lionel had given her as a silver wedding present. Half-past ten. Henry would probably have been in his office for two hours. He was terribly conscientious. 'Mrs Percival wants me to look over her menus for the week. I've got a minute.'

'I've been reviewing your portfolio, Mama . . .'

'That's good of you, Henry.'

'. . . and I think you should sell half your holding of Glaxo. Do you want me to arrange it for you?'

'If you really think it's necessary.' But she knew he would not have telephoned otherwise.

'I've been studying the annual profits and I don't believe the company has a solid future.'

'Very well, darling.' She'd glanced down at that point and read 'Chicken à la King' in Mrs Percival's galloping pencilled script. 'How are you?' she asked perfunctorily, and frowned suddenly. Mrs Percival was getting lazy. Surely they'd had vanilla mousse with sponge fingers only last week?

'I have a bit of a headache,' he said, which was very unlike him. He never complained. But, then, he'd never had a serious illness in his life.

'A headache?' She would ask for stewed rhubarb, instead. There was masses in the garden that needed eating and, besides, Lionel loved the astringent soft taste of it, providing there was plenty of sugar and cream.

'Mmm.'

'Bad?'

'Quite bad.'

She should have been alerted then. But all she said a little impatiently was, 'Take an aspirin. No, take two.'

'I already have,' said Henry, who disliked taking medicine of any sort. 'An hour ago. And I took two more early this morning.'

'It's very muggy,' said Eleanor, looking out of her French windows at the day trembling with damp heat, the miasma of hovering midges. Not a good morning to work among her shrubs and plants, perhaps. She'd busy herself in the garden room instead, where there were seedlings to be potted out. 'I'm sure you'll feel better soon.'

An hour and a half later, he was dead. And a week after that, he was laid in the ground in the chapel two hundred yards from where she was sitting pondering over a list of meals they'd be unable to eat when the time came.

Henry was gone but simultaneously, from the other side of the stage, fear had made an entrance. He'd stay till the curtain came down. There was no escaping him and she knew it.

For the rest of her life, she'd anguish over failing to listen to Henry. But, in fact, there was every excuse. There'd been scant tenderness and sympathy in her own upbringing and how could you know unless you'd been shown? Besides, the doctors confirmed that, almost certainly by that stage, nothing could have been done for Henry.

But after his death, she changed. Each time a member of her family suffered the slightest sickness, she became quite abnormally anxious. She knew now that a cold could escalate into pneumonia; a cut could result in septicaemia; and, of course, a simple headache could herald a fatal brain aneurysm that might have been ticking away for years. Besides, if one cataclysm could happen, who was to say there wouldn't be a second or even a third?

And, just as trust in the security of the future had failed, she no longer felt envied, either. The long run of luck had been broken: Lionel's distinguished career, their own happy relationship, the successful sons, the daughters' very different but seemingly satisfactory marriages.

To the outside world, however, her imperious confident shell had never cracked. She was a hard woman, people said – which was just as well, they'd add soberly. She was the hidden power in the family, the steel hand in the velvet glove, a matriarch who was anything but soft.

But the reality was that, led by Lionel, the family started to protect her. They learnt to read the horrible anxiety in her eyes, measure the rising panic in her voice. And, though no such decision was ever articulated, because they didn't behave like that they silently carried a unanimous vote against ever telling her bad news.

It didn't work, of course. What happened was that her intuition, which had always been powerful, became ever more finely tuned. And, however hard they tried to keep unpleasantness from her, she learnt the trick of discovering it for herself.

Her husband would tease her for stating the opposite of what she really meant. But didn't all of them do the same?

'Simon's business will pull through,' Lionel had assured her with an uneasy glance, on his return from lunch at the Reform, so she knew that the garage was in real trouble.

'I've no worries about Charlie whatsoever,' Tom would insist with his mixture of fierceness and joviality, and therefore she understood he was increasingly anxious Charlie wouldn't make it as a practising barrister.

And Camilla? From titbits dropped by various members of the family, she'd gathered that her elder daughter had turned up at Simon and Suki's when Max and Kitty were there. 'How nice,' she'd prompted, on telephoning the house to find out more. She meant it in all sincerity. But Suki's response – over-effusive agreement – had alerted her.

'Lovely!' said Suki. She seemed to be searching for more words. 'A real surprise, after all this time.'

'So she just turned up, did she?'

'Mmm, yup – just like that.'

'Strange,' said Eleanor and let a silence fall, but nothing came of it. 'I've been trying and trying to phone her,' she complained, 'but that foreign housekeeper of hers always says she's out.'

'Oh yes,' said Suki as if she'd suffered the same experience; and there was another yawning pause.

'So how was she?'

'Fine,' said her daughter with a nervous laugh. 'Fine,' she repeated as if trying to convince herself, too.

So something very significant had happened that evening. But nobody would enlighten her.

'And Max?'

'Max was – you know . . . okay . . .'

So Max was sliding ever further out of control. She loved her grandchildren dearly and equally (which might have surprised some of them). She longed to comfort Max while gently guiding him. But whenever she attempted to do this, the words emerged wrong. It was the same with Liza. She was deeply proud of her ambition and zest for life as well as her beauty. '*So why do I always make her feel her dream of fame is worthless?*'

'*I can't connect,*' thought Eleanor. '*That has been my greatest fault, or handicap. I am far from stupid, but some things cannot be learnt and anyway I'm on the last lap.*'

And now? She found herself more fearful than ever. Her intuition was telling her that something was about to happen which would be worse than anything that had gone before. How did she know?

'*Aren't I a witch?*' she thought with weary distaste.

 Chapter Thirteen

Tom's house in London was not a relaxing place, but Suki and Simon were used to that by now.

'No no no!' they heard him shouting from inside, even as they rang the bell and studied the newly painted red front door. When he opened it, he failed to greet them, holding up a warning hand instead so he could continue listening to the alternate squeaks and groans issuing from upstairs. They stood in the hall, clutching the bottle of wine they'd brought and waiting. 'E major!' he shouted once at the top of his voice and, when the noise had come to an end, he told them: 'That girl's got real talent, if she'd only work at it.'

After that, he said: 'Hello!' and kissed Suki warmly as if now he'd finished monitoring his daughter Miranda's violin practice, he could show how pleased he really was to see them.

At that moment, Becky darted out from the kitchen, where she'd been taking a telephone call. She smiled apologetically at them as she told her husband, 'We're going to a black tie dinner at the Farmers on the fifth, darling – I checked the diary.' And only after that did she properly welcome her guests.

They were family, of course. Perhaps it was a compliment to be treated so casually. However, as always, it had the effect of lowering their spirits before the evening had even begun – especially as, most unusually, they'd hardly exchanged a word on the way there.

As they entered the drawing-room, Tom said casually, 'I think I'm at last making headway with the parents.'

'Oh, really?' Suki had guessed Tom would talk about trying to move Lionel and Eleanor from their house even though there was a specific agenda for this occasion. It was becoming an obsession with him.

'*They* can't manage that place on their own!' Tom gave the impression it was absurd, even amusing, for anyone to think otherwise.

'They seemed to be doing fine, last time I was there,' Suki observed mildly.

Tom shook his head sorrowfully. 'They're not, you know. And I think – *I think* – it's better to make a decision now, before there's a catastrophe.'

'Such as?'

'Falling down those stairs,' he said immediately, as if he'd prepared for this.

Becky instantly backed Tom up. 'Actually, I very nearly fell down them myself.'

'Beats me why all these old people want to turn their houses into death traps. Uncle Hector's exactly the same.'

'You're just going to have to wait for the money,' Suki told him with a faint smile. 'We all are. So leave the parents be.'

'I don't know what you're talking about!' Tom blustered.

'Believe me' — Suki sounded very weary and there was something oddly final to her tone — 'we've always needed the cash more.'

Grand furniture that had once adorned Lavenham sat a little uneasily in these more modest dimensions. A huge uncomfortable oak settee took up almost one wall; a mahogany bookcase scraped the ceiling. There was more of the same in Tom's country house: forceful reminders of the inherited wealth and importance once enjoyed by the family.

When his parents visited, they'd look a little sorrowfully at their old furniture, even though they'd seldom used it themselves. 'I always loved that desk,' she would say, though she'd only ever watched her mother-in-law write at it and had not been left with kindly memories of that chilly evasive woman.

Through the French windows, Suki and Simon could see Tom and Becky's garden, which was in another class from their own, where patrolling cats ruined grass already thinned by the shade cast by an old pear tree and wooden fences leant ever more drunkenly each year, their struts rotted by spring rain. This was a proper landscaped garden — big for London and well proportioned where theirs was long and narrow — with a stone wall perimeter and trellis dividing up the various sections: dense springy lawn with herbaceous border directly behind the house, roses and other shrubs in the middle section, vegetables at the secluded end. It resembled the layout of Uncle Hector's garden in extreme miniature. His influence was extraordinary. 'Worth a-a-ll the trouble,' Tom would drawl, exactly like him, as he hoed and watered his vegetables — even though, just round the corner, there was an excellent and inexpensive greengrocer. Anyway, he had another house in the country, where it made far more sense to be self-sufficient.

Tom filled all their glasses with hock. 'What do you think?' he asked. But before they could answer, he gave his own verdict: 'In my opinion, this is a real find.'

Suki and Simon had brought some good Sauternes but, after removing the wrapping, Tom had examined the bottle with the air of a schoolmaster hovering between a B minus or a C plus. It had annoyed Suki, as Tom and Becky never contributed wine themselves.

They got their own back by tasting his hock with similarly critical expressions.

'Fine,' Simon pronounced eventually, but he frowned a little, as if the wine had only just passed muster.

Tom let it go. 'Got an extraordinary letter from Camilla this morning,' he said.

Becky tapped the side of her head dramatically. She was joking, of course.

'A letter?' echoed Simon. He should have known the family well enough, by now, to be unsurprised. They disliked direct confrontation, preferring to set out gripes on paper. These were almost invariably ignored at the time; but the unwritten responses festered and would sometimes come out months later in other communications concerning entirely separate issues. 'For your information,' Tom had penned not long ago as a postscript to a letter to Suki complaining about an unusually large gas bill at Chepstow Place (part of which he was obliged to pay for Charlie), 'we did say thank you for the crystallized ginger you so kindly gave us last Christmas.'

'What did the letter say?' asked Suki.

'Oh, some absurd stuff about my having encouraged Charlie to tell Max to abandon her. Actually called me a despot!' Tom looked honestly astonished. 'As if I'd *want* distraction for my son at a time like this!'

'Well, she doesn't exactly do much, does she?' observed Becky, thinking of how busy her own day was what with ferrying the girls round to all their extra lessons and taking care of Tom's many needs, too.

'Bit of shopping, followed by lunch, followed – very swiftly – by several G and Ts, shouldn't wonder,' said Tom.

'*I'd* drink,' said Becky, glancing meaningfully at her husband, whose fidelity, so far as she knew, was unimpeachable.

'We couldn't have asked her here tonight,' said Tom. 'Don't want a repeat performance of what happened at yours.'

'No fear,' said Simon, with a faint smile.

'We've business to do. Nobody's mentioned this to her, I hope?'

They hadn't. But, then, nobody had had any real contact with Camilla since the dreadful scene she'd made at Suki and Simon's. It was all so embarrassing – and for her, too. She'd have been mortified once the drink wore off. They felt very sorry for Camilla. But it was a relief, really, that she was keeping away.

The two couples were meeting to discuss Uncle Hector's imminent seventieth birthday party, which – they'd stressed months ago in more than two hundred roneoed letters to family – must be kept a secret. 'DO NOT TELL HECTOR!!!' had been typed in purple capitals at the top of every one. It had been Suki's idea to give him a surprise celebration. It was to be held at the Hyde Park Hotel, which was appropriately spacious, and a young quartet had been engaged. Tom was treasurer. Families had been asked to contribute fifteen pounds per head; but there was already a shortfall, as he was about to point out fiercely. And it was all very well insisting on champagne . . .

However, he wasn't quite ready yet.

'Anyone been round to Chepstow Place lately?'

'I talked to Kitty on the phone the day before yesterday,' said Suki. She was thinking that – since Simon's appalling revelation – the conversation with her daughter seemed to have taken place in another life.

'Oh, how is she?' asked Becky perfunctorily.

'All right,' said Suki. It wasn't true. Kitty's voice had had a flat hopeless note to it. Suki assumed she was unhappy in love, though her daughter never confided in her about such matters. Kitty should marry soon, thought Suki with none of her usual energy.

'High time Max left,' said Tom.

'I know,' Simon agreed with a smile. 'Those two were such a contented couple. They didn't need anyone else.'

'What on earth are you talking about?' Tom sounded really angry, suddenly.

'Nothing, nothing!' Simon was honestly astonished.

'Now, darling,' said Becky soothingly. But secretly she was pleased, as always, when a private worry was commandeered by Tom. 'Time for dinner?'

'They're first cousins!'

'Of course they're first cousins,' Simon agreed, still none the wiser, and tried to catch Suki's eye. But she wasn't responding. She'd avoided his looks all evening. '*I don't blame her*,' he thought, with a quite new sense of shame.

'We are meant to be discussing the party,' was all Suki said, dully.

But she was thinking about Uncle Hector and secrets.

She'd been with him that very day – though she hadn't revealed this to Simon yet.

After the bombshell he'd dropped the evening before, it had felt entirely natural and sensible to seek out her uncle. After all, wasn't he the wise elder of the family and fierce guardian of the whole crucial complicated structure? And hadn't he always adored *her* in particular? Tom had once suggested she was the type of woman that he wished he'd married himself ('an earth mother', he'd said). Uncle Hector would surely know what to do.

In her anxiety, she'd not thought to telephone beforehand. It was only after that disturbing and almost inevitable moment of feeling lost – just before the dark jigsaw arms of the monkey puzzle tree loomed over the country lanes and, moments later, the wheels of her car were crunching the gravel in the forecourt – that she remembered the busy complicated life of the house.

The front door was always open because the place was never unoccupied. Suki caught a glimpse of an aproned young girl, carrying a bucket and a mop, as she entered the chilly hall with its familiar aroma of dried lavender and beeswax, its contradictory mixture of bleakness and busyness. The old flagstones were swept and washed each day, the glossy surface of the bare mahogany stairs maintained just as her grandparents' was. There were sounds coming from all over the house: saucepans being set down with a solid clunk in the stone sink in the scullery, the whoosh whoosh whoosh of a stiff broom against a hard grainy surface, and – upstairs – the thumping flurry of un-slept-on mattresses being heaved over yet again, sash windows eased up so that rugs aired only yesterday could be flung across sunny sills once more. All this for just one person, Suki marvelled. She'd had to dispense with her own cleaner months ago.

Merriweather was in his kitchen, of course. He was making his legendary shortbread, which tradition dictated must always fill a silver box on the sideboard in the dining-room. He had an unusual tin instrument, rusting at the edges, for achieving the correct shape. '*So that's what he looks like when he's happy,*' thought Suki as she watched him punching oblongs out of a speckly expanse of pastry.

He disliked surprises. He didn't ask what she was doing there or even address her as 'Miss Suki' as usual. His contented concentrated expression had vanished. He suspected, quite correctly, that – as it was now noon – she would be staying for lunch.

'Hello, Merriweather . . . Is Mr St Clair around?'

But he pretended deafness, turning his back on her to open a door in his antiquated range so he could insert his tray of shortbread. There was a sudden blast of heat, an acrid stench of ancient fat.

She could hear shouting in the distance and, following it, found her uncle by the enormous cedar set in a clearing at the very end of the garden.

He had his back to her. He and his head gardener were poring over a knobbly eruption of deep yellow toadstools at the tree's base. Mouthing the words, nodding dramatically at the same time, Partridge informed Uncle Hector: 'Need to take care of them spores, too.'

'What's that, Partridge?'

Partridge said quietly, perhaps for Suki's benefit: 'He will carry them dodgy old bits of wood about in his bucket, spreading infection.' Then he bellowed at the top of his voice: 'Them fruiting bodies!'

Uncle Hector sounded very puzzled: 'Shooting bodice?'

Partridge gathered up his strength once more. 'Stump'll need a dose of the ammonium sulphate!'

'What's that, Partridge?'

It was at this point that Suki touched him on the arm.

It was wonderful to see his sudden incredulous delight. Then, like a cloud passing over the sun, sadness eclipsed it. 'Honey fungus,' he said, his face puckering up like a baby's. They were dreadful words to Uncle Hector: curse of all the growing things he loved most, destroyer of the exquisite creeper that had once flowered all round the window of his Wisteria Room. 'It'll have to come down.'

'Oh no!' exclaimed Suki, momentarily distracted from her own troubles. She couldn't imagine this place without the old cedar. It had, after all, given the house its name. It was as much a part of Uncle Hector's as that other tree beloved by all his family, who knew, when it loomed above, that their journey was over.

Uncle Hector nodded. 'Otherwise it'll spread.' He looked utterly miserable.

'Could go to the monkey puzzle,' Partridge warned, for Suki's ears alone; and added, chattily, 'They enjoy them trees, they do.'

Uncle Hector was always consulting his watch. Now he was made aware of an even more pressing worry. 'Have you said hello to Merriweather?'

Suki immediately burst into tears. It was because of the relief of seeing him – her dear fussy old uncle – and finding everything in his regimented world so comfortingly predictable. Instantly she saw real alarm in his face. Coming all this way to see him and then crying in front of a servant must signify catastrophe. In his mind, that could mean only one thing. Did she imagine that he was starting to look at her quite differently, with a strange disapproval verging on distaste?

He hustled her away from curious Partridge and into the cool innards of the house. Then he left her on her own in the drawing-room while he went to have a word with Merriweather about lunch.

Suki heard their raised voices coming from the kitchen. Some mutinous muttering about a wasted pancake countered by a brisk suggestion from Uncle Hector – who didn't know the first thing about cooking – to make use of the fresh eggs from the hens for a change.

Then, still in his old blue work overalls (because he was so anxious to discover what this was about) and looking very out of place in his formal drawing-room with its beautiful old rugs and good pieces of furniture and excellent paintings, he fiddled with his hearing-aid, which took several minutes because his hands were trembling so. 'Bugger bugger bugger ...' he muttered very loudly and crossly as if, all of a sudden, it didn't seem to matter swearing in front of his favourite niece because she'd come crashing down from her pedestal.

Finally he was ready to hear the full story, his face folded into miserable lines of disappointment and disapproval.

'The evidence was staring them in the face,' Tom complained as he took a spoonful of Becky's ice cream, made from the blackcurrants in their country garden. 'But no, they wouldn't have it. They were out for hours. When the foreman delivered the verdict, I couldn't even *look* at the poor coppers who'd brought it to court. Imbeciles! I tell you, if *I* ever knew I was guilty as hell, I'd elect for trial by jury.'

As a QC specializing in criminal law, Tom represented dishonest or positively wicked people all the time. 'What do you do if you know they're guilty?' Suki had once asked. 'I'm not supposed to know that,' he'd replied with a tight smile. He was busier than most – but never failed to point out that, as a freelance, he couldn't afford to turn work down.

'You promised not to talk shop,' Becky reminded him with a pout.

'Sorry, my love . . . This ice-cream is excellent, by the way . . .'

'We are meant to be talking about the party, darling.'

'You're perfectly right, my sweet . . .'

'So what about a nice tomato salad to start with?' Becky suggested, remembering the pact to discourage overspending that she and Tom had made beforehand. 'Or soup?' They worried about money all the time. It was true that they had two nice houses and at least a couple of good family holidays abroad a year and there'd been private education for all the children. But they weren't rich, for God's sake!

'Too ordinary,' said Suki. 'How about smoked salmon?'

It had been astonishing and gratifying to see the change in Uncle Hector.

Once she'd begun to explain, she became his favourite again – the darling niece possessed of all the qualities in a woman he admired most. Not that he wasn't worried! As he grasped the nub of why she'd come rushing down here without warning, he shook his head in disbelief.

'Why didn't you say something?' He was hurt. 'Why didn't you come to me at the beginning?' Then: 'What's money for?'

Lighting must be kept to a dim eye-straining minimum, housekeeping expenses pared to the bone, the young eternally nagged about the cost of things and, above all, capital must never be touched. However – in a situation like this – Uncle Hector could demand in all sincerity, 'What's money for?'

But at which point during your gradual slide down the precipice were you entitled to ask for it?

'Now,' he said, holding her hand tightly, patting it every so often for encouragement, 'we're going to have to think really hard about what we're going to do. But first I want you to tell me exactly what he said . . .'

 Chapter Fourteen

'It was one of those moments that define your life,' Simon had begun, watching Suki very carefully for her reaction. 'You're faced with a temptation: a solution, if you like. You can either seize it – or not.' And, waiting in dry-mouthed terror, Suki had found herself wondering, 'Is this how men always explain it to their wives?' Suddenly, the whole of her marriage seemed a sham and the confusion was almost as painful as the betrayal. Who was this man she'd lived with for a quarter of a century and considered to be her greatest friend? If it had taken him only a second to turn his back on her, what had been the meaning of that great slice of her existence, so rich and satisfying at the time?

It had seemed so inappropriate to be having the conversation in their bedroom, yet it was where every significant discussion had taken place.

She'd realized, at supper, how strangely nervous he was. He should have come home in fine spirits after the lunch with her father at the Reform, but instead he'd shouted at Phil – which he never did – and then she noticed that he kept glancing at her as if trying to work something out.

He was wondering how she'd react to this blow, of course. She knew it for sure when he suggested taking whisky upstairs with them.

There was no question of getting ready for bed this time, discussing finer details between the sheets. He'd decided they'd talk like uncomfortable guests: she perched on the stool of her dressing table, facing away from her mirror so she couldn't see her frightened face; he seated formally on one of the chairs where he'd drape his clothes. It was very painful for her to appreciate, all over again, how nice-looking he was. If Anthony could manage to attract women like flies, she told herself miserably, she was deluded to expect fidelity from Simon.

And then he'd asked: 'Do you remember that party we went to a few months ago at the Oriental Club?'

And Suki thought: '*So it actually happened with me there. I'd never have believed such a thing possible.*'

They didn't go to that many smart parties and this one had been fun, with delicious food and drink and the vigorous rising hum of a successful gathering. '*How strange,*' thought Suki, '*that I can remember the shrimp mayonnaise canapés exactly and yet I've no memory of <u>her</u>. I know exactly who he likes and why. I'm never surprised by his impressions when we discuss people afterwards because invariably they echo my own – or perhaps it's the other way round. Why didn't I pick up some resonance? What instinct failed me?*'

She remembered that an over-active hostess had separated

them almost immediately: introducing her to a career woman
with whom, of course, there was nothing in common. And
while the woman had droned on about her job as a successful
advertising copywriter – 'remember the margarine and
buttercups?' – she'd discreetly searched for Simon among the
sea of animated heads and located him talking to a man of
similar age with receding dark hair and a long and narrow face
edged with a wispy fringe of beard that managed to achieve a
look both effete and lupine.

'Who was that?' she'd asked without great interest, when they
were eventually reunited.

'Only someone I was at school with,' he'd replied in
similar vein. And then he'd added, turning his mouth down,
as if the information were utterly unimportant: 'Actually he's
an earl.'

'Simon had a good education,' Suki told her uncle, repeating
what her husband had said, mimicking the helpless charming
shrug.

Simon hadn't needed to explain – and neither did Suki for
Uncle Hector – that because his soon to be impoverished
parents had sent him to Harrow, he'd been thrown together
with boys who would, in future, have money and connections.

By now Uncle Hector's exhausted disgusted expression had
metamorphosed into one of concentrated concern. It was
extraordinary how it happened (odd, too, the way he now
seemed to find no difficulty in hearing every single word). One
moment he was staring silently down at his lap, resembling an
ancient hostile tortoise. The next, he'd realized – just as she'd
done, at precisely the same point – that this would be no tale of
infidelity and betrayal, after all.

It was about stupidity and greed. Shortly he'd understand that a member of the family – the husband of his favourite – had broken out of the corset of conventionality and fear that usually restrained people like them from breaking the law. '*Especially not people like us,*' Uncle Hector would correct himself very grimly.

'Have you any idea what it's been like for me?' Simon had asked his wife. 'I mean, to know that, however hard you work, you're going slowly bust and there's absolutely nothing you can do about it.' He'd added, 'You must have known I was worried . . .'

'Of course I did!'

'Why didn't you say anything, then?'

'Why didn't you tell me?'

'I didn't want to worry you.'

It seemed that his old schoolmate, Rupert Fortescue – formerly Viscount Belton – had recently inherited an enormous estate in the West Country. The earldom was less relevant, so far as Simon was concerned. He told Suki that he'd happened to spot the death notice in *The Times* a few weeks before the party and instantly remembered a long ago weekend and the isolation of that grand location, the acres and acres of unused space. Why shouldn't he take advantage of dim amiable Fortescue's good fortune?

'When I saw him unexpectedly like that after all those years,' he explained, 'it was as if I heard a voice in my head.'

'What did it say?' Suki had asked, so relieved by now that she was able to be curious.

He'd failed to answer. It had been the devil's voice, of course, though he'd never have put it like that. '*There's your solution,*' it had whispered.

But if he was truly honest (which he wasn't altogether with

Suki), hadn't there been another ingredient? A feeling that he was owed for all that had been taken away? Perhaps some deep and shameful part of him had wanted to implicate the new earl, who'd had it so very easy, by comparison. *'Serve him right!'* said the same secret voice.

Straight away, surrounded by shrieking guests, he'd asked his fellow Harrovian if he could do him a favour. Fortescue had cupped a hand round one ear, grinning amiably and showing his receding gums, and Simon had had to spell out the request at the top of his voice. ('Do you think anyone else heard?' asked Suki anxiously, already thinking ahead.) Without a moment's hesitation, Fortescue had agreed.

Simon thought he could understand why. They both shared the same harsh but increasingly glorious memories. For Fortescue, this bond meant that trust was unquestioned and – because he himself had steadily become richer (though not through his own efforts) and was unimaginative – it would not occur to him that a contemporary might tumble into genteel poverty and then teeter on ruin. Besides, there were no indications. Granted, it was a bit of a surprise to learn that an old Harrovian had become a second-hand car dealer. But Simon still had all the poise and mannerisms of his class and, despite a gap of almost thirty years, was completely recognizable.

'D'you ever go back to the old place?' Fortescue had asked him, but straight afterwards recalled that he'd never seen Simon at any school reunions.

'No, actually,' Simon replied with an easy smile, as if being reminded of all the privilege he'd once enjoyed wouldn't matter to him at all.

*

'Oh my dear!' Uncle Hector exclaimed at this point. 'Have you said anything to your father?'

Suki shook her head and saw a look of dreamy pleasure briefly light up his face. Immediately afterwards, he appeared a little ashamed. The fact was, he'd felt unloved as a boy and any indication that he was cherished was as startling and delicious as an embrace.

And then Merriweather interrupted them: 'Lunch.'

'Lunch is served, is it, Merriweather?' asked Uncle Hector very pleasantly, filling in the customary courtesies for him.

Merriweather failed to reply, having already said as much.

'I must get out of these,' said Uncle Hector, indicating his overalls.

Once he'd changed, they'd continue in the dining-room with the double doors closed. And he would strive to keep his voice down.

Simon had fed Fortescue a cock-and-bull story about having to deliver a couple of cars to clients in the area: needing them on the spot, but also requiring time to finalize paperwork. Would Fortescue temporarily house them for him? A brighter man would almost certainly have smelt a rat. 'No problem, dear chap!' He had at least two enormous barns, he'd told Simon, either of which might be ideal. 'Only too pleased,' he'd said, and repeated it several times. He'd always been amiable.

'But I have a barn,' said Uncle Hector wonderingly, as if watching himself say the words from a distance.

But before she could digest the shock of this, Suki rushed on with her story, anxious to get it all out. 'He told me he had to go away for the night. He said it was to do with work. But afterwards I thought, I thought . . .'

Uncle Hector stopped her. 'No, no, no!' Such fears mustn't be articulated. It would upset him far too much.

All on his own, Simon had loaded his two costliest cars on to a transporter and, leaving his garage unlocked so as to back up the story he would tell the police, set off for the West Country. He'd feared being conspicuous but, as it turned out, was only one of scores of nocturnal travellers piloting enormous unwieldy vehicles through mist and dark. Did any of those other drivers cross a crucial boundary in the course of their journeys?

Luck had seemed on his side. Once he'd settled the cars with the help of an estate worker (roused from his bed but more than happy after a large tip), he'd driven straight back to London again. He'd returned home to bath and shave (and soothe Suki, who'd missed him dreadfully in their one and only night apart), and then he'd set off for his garage, just like any other morning.

When he'd phoned the police to report a break-in and robbery, he'd sounded honestly shocked and angry – as if he'd successfully thought himself back into the skin of the gentleman salesman everyone saw him as.

Uncle Hector said, picking at a lumpy beige omelette with a frill of blackened egg white: 'Come to think of it, your father *does* know about it!'

'That's impossible!'

'Yes, it's coming back to me now . . . Simon told him about a break-in at the garage when they had lunch together.'

'Why should he have done that?' asked Suki, mystified. The gap between the husband she'd believed she knew so well and the man who'd committed a crime was yawning ever wider. It felt like stumbling into a horror film.

'Mmm, at the Reform,' said Uncle Hector, fitting bits and pieces together, already looking ahead, searching for a solution like a man with a flickering torch on a dark night. He was thinking, '*Charming chap, good worker, excellent husband and father . . . Not a first-class mind, though. No. Not so dependable really, either. Oh dear, oh dear! Darling Suki is going to have to be very strong.*' Out loud, he said: 'The police aren't suspicious, are they?'

'He didn't say so.'

'Then he must have told you because he'd made the mistake of telling your dear father,' said Uncle Hector. 'No flies on *him.*' He patted her hand. 'I'm talking about Lionel, of course . . .'

The police had asked Simon a lot of questions. But he'd handled them well, he'd told Suki, eyes cast down in secret satisfaction, a hand over his mouth to hide any suspicion of arrogance.

He understood, he told her, that they'd already put in a report. If all went well – and there was nothing to indicate that it wouldn't, he said confidently – then the insurance would probably come through in a couple of months.

'But you can't!'

He'd stared at her blankly. How handsome he was, she'd reflected sadly, though aware – for the very first time – of the lack of strength in his small features, the lie behind the candour of his gaze.

'I won't be a party to this, Simon.' How painfully hard it had been to say it but she'd known she was right. It was wrong of him to have involved an innocent schoolfriend, too. Above all, she knew that everyone in the family – people of integrity – would agree with her. That had been almost the worst part of learning about Simon's dishonesty: the knowledge that she was not the only one to have been betrayed.

'But he did it for you,' said Uncle Hector triumphantly.

Suki looked at him with her pale and anxious face, her eyes sore from lack of sleep.

'For the very best of motives,' her uncle went on, rubbing his hands together energetically. 'He was only trying to protect his family. Poor chap. None of it's his fault really . . . He's had a terrible time lately what with the mess the country's been in. Must have been worried sick.'

'I suppose,' Suki agreed with a troubled frown. 'He seemed so confident the business would pick up. He told me not to worry . . .'

'Quite right!' boomed Uncle Hector. 'Quite right!'

Over tiny dripping cups of Nescafé served in the drawing-room (Merriweather had slopped the coffee when he banged the tray down), she asked: 'What shall we do?'

'We'll think of something.'

'We?' She looked scared again.

Uncle Hector patted her hand. 'Don't worry. This stays with me.'

If Simon had only come to him first, he thought. Of course, he would pull whatever strings possible. But if, despite his best efforts, the worst occurred (which it must not, he thought fiercely), then the whole family would mass ranks. They'd be there in the background, offering support, while sending messages to the outside world that (a) it could have happened to anyone and (b) this was not something they wished to discuss.

He sighed heavily. Then, reminded of something far more cheerful, he said, 'You *are* a darling to have thought of this birthday party for me. Such a lovely idea. I knew it was you.'

'Birthday party?' echoed Suki, summoning incredulity with an effort. 'I've no idea what you're talking about.'

For reply, Uncle Hector passed across a letter in scrawling black handwriting, spattered with exclamation points and dashes and underlinings. It was from third cousin Harriet, whose passion was correspondence. '*So* looking forward to your party, dear Hector!' it said. 'Now – can I bring anything?'

 Chapter Fifteen

As Liza pushed through the revolving doors of the Savoy, she had a very clear picture of the solution to her problems. He would be tall and slim, handsome in a pale and non-threatening way – very much as her father had looked, in fact.

There was nobody of that description in the American Bar. There was, however, a person who looked like a large elderly pig. Big and plump with receding grey hair and a faint smile on his stiff florid face, he was sitting at a table reading the *Evening Standard* and sporting a red carnation with the bemused air of a man wearing a paper hat at a party. Watching from a safe distance, half-hidden behind a door, Liza thought he looked like someone her grandparents might know. Then he licked a finger before turning a page and she revised the opinion.

In spite of his promise to position himself well
beforehand, there was no sign of Max. Liza decided without
hesitation to pass on this meeting. But should she hang
around, all the same, and wait for her cousin? It would be fun
to have a drink here and, though she was broke as usual, Max
always had money.

As she was vacillating, the pig glanced up and very scarily not
only spotted her skulking behind the door but also saw straight
through her attempts to disguise herself. He smiled and
beckoned, and – impressed by his magician-like powers – she
found herself complying.

'You must be Liza?'

'Maybe.'

'Talented young soprano?'

'Possibly.'

'Then it could be' – he smiled without warmth – 'I'm your
patron.' He held out his hand. 'Felix Munro.'

Even though he was repulsive, vanity made Liza pull off her
headscarf and shake out her blonde hair as if unwrapping a
present destined for someone else. She also removed the floor-
length black coat she'd borrowed from her mother. She used
to like black but hated it now. Besides, she knew she had a nice
figure.

'What will you drink?'

'A Manhattan,' said Liza as casually as if she drank them
every day. It was time to claw back some measure of control.

She didn't like the amused and curious way he was studying
her: even though it seemed measured as if, quite deliberately, he
never did anything at full capacity. She glanced round again to
see if Max had arrived.

'Looking for someone?' He didn't sound especially

interested. He'd taken the opportunity to assess her legs, though. He wasn't even ashamed to be caught in the act.

'Why, should I be?'

He shrugged in a manner that suggested he held all the cards. 'So, Liza . . .Why don't you tell me about yourself.'

Max was nearly always late but had really intended to keep his promise this time. It was sheer bad luck that, just as he was leaving, his grandmother had telephoned. At least it wasn't his mother, though. He only answered it in case it was Liza with a last-minute change of plan.

'Who is that?'

'It's Max.' He sounded very childish. His grandmother had that effect on him.

'Max,' she repeated as if mentally shuffling the deck of grandchildren into place. Then: 'How are you, darling?'

'Fine,' muttered Max, responding to the endearment, despite himself. It was a quarter past six. He'd intended to be at the Savoy fifteen minutes ago. He asked politely, eyes rolling wildly, 'How are you?'

'Your grandfather and I are *vay* well.'

His grandmother wouldn't refer to the evening at Kitty's parents, of course – she never talked about personal stuff like that. But he guessed she probably knew all about it. It was like pass the parcel in their family: one person handing on a juicy piece of gossip to the next, pausing only to unwrap a layer. He cringed as he remembered the unspeakably dreadful scene at dinner and then his mother shrieking at him so all the neighbours could hear. His dominant impulse had been to run away from everyone who'd ever known him, but that was impossible, of course. So he'd done his bad boy zombie act, which was the next best thing. He'd tried to ignore the shocked reaction of Uncle Simon and Aunt Suki. ('Heartless!' they'd probably said later.) For a moment he'd felt as if he truly was made of stone, and it was satisfactory in a weird sort of way. First he'd deliberately terrified Kitty with his reckless driving and then he'd heard himself say those unforgivable things to her. When they got home, he'd observed her rush into her bedroom and shut the door and knew for certain she'd be sobbing her heart out. '*Good!*' he'd thought, mostly because she'd witnessed what he'd suffered and therefore deserved punishment. But when Charlie had asked him what sort of evening they'd had, he'd replied casually, like just now, 'Fine.'

'What have you been up to?' his grandmother asked.

'Um . . . not much . . .'

'Not much,' she repeated like a judgement.

'Just, things, you know, Grandma . . .'

There was a pause, then: 'How's the real tennis going?' in that soft indulgent tone with a hint of hauteur.

'Fine,' muttered Max again.

'Are Charlie and Kitty there?'

'Not yet.'

'Ah,' said his grandmother with meaning, 'they'll have been working at their jobs, poor darlings.'

He'd not questioned his mother's version that night, mostly because he could see that Aunt Suki and Uncle Simon believed it, too. His father with all those women! Oh, it was disgusting! But he wasn't going to give him a chance to tell his side of the story. It was like refusing to open the letters. There was a whole pile of them now at Chepstow Place. '*Please open this, Max,*' his father had written on the envelope of the latest.

Sometimes he wondered why he hadn't destroyed them.

He'd picked on Kitty because he had to direct the savagery somewhere. He knew it was unfair. But Kitty was probably the one person on earth he could be certain would never reject him. He tested Charlie's affection also, though to a lesser degree. He played his radio late at night knowing perfectly well it was distracting. Did he *want* them to throw him out?

Only Liza was treated circumspectly: probably because he recognized she was as self-centred as he. She was a frivolous girl, his grandmother had once said – her voice very light and amused, as if really she were paying Liza a compliment.

And now, in the same spirit, she paid another. 'I'd better let you go, Max. I'm sure you have far more important things to do than talk to your grandmother.'

'You'll have dinner with me,' said the pig. There was no question about it. He'd decided in his jaded complacent way that this was how the evening would continue.

It had probably been a mistake, thought Liza, to tell him she sang in a pub; but she'd wanted to stress her energy and commitment. 'I'd really like to go to music school.' She tried to sound hopeful and also encouraging.

But the pig seemed more interested in her family. So she told him that her father was a QC and one of her brothers was training to be a lawyer. The other one hadn't made up his mind yet, she said – he was a bit of a playboy, actually, she'd added with a fond smile. Her sister was a secretary. Describing how she still lived at home with all of them nearly brought tears to her eyes.

'Do they know you're here?'

'Of course!'

He looked doubtful, though still faintly amused. 'Girl like you?'

Liza appeared very knowing and poised as she attacked her third Manhattan. But inside she felt despair. If only the family encouraged her ambition more. Was it foolish to harbour such dreams? She wanted success and fame so badly that it hurt, but each day was confronted with the reality of her existence, which was looking after old women for a pittance. Uncle Tom was always saying the twenties were the best years of your life. Liza couldn't understand it, really, because Charlie and Kitty and Max were all unhappy in their different ways, too. When she thought about Kitty's misery, she felt very guilty, even though it was Max who'd started it. And now it had become like the ganging up they'd never engaged in as children: crowd behaviour, rounding on the most vulnerable, as shameful as it was hurtful. *'Join the club!'* thought Liza, wallowing in her own disappointment.

The drinks tasted very fruity and sweet. She'd been thirsty as well as nervous and the combination had made her drink too fast. 'I must just . . .' She tried to rise to her feet, staggered, sat down heavily.

'Dear, dear!' said the pig.

'I'm quite okay,' she assured him sternly.

'We won't have dinner here.'

Liza tried to think clearly. 'Careful . . .' she thought. Carful? Earful? What had happened to Max? If he still hadn't arrived by the time the pig asked for the bill, she'd make an escape via the ladies' room. The sketch of a plan unfurled by fits and starts in her woozy mind.

'There's a nice little Italian nearby . . .'

The pig caught a waiter's eye and executed a confident scribble in the air with a podgy liver-spotted paw and Liza seemed to notice her white soft little hands for the first time.

'It so happens, my dear, that I only live round the corner.'

'I must just . . .' Liza repeated.

To her relief, there was a telephone outside the ladies' room. She decided that, after her urgent visit to the lavatory, she'd ring the flat in Chepstow Place. Even if Max wasn't there, Charlie would be. He never went out now. As she washed her hands, she thought of decent kind Charlie with longing – and was confronted by a flushed and wild-eyed blonde. '*Oh God!*' she thought, appalled. '*That can't be me!*'

But after she'd splashed her face with cold water and sluiced plenty into her open mouth, too, she felt better. Her mascara had been rinsed off. She could see in the mirror that she looked a lot younger now. Falling into the role, she rubbed off her lipstick with her handkerchief and flattened her hair. 'I could be his granddaughter,' she told her new reflection, sounding truly shocked.

She found enough small change for the telephone in her handbag. '*See?*' she crowed to herself. Not so drunk, after all! She put the money in, dialled the number, heard Charlie's wary voice (because it might be Aunt Camilla again). 'It's Liza!'

'What's going on?' A hand was laid on her shoulder from behind.

'Liza!' she heard Charlie say on the other end. 'Is that you, Liza?' He didn't sound particularly anxious but, then, he'd no idea where she was. And then she remembered that he didn't even know about the advertisement she'd placed.

'It's okay,' said Liza quite calmly. 'I'll ring you later.'

She'd have to go for dinner now but straight afterwards would extricate herself. She'd feign illness, if need be: she was confident she could talk her way out of any situation. She'd no money for a taxi, of course, but it wasn't in her nature to worry. The death of her father had been cataclysmic but it seemed set apart, different. It didn't mean more bad things were likely to happen.

'I've had a better idea,' said the pig as they walked out of the hotel. She felt his inexorable grip on her elbow.

'*Food*,' thought Liza serenely. She could do with some. As a matter of fact, she told herself, she'd earned an expensive dinner. And when it was over, there'd be a whole plethora of horrors to regale the others with. She saw herself back at Chepstow Place sparkling away, stressing the daring of it, making them laugh like always.

The minute she saw Max, though, there was nothing but relief. It was so typical of him to saunter to the rescue at the very last minute. It occurred to her that probably this had to do with discouraging people from expecting too much of him. They'd a great deal in common, really.

'Here's my brother,' she told the pig blithely. 'Gotta go now.'

'You're pissed,' Max told her as they walked along black glittering streets in search of his car. It had rained while she'd been indoors and the air was suddenly renewed.

There was a dull boom from somewhere in the distance. If either of them followed the news, they'd have been aware that two IRA bombs had exploded in separate pubs in Guildford a few days before. Five people had been killed and many more injured. But it didn't even occur to them that this might be another bomb. They were quite extraordinarily oblivious of what went on outside their world.

'He shouldn't have let me drink all those Manhattans,' Liza grumbled. She tripped on the hem of her mother's black coat and Max caught her.

'How many did you have?'

'About six,' she said, exaggerating as usual.

Max whistled. 'What do you want to do now?'

'I don't know . . .' She wished that she wasn't looking so bedraggled and childish and dreary. It meant they couldn't go to a nightclub. But at least she could amuse him. With her perfect ear, she mimicked the pig: 'It so happens, my dear, that I only live round the corner . . .'

'I hate men like that,' said Max with real violence. 'How old was he, anyway?'

'I think he was a white slave trader.'

'Older than Grandpa.'

'One more minute and I'd have been abducted.' For the second time that evening, she almost made herself cry. 'I could have disappeared off the face of the earth, Max!' It was easier than admitting that, though interest had been shown in her, it certainly wasn't for her singing. The episode made it even harder to contemplate working for Mrs Withers, aged eighty-nine, whose very occasional bathing was ruled by a cantankerous boiler. She had six cats, too, and insisted on Liza regularly changing the sodden ash in their trays.

Liza felt cross and drunk and very sorry for herself. She tripped again and once more Max caught her.

'My mother's having an affair,' she told him and, too late, clapped a hand over her mouth. Even in her drunken state she felt guilty for betraying her mother, though, to her chagrin, she'd certainly not been confided in.

She'd intended to create a bond without actually spelling it out. Because it seemed Uncle Ant had affairs – loads and loads of them, Kitty had informed her with a grimace. 'It's the real reason Max is upset,' she'd explained (though it was Kitty who appeared distraught).

Max said nothing.

Liza looked up at his beautiful blank face and unreadable dark eyes and thought about even ancient people having affairs, and took the astonishing decision to kiss him.

His lips felt very soft but passive. He seemed frozen, waiting. But he didn't pull away. It was as if he were waiting to see how she'd proceed next.

'*It's like kissing me!*' thought Liza, not fully understanding what she meant and far too drunk to consider consequences.

Chapter Sixteen

Kitty heard the whispering in her sleep – her name, repeated over and over again.

Dreams have a trick of adapting to outside stimuli. For a moment, she believed that Max was calling her, and instantly her brain concocted a complicated explanatory back drama in which he'd always been a player.

'Wake up, Kitty! Please!'

Fully conscious at last, a little regretful to be woken, she asked in her normal voice: 'What's the matter?'

'Sshhh!' said Charlie. She could hear his breath coming in ragged gasps.

The sounds and feelings of the previous evening were coming back to her now: the outrageous unbearable pictures, the anguish and jealousy and, finally, the anger. There was every reason to have dreamt about Max.

She'd been awoken by the metallic clunk of keys dropping, laughter incompetently stifled, a door opening and shutting, more whispering. After that, there'd been the clatter of shoes kicked off, then the squeak of bedsprings building to a regular rhythm until it was impossible to deny what was happening next door. She'd put her pillow over her head. Later, there'd been more whispering as if some sort of an argument were taking place. It was strange how whispering removed the distinction from voices even if you knew exactly to whom they belonged. Then there was the stealthy sound of feet creeping along the narrow hall carpet like big clumsy insects and the sharp click of the front door being pulled to. She'd had to resist the impulse to run after Liza and confront her.

'I can't think!' Charlie was whimpering. 'I can't think, Kitty!'
She reached out a hand for the switch on her bedside lamp.
'Don't!'

But it was too late. Light had already defined her little room with its mish-mash of spoilt or rejected furniture from the old family house, Lavenham: stuff for grandchildren, who must learn to prize good things. There was the too big mahogany chest of drawers, one side of which had been badly bleached by the sun, the Georgian dressing table with a mirror from a later period that didn't fit, the Chinese prints of birds her mother had insisted would look quite lovely but were unsuitable for a bedroom. (The stork perched on a bamboo, smug yet quizzical, depressed Kitty every single morning.)

It was five o'clock, she saw from her watch, and the sight of Charlie was a shock. His eyes were red and swollen. He looked very embarrassed, humbled to be viewed in such a state.

'What's happened? Tell me.'

He sat down on her bed and put his head in his hands. 'I set my alarm . . .' he began. He'd been setting it for four o'clock in the morning since Max had arrived and its tinny peremptory buzz sometimes woke Kitty, too. It was the only way to cope with the workload, he'd apologize.

'And?'

He couldn't answer. He was still catching his breath in great sobs. The only other time she'd seen him cry was when, as a ten-year-old, he'd jumped on to Uncle Hector's pitchfork.

'What's happened, Charlie?' she repeated, very tenderly. 'I can't help unless you tell me.'

'I don't know,' he said, sounding helpless and scared.

She put her arms round him and, to her consternation, he reacted by kissing her neck roughly, as if his previously shy and gallant self had been swept away by whatever emotional short circuit had caused this loss of control.

'Tell me . . .'

'I woke up like this,' Charlie sobbed. 'And, I dunno why . . . I can't stop.'

It touched her that he'd suffered for an hour before waking her. She embraced him more cautiously, beating him on the back like he'd so often done to comfort her. 'What should I do?'

'Just – don't go away.'

'No, I mean, should I phone your ma and pa?'

'No!' He sounded horrified.

'Would a hot drink make you feel better?'

He raised a watery smile. 'You and your hot drinks!'

She boiled milk in the little kitchen, put in two spoonfuls of Horlicks and one of sugar, just as he liked. She rejected the Law Society mug his father had given him in favour of one proclaiming 'The Boss' – a present from herself.

He was lying on her bed in his blue and white pyjamas when she returned. He'd even tucked himself under the quilt (pink, with white sprigs and scorch marks, also from Lavenham). 'Sorry,' he said, making an embarrassed face, but didn't move. Tears were still leaking out of his eyes. He looked exhausted, puzzled, fearful: as if watching himself from a distance.

'I don't think you should try and work any more.'

'I can't!' he said immediately, sounding as panicked as if she'd suggested the opposite.

'I think,' she went on very soothingly, 'that you should go back to your own bed and try and get some sleep. And if you don't feel any better later . . .'

'Couldn't I stay here?' he pleaded, as if this was the only thing that might help him. 'I don't mean . . .'

It hadn't even occurred to her. But now she thought, '*Why not?*' What did it matter if Max jumped to conclusions in the morning? Let him.

Arranged end to end in her not very comfortable single bed, Charlie's enormous feet jerking spasmodically every so often, neither of them got much rest. He hadn't been able to sleep for weeks, he confided in a hoarse whisper. He'd felt as if his head was about to explode and now he'd developed a twitching eyelid that was driving him crazy. Actually, he went on wonderingly, as if the comparison had only just occurred to him, he felt like an elastic band that had been stretched and stretched until finally it had snapped. You could hear the break in his voice, in the night.

'You know when the tube went in that old television . . .'

'Mmm.'

'. . . and suddenly there was just this white line running across the black?'

'I remember.'

'That's what I see when I shut my eyes.'

'It doesn't mean anything,' said Kitty comfortingly, and secretly closed her own to see if the same thing happened (which it didn't).

Once he hugged her feet and said, 'I don't know what I'd do without you, Cuz.'

'You don't have to,' she told him briskly. Then, 'Charlie . . .'

'Yes.'

'Did you . . . hear anything at all before you woke me up?'

'What?' he asked incuriously.

She didn't explain. He couldn't have slept so badly, after all.

In the morning, she telephoned Charlie's chambers and told them he had a feverish cold – a temperature of over a hundred, she went on, crossing her fingers. The clerk expressed concern, but it didn't stop him from asking when Charlie was likely to return.

'As soon as the fever's gone – probably a couple of days.'

After that, she made Charlie eat a boiled egg and, like a mother, cut his buttered toast into fingers. He looked a little shamefaced, sitting in his pyjamas in the sun at the scarred old table in the sitting-room.

'Don't you have to go to work?'

She smiled at him. 'I've called in sick. I'm getting out of choir practice this evening, too.'

Charlie made a pained apologetic face. He knew how much her singing meant to her.

'This is far more important.'

After breakfast he went straight back to her bed without permission as if confident she'd understand that the memory of her warm proximity was the greatest of comforts.

Kitty was waiting for Max to get up. She had resolved to tell him he was no longer welcome at the flat.

At twelve o'clock he emerged from the study looking rumpled in oddly childish flannel pyjamas and Kitty wondered if, every day, he rose this late and stared out of the window for long minutes while he yawned and scratched his head, as if locked in profound, creative thought. He'd left the door open and she caught sight of his untidy bed, the room strewn with clothes.

She followed him into the kitchen, but, instead of making her prepared speech, found herself saying, 'I've taken the day off.'

He glanced at her without interest before opening the refrigerator door and concentrating his attention on the contents. He looked like a beautiful, exotic animal that had wandered in from outside.

Ever since they'd shared the flat, Kitty and Charlie had allocated a sum of money each week to cover housekeeping expenses. They called it the pot ('Since we can't very well call it the kitty,' said Charlie). These days, it paid for Max's food, too. He particularly liked Grapenuts, Kitty had discovered, and also salami. Sometimes she'd hear the vroom of his sports car gobbling petrol as it accelerated off up the street and wonder why it never occurred to him to contribute.

She watched him finish the last of the milk. She would have to go out and buy more.

'The thing is, Max . . .'

He looked up from his glass. He sported a dashing little moustache of cream.

'. . . Charlie's not well. I'm looking after him.'

It was Max's style to wait to be told, rather than ask questions. It was a form of self-defence and Kitty knew that, really. But, because he'd hurt her so greatly, she now interpreted his silence as a lack of concern for Charlie. '*He couldn't care less about either of us!*'

She'd definitely decided to ask him to leave, hadn't she?

So what stopped her?

Max went out at about two. Before that he took all the hot water, which meant Charlie couldn't have a bath later. And afterwards, he ate the cheese slices Kitty had been planning to grill on toast for lunch.

She made herself ask, 'What happened last night?'

For a moment, as he turned his basilisk gaze on her, she was actually afraid.

'Wasn't Liza going to meet her sugar daddy?'

'Oh yes,' he said, after a moment, as if it had all been quite unimportant.

'What was he like, then?' asked Kitty, and even felt able to smile in a friendly sort of way.

'Ancient,' said Max with a scowl.

It so happened that, the same day, Tom bumped into the head of Charlie's chambers, a friend who'd helped arrange the pupillage, at a lunch in Middle Temple Hall.

'Sorry to hear young Charles is under the weather,' he said when they'd exchanged pleasantries.

'What?' Tom looked very puzzled. 'I didn't know.'

'A bad cold, I gather.'

'Ah!'

'I must say, I have noticed he hasn't been looking too well lately.'

'Strong as an ox,' Tom assured his friend vigorously, rubbing his hands together. 'Strong as an ox.' He waited to be complimented on having such an industrious and brilliant son, who'd hitherto never taken a single day off and was such an asset to the chambers. But nothing came. His friend started talking about a fraud case that had commanded the headlines recently. And, though Tom joined in the discussion with his usual interest and energy, part of him felt strangely apprehensive. He made a mental note to telephone Chepstow Place as soon as he got back to his own chambers.

It was Tom's style to attack difficulties rather than try and understand them. He liked to say there were no problems, only indecisions. Of course he wasn't going to accept that Charlie was too ill to go to work.

'I'm afraid he's asleep,' he was told by Kitty.

'Well, wake him then!' he ordered with an unconvincing laugh.

Kitty found she could easily summon up the strength that had failed her when trying to confront Max. For all his bluster, she wasn't afraid of her uncle. He was like an overgrown child, the way he tried to control everybody. She was resolved to protect Charlie, while giving nothing away. 'He couldn't sleep all night, actually.'

'It's only a cold, isn't it?'

'A very bad cold. And a temperature.'

Tom let a pause fall. 'What temperature?' he inquired in an unusually quiet tone but with a hint of menace.

'About a hundred and three, I think.'

'That's all? You don't peg it till you get to a hundred and five!' He continued with his characteristic blend of fierceness and joviality: 'And when do you *think* he's going to wake up?'

'Dunno . . . Shall I get him to phone you?'

'You do that, young Kitty.' Without really intending to, he could sound as intimidating as a Mafia boss. 'You make sure and do that.'

Becky telephoned within five minutes, sounding concerned and harassed. Tom must have contacted her almost immediately. He was like a tornado, thought Kitty, the way he stirred everyone up.

'Has the temperature gone down at all?'

'I don't know.'

'Is he still asleep?'

'Yes.'

'Better not wake him, then . . .' But Becky sounded uncertain. 'I would come round, but the thing is we've a dinner party this evening.' Her voice changed a little. She was unable to conceal the pride. 'Two high court judges. And I haven't even started the Beef Wellington yet.'

'There's no need. I'm looking after him.'

'Dear Kitty,' said Becky, 'I'm so glad you're there.' She sounded as if she truly meant it, for once.

Charlie genuinely fell asleep at about half-past four and, after she'd cleaned the kitchen, Kitty found herself wandering into Max's room, half against her will, much as she'd catch herself touching his just-used washing things.

There'd always been servants at his parents' house. No wonder he dropped his clothes all over the floor and never emptied ashtrays. But, under the musty blanket smell of old cigarette stubs, she could discern the very faint lemony scent of his aftershave. It was like glimpsing the old sweet boy beneath the atrocious behaviour.

Then her eye was caught by an opened letter. Like all his possessions, it had been carelessly treated: left balanced on the chest, whose drawers were pulled out, spewing socks and ties.

Kitty didn't believe in reading other people's correspondence. But the temptation was too great. To her astonishment, the letter was from Uncle Ant. He wrote all the time, but Max would let the unopened envelopes pile up for all to see.

'My dear Max,' she read, 'I know you don't understand any of this and it's very hard for me to explain. But you have to know that I love and miss you . . .'

Kitty stopped, feeling as guilty and intrusive as she should have been to start with. And just then, Charlie awoke and called like a child scared by the dark: 'Kitty! Kitty! Where are you?'

'How are you feeling?'

Charlie shook his head despairingly, closed his eyes once more.

'Your parents keep phoning. You're going to have to speak to them soon.'

'What do I tell them?' He sounded terrified. 'My dad . . .'

'I'll talk to my ma,' Kitty suggested very calmly. 'She can handle him.'

Besides, as a godmother, Suki had always had a special relationship with Charlie.

Chapter Seventeen

Liza said with a dreamy slightly edgy note to her voice that should have warned her mother: 'Do you think they watch us?'

She and Jane were drinking tea in their kitchen. Liza had woken up late, complaining of a hangover, and cancelled an appointment she'd made with her agency to go food shopping for one of the clients. 'It's always the same stuff,' she'd complained. 'Tins. Condensed milk. Baked beans. Spaghetti.'

'Who?' asked Jane with an absent smile because, though ostensibly trying to read the newspaper, she was thinking about Anthony. It was annoying that Liza had decided to take the day off because they'd planned to meet later. Anthony would be unable to come to the house now, of course. They'd be obliged to meet in a restaurant, and she did not look forward to it. Anthony's grand expensive places forbade intimacy and, denied the touch of his skin, the other women became painfully obtrusive. Jane would come away feeling unhappy and deprived and hearing that sad disappointed voice in her head, '*What on earth are you doing with him?*'

'Pa . . . *and* all the others.'

'I don't know, darling,' said Jane, forcing herself to concentrate. She disliked having this sort of conversation with Liza, mostly because she became so troubled. She herself would attempt to remain very calm, almost as if they were discussing somebody with whom she'd never had any sort of profound connection.

'He didn't want to go,' said Liza very definitely.

'Of course he didn't.' It was nothing but the truth.

'So his spirit would have stayed, wouldn't it?'

'I suppose so, darling.'

'So do you think he's still here, watching everything we do?'

'I don't think anyone knows that for sure,' said Jane very serenely, while thinking, '*What made her say that?*'

'Why did you say his spirit would have stayed, then?'

'*Oh dear!*' thought Jane. '*I can't cope with this.*' But out loud she said very tenderly, looking at her daughter's pale skin and light hair, 'Even if Pa isn't actually watching everything we do, he *is* here, in a sense, because he's part of you.'

Liza was looking at her hopefully now.

'You've half Pa's blood in your veins and half of his genes,' she went on. 'You've the same hair he had, the same eyes, the same smile. He'll always be part of you.'

'It's not enough,' muttered Liza.

'I find it very reassuring,' Jane said with a smile, even though she agreed with her daughter. She thought uncomfortably, '*Where does Liza's wildness come from? Not me. Not Henry, for sure.*'

They'd striven so hard to be good parents, reluctantly applying discipline when all else failed. But Liza was like a blade of grass growing through concrete: astonishingly single-minded and wayward.

Her job in the pub was coming to an end and there were no more singing engagements lined up. Jane could feel the disappointment as acutely as if it were her own. Liza wanted instant success but she was only twenty-one. She must learn to accept setbacks. It was part of growing up.

'What were you doing last night?' Jane asked to distract her. She was thinking, '*She ought to be using this time to practise her singing, but she'll get cross if I tell her so. Oh dear oh dear, I couldn't love her more but do I indulge her too much now Henry's no longer around? And I shouldn't be sitting here, drinking tea. I should be getting myself a job. But then I wouldn't be free in the afternoons any more. Anyway, someone has to walk that wretched dog.*'

'Nothing much,' Liza replied. The puppy was in a deep slumber on her lap. It looked very young and innocent. Early that morning it had ripped a hole in her mother's favourite patchwork cushion and efficiently rootled all the feathers out until the kitchen resembled a field of flowering dandelions. It had left a pile of excrement in one corner, too – exactly where it had deposited the last lot the night before. For such an untrained animal, it had an odd sense of order.

It was Jane who'd cleared up, of course, because Liza was still in bed.

'You got back jolly late.'

'Did I?'

'Where were you?'

'I only met Max for a drink at the American Bar at the Savoy.'

'Only!'

'It's not so special,' said Liza kindly because, so far as she knew, her mother never went to glamorous places any more.

'So you two just decided to meet up there, did you?'

'Mmm.'

'Why was that?'

'It was Max's idea,' Liza told Jane with an innocent look.

'Why not the others, too?'

'Dunno really. We don't do everything together.'

'You used to . . . Anyway, did you have fun?'

'It was okay.'

'Only okay? Did he – mention his father at all?'

'Nope. Why?'

'Oh, no reason. How is Max, anyway?'

'Fine,' said Liza, sounding severe.

'Do you think I ought to redecorate this room?' asked Jane, noticing the grease marks on the yellow paint around the stove.

'No!' said Liza in fright, because, since her father had gone, she'd refused to allow a single aspect of the house to be changed. All his clothes were still upstairs – his suits hanging in a neat row in his wardrobe in the master bedroom, his polished shoes set out in lines beneath. His perfectly furled umbrella stood to attention in the stand by the front door. Even the black trilby he'd occasionally worn still hung on a hook. They could see its dark disembodied shape through the frosted glass when they returned at night.

'Isn't that Henry's hat?' Anthony had asked Jane very gently, the last time he'd come.

The telephone rang and she jumped up to get it.

But it was too late. Liza had anticipated her.

'Aunt Becky,' she said as she handed it over. She wore a faint smile. She knew very well that her mother had been expecting another caller. She was on the case. It was only a matter of time before she unmasked him.

When Becky was agitated, she talked too fast. She sounded aggrieved, too. 'Actually, it was Liza I wanted to speak to, Jane.'

Jane raised her eyebrows, waved the receiver at Liza, who shook her head strenuously. 'Sorry, she was just on her way out.' Funnily enough, she suffered no guilt when lying on behalf of her daughter.

'Oh dear!' Becky rushed straight on: 'Charlie's not well – he didn't go into chambers today. I've spoken to Kitty and I've been trying to phone again but it's always busy and I was wondering if Liza knew anything?'

'What's wrong?'

'A cold, Kitty said.'

'Oh, everyone's had them.'

'Have they?' Becky sounded as if she longed to believe her. 'It's just that Tom . . .' Her voice tailed away.

Jane thought: *'Poor Becky. And poor poor Charlie. He's not even allowed to take the odd day off.'*

When the doorbell went, Kitty assumed it was her mother. She'd taken the phone off the hook after she'd called her, as a precaution in case her uncle rang again.

In fact, it was Liza in one of her very short skirts. She veered between shocking and decorous, as if confused by the mood of the seventies. Was she really as liberated and ambitious as she liked to proclaim? Or, secretly, was she as conventional as her family? She wore dark glasses, too – she liked to advertise her hangovers – and carried a big bag of grapes, which she was picking at.

'Charlie's ill,' she said, by way of explanation.

'How did you know?' asked Kitty.

Liza shrugged with her usual confidence.

Kitty stared accusingly at her cousin. Moments passed and then, trembling inwardly, she heard herself ask: 'How did you get on last night?'

Liza kept her dark glasses on (probably deliberately) so it was impossible to read her reaction. 'Okay,' was all she said after the slightest of hesitations.

'Max isn't here,' said Kitty even more coolly.

'I haven't come to see Max.'

'Haven't you?'

'What's this?' Liza sounded genuinely astonished. She went on very smoothly: 'What time did he get back anyway? Did he tell you I drank about a dozen Manhattans? I promise you, I was seeing double. He wanted to go to Annabel's but I'd put on all that dreary gear for the pervert so I got him to drop me off.'

Once, when they were six, she'd taken Kitty's bar of chocolate. 'I haven't!' she'd insisted, outraged, when charged. There were sticky brown marks all round her mouth and everyone had a go at her. There'd been tears, too, but she'd never confessed to the theft.

Now, she took off her dark glasses with a flourish. She had beautiful eyes: watery blue, like her father's had been. They looked very round and innocent. She stared unflinchingly at her cousin then smiled sweetly and headed for Charlie's room.

'Actually,' said Kitty, with all the embarrassment Liza should by rights have displayed, 'he's in my bed.'

*

Suki arrived shortly afterwards with the cake she'd baked for Phil's tea. Walnut and coffee was his favourite, but she wouldn't tell him he'd been robbed.

Charlie was back in his own bed by then but, instead of sitting beside him like Kitty, Liza was standing by the door as if afraid that whatever was afflicting him might rub off on her, too.

'What's up, old chap?' As Suki asked the question, she looked curiously round the room. She'd never shared a flat herself. She'd married so young that she couldn't conceive of being independent. '*What would have happened to me if Simon hadn't wanted to marry me?*' For the very first time, she found the idea less terrifying than interesting. It was as if the familiar picture of her husband as saviour and protector was gone forever now.

This room looked almost as bare as when the two young cousins had first moved in. There was a big and rather battered-looking old wardrobe with a dull key sticking out of it, a small painted chest of drawers where Charlie's hairbrushes were arranged, law books and papers piled in heaps, a sober work suit draped over a bentwood chair, and a single divan that was probably extremely uncomfortable, thought Suki, like all the beds from Lavenham.

To her horror, Charlie started sobbing, as if quite undone by her warm sympathy.

She saw Liza make a sudden movement as if she only wished to escape, but showed none of her own dismay. 'It's okay, darling . . .' she took Charlie in her arms and rocked him to and fro. 'It's okay . . .' She guessed that he was mortified to be seen in such a state.

She didn't know that he was thinking how like Kitty she was

with her long flowery dress and schoolgirl fringe, though a good bit plumper. She smelt of sugar and butter. It was deeply comforting to be in her embrace.

'Sorry, sorry . . .'

'No need.' In fact, Suki found it a relief not to have to think about her own problems for a change. 'Now, why don't you tell me what this is about?'

But Charlie couldn't answer. He merely sobbed.

'He's overworked,' said Kitty, who'd been silently observing this scene. 'He never ever stops, Ma. He works all evening and then he sets his alarm for four in the morning and starts again.'

Suki nodded, thinking, '*That's how Tom operated, too. I remember he did it for weeks and weeks before his bar exams. And he told me once he'd never felt more alive, before or since.*'

'I was okay till this morning,' Charlie muttered.

'Were you really, old chap?'

'I can't concentrate,' he told her miserably. 'I try so hard. I stare and stare at the page, but I can't make any sense of it. I just see these words that mean nothing. They're like those marks on ancient tombs, you know?' He fixed her with his mournful eyes. 'I sound really pathetic, don't I?'

'You don't sound pathetic at all,' Suki assured him briskly. 'Kitty's phoned the doctor, hasn't she? I expect you need a tonic. Can't go on beating the old brain for ever.'

'Can't I?' he asked hopefully.

'It's not a horse.'

'No.' He smiled weakly but then, to Suki's consternation, his eyes filled with tears once more. 'It's him, too,' he sobbed. 'He never speaks to me. He never even looks at me.'

'The barrister he's working for,' Kitty supplied.

'Oh, they're all like that,' said Suki for comfort. But she was remembering how helpful Tom's pupilmaster had been. He'd described him as the best pupil the chambers had ever had (as Tom continued to remind the family) and they were still friends.

'I feel like I don't exist.' Charlie sounded wretchedly bewildered. 'But he gives me all this work. He just seems to assume I know what I'm meant to be doing.'

'Do you think he's having a nervous breakdown, Aunt Suki?' asked Liza from the doorway, sounding very kind and concerned. But Kitty and Suki shot her identical angry glances.

'Shut up,' said Kitty, most surprisingly.

Suki could see now that she'd have to talk to Tom. She wasn't looking forward to it one bit.

 Chapter Eighteen

Hector leant forward, his face all furrowed up with anxiety, and asked, 'What exactly is the matter with Charlie?'

But Lionel said very confidently, 'Charlie will be all right.'

It was exactly what he'd said to Eleanor, who had immediately concluded that Charlie was in a very bad way indeed.

'What do you mean "will be"?'

'Charlie *is* all right,' he'd amended, cursing himself for his mistake.

'You said it was a cold?' Her voice had started to rise; there was that familiar look in her eyes that never failed to spark sympathy and anguish in him. 'But he's been off work for days now.'

'It's a bad cold.'

'Charlie's not like that,' she went on, as if she'd not heard.

'You know he's not. He's such a conscientious boy. He never takes time off.'

'My dear,' Lionel had said very slowly and soothingly, 'I've just spoken to Becky who has just spoken to Charlie. He's in bed with a fever and a bad cold.'

'He is getting better?'

'As I say, it's a bad cold.'

'What does the doctor say? He *has* seen the doctor?'

'Of course.'

'Well, I think they should think about getting a second opinion.' But she sounded a little calmer. If Charlie's mother was satisfied, then perhaps there was no need for panic after all. But she'd telephone Becky in a while, just to make sure. She'd find out exactly what the temperature was. She might even consider taking a train to London herself.

As for Lionel, it appalled him to envisage Eleanor's reaction if told the truth.

However, he couldn't have been more wrong. When Eleanor discovered the real reason why Charlie was off work – as she was bound to do eventually – it came only as a relief. So Charlie had had a wobble! The young were very sensitive – very – and he'd been working far too hard. The poor lamb! All he needed was a break.

She couldn't think why Lionel had so needlessly worried her with a silly fib.

The two old brothers were seated in leather armchairs in the morning room at Hector's club, the Travellers, having just enjoyed lunch. It was a monthly tradition. They'd alternate between here and the Reform, those enormous grand houses next door to each other in Pall Mall, chewing over family business along with the nursery food, pronouncing judgements while gently (and quite automatically) engaging in the usual sparring. Lionel, first to join a London club, had offered to put Hector up for the Reform. It made sense because, as a solicitor, Hector was in the same business. But it wouldn't have done, of course. He must have his own club, which would, without doubt, be superior.

When had the pattern been set for this lifetime of striving against each other? Was it when Hector, supposedly the less intellectual son, had achieved an honours degree in classics and their mother had protested, astonished, 'But you're the wrong one!'? Or was it far earlier when twelve-year-old Lionel, creeping down the grand staircase at Lavenham, had heard his father tell a dinner party with the usual crusty authority, 'Mark my words, it won't be Lionel who makes money . . . Hector's little choice as the second son.'

And now there was another private gripe for Lionel. Two years ago, when he'd reached seventy, he hadn't been given a surprise party – just a nice lunch at home with immediate family only. And he'd known about it for weeks and Mrs Percival had done the cooking. '*Oh, I know, I know!*' he reproved himself. *He* hadn't given an increasingly expensive party for the whole enormous clan every summer for the last thirty years. And Hector had no wife and children of his own, so his life was the family. But the unfairness niggled, all the same. He loved his brother deeply, but was he similarly adored for himself? He feared not.

Age had brought them increasingly close. They'd shared so much, even the things they'd never discussed. When they were eight and six, Great Uncle Walter had taken them for a picnic on Corney's Hill – just the two of them ('So kind,' said Mama sternly, 'of course you must go') – and, suddenly, laid out on the grass in the sunlight, was a long pink sausage (but attached to Great Uncle Walter). The little boys had not exchanged so much as a glance and, as for that formidable old buffer, the master of the local hunt, he'd said nothing, done nothing further, as if just showing them his power was satisfaction enough. Next time they'd dared to look, the sausage had been put away in Uncle Walter's enormous tweed plus fours. What had been the point? It remained one of the great mysteries of their childhood.

Now Hector wore the look his brother was learning to fear: a muddle of anguish and guilt as if he were pushing himself inch by inch to the edge of a new conversation, where painful truths might at last have to be admitted. At least he'd inserted his hearing-aid properly, for once, though this carried no guarantee he wasn't about to shout.

'What exactly did the doctor say?'

'Nervous exhaustion,' muttered Lionel, because it was humiliating to have to articulate such a thing about one's grandson. But he would never have considered lying to his brother.

'What's that?'

Lionel looked round nervously but the only other occupant of the room, a retired accountant, was fast asleep. Raising his voice fractionally, elaborately mouthing the words, he said: 'The doctor thinks Charlie has over-stretched himself.'

Hector got the meaning that time. But he stared at his brother blankly. Both of them had been willingly over-stretched for their entire working lives. How, otherwise, could they have hoped to amass such marvellous trappings of prosperity?

'I don't understand it, either,' Lionel admitted, sounding miserably bewildered. 'It's only a pupillage . . .'

'Indeed.'

'When one remembers Tom . . .'

Hector nodded, thinking of his forceful and very successful nephew. It had always been clear to him that Charlie was a gentler, more sensitive character: it was one of the reasons he'd become such a favourite. But for the boy to have collapsed in a wretched heap like that! It was disturbing. They would have to think about this most carefully, Lionel and himself. It might involve approaching a subject regarded as out of bounds for nearly half a century now.

But before Hector could articulate this, Lionel said very nervously and quickly, almost as if he'd read Hector's mind and was trying to forestall him, 'Suki told Tom Charlie needed a rest. But he won't hear of it!'

'What?' Hector's hearing-aid had slipped out again and he was craning forward to catch the words as the clock on the mantelpiece chimed once, signalling that it was half past two.

Lionel mouthed the name, making his mouth into a gasping 'O' like a goldfish surfacing for air.

'Ah!'

The brothers considered the problem of Tom as they sipped the bitter dark coffee that was always left for too long on a side table and never properly hot. Like the overcooked nursery food, it wasn't really important.

Tom refused to acknowledge that Charlie was suffering from work-related stress and consequently was making things very much worse.

He'd stand over the bed where Charlie still lay after a week, mortifying tears leaking out of his sore eyes, and shout. Fresh from the courts where, by rights, his son should have been, too, trembling with fear and fury in his black suit, Tom would rant for hours, trying to instill gumption. Charlie should be ashamed of his pathetic behaviour! This business was about making a mark and being available. As if he didn't know! He worked like a slave to keep all the balls in the air. And look at him, he said – *he'd* never cracked up at the first bit of pressure, his energy was limitless. The chambers were being very patient with Charlie, thank God, and they were still under the impression this was a mere cold, but if it was allowed to continue . . .

'What's the matter with him?' Tom would demand miserably of Becky, the only person in the world allowed to witness his soft side. 'And why does he cry like that?' He sounded near tears himself.

She was very hesitant. 'Perhaps he really isn't well, darling.'

'What do you mean?'

How fierce he could be. Even she quailed a little. 'Charlie's always been such a good boy. He's exhausted. He's just had a blip.'

'A *what*?'

'I'm not saying Charlie's had a breakdown,' Becky rushed on, without thinking. It was exactly what she meant, of course.

'What Charlie needs,' Tom interrupted, sounding very cold, even disgusted, 'is a good kick up the backside. The boy's lazy. He's no backbone.' Then Tom, the proud father, actually said, 'I'm ashamed of him.'

'You don't mean that.' Becky sounded as soft and gentle as a dove.

'I've every right to be,' said Tom miserably. Then he buried his head in Becky's bosom. 'I only want the best for him,' he muttered.

'I know you do, darling. And so does he, really. He knows you love him . . .'

'Do you think so?'

'I know so.'

'There's such a short time to do it,' said Tom very soberly when he'd recovered himself. 'Such a small period of opportunity when you have to get your life right. And you only realize it later. It's him I'm thinking about, my darling. You do understand that, don't you?'

Hector said, staring very steadfastly at his brother, 'I think you may have to have a word with Tom.'

Lionel's reaction was extraordinary. He went pale; he shook his head violently. He looked as if he'd seen a ghost.

'Perhaps *I* should, then.'

'No no no!' protested Lionel with such vehemence that the sleeping accountant awoke with a snort.

He and his brother had entered into an agreement, hadn't they? It had been unspoken, like so much else between them, and so very long ago that it was almost forgotten. But now, suddenly, Hector had got it into his head to dig it up once more. The mere thought made Lionel shiver. It couldn't happen! It mustn't.

 *Chapter Nineteen*

The voice managed to be both authoritarian and vacillating, in between many long pauses during which an unseen dying bluebottle buzzed feebly at a closed window. 'And after due reflection we would prefer to temporarily withhold our offer until matters would appear to be more fluid . . .'

'Excuse me,' Kitty interrupted with a sweet smile.

Old Mr Chapman's reaction was not encouraging.

'Isn't that a split infinitive?' Her pen poised above her notepad, Kitty added helpfully, 'temporarily to withhold . . .?' with a faltering question mark.

Which misguided person had first propounded the theory that showing this sort of initiative was a good idea and could even lift secretaries out of the typing pool and into far more rewarding careers?

Old Mr Chapman stared at Kitty, whom he'd asked to take a

letter just as she was putting the cover on her typewriter and preparing to go home. The look – first surprised and even thoughtful (as if a worm had uttered) and then increasingly threatening – said it all. He was not employing her for her opinions.

Holding his gaze, Kitty just as mutely replied, 'I may not have had a particularly good education but I do come from a family where we know about grammar.'

In the end, purple with fury, he spluttered, '*Will* you kindly do as you're asked?'

She'd pay for the folly the next day. She didn't know why she'd bothered. She'd far more interest in Charlie's work than her own, which had never been more than a fill-in until her real life of marriage and children began.

It was her parents who had encouraged this attitude, of course. Even in the mid-seventies, spinsters did not command respect from the St Clairs, whatever their other achievements. It so happened that one had become a renowned expert on bees and another had exhibited her exquisite embroidery all over the world. But inside the family, they were gently mocked: 'Bees can't answer back' . . . 'Just a lot of stitches' and so on.

Anyway, was marriage to be so desired? Even her parents' seemed troubled now, like a formerly clear and beautiful recording with a scratch that became a little more pronounced each day.

'*But what will happen to me if I don't get married?*' thought Kitty.

She heard Max's voice as she put her key in the lock. Very quietly she shut the front door behind her and stood listening.

It came from Charlie's bedroom, strangely full of energy and enjoyment: '. . . happy indeed I was, if pleasure be happiness. So

I lived and so I died. And now that I am dead they have set me up here so high that I can see all the ugliness and all the misery of my city, and though my heart is made of lead yet I cannot choose but weep.'

In the flimsy tiny hall, Kitty heard Charlie's hoarse interruption. He sounded very eager: '"What! Is he not solid gold?" said the Swallow to himself?'

He and Max chuckled: Charlie pleased he could still depend on his memory, Max delighted for him. Or so Kitty surmised.

It had been Uncle Hector who'd first introduced the four of them to 'The Happy Prince', and for years and years it was their favourite story of all, even though, for some never explained reason, their grandmother disapproved. When they stayed at Cedar Manor, they'd nag him to read it to them as often as they begged to see his false leg. The ritual was always the same. They'd be freshly bathed and curled up on Max's bed in pyjamas and dressing-gowns and Uncle Hector would be sitting upright on a nearby chair, the awesome giveaway ridge of his prosthesis under the twill knee of his right trouser leg.

They always ended up on Max's bed. It was because nobody could resist him when his girlish eyelashes fluttered towards his cheeks like sooty fans and he pleaded in an exhausted voice, 'I'm *so* tired. And I *am* nearly the youngest.' It meant he could stay put in comfort while the others must brave cold and scary corridors when the time came to go to bed. 'You're all tyrants,' Uncle Hector informed them sternly, but he would read until Max's eyelids closed and his mouth stopped rhythmically sucking his thumb, and then he'd gently remove the thumb and make the others tiptoe out.

*

Kitty appeared in the doorway, arms weighed down with bags of food bought on the way home, and Max halted in mid-sentence.

'Oh, don't stop!' said Kitty very enthusiastically. 'I love that story.'

But he shut the book with a snap as if the last thing he wanted to give her was the sight of him being kind.

'Shepherds' pie!' she announced, shaking her plastic bags so they rustled. 'Are you home for dinner, Max?'

He appeared not to hear for a moment. Then he replied very coldly, addressing the wall to one side of her, 'No, I'm going out.'

It was Charlie who asked, 'Where to?'

'Liza wants to go to the new Bond,' Max told him in the friendliest way possible as he put on his leather jacket and patted the pockets to check he had money and keys. '*The Man with the Golden Gun.*'

So it was still on: the two of them peeled off from the old inseparable gang of four in a relationship threaded with new secrets.

When Max's car had roared off down the street, Charlie said, 'My mother was here today.'

'Oh?' Kitty was thinking in a self-pitying way, '*I'd like to have gone to that film.*' Besides, there was nothing interesting about his piece of information. Aunt Becky came round to the flat all the time.

'Uncle Hector phoned her.'

'What about?'

'He wants me to go and stay for a bit.'

Kitty digested this. 'Well, that's a good idea, isn't it?'

Charlie made a pained face. He seemed pitifully lacking in confidence.

'It'll be fun! You need a break.'

'You don't think that . . .' Charlie bit his lip '. . . I ought to be trying to work things out here?' He gazed at her with anguished eyes. It was part of his character to want to be seen to be doing the right thing, to feel that struggle was required.

'You need peace,' said Kitty, which was the closest she'd get to telling him he should be at a distance from his father.

'It just seems so – pathetic of me.'

'Charlie! It's not your fault you feel like this.'

'No?' he asked doubtfully.

His father had informed the chambers with his usual authority that pneumonia had developed. They obviously believed it because they'd sent a nice card, so a back-up letter from Charlie's GP (which would be difficult, if not impossible, to arrange) might not even be necessary. In the meantime, Charlie's rival pupil (who'd signed the card) was streaking ahead unimpeded for the coveted position of junior tenant. 'Fortunate chap,' Tom had observed, unamused.

Stuck in the flat all day, Charlie didn't spend his time in bed any more. He was constructing a house out of matchsticks. It was ambitious, a little reminiscent of Cedar Manor. Yesterday, he'd spent a whole afternoon adding minute pediments and, in the evening, his father had caught sight of the house resting on the table in the sitting-room.

'What's *that*?'

'It's good for him to do things with his hands,' faltered Becky, who was hovering behind, as usual.

'He's not a bloody – BASKET CASE!' For one awful

moment, it seemed as if Tom was about to strike the house and return it to matchsticks. But the fact was, for all his fierceness, he was appalled to see his son like this. He hadn't meant to sound so rough and was pained when Charlie winced and shut his eyes as if he were truly afraid.

'It's good for him,' Becky had repeated more firmly. Then she'd taken Tom by the hand and led him away.

'By the way,' said Charlie, remembering, 'there's a quiche Lorraine. She put it in the fridge.' His mother brought food all the time, as if she still didn't trust Kitty to take care of her son in this respect.

'I'll miss you.'

'Ditto,' he said with real feeling. There was a lost look in his eyes as he went on, sounding honestly perplexed, even a little scared: 'Some people . . . they behave as if they're frightened of me!'

Kitty thought of being alone in the flat with the two other cousins and a sense of deep loneliness swept over her. 'Charlie . . .'

'Mmm . . .' He was contemplating the construction of a chimney now. It would snake up the side of the house like a long angular arm attached to a body. For a moment, he looked utterly contented.

'What do you think about Max and Liza?'

'What about them?' He sounded absolutely indifferent.

'Haven't you noticed anything?'

'Mmm?' He broke a match into three pieces, frowned slightly as he considered them.

'I think there's something going on there . . .'

But he wasn't listening.

'That night Liza went off to the Savoy . . .'

'Mmm?'

'When she met that old perve – *you* know. It happened then.' At last she had his attention. He frowned. 'Max and Liza?'

Kitty nodded. 'I heard them. They were here.'

'You mean . . .?' He looked utterly incredulous.

'I think so.'

'But it would be like, like . . .'

'*You and me*,' thought Kitty. Except that, according to the law, first cousins were permitted to sleep together and even marry. Had he forgotten his astonishing suggestion the night Max had moved in?

'Max would have told me,' he insisted with his old confidence.

'Would he?'

'Oh yes!' He meant that there were no shadows between him and Max. Unlike Liza, who'd shied away from him since his breakdown, Max had been friendly and supportive in his fashion. It was almost as if he – who was such a master of detachment – understood what it was like to feel out of control and fearful.

'Liza hasn't told *me*.'

Charlie frowned. 'You know what Liza's like . . .'

Kitty nodded, wondering if he was beginning to believe her now.

For all her charm, Liza was a dissembler and a troublemaker. But she was also a risk-taker who delighted in shocking. And she was aware of Max's beauty all right. 'He could be a film star if he wanted,' she'd observed not long ago, a thoughtful look in her pale eyes.

Kitty knew that unless her mind was going (like Charlie

clearly feared his own was), she couldn't have been mistaken. Like a lawyer, she assembled the evidence. The unmistakable sounds of love-making coming from the study Max had appropriated as his bedroom; the fact that Liza and Max were known to have spent the evening together and had never denied it; the certainty that Max didn't have girlfriends because they'd have known about them by now.

She thought of the four of them in Uncle Hector's barn long ago, playing in the hay. Only her relationship with Charlie had remained as uncomplicated and rewarding. Dear Charlie, who needed protection from his father so desperately: who had every chance of recovery if given enough comfort and encouragement. There was no man she loved and trusted more and tomorrow he'd be gone.

'Charlie . . .'

He turned his kind exhausted brown eyes on her, ready to fall in with shepherds' pie or quiche Lorraine or whatever else she felt like suggesting.

Chapter Twenty

When the telephone rang at half past one in the morning, Simon answered it on his side of the bed. And as consciousness hit, in the second before the caller spoke, was convinced it was the police. He'd started dreaming about them now: Detective Inspector Calder and Detective Inspector Dodd. Caller and Plod, he nicknamed them for Suki, giving the impression that it was all faintly amusing and beneath him. They'd visited the garage twice, sliding in when least expected. The second time, they stood and watched while he tried (without success, as it happened) to sell a four-year-old Peugeot with a temperamental ignition, and glanced without expression at the group photograph of Suki, Kitty and Phil on his desk. He thought he'd carried off that informal interview pretty well, considering. Mr Winslow-Carter, they called him every two minutes — as if rehearsing for a more important scenario.

'Who is it?' muttered Suki, suddenly as awake and afraid as he. She'd confessed to telling her uncle the truth about the missing cars. He'd been very alarmed at first, but afterwards – just like her – started pinning hopes on Uncle Hector, who possessed powerful connections as well as a magical reputation. 'Any news?' he would ask, seemingly casually, when he came home at night. Suki noticed he had a new expression now: half amused, half distasteful. He hated himself for what he'd done, obviously. The mystery was how it had happened in the first place.

'Your sister.'

'Oh good!' said Suki with real relief, even though it had been wonderful to be deeply unconscious for once, removed from their problems for a while. 'Let me talk to her.'

Camilla was drunk again, thought Simon as he passed the receiver to Suki. '*Awful thing alcohol!*' He cuddled against his wife's back, breathing in the vanilla scent of her soft body. '*Brings out the aggression in people.*' He liked his wine all right, but '*At least I'm not an alcoholic.*' It wasn't the first time Camilla had phoned them in the middle of the night. Suki was much nicer to her than Tom.

'I'm sure that's not so,' he heard Suki say soothingly. Somewhere outside in the darkness, in the grid of narrow back gardens, a cat yowled suddenly and he shivered, reminded of the fearsome world he'd stumbled into.

There was a burst of distorted jabber from the other end of the telephone. Camilla sounded very worked up. What an impossible woman she was! That appalling scene she'd made the evening Max was here! Okay, she had every reason to feel upset with Anthony! But imagine Suki behaving in such a way! It was unthinkable. Simon thanked his stars that he was married to such a sweet and diffident woman.

'What would he gain from such a thing?' he heard Suki ask gently.

More jabber. He felt a movement as Suki held the receiver at arm's length.

'I can't believe that,' she said – again very carefully – but it provoked a torrent. Simon pictured his sister-in-law simmering in her grand and silent house, prowling its thick carpets, returning again and again to the drinks tray. It occurred to him that she must have loved Anthony far more than she'd ever let on, to have allowed the break-up to get to her like this. Funny. To him she'd always given the impression of being a little bored with her husband, embarrassed by his difference from the rest of them. And now, of course, to compound the humiliation, she'd lost her son as well. Simon knew that if ever he lost his own family, he would be destroyed. No question.

Suki said, 'You must be mistaken, Camilla . . .' Then suddenly, 'Hello, hello? . . . She's rung off!'

'What was all that about?'

Suki switched on a lamp because this was serious and she wanted to observe his reaction. She never wore anything in bed. It was another of her rules for staying happily married. Her skin looked luminous and luscious in the soft pinkish light but her face was greasy and strands of her long hair adhered to it. She'd started wearing night cream some months back even though she knew perfectly well that he hated it. 'You'll be glad in the end,' she'd insisted.

'You're not going to believe this!' As usual, Suki paused for effect. 'She says Anthony's trying to kill her.'

'*What?*'

'Well, of course I don't believe it either!' But there was a miserably doubtful note to her voice. These days, certainty was going down the tubes. If a husband who'd always appeared to possess the right values could turn to crime, anything was possible.

'And just how is he going to bump her off?' Simon seemed amused. She knew as well as he did, of course, that this was drunken rubbish.

'She says he tried to run her over in his car.'

'The Rolls? So the chauffeur's in on it, too, then? Dear oh dear . . . She's been reading too many cheap thrillers.'

'What does it all mean, darling?'

'It means . . .' He shrugged, raising an imaginary bottle to his lips.

But Suki looked unhappier than ever. 'Should I phone Ant, do you think?'

'What, now?'

'She sounded dreadful, Simon.'

'It'd look a bit odd.'

Suki bit her lip. He was right. Since they'd heard about the womanizing, Anthony had telephoned a couple of times, sounding as warm and affable as ever, and in cowardly fashion she'd pretended to be busy. She'd promised in a falsely friendly way to ring back, and never had. And now it was too late. He'd got the message. As one, the family had taken Camilla's side. What else did he expect?

'I can't talk to the parents,' she said.

'No,' he agreed, thinking of the spin his mother-in-law might put on it.

'Maybe Pa?' But even as she made the suggestion, she turned her mouth down, rejecting it. Her father doted on Camilla. It would be unfair to inflict such distress on him, at his age.

'Poor little sod,' said Simon as he'd said so many times before about Max.

'Mmm, it's not fair,' Suki agreed automatically.

It was the end of the conversation. He touched her cheek, grimacing. 'I hate this stuff. Why don't you just take it off?'

Suki obediently fumbled under her pillow for a tissue even though what she really desired was to be allowed to sink back into sleep. Even so, how marvellously handsome he looked in the rosy light: so fit and youthful, with a lock of fair hair falling over his face. What extraordinary luck, she'd always told herself, that he had chosen her. But sometimes nowadays when they were this close – his warm skin pressed against hers, the familiar feel of him rooted in her flesh – she'd sense a strange and terrifying emptiness. Because of one stupid, ill-thought-out impulse, he'd pitched all those he should have protected into chaos and terror. Had he not considered them for a second?

She found that she was starting to look at everything differently now: re-evaluating their relationship from the beginning. For example, was it really her goodness – as he'd always maintained – which had caused him to pick her above all other women? ('One man saw the pilgrim soul in you,' he liked to quote to her.) Or had it actually been the grandeur and solidity of the St Clair family that he'd found so attractive?

The next day, Suki telephoned Jane. She needed to talk to her, anyway, about table arrangements. Uncle Hector's party was getting very close now and Jane, who was artistic, had agreed to make the place cards.

First things first, though.

'Jane, have you seen Camilla at all lately?'

'No.' Jane seemed oddly taken aback, but Suki dismissed this as unimportant even when her sister-in-law faltered, 'Why?'

'She hasn't been phoning you in the middle of the night or anything?'

'No.' Jane sounded very faint. 'Why should she?'

'And I suppose you haven't seen Anthony either?' Suki pursued.

There was silence from the other end. But it never occurred to innocent Suki that Jane feared for one awful moment that her secret had been discovered and she was now the butt of sarcasm. Or that she herself saved the situation by rushing on, 'The thing is, we're all a bit worried about her.'

Jane was a darling, of course, thought Suki, but she wasn't proper family. So she was reluctant to describe in detail her disturbing conversation with Camilla the night before. 'It's terrible for her being alone in that house,' was all she said. 'And most of us feel tempted to have a drink or two when we're miserable, don't we?'

'That's true,' she heard Jane agree, sounding subdued.

'I just hope to God,' Suki went on in a heartfelt sort of way, 'that she doesn't make a scene at this party.'

It loomed like a tapestry in progress. With luck, on the night, all the family would see was the splendidly complete picture. Only she and Tom, who'd toiled away for weeks, would know about the messy jumble of threads at the back: the quartet which had threatened to cancel because of a more distinguished booking (until Tom had weighed in with talk of writs), the horrifying last-minute discovery that the chosen caterers had once caused salmonella poisoning (which provoked even darker threats).

Seated at her desk in her house, Jane said: 'I've done your place cards, Suki.' There were a hundred and fifty of them and they lay in front of her in alphabetically arranged stacks. One person was missing from the guest list but she'd made a secret card for him, too.

Number one hundred and fifty one, inscribed with loving care. As she listened to Suki talking worriedly about food and music, Jane laid his card next to hers and, after that, encircled the two of them with a grand sweep of jumbled up family.

It was impossible, of course! And, anyway, why would he choose to be with her, rather than one of his other women? What was she doing even playing with the idea?

Chapter Twenty-one

'Darling Charlie,' wrote Kitty. Then she stopped at exactly the same point as she'd done in her previous three letters, which lay scrunched up in a wastepaper basket at her feet. She felt very alone in the tall sliver of drawing-room with its chipped paint, its assorted collection of uncomfortable old furniture, its leafy view of dusty plane trees; and her mood was intensified by the mournful sound of a milk float wheedling its erratic stop-start way up the street. This part of the city emptied at weekends, with most of the young flat-sharers disappearing to far more luxurious establishments in the country where they were treated by parents like returning warriors.

'*I miss him,*' thought Kitty, picturing Cedar Manor and big properly proportioned old rooms and the hidden bustle of servants and the mingled scents of lavender and beeswax. She had the feeling that if she could be somehow magically transported to that kingdom of her childhood, she'd find the old Charlie waiting for her, as if nothing had happened.

She could almost make herself believe it hadn't. That following morning, early, Aunt Becky had arrived to drive him to Waterloo station. There'd been no chance for discussion, or even to say goodbye. And if he'd tiptoed into her room and gently kissed her on the forehead, she might very easily have dreamt that, too.

He'd be washed and shaved by now and dutifully eating breakfast at the long highly polished table in the cold dining-room – she could see him clearly in the jeans and navy pullover he wore for weekends. There'd be cold toast and watery coffee and a pot of old marmalade that needed using up and Uncle Hector would already be gearing himself up for the host of tasks set for the day. 'What are you planning to do with yourself, dear fellow?' he'd be booming, looking fretful. He'd insist that Charlie mustn't fritter away his time, even if he'd come for a rest. He'd put him on to pulling up dandelions or some such soothing and pointless work.

Kitty thought, '*I could easily have called him "darling" before,*' but knew this was not true. 'Dear Charlie,' she'd have written for sure, and meant it from the depths of her being. Dear dear Charlie, beloved cousin and friend.

'*But I can't call him "dear" any more,*' thought Kitty in a kind of despair, '*and yet I can't seem to make myself call him "darling" either. Oh God, what have I done?*'

The person she'd known and loved for all of her life, who comforted and cheered her in a way nobody else could, had been eclipsed by a stranger. When Kitty thought of how it had transpired, a mixture of shame and loneliness overcame her. She would remember Charlie's face coming nearer and nearer until at the point of a new and quite different intimacy – their first kiss – she no longer recognized him. It was astonishing how different he'd looked close up: his eyes very expressionless and staring, his lips puckered into an absurd shape. *'Did I look like an octopus to him, too?'* Kitty wondered. Oh why hadn't they just exploded in laughter at that point and abandoned the whole plan?

'Oh God, oh God, oh God,' she thought, and her pen squiggled out of control, ruining yet another sheet of good writing paper.

She hadn't heard a word from him since and was very sure what that silence meant.

'My dear Charlie,' she began afresh. That seemed better. He *was* dear to her.

She squeezed her eyes shut again. It had all been her fault. It couldn't have happened.

They'd been drunk, of course. At least it could partly be blamed on alcohol.

With the flat to themselves, they'd consumed two bottles of Hirondelle red wine with the whole of the shepherds' pie she'd cooked and the quiche Lorraine his mother had brought, too. She'd made her suggestion by then so it was no wonder, really, that they'd eaten and drunk like maniacs.

'Charlie . . . do you remember what you said that night?'

'Yes,' Charlie had responded, with an odd look on his face. He knew exactly which night she was referring to, of course, and what was said. That was the thing about knowing each other so well. Talking was hardly necessary.

'Well,' she'd gone on bravely, 'I've been thinking and, um, actually, I think it's rather a good idea.'

He'd hesitated, appreciably. 'You do?'

She'd stared at him over the rim of her wine glass. 'Mmm . . .'

What he'd said next had taken her aback: 'We're not thirty yet!'

Did he mean he wasn't desperate enough yet to settle for her? He must have recognized the hurt on her face because straight away he'd said very gently: 'Have to think about this a bit, Kit.'

But after a lot more wine, he kept casting her shy interested glances as if he were more and more coming round to the idea. Perversely, that made Kitty have second thoughts herself and their supper proceeded a little formally and hesitantly, as if they were strangers on a first date. At one point, Charlie seemed about to say something and very deliberately stopped himself; and she wondered if he'd been on the point of launching into one of his tales of rejection by some other girl.

She could very easily have called it off at that stage – '*Oh God, why didn't I?*' – but then he'd said thoughtfully, with that familiar little frown, 'I'm actually starting to think you may be right . . . Cos they are getting on awfully well these days.'

And instantly, she'd envisaged Max and Liza – not in separate seats in some darkened cinema but entwined in Max's car in some private place – and, fired by jealousy and alcohol, had straight away got up from the table and kissed Charlie on the lips. '*So there!*' It had been like leaping across an abyss.

'I hope you're having a nice time staying with Uncle Hector . . .'

'*Oh my God,*' thought Kitty, biting her lip, '*this is so weird! And we've got the same grandparents, too!*'

'It's been very quiet here . . .'

'*Why am I writing boring stuff like this to him?*' thought Kitty. '*Charlie?*'

'What are you doing?' asked Liza.

She'd wandered into the room in a borrowed nightdress: one of Kitty's sensible winter affairs, with a high frilly neck and long sleeves. Her fair hair fell round her shoulders like a waterfall. She looked prim as a Victorian maid.

Yesterday evening she'd turned up for supper, as was her habit now. But there was no indication of any sort of intimate involvement with Max. They'd appeared extremely relaxed with each other, but that was all. It was for her benefit, Kitty told herself a little wearily. At eleven o'clock Liza asked if she could stay the night, making it sound a most reasonable request since Charlie's bed was now free. And she'd definitely stayed in Charlie's room all night on her own because, this time, Kitty was on watch for sounds of love-making.

'Nothing much,' Kitty replied as she scrunched up the latest letter and threw it away.

'Who were you writing to?'

'Nobody.'

Liza's glance flickered meaningfully towards the mass of stiff white peaks in the wastepaper basket. But Kitty ignored this, making a mental note – at the same time – to dispose of them.

'How's Charlie?' asked Liza after a moment.

'Okay, I think.'

'Haven't you talked to him?' She wore a little smile, as if she could see straight through Kitty's pretence at nonchalance.

'Not recently.'

'That's strange,' said Liza, seemingly still amused.

'Why?'

'*Charlie?*'

Kitty looked away, trying to banish the pictures flooding into her mind. Had she and Charlie really lain together naked in his bed ('Not mine,' she'd insisted for some reason), performing the same dance rehearsed on so many uncaring strangers? It had felt so odd and awkward at first, as if it could never happen; and then she'd decided that the only way to cross this second and far more terrifying boundary line was to treat gallant decent Charlie like those cold-hearted bastards who'd gone before. 'Fuck me!' she'd heard herself order him (to her deep shame now), and imagined Charlie flinching in the darkness because he hated women swearing, and most especially her. 'Righty ho!' he'd agreed, sounding a little surprised. But, once past his initial shock, he'd gone at the sex so enthusiastically that, at one point, Kitty had gasped, 'Hang on a mo . . .' At the moment of climax he'd called her 'baby' (which seemed odd as he was actually a month younger).

'You've gone all pink, Kitty!'

'Have I?'

Liza regarded her kindly. 'Why don't you let me iron your hair for you? It'd look much nicer straight.'

'*It was Max I really wanted.*' Admitting it at last felt more sad than shocking for Kitty though it didn't diminish the guilt. She'd secretly coveted one cousin, but slept with another. It had been very unfair and definitely unwise. '*But why do I feel so confused?*'

It should have made her blush all over again when Max appeared in the doorway. But he wore his childish flannel pyjamas and his familiar self-absorbed expression and he stroked a non-existent beard as if pondering some obscure problem and, as usual, he took all the milk. And a strange thing happened. Instead of openly lusting after Max, Kitty found herself more than ever missing Charlie.

The telephone started to ring as it always did at that time and the cousins exchanged glances.

'I'll deal with this,' said Liza.

Kitty and Max listened to her innocently informing Camilla that Max had gone out for a coffee. No, she didn't know what time he'd be back. Possibly he'd be away for the entire day. 'I can't help that,' she said at one point and had to hold the receiver at a distance because a burst of jabber indicated Camilla was reacting strongly to the cheekiness.

Kitty watched Max for signs of distress or guilt but he appeared absolutely unmoved.

'I think she'd been drinking,' Liza remarked casually as she put the phone down. It seemed she could get away with saying things like this to Max now. Did that indicate a new intimacy? But before Kitty could give it proper consideration, Liza changed the subject.

'I'm not particularly looking forward to this party.'

They all considered the prospect of Uncle Hector's surprise birthday celebration, only a few days away, the vast throng of family seen so recently in the summer.

'No,' Max agreed sombrely. His mother would be there of course (because the invitations weren't up to Uncle Hector this time) – though not his father, who was no longer regarded as part of the family. And everyone would ask with concerned though expectant expressions, just as they'd done a few months before, 'What are you doing with yourself now, Max?'

'Mum's bought herself a new dress,' said Liza. 'She's always buying clothes now.' She glanced at them with a mischievous disgruntled expression. 'And I found this bra the other day . . .'

'I'm always finding them,' Max responded with an air of comic gloom.

Liza pouted. 'It's not funny!'

'It doesn't mean anything,' said Kitty soothingly, remembering that her white 34A Wonderbra was still hanging from the plastic clothesline above the bath.

Liza nodded meaningfully. 'I *know* she's having an affair,' she told Kitty, and made it sound strangely like a warning.

'*Dear Charlie*.' Kitty saw him whacking her on the back for comfort, tinkering with his matchstick house, crying in her arms – the best brother imaginable. And now she'd lost him. At the same time – also through her own stupidity – she'd become involved with another bastard. '*Because that's how men always always behave to me afterwards*,' thought Kitty, feeling very bewildered and helpless.

# Chapter Twenty-two

The sounds, as he gently surfaced out of sleep, were quite different from London ones – and isolated, set against a backdrop of silence. The morse-code-like cooing of woodpigeons – two protracted notes, one short; the anguished complaints of a cow far away in the fields around the estate; the echoing repetitive thwack of a piece of wood being hit very precisely with a hammer for some reason in the distance. Nearer at hand, there was the brisk hollow tap of heels on stone and parquet as the table in the dining-room was formally set for breakfast and the scraping of slices of toast which had been imprisoned in the greasy basket-like flat contraption under a lid on the kitchen range. It was all deeply comforting – as would be Uncle Hector's genial predictable roar, promptly at a quarter to eight, 'Chaa-rlie? Time for lazy guests to GET UP!'

It felt wonderful to have been removed from the pressures

of the city. His mother still telephoned every day, of course, and the grandparents kept in touch, too. But Uncle Hector didn't bully him to tackle his chambers work, taking the view that he needed a rest from all that. On the other hand, he expected him to fill his days with useful pursuits like helping in the garden and, in fact, Charlie had found it very therapeutic to spend a whole morning digging out a rotten stump.

He was still anxious, though, and there were strange terrifying moments when it felt as if his head was in a vice and being squeezed. But each day these sensations lessened. Sometimes, he'd imagine his old exhausted self still crouching over a pile of papers on his bed at Chepstow Place while the dawn came up and feel a little guilty for abandoning him.

It was interesting to be part of Uncle Hector's daily life, seeing all his odd routines and the discipline and sweetness close up. Witnessing the amount of pain he dealt with so impatiently and even angrily, it was hard to go on feeling sorry for oneself.

Charlie would stay up later in the evenings, sitting on his own in the badly-lit drawing-room, reading or staring into the dying fire. 'Not too long,' Uncle Hector would warn gently as he patted his great-nephew on the shoulder with one hand, while leaning on his stick with the other. 'You need your rest.' And then Charlie would hear his slow progress up the wooden staircase, the long halts every so often and Uncle Hector crossly muttering 'damn!' as if spurring on a horse.

Last night on his way to bed, passing the open door of Uncle Hector's room, Charlie had glimpsed an eerie spectacle in the dim light from the landing: his great-uncle's false leg, still formally attired in a navy blue sock and suspender and one of his highly polished black shoes from Church's, standing to attention by the spartan single bed where its owner lay deeply asleep.

Uncle Hector was on the telephone a lot (which he hated) and often seemed unusually preoccupied after these conversations, his face furrowed and miserable. Yesterday afternoon, pulling up chickweed from a path behind the house, as instructed, Charlie had heard his great-uncle's voice booming from a distance, 'SURELY YOU KNOW SOMEONE IN THE DPP'S OFFICE?' Soon afterwards, his grandfather had turned up for tea and Charlie had been told kindly but briskly that his two old relatives needed to talk in private.

He'd decided to pay a visit to the barn – which seemed very forlorn without his cousins – and so had not overheard any of their booming conversation. But he'd returned just in time to catch his grandfather, sunk in fierce contemplation, climbing back into his Bentley. 'Ah, Charlie!' he'd exclaimed, with his sudden smile, as warm and unexpected as the sun lighting up a frosty landscape.

But there was no wake-up call from Uncle Hector this morning and when Charlie descended to the dining-room only ten minutes late he found him very agitated.

'Damn, damn, damn! I knew this would happen!' He limped to the window, a backless leather slipper dragging from his false foot, which was dressed, as usual, in an unwrinkled dark sock. 'And look what THOSE WRETCHED VERMIN have been up to in the night!'

Uncle Hector loathed the moles almost as much as the honey fungus that had laid a death sentence on his beautiful old cedar tree – more than Edward Heath (who'd let down the Tory party and numerous people like himself) or Harold Wilson or television (it was a damned good thing, too, that they'd shut it off at ten-thirty during the three-day week) – but not as greatly as people who put their own happiness before their children's. However much arsenic Partridge laid down, the moles would return, desecrating the precious emerald lawns that had been rolled and mowed to perfection for nearly forty years now. Finding their dark eruptions always ruined Uncle Hector's mood. It was as if they were cocking a snook at him.

To compound the misery and irritation, it seemed that Merriweather had been right about his health. For months, the servant had warned with grim certainty that his back would give out. Now he'd retired to bed and one of the two girls from the village who came in each morning to do the cleaning had made breakfast. But it wasn't satisfactory. Charlie could tell from Uncle Hector's impatient sighs and frowns. A fresh pot of marmalade had been put out instead of the almost empty one which needed using up. Unnecessary effort had been put into forming ridiculous curls of butter, which had then been arranged on a Spode saucer nobody was allowed to handle except himself. Obviously none of these girls could be trusted. Where would lunch and tea and dinner come from? Oh Lord!

Charlie considered the problem as he munched toast that was less burnt-looking than usual. 'We could always have picnics,' he suggested.

'PICNICS?' Uncle Hector sounded as if he'd never heard the word before. And, anyway, Charlie could perceive as well as he that rain was now seeping down outside.

'In here, I mean. It might be fun.'

But Uncle Hector cast him a pitying though tender look before muttering gently, 'Oh dear, oh dear, that would never do!'

'Restaurants?' said Charlie to himself.

'What's that?'

Charlie dismissed the London thought. 'Or – *I* could do the cooking.'

His great-uncle looked dumbfounded. Men didn't cook! Except that, of course, in this establishment, one had been doing the catering for almost half a century. What he really meant, of course, was that men like Charlie didn't cook. But this was an emergency. '*Can* you cook?' he asked, looking very troubled.

'I've watched Kitty do it enough times,' Charlie replied almost to himself. 'She'll never let me, though.' He boomed confidently: 'Of course I can!'

It might be good for Charlie, thought Uncle Hector. It was important for him to feel useful. And probably it would only be for a couple of days, until Merriweather recovered. It would certainly help *him*. It seemed very bizarre, though. It would definitely be best not to mention anything to Tom.

Charlie surveyed the contents of the larder: two fat stripy slugs nestling in a proprietorial way on a raw cabbage and, under a fine mesh cover, part of a crusty mauve ham and a few turnips. It looked as if Merriweather had been planning to combine these ingredients (though probably not the slugs). There was a slightly unpleasant smell, too, and Charlie thought of the market garden outside still trailing the vestiges of luscious exotica like a woman packing up her summer wardrobe.

'Oh dear, oh dear, oh dear!' said Uncle Hector, thinking of the pennies that had been lost at the market. But the cobs of sweetcorn Charlie had boiled for three minutes in salted water then slathered in butter were delicious, and so were the sliced carrots to go with the fluffy (and very fresh) omelettes he'd cooked.

'Is it all right?' he asked.

Merriweather had appeared astonished when Charlie had carried a tray into his dark, poky little quarters. He wasn't used to being waited on, of course. The bedroom was windowless, with the standard house lighting, and smelt very stuffy. There were no books to be seen, though Merriweather's spectacles were lying on the narrow and extremely uncomfortable-looking bed. However, to Charlie's surprise, there was a small black and white television propped on a pile of old telephone directories. He also absorbed a tiny photograph (also black and white) of a young man with very short hair in soldier's uniform in a cheap frame on the unpolished chest of drawers. Merriweather hadn't thanked him, though he'd silently and meaningfully jabbed a gnarled finger at the sweetcorn.

Uncle Hector smiled at Charlie. 'Very much so,' he replied, noting with pleasure that his great-nephew looked happier than he'd done for months.

'If it's okay, Uncle Hector,' Charlie began very hesitantly, 'I thought maybe I could borrow the Daimler and go off and do a bit of shopping this afternoon.' He added, 'There's not much in the larder, actually.'

Dinner turned out to be even more scandalously delicious.

Charlie had roasted a chicken, which was simple. But, from Uncle Hector's awed reaction, he might instead have solved a problem of quantum mechanics.

'Oh dear, oh dear!' He'd obviously enjoyed the globe artichokes, too, with the same vinaigrette dressing Charlie had watched Kitty make. As usual, marvellous wine had been brought up from the enormous cellar – Uncle Hector had tottered down there himself, on his stick – and by the time they'd reached the pudding course (stewed rhubarb, also from the garden) both of them were very happy. They ate some of Merriweather's famous shortbread, too, more out of duty than enjoyment. ('He's not going to like this,' had been Merriweather's only muttered comment when Charlie delivered his supper tray.)

Halfway through the artichokes, Tom telephoned.

'Can you ring back?' Uncle Hector boomed. 'We're having dinner.'

Tom could not, apparently: it seemed he and Becky were already late for an important engagement so he needed to talk to his son now.

'He'll ring you tomorrow,' said Uncle Hector very firmly, already replacing the receiver.

It seemed to Charlie, flushed with alcohol and triumph, that this was the perfect moment to break his news. Perhaps it would become real to him, then. Until now, a confusing mixture of emotions had made him put the memory of that extraordinary last night at Chepstow Place on hold. Kitty? In retrospect, it felt both wonderful and shocking. He was far closer to her than to either of his sisters.

He felt deeply connected to his great-uncle as they sat in their sober suits and ties at one end of the long polished table. It was Charlie who'd arranged the treasury of gleaming silver that protocol dictated must be displayed for every meal, however meagre, even if only one person was eating. All round the walls, priceless oil paintings badly in need of cleaning overlooked them. Uncle Hector had been a saviour to him. Hadn't he earned the right to hear this before anyone else?

Then something stopped Charlie. It was almost as if a watchful wraith, passing behind his chair in the candlelit gloom, had laid an icy hand over his mouth in warning. He shivered and bit his lip. He even turned round for a moment before smiling faintly at his own foolishness.

'Cold?' asked Uncle Hector, instantly solicitous.

As usual, the fire in the drawing-room had been lit after the sun had made a blazing majestic descent behind the doomed cedar tree. The girls from the village had also arranged a decanter of cognac and glasses on a side table. Charlie knew that, after he'd snuffed out the candles in the dining-room with the silver hood on a stem kept in the sideboard, the rest of the evening would be spent mostly in silence, he and his great-uncle reading their separate books (his was an old favourite, *Huckleberry Finn*), occasionally exchanging affectionate glances. 'Ha!' Uncle Hector would say every so often, as if letting out the last remnants of irritation with the day.

But tonight turned out to be different. They talked and nobody else heard the volley of bellowing because apart from Merriweather, stuck in bed with his fuzzy old television set and – together with most of the nation – watching Morecambe and Wise, the house was empty.

Confronted by the big portrait of Samuel St Clair which hung over the drawing-room mantelpiece, Charlie found himself asking idly, 'How did you get on with your father, Uncle Hector?'

How wise and sad his great-uncle looked as he gazed at him over the rim of his brandy glass. He appeared to be making a decision. 'I didn't, really,' he said finally. 'Your grandfather had a much better relationship with him.'

'Why?'

'I suppose because Lionel was a more satisfactory son.' Uncle Hector seemed to shrink into his faded pink armchair with its reinforced arms of newer material, a dull shine of old brilliantine darkening the backrest. 'Cleverer . . .'

'No!' protested Charlie in polite disbelief.

'Oh yes!' Uncle Hector nodded sadly. 'Not quite so conscientious, maybe. Far better at cricket and all the things that mattered . . . And I wasn't a particularly attractive child, you see.' He added, almost in a whisper, 'But then, I'm afraid *I* didn't like my father very much.'

Could he really have said it? And, if so, why had he arranged it so that, for four decades, he had continued to see his father every single day? Charlie stared at the hooded eyes and thin lips, recoiled from the autocracy that now seemed to seep through crusts of paint. Not a nice face – though this had never occurred to him before. Neither had he heard of anybody in the family admitting to such dislike. They were entitled gently to mock each other and sometimes disapprove. But family was sacred, especially to Uncle Hector. That had always been understood. Charlie sat very still and heard minutes ticking off on the heirloom gold clock on the mantelpiece. But it seemed that was all his great-uncle was going to say on the subject.

'*I'll have to think about this,*' thought Charlie, while keeping an interested polite look on his face. He went on, 'What about Nancy?'

'Nancy?' All of a sudden, Uncle Hector seemed quite extraordinarily alarmed.

'Great-Aunt Nancy,' Charlie corrected himself.

'What about her?'

'I meant, what was my great-grandfather's relationship like with *her*?'

More long moments passed. Then Uncle Hector said, 'You have to understand that Nancy was beautiful.'

Beautiful? Charlie mouthed the word, eyebrows raised. For how would he know? There were remarkably few pictures of his great-aunt around. Perhaps people hadn't taken many photos, in those days.

'Oh yes,' Uncle Hector confirmed, nodding gravely, as if beauty were a burden, 'and clever. And more alive than anyone I've ever met.'

'So . . .?'

'Of course he loved her. How could he not? Everyone loved Nancy.'

'What a tragedy,' said Charlie politely.

'What's that?'

'Tragedy,' Charlie mouthed.

'Oh yes,' Uncle Hector agreed, staring into the distance and looking very old and spent. His mouth wobbled for a moment. 'Oh yes.'

Very soon after that he ostentatiously removed his hearing-aid so Charlie couldn't question him further, fumbled for his stick and rose groaning from his chair. He replaced the equipment in his desk where it was always kept and laid a parting hand heavily on Charlie's shoulder even though the clock wasn't due to ping for another twenty-five minutes to signify bedtime. The conversation was over and Charlie wished profoundly that he could discuss it all with Kitty.

 Chapter Twenty-three

The street had seen Jane's affair develop from the beginning and at one o'clock on Friday – Anthony's usual time for visiting – there was an air of expectancy as palpable as the drizzle that seeped from the moulting sycamore trees, leaving a veil of stickiness on car windscreens. Folds of greying lace curtain stirred in the ground-floor windows opposite as Mrs Murphy settled herself for a good view of the Rolls and the chauffeur; and, though he usually made himself a cup of tea about then, the old man next door found time to lean on his gate and comment to all who passed on the shocking state of the pavement and the capriciousness of the weather.

The street had witnessed the events of the past year with sadness and sympathy. The businessman setting off one morning so neat and brisk, never to return; the little family smashed overnight; the loneliness that had fallen, as suffocating as dust, and the courage in the face of such loss. 'Always had the time of day for you,' remembered the leaner on the gate. 'Everyone deserves a bit of happiness,' said Mrs Murphy, moving the conversation on a notch. 'And she's a lovely lady,' the old man agreed. Because they could all see what was going on. It was soon, certainly, but life must continue. A decent period of mourning had been observed. And hadn't they all been shown how transitory this existence could be? It was over in a blink.

They were fascinated by Anthony: impressed and also puzzled, though he seemed quite oblivious to them. Where had all that flash and wealth come from? Could it be possible he was a super-criminal? Come to that, where did the chauffeur disappear to, in the meantime? They couldn't ask any of these questions, of course. More mundanely, they guessed that Anthony was married but, in this instance, found the situation oddly hard to condemn. It was because Jane was so transformed: her cheeks rosy again, her eyes bright and interested. It was such pleasure to see that remarkable recovery. They'd continue to observe. Sooner or later, they were sure, all would be revealed.

'*Happy*,' thought Jane, inside the house. '*Happy happy happy*.' She hummed as she lit the candle on the mantelpiece in her bedroom, where each colour and shape seemed more intensely agreeable, breathed in the scent of sandalwood with extravagant pleasure, caught her reflection in the glass. How very much nicer she looked, these days. How delicious everything was. '*My lover*,' she thought.

But when he arrived (to the relief of the watching

neighbours) he was pale and sombre. He didn't even apologize for being half an hour late. 'We must talk,' were his first words.

'Of course,' she agreed with a gallant smile, while wondering bleakly if Mrs Murphy had noted the lack of champagne, too.

'I'm sorry,' he began, shaking his head as if he wanted only to be done with this ordeal.

'It's all right,' she replied, too quickly. She could actually feel her heart sinking – the cliché was true – and the loneliness gathering around once more like fog.

'No, I mean . . .'

'Really!' she assured him brightly.

It was all right, she meant, to have made her feel, briefly, that she was in another skin. Because of the nature of what he'd given, he would be absolved for breaking it to her that there'd be no more. In fact, she'd always known this was coming, having learnt most bitterly not to count on good things. Their affair might have been all the sweeter for that.

They should have talked a long time before, thought Anthony. He knew it had been remiss of him, and probably selfish, to fail to make his position clear. He winced, thinking how many times he'd been dubbed selfish. (Even that morning the word had been shrieked at him.) But it had been like entering a different world to come to this tranquil house, this gentle woman, on the other side of London. Somehow he could forget the other stuff. And besides, she never asked questions – which was odd really, it occurred to him for the first time.

'Let's stay here, shall we?' he suggested, leading the way into her sitting-room. And then he sat down on one of the chairs, leaving the sofa free.

It was the end. Jane knew it for sure now. *'He can't even face sitting next to me!'*

'Oh, life!' she heard him begin with a heavy sigh. And then he put his head in his hands.

'I'll say it for you,' she thought as she watched him. *'You were amusing enough for a time, but now someone else has come along. Even I can't manage limitless women. There has to be a turnover.'*

'I'm sorry,' he said once more.

And Jane found herself thinking savagely, *'Why?'* She'd never demanded exclusivity. She'd taken what was on offer in a kind of ecstatic trance. She thought of being shut up again in the same dark room he'd rescued her from; and one part of her wished he'd straight away leave so as to get this over with. But there was a shred of comfort in knowing there was no way he could guess her thoughts. She made herself continue to sit very passively, and even smile faintly, while he sighed and muttered as if it were he who'd been wronged.

'Drink?' he heard her ask and forced himself to return to the present.

'Sorry,' he repeated yet again. 'I meant to bring some.' He thought of the morning he'd had. No wonder he'd forgotten the usual champagne.

She smiled at him, though she was very pale, he noticed. Was she ill?

'Is whisky all right?'

'Whisky?' He made himself smile back. It felt so tight. It was because he felt as if he was holding a hand-grenade. Any minute now and he'd change her landscape forever.

After he'd emptied his glass, he observed, as a starting point, 'We don't talk much, do we?'

'We don't,' he heard her meekly agree.

'I wonder what you think of me . . .'

She kept the same fixed smile on her face.

'. . . coming here, week after week like this, taking advantage of your kindness . . .'

'*If I got through that far greater horror,*' thought Jane, '*I ought to be able to endure this.*' But she felt as if every atom of control she'd summoned for Henry's funeral was slipping away: as if the grief she'd managed to suppress then, for the sake of the family, was about to pour out in a great uncontrollable mess. However, all she said quite tersely was, 'Not kind.'

'No?'

She thought: '*Why does he look taken aback?*' But she remained silent, even as she heard the puppy, shut in the kitchen, yelping with fury.

Anthony watched her shake her head with a set expression and felt surprised and more than a little hurt.

'That's how it's appeared to me, at any rate,' he told her very gently, 'and I thank you.'

What happened next astonished him. He watched her expressionless face start to come alive: the dead pallor replaced by a kind of desperate excitement.

He paused. 'It's you who's got me through all this, this . . . Oh God! You don't really want to hear about it.'

At that, Jane rose from her chair and went to kneel in front of him and take his hands. 'Tell me,' she said very tenderly and

firmly, almost exactly as if talking to Liza when she'd got herself
into a state.

'At a quarter to nine today,' Anthony began, 'when I came out
of the club, my wife was waiting for me . . .'

Later, it struck Jane that he could have been about to break
it to her that he was going back to Camilla. But in fact this never
occurred to her. It was because he looked so fearful and
anxious – exactly as he must have done that morning – as if
reliving the shock and horror of it all.

She pictured him issuing from Brooks's, freshly bathed and
shaved and smelling of delicious aftershave, elegantly parcelled
for his day and thinking about practical matters like meetings,
already making decisions. When someone had shoved him in the
back, he'd at first believed it was a mistake. But then the shouting
had started and, very soon, he realized it was directed at him.

'You have no idea what she said!' He shuddered. 'Shrieking
at me, pointing at me! And in front of complete strangers! What
on earth did they think?' For the second time, he said, 'Oh God,
you don't want to hear all this!'

'I do,' said Jane resolutely, picturing him cowering under the
abuse: a well-dressed man in a smart West End street full of
similarly elegant strangers.

'I'm not sure I know how to explain.'

'Try,' she suggested very gently.

'When we first met' – he shrugged helplessly – 'she was so
very . . .'

There was no need for him to say the word. It hung before
them like a neon sign – the way Camilla had always been
defined. 'Look at me!' it blinked, outshining all else, attracting
people like flies trying to absorb the light.

'Sweet, too.' For a second he had a dreamy proud expression as if remembering halcyon honeymoon days closeted with all that beauty and Jane felt a pang of quite unreasonable jealousy.

'I think she was desperate to get away from her mother,' he said. 'Not that she wasn't . . .'

Quite. The one thing everyone knew about the marriage was that it had been a love match.

He was stroking Jane's hair absentmindedly by now. 'We'd been married for about six weeks,' he told her, 'and she threw a silver teapot at me.' He sounded very matter-of-fact. 'Actually, it was a wedding present. She'd just unwrapped it. I'd made some silly joke at her expense – just a tease, but maybe a little thoughtless of me, in retrospect – and, next thing I knew, something heavy had struck me on the head.'

Jane gasped.

'It knocked me out and cut my head open. Poor girl was devastated.'

'I should think!'

He shrugged. 'She drove me to casualty, where they gave me ten stitches – she was in a terrible state. Lovers' tiff, I told myself. And, you know, all the strain of that big wedding . . . Anyway, once she saw I was all right, she made a joke of it. She even told her father and, I remember, he actually ended up laughing too, as if it was something funny and different that she'd done. "Good thing we're so rich," she said. "I'll never have to make my darling husband tea."'

'So I forgot it – till the next time. We were having supper together – pleasantly, I thought – and all of a sudden she emptied a bottle of champagne over my head.' He looked a little regretful. 'Vintage Dom Perignon.'

'What provoked that?'

'No idea,' he said. 'Half the time I never even knew what I'd done wrong and I really tried, you know. Those moods of hers,' he went on, 'she's good at covering them up. Or at least, she used to be. She was sweet as anything when other people were around.' He paused. 'Once I got so worried about it, I tried to talk to Hector.'

'Hector?' she echoed.

He looked helpless. 'That's who everyone in the family goes to, isn't it?'

'What happened?'

'I got the very strong feeling he disapproved.'

'He probably thought you were being disloyal.'

'You think?'

'Mmm. It might have been all right if Camilla had gone to him . . .'

'Which she never would have, by the way.'

It was novel for Jane to be discussing the St Clairs so objectively and from the same standpoint. It lessened the family's power, though there remained a sense of disloyalty.

'Of course,' Anthony went on, 'her mother would say she was highly strung. She's probably still saying it.' He looked at Jane with the shiny black eyes Max had inherited. 'Is it highly strung to smash something every time you can't get exactly what you want? Or phone up my business contacts and tell them I sleep with everything that moves? Or blacken me to my beloved son so he never wants to see me again?' He was trembling with emotion, as if – thought Jane – he hated himself for finally coming clean about his marriage.

It had ended, he explained, when Camilla informed him he was mentally ill and should see a doctor. It had all been so different from what he'd hoped for, he said sadly: a family life with lots of children, a haven. But he'd stuck it out for years and years for the sake of Max and because he believed in marriage, he told Jane. But he'd realized then, he went on with tears in his eyes, that he could not stay for one single more minute and, when he informed Camilla, she'd thrown a stack of plates at him, one by one. They were his favourite plates with paintings of wild flowers on them – though that was beside the point – and poor Max had heard it all.

She must have telephoned the *Daily Mail* straight afterwards, he said, because the next morning a reporter contacted him at his club. He'd refused to comment, of course. Just like the St Clairs, he hated the press.

Later, Jane said, 'She told the family about other women, too.'

They were in bed by then. The street had observed the curtains of her room being pulled shut and after that, half relieved, half a little affronted, got on with its business.

'Ah!' There was a wealth of meaning in his tone. Finally he understood why all those people, who'd professed such fondness for him, had suddenly avoided him as one. 'When?'

'The night she came round to Suki and Simon's.' Jane hesitated. 'Max was there.'

'Max?' He sounded quite panic-stricken. 'Oh Lord! Why did no one tell me?' But he already knew the answer. 'You, though, Jane . . . Why didn't *you* tell me?'

She was silent.

'Don't tell me you believed it, too!'

'I feel terrible,' she said miserably.

'No, no, it's not your fault!' He sprang up and started pacing the room, stark naked. 'I must think what to do. Poor little chap! As if things weren't bad enough already!'

'Should I get Liza to say something?'

'No!' he said immediately, then smiled a little apologetically. He hadn't meant it to sound so emphatic.

'Would you like *me* to try and talk to him at Hector's birthday party?'

'No,' he said again, far more gently, but he smiled at her gratefully. 'You know how Max is with his mother . . . It's a question of loyalty.' He looked quite powerless and it occurred to Jane that, despite his obvious difference from the family, he was just as wary of confrontation.

Jane pictured Camilla pacing her lush prison of a house, mind churning with poisonous thoughts behind the mask of her beautiful face, and felt pity and fear in almost equal measure.

'What happens if she finds out about this?'

'Us?' he asked, and Jane felt almost faint with delight. 'She won't. Promise.'

Chapter Twenty-four

There was always a whiff of mothballs when the whole family got together. You didn't notice it so much at the summer party, where it was overtaken by agreeable natural fragrances. But in an enclosed space it became almost solid. Some of the fumes stayed in the cloakroom, buried in the ancient fur coats (which the moths had already got to, by the way). The rest drifted into the enormous room that had been hired, along with the creased old dresses and wraps, making the young ones wince. For an occasion like Uncle Hector's birthday party, the jewels had been removed from the bank: heirloom diamonds and rubies and emeralds in old settings, which cost too much to insure now. It made no sense, really, for poorer members of the family to hang on to these treasures, showing them off very occasionally for a few hours like dispossessed monarchs. But it was considered a duty to preserve them for the next generation – and irrelevant, really, that it wasn't the kind of thing the young liked to wear any more.

Liza was a case in point. She sported clip-on plastic daisy earrings to go with the very short dress she'd selected even though Jane had emphasized this was a formal occasion. Watching her daughter with the usual mixture of pride and concern, she realized she should have known better. The sure-fire way of controlling Liza was to ask her to do the opposite. But Jane noticed to her surprise that Max, by Liza's side, looked spruce and respectable in a black dinner jacket. Was the effort for his mother? Or did he have some secret leaning to conform, after all?

But there were some older members of the family who would on no account dress up and this had become accepted. Crazy Claude – never out of his moulting khaki corduroy suit – was one. He'd bicycled to the hotel in a dream, arguing with an imaginary defendant, a cluster of stuffed carrier bags slung over his handlebars like balloons. As usual, he saw any family occasion as a chance to pick Lionel's brains, once the foolishness was over with.

Tom had asked everyone to assemble at half past six. Uncle Hector would arrive at seven. He'd been told that in celebration of this landmark birthday, a trip to the theatre was planned – Stoppard's *Travesties* at the Aldwych – and there'd be drinks beforehand at the Hyde Park Hotel.

'THE THEATRE?' Uncle Hector had queried on the telephone, with a smile at Charlie in the background. He hadn't been for years now. What was the point of paying an exorbitant price to sit in the same uncomfortable seat for hours on end, when you couldn't hear a word? Anyway, he disliked contemporary plays.

'Everyone's talking about it,' Tom told him, though Stoppard was not to his taste, either.

Charlie was to drive his great-uncle up to London in the Daimler.

'Black tie would be best,' Tom advised.

'BLACK TIE FOR THE THEATRE?' Uncle Hector had winked at Charlie. 'Is that strictly necessary?'

'We'll be going to Claridge's for a late supper. Didn't I tell you?'

'I thought nobody dressed up nowadays.'

For some members of the family, fifteen pounds was a lot. They were determined to get their money's worth and already making heavy inroads into the trays of champagne circulated by impassive waiters. They were wondering what was for dinner. They were going to enjoy themselves.

Jane was thinking about what Anthony had told her the day before.

'This business with Camilla,' he'd begun casually. 'It's not exactly the best moment for it to have happened . . .'

His business had been facing crisis for some time, he explained. The city had lost confidence and it was no wonder, really, seeing what a hash the economy was in. There'd been no real growth for years. He'd borrowed massively on the strength of completing a particular development – an enormous block of flats in Chelsea – and now the bank was foreclosing on the debt.

'How much?'

He'd shrugged, couldn't seem to bring himself to utter the

figure. 'The sum is unreal,' he'd said, and even smiled faintly. 'I'll probably get wiped out.'

But she could tell that he didn't mean it: was probably already planning a recovery. It was part of his resourceful nature. Besides, he was hardly behaving like someone on the brink of ruin. She thought of the chauffeur-driven Rolls that still delivered him to her door. Perhaps pretending you were as rich as ever was as effective (and necessary) as behaving like a beauty.

'This might be good for me,' he'd said. 'Stop me from getting complacent.'

'And Max?'

'Perhaps,' he'd said slowly, 'having a bit less money will be the making of Max.'

And now there was the prospect of meeting Camilla again, with the full knowledge of just how volatile she could be.

Jane glanced round nervously. No sign yet. But, then, beauties liked to make an entrance.

Kitty stood with her parents in a throng of people, sipping champagne and dealing with the usual volley of questions. It was a pity, she thought, that she couldn't silently hold up one prepared placard after another: 'Still in Chepstow Place' ... 'Yes, still sharing with Charlie' ... 'No, haven't moved from the chartered accountants.'

'And do you enjoy the work?' a second cousin once removed asked.

Kitty thought, '*I wish I was anywhere but here. I wonder if he's feeling as peculiar as I am about what happened – with half of me wanting to blot it out, pretend it never happened, and the other half anxious to see him again but in a quite new way. I'll know how he's feeling as soon as I see him because I always know exactly what he's thinking. But if he has that sheepish shambling look, am I going to be relieved or disappointed?'*

'I hear Charlie's not been well lately,' said Cousin Margaret, sounding very concerned.

'Nonsense!' boomed Tom.

'Well, he has had pneumonia,' Becky corrected him, looking flustered.

'Pneumonia?'

'Only a touch,' Tom conceded.

'But he's all right?' Cousin Margaret pursued, even more anxiously. There was a gash of scarlet lipstick painted two inches below her lower lip. It appeared, from a distance, as if she had two mouths.

'Of course he's all right!'

'He's much better,' Becky added, glancing at Tom. 'He'll be fine,' she went on, her voice raised like a child's. 'You know he's bringing the guest of honour?'

'Hector?'

'Yes, Charlie's been staying there.'

'Staying with Hector? Whatever for? I thought he'd been ill.'

'He'll be home very soon,' said Tom, turning away, abruptly terminating the conversation.

Suki thought, watching her handsome husband throw back his head and give his charming easy laugh, *'How can he behave so normally? How can he be so happy?'*

At least three people tonight had already asked her in a concerned way, 'Everything all right?' Even Phil, who never noticed anything, had patted her shoulder in the car. 'Mum,' he'd

said, in the same abrupt embarrassed way he so irritatingly
cleared his throat.

Each moment, she waited for the knock on the door, the
men in dark suits, the arrest that must surely come, and it
showed in the circles under her eyes, the weight loss (the only
advantage). 'I'm working on it,' Uncle Hector assured her,
whenever she ventured to ask if he'd thought of a solution yet.
But he sounded worried to the point of tetchy. With his
connections, not to mention the legal influence of the family,
surely there was something he could do?

This was the world Simon loved, of course, she reflected
sadly – these agreeable and civilized surroundings where the
right accent ought to guarantee the right job and men deferred
to women (while remaining confident of their own superiority).
The St Clairs knew who they were for sure – after all, there were
enough of them – and this was probably their greatest strength.
No wonder he looked so relaxed. He must feel like an exile
invited to visit his old homeland.

She wondered how the family would react if they knew what
sort of dishonesty he was snared in. *'And they're going to! I know
they are!'*

Simon had broken it to her on the way to the party that his
old schoolmate, Rupert Fortescue, had been in touch. 'About
those cars . . .' he'd begun. They couldn't stay in his barn
forever, he'd said. Apparently, he'd been surprisingly firm in
his hesitant overly polite public-school sort of way. Quite
reasonably, Simon told her, Fortescue wished to know his
plans.

Lionel and Eleanor made a stately entrance at ten to seven.

No Camilla. Eleanor had checked immediately, though

nobody would have guessed from the calm, cool way her blue gaze roamed over the gathering.

They'd discussed the problem, in their fashion, in the car on the way up from Hampshire. They knew Hector was still furious with Camilla but he'd no control, this time, over the guest list. Camilla was family.

'It'll be good to see Camilla.'

'Mmm, how long is it?' Someone honked at them furiously, but that often happened. Lionel drove slowly, on the crown of the road and low down in his seat. If passengers were in the back, he'd swivel his head to talk to them. Last week a young man overtaking had leant out of his window and shouted that he was a useless old twat. Lionel had majestically affected not to notice. But he'd looked up the unfamiliar word in his Penguin dictionary and used up a last-minute 'w' at Scrabble a few days later. TWAT. Useful. 'Slang for fool,' he told Eleanor, who'd not been in the car at the time.

'Too long.'

'We've talked to her . . .'

'I suppose.'

Camilla had telephoned the night before last just as they'd got to bed – something about tiresome neighbours that they couldn't make head or tail of. She'd sounded very agitated and angry, poor darling, but this was understandable. Women needed the protection of marriage, Lionel pronounced, and – Hector was right – if children were involved, the contract should be for life, whatever the circumstances. No wonder Camilla was in a state. It was no fun to find herself adrift at her age.

'This has been a trying business.'

Eleanor had nodded, feeling the heavy diamond and emerald

pendant earrings that had belonged to Lionel's mother pull at
her ear lobes. The screws were too tight, but she couldn't risk
losing them. She'd marked them down for Camilla in her little
black exercise book, but maybe she'd change her mind and leave
them to Suki instead.

'We've done our best . . .'

Perhaps Camilla wouldn't turn up for the party, after all. It
might be as well for Max, who was looking so much better,
though they noticed that even he – who always appeared so
impervious – cast the occasional anxious glance at the door. Oh
dear, oh dear, oh dear. A trying business, indeed.

Charlie said, 'Ready for this?' And, at the same time, thought,
'*Am I?*' He believed he could deal with his father. He knew he
wouldn't dare have a go at him in front of all those people. As
for Kitty, his heart fluttered in an unfamiliar way at the prospect
of seeing her again. He'd found himself humming earlier in his
bedroom at Cedar Manor as he bent his knees and struggled to
knot his bow tie in front of the mirror on the dressing table.
He'd knocked over an ornament as he did so: a porcelain basket
filled with miniscule pieces of porcelain fruit. He was hoping to
be able to mend it in secret later.

'What's that?' Uncle Hector hadn't put in his hearing-aid
properly yet.

Charlie boomed the question and it ricocheted around the
confined space of the Daimler.

'Ready,' Uncle Hector confirmed with a smile.

'Remember, we're only coming for a drink.'

'What's that?'

Charlie brought the car to a halt in front of the hotel and
turned to face his great-uncle. His mouth gaped like an idiot's,

his eyes popped open, his arms shot out. 'Surprise!' he bellowed.

Uncle Hector patted Charlie on the knee. It was good to see him act like his old self. The dear chap had been such a help to him: he didn't know how he'd have managed otherwise. And the strange thing was, Charlie seemed to enjoy behaving like a servant. His meals were becoming more and more delicious. The only time he regressed was when his father telephoned. It was painful to see the change in him then – the anxiety that sprang up in his brown eyes, the quiet despair that descended like a pall. But very soon now, Charlie would have to resume his life in London and the interrupted pupillage. And then Merriweather, whose back was surely on the mend, would take up the reins of power once more. Uncle Hector found he was dreading it. Dreading it.

'And you don't know about the picture, either,' Charlie reminded him as he opened his door and prepared to lever his great-uncle out.

Uncle Hector smiled. Of course he didn't know that the family had clubbed together and commissioned a painting of Cedar Manor for a present.

Only three people had told him so far.

They'd requested the staff to shut the doors to the ballroom. Then there was a bit of giggling from the young ones and a lot of shushing from the older ones and the whole big gathering gradually fell silent.

They all heard Uncle Hector's booming voice outside – 'We mustn't be late for the theatre, Charlie' – and smiled ecstatically at each other, even the handful of old ones like Cousin Harriet who'd given the game away weeks ago now.

'Happy birthday!' they chorused as the doors were opened.

To Uncle Hector's credit, he looked properly astonished and, after that, delighted.

And so satisfied was everybody by his reaction that only a few people noticed when Camilla slipped in – too late to attract any attention after all.

Charlie said, 'I got your letter.'

The nervousness had faded away as soon as he'd spotted her: familiar Kitty, though secretly different. He glanced round quickly to see if anyone had noticed that he was grinning like an idiot. The proof that that extraordinary night had happened was folded in a hidden pocket of his dinner jacket. 'Darling,' she'd written.

'You look okay,' she responded. But she seemed a little embarrassed by the eager joyful way he was behaving because she kept looking about her, too.

'I'm fine now.'

'Really?'

'Truly.'

'You could have written back,' she told him a little sternly, with a frown, and it occurred to Charlie that it was almost as if she were trying to turn him into something he was not: a man who could take advantage of a girl then pretend it had never happened.

'I know,' he admitted humbly. 'I did start to.'

She was wearing a long not very well-cut blue silk dress that didn't flatter her colouring. But Charlie only thought how nice she looked. He was thinking of the softness of her mouth and the sweetness of her naked damp skin, so close to his that they'd created suction noises. But it had been awkward to begin with, in spite of all the alcohol. Then, all of a sudden, she'd ordered 'Fuck me!' in a strange deep growl and pulled her top over her head. One of the pads had come adrift from her bra (the same one Charlie had seen drying in the bathroom so many times), and a half moon of foam had reared up like a last-minute warning finger. '*What?*' she'd asked, struck by his wandering eye, and then, in her normal voice, 'Oh God!' For a moment, they'd stared at each other blankly as if uncertain whether it would be a good or bad idea to treat this as a joke. Then they'd simultaneously dived for the light switch.

It was true that he'd attempted to write to her. He felt guilty about not telephoning, either. But it was such a performance making a call from Cedar Manor. For a start, it was hardly private. At least she was aware of all this. It had to be one of the advantages of belonging to the same family.

He stammered: 'It didn't mean . . . I mean, I *have* been really busy . . .'

But Kitty raised her eyebrows in an ironic sort of way as if she didn't believe him.

'It's been great staying with Uncle Hector, actually. Apart from . . .'

Then Charlie stopped this inarticulate burbling because he'd noticed that, all of a sudden, Kitty looked very apprehensive – as if she feared that, any minute now, he was going to tell her it had been the most dreadful mistake. '*As if!*' thought Charlie. As if he'd ever treat her like that! He'd take the bull by the horns – be strong-minded, for a change. After all, he reasoned, it was better to sort things out between them now.

'Did you mean it?' he asked urgently. He thought afterwards that he must have guessed this would be their last real chance to talk.

'What?' she asked, but he could see from her expression that she was stalling. In fact, she seemed not to be looking at him at all, but somewhere over his shoulder.

'*You* know.'

'Absolutely!' she told him, as if she'd made a snap decision, and she smiled at him encouragingly and even grasped his hand.

'Okay,' said Charlie equally decisively, beaming back – and, the very next minute, felt a firm hand on his shoulder and turned to face his father.

The quartet started playing in the background – graceful strains laid tentatively across the hubbub. The young performers, fresh out of music school, were upset to throw Mozart and their talent away.

They hadn't been due to start until dinner, when people were meant to listen while they ate. But just now, Mr St Clair had ordered them to begin.

'Now?'

'Now!' It was extraordinary how furious he looked, this big man all done up in uncomfortable-looking evening clothes – but hadn't he already threatened them with legal action?

'But . . .'

'Just do it! Please!'

They couldn't know the anger wasn't directed at them: that, on seeing his son again, all Tom's misery and upset had come flooding back. They just happened to be in the line of fire.

Max watched his mother out of the corner of his eye, while fielding the usual questions. Hampered by the crush of family, she was surely working her way round to him. But thankfully, because everyone seemed to want to greet her, she was making slow progress.

He could see that she'd made an effort for the party. Her hair was in a shiny loaf shape (so she must have been to the hairdresser) and she was wearing one of her beautiful filmy dresses. From a distance she looked like the glamorous mother of his childhood who'd suffused his bedroom with fragrance when she kissed him goodnight, to linger like a ghost in place of the conversation there should have been. Then he noticed that, like a hurricane, she seemed to alter each group she joined.

She appeared to be indignant about something: most likely his father again, thought Max wearily. As if everyone hadn't had a basinful of that stuff! She came right up close to people as she talked and he saw them back away as diplomatically as if she suffered from bad breath. (Well, she definitely did smell different these days, he reflected.) But their expressions were wrong: uneasy, the party jollity punctured. And when she passed on they regrouped, speaking intently to each other with serious faces, like survivors.

'For the time being,' said Max politely in answer to another inquiry about his life, and watched his grandmother absorb the situation from the opposite side of the room and, like a stately old ship, navigate an immediate and effective passage through the sea of guests. He saw her touch his mother on the arm and her lips moved. 'Camilla,' she might be urging in her cool firm way, 'take a grip on yourself, child.' Except that none of them ever actually came out with things like that. You were meant to pick up on the anger and disappointment like receiving radio waves. If you were good like Charlie and Kitty, you resolved to do better next time.

His mother wasn't being good now, though, and perhaps she

never had been. He saw her shake her head like an angry
bullock, as if rejecting this festive gathering and, along with it,
the silent demands and expectations of her whole family. Why
had she come, then? Nobody would have minded if she'd
stayed away. She was going to spoil the party, just to make a
point. She might even start on his great-uncle.

His mood lifted as Liza joined him.

'I've just seen Uncle Tom,' she said with her mocking smile.
'He's been telling people his speech is exactly two thousand
words long, with some witticisms.'

An hour and a half later, after the big flaming cake had been
brought in, Charlie stood up to say a few words of appreciation
on behalf of the younger generation. It had been the last-minute
idea of his father, whose own speech had chronicled the various
triumphant phases of Uncle Hector's life. The guests were
longing for the promised jokes and, when they came, laughed
too early and hard. 'What's that?' Hector could be heard asking.
It didn't matter, really. Tom's attention to detail, which made him
such a brilliant advocate, was a disadvantage on this sort of
occasion though everyone clapped dutifully at the end.

Charlie hadn't been keen, at first, to say anything. 'Don't be
a wimp,' his father had told him in a low furious voice,
somehow managing to convey both contempt and boredom.
But his mother had urged, 'You are the eldest grandson, darling.
And Uncle Hector would appreciate it so much.'

'What shall I say?'

'Just — whatever comes to mind.' She'd beamed
encouragingly at him as if she believed it would restore his
confidence to do something important and knew he'd rise to the
occasion.

It wasn't easy standing up there, looking at a mass of old evening dresses and dinner jackets, an expanse of still expectant faces, and for a moment Charlie felt the terrifying and familiar beginnings of panic. He told himself he could do this.

'I know my great-uncle is seventy years old now,' he began in his ordinary voice.

'Speak up!' shouted several voices from the back.

There was no point in repeating it. Everyone knew Uncle Hector was seventy. It was, after all, the reason they were all there.

'Uncle Hector has many wonderful qualities,' Charlie told everyone, turning up the volume. He could see his great-uncle beaming, so he could probably hear him all right now. 'But I think his greatest quality of all is that he's like a young person himself. He's always interested. He's always on your side. You can talk to Uncle Hector about anything.' Charlie faltered. How on earth should he go on?

'He's also one of the two kindest people I've ever known.' Charlie paused again, realizing he'd created a natural introduction to what he was suddenly impelled to say next. Afterwards, he couldn't understand what came over him. Hadn't they agreed the night it began that it should all be kept secret? It had something to do with the ominously disappointed way his father was staring at him. The strange thing was that, in spite of the vast presence of the family, he was really speaking to Kitty. It also occurred to him that perhaps he could give no finer present to his great-uncle, who was so fond of them both.

Kitty sat frozen with embarrassment, staring down at her lap, sure that everyone was ponderously turning as one to inspect her. 'What did Charlie say?' she heard one of the old ones trumpet. 'He says he and Kitty are to marry?' 'Tom's boy and Suki's girl?'

Then the laughter began: at first soft, even melodious, then increasingly strident. Aunt Camilla laughing her head off as if Charlie had just made the greatest joke of all.

When Liza rose to her feet, Kitty feared worse. Another speech? A round of cheers? But to her very great relief, Liza simply started singing. 'Summertime' didn't seem inappropriate in October, just beautiful and nostalgic, and gradually the scandalized whisperings died away. 'Isn't that poor Henry's girl?' Kitty heard someone ask, again too loudly, and there was a chorus of shushings before the same person pronounced, surprised, 'A really pretty little voice.'

'*Bless you!*' thought Kitty. It was like being given a reminder of why Liza had always been such an essential part of their foursome. She was the wild one who dared translate fantasy into action: a counterpoint to Max's passivity and Charlie's and her own caution. Dear Liza. It was clear that, beneath the petulance and immaturity, she also possessed a heart.

The party broke up soon afterwards.

On the long drive back to Cedar Manor, his painting carefully stowed in the back, Uncle Hector talked a little about the party. 'Wonderful!' he said, and 'Splendid!' But mostly he sighed and shuffled in his seat as if in pain. And, to Charlie's consternation, he didn't refer to his announcement once.

Chapter Twenty-five

'Thank you, Cuz!' muttered Kitty.

Liza shrugged. Kitty would have done the same for her, she implied, looking flushed and pretty. 'Was I really okay?'

'Wonderful!' Kitty thought, *'I couldn't have stood up in front of everyone like that! I can only perform as part of a group. Perhaps that's another crucial difference between Liza and me.'*

Then Liza remembered what had provoked her recital. She asked, round-eyed and fearful: 'D'you think Charlie really has gone nuts now?'

She'd swooped on Kitty for a private moment as everyone was collecting up coats to go home. Glowing with goodwill, she'd dropped half a crown in among the sad collection of pennies in a saucer and received an astounded beam from the elderly female cloakroom attendant. It was one of the menial jobs she'd done herself while waiting for her dream of fame to be realized.

But, to her astonishment, Kitty merely gave an unhappy smile.

Liza frowned. 'Kitty?'

'It's true, Liza.'

Liza's mouth fell open. Then she said: 'How *could* you?'

Kitty stared at her cousin in amazement. How dared she, of all people, ask such a question?

'Charlie!' Liza went on. '*Charlie!* It's like, it's like . . .' Shaking her head, she seemed to be searching for a parallel to convey the full strength of her upset and distaste.

'You and Max,' said Kitty very coolly.

But Liza never even hesitated. 'Exactly,' she agreed, nodding enthusiastically. She met Kitty's eyes easily. Nobody could have appeared more innocent.

Max kept his distance. But Kitty had caught sight of his astonished face at the exact moment when Charlie made his announcement. He'd appeared almost foolish: Max who prided himself on his inscrutability.

The grandparents approached to say goodbye. 'Kitty,' said Eleanor. She paused with a tight bright smile, as if waiting for the correct words to materialize. 'You must come down soon.'

Lionel looked shell-shocked. He and Hector had identical grim frozen expressions. Kitty had noticed them arguing a short while ago, over by an abandoned table while waiters darted deftly round them, removing plates smeared with birthday cake, gathering up glasses. 'You must!' she'd heard Uncle Hector boom. And after that, she'd seen her grandfather shake his head as mutinously as a child, as if this wasn't the first time he'd refused such an order from his brother. They didn't say the usual affectionate goodbyes. Her grandfather wouldn't even look at her great-uncle. Had they been arguing about her?

What nobody realized, thought Kitty miserably, was why she'd encouraged Charlie earlier that evening – given him the go-ahead (as it had turned out) to announce their engagement. 'Did you mean it?' he'd asked, referring to a drunken exchange of promises made that extraordinary night (and meant to be kept secret). 'Absolutely!' she'd assured him with a smile. It was because, over his shoulder, she could see his father approaching: Uncle Tom in his uncomfortable dinner jacket, weaving through crowds of cousins, intent on joining them and almost certain to upset Charlie all over again.

And now look what had happened!

Eleanor asked Lionel, 'What was all that about?'

She seldom asked direct questions and it fazed Lionel. It was lucky he could pretend all his attention was on negotiating a roundabout. 'What, my dear?' he asked after a moment, ignoring a blast of furious honking from behind.

'You know vay well what.'

'Ah!' It was lucky he had a good excuse for keeping his eyes on the road (especially as another car had drawn alongside and its driver was making a vigorous but unfamiliar gesture.) He could feel her cold resolute stare boring into him. It was most discomforting, as she well knew.

'We should put a stop to this, Lionel,' Eleanor said after a pause lasting more than a dozen miles. Was she referring to the extraordinary announcement of an engagement between two of their grandchildren? Or her own maddening habit of stating the opposite of what she really meant? Or – with her legendary intuition – was she finally tuning into the existence of a secret deliberately kept from her for all of her married life?

'Just what Hector was saying,' said Lionel, ducking the issue.

She relapsed into silence while she ruminated on this.

Lionel was sure she'd not let it drop, though, and he thought wearily, 'Perhaps Hector's right. Maybe one of us has to say something now.'

But he could hardly bear to think about it. As for being forgiven for his silence . . . He knew very well that was out of the question.

For Jane, the drama afforded a good excuse to telephone Anthony. Since the party had ended early, it wasn't too late. Charlie and Kitty! Positively incestuous, thought Jane, who was in love with her own brother-in-law. Charlie's bombshell had been all the more surprising because Liza hadn't known and nor, very obviously, had Max. What was happening to them all?

There was another reason for making contact. She could give Anthony positive news of his son. 'He looked wonderful tonight,' she'd say. 'I think it's good for him being in that flat.' And she could relay Liza's triumph: 'She really can sing!' '*If only somebody would give her a chance*,' thought Jane, '*then all that restlessness and frustration could be channelled in a positive way.*'

And perhaps she should also tell Anthony about Camilla, whose behaviour had been distinctly disturbing. She'd looked so angry, and that eerie solitary laughter had been reminiscent of someone or something: a famous portrait of inappropriate, alarming mirth. 'Drunk!' Simon had muttered just before Liza created a diversion, and Jane had watched the shocked realization ripple round the family – even though none of them had exactly held back on the champagne (the more so because they'd paid for it themselves).

But the porter at Brooks's informed her that Anthony was out and her happy new confidence started to waver. '*You have only his word for what happened,*' said that insistent and mournful voice in her head.

'Would you like to leave a message?'

'No message, thank you.'

 Chapter Twenty-six

'You know I'm not happy about this,' Suki told Simon with a frown that was imperceptible in the darkness, 'but I'm not exactly unhappy either.'

It was an advance in their discussion, hours after the initial shock.

There'd been no proper chance to talk to Kitty after Charlie's announcement: just a snatched moment, with family milling round. Without conferring, they'd decided that Charlie had made a clumsy and ill-judged attempt at humour. Either that or, despite seeming so recovered, he was in a very bad way. 'It's not true, darling,' they'd told Kitty confidently and were horrified when she nodded, looking more scared than happy. They'd wanted to take her home with them for the night and talk about it all but she'd insisted on going back to the flat in

Chepstow Place with Max and Liza (who seemed to have moved in, too, for the time being).

Getting into bed, Simon said, 'We must sleep on this.'

But it was a myth you could do any such thing. They were restless for hours, just as they'd been for days now, but at least they were kept awake by a different worry. And, once the discussion started it was untainted – for a change – by shame or disappointment. Furthermore, because the problem involved one of their children there was the tentative unvoiced hope, on both sides, that if they continued in this very normal fashion the old trust and closeness might be restored.

They examined the engagement from every angle, becoming increasingly positive as the night wore on.

'I suppose,' said Suki slowly, 'he might actually be a good husband.' But she was thinking, '*What is that?*' For years and years, her whole family had regarded Simon as a good husband and now he threatened to disgrace them all.

She could feel his familiar shape beside her and picture his fair untroubled gaze as he stared up at the invisible ceiling. It was uncanny how he hadn't aged, though this had never struck her before. Even tonight, it had been remarked upon. Suki thought a little resentfully: '*I know I have – especially lately.*'

'Charlie? A good husband?' He sounded doubtful.

'Don't you think so?'

'Why do you say that, Pudding?'

'*He's really trying to get back to how we were,*' Suki conceded. Out loud, she said: 'Well, he's a dear old thing, isn't he?'

'That's certainly true.'

'I know Kitty never tells us a thing about her private life but I've the feeling she doesn't always choose well. And . . .' Suki paused. 'She needs someone nice.'

'She does indeed.'

'And he's reliable.'

'Do you think so?' Simon gave a faint involuntary snort –
'*Hardly!*' he thought. Was it reliable to crack up at the first sign
of pressure? Or wreck a delightful and significant family
occasion because you wished to draw attention to yourself? But
he let it go for now, merely asking in his meaningful intimate
way, 'Is that enough?' He knew she would understand. He was
thinking about romance and all the special reasons he'd
discovered for loving her.

But Suki queried a little sharply: 'You don't think so?'

'What?' asked Simon, thoroughly taken aback.

'*I* think reliability is extremely important,' she told him with
surprising firmness. She added, 'Just about the most important
thing there is' – and might or might not have been aware of him
flinching beside her in the darkness.

('Weird!' Phil had pronounced on the way home. But both of
them had vigorously objected.

'No, it's not!' Suki had said. 'There's nothing to stop first
cousins from marrying. It's a lovely idea!'

And Simon had agreed in the treacly way that instantly
caused Phil to clear his throat. '*I'd* have married Mum if she was
my first cousin, I can tell you!')

It *was* weird, though! Charlie and Kitty had grown up
together like siblings. They couldn't get their heads around it.

'How did it happen?' asked Suki wonderingly.

'*How does anything different happen?*' thought Simon. '*It's because
you take a leap into the unknown. For a moment, you forget how you're
expected to behave.*'

'Do you think . . .?' Suki began. She knew it was unnecessary
to continue. That was the thing about being married for so long.

'No!' Simon couldn't bear even to consider it, though another part of him was very thankful they were on easier ground. 'Of course not!'

'Something must have happened . . .'

'If you ask me, Pudding, he came up with the idea on the spur of the moment. Attention-seeking, or some such. We all know he's been a trifle flaky of late. Didn't you see Kitty's face? The poor love was mortified.' He added firmly, 'Mortified.' The fact was, he couldn't bear to think of his daughter sleeping with any man, let alone Charlie. He'd like to meet the suitor who was good enough. They both would. It was high time he made an appearance.

Becky and Tom stayed awake half the night, too. Tom cried in Becky's arms – savage heaving sobs of disappointment and dismay. The treasured son he'd invested so many hopes and dreams in was disappearing by the hour – to be replaced by this inadequate, embarrassing and frankly loopy person who'd just ruined Uncle Hector's birthday party, wrecked it after all those weeks of hard work.

'He didn't mean it like that,' said Becky, the soother and peacemaker. 'You mustn't think he was getting back at you. Of course he wasn't. Didn't you see the look on his face? He thought everyone would be so pleased. Including you. You know how Charlie is? He's like Boomerang,' she went on, thinking of their Labrador, who would wag his tail in happy anticipation as he brought in dead eviscerated rats as gifts.

Becky paused, feeling the weight of his head against her shoulder, his body slack against hers. How sweet it was to feel so trusted and depended upon. For all their famous happiness, Becky didn't believe Suki and Simon's marriage was as profoundly close as hers. Intimacy was surely about comprehending the full range of a person's soul. '*And I do* . . .' Knowing quite how difficult Tom could be only made her love him more. In her opinion, his occasional pushiness was entirely the fault of his mother, who'd frowned on failure and never been satisfied. '*Cold*,' thought Becky, thinking of the way Eleanor criticized without words. She envisaged Tom as a child – under-loved, anxious to please – and believed she understood it all.

She was the only one he apologized to, ever: the sole person capable of controlling him. 'Was I really awful?' he'd humbly ask, after he'd savaged someone with Leftie views at a dinner party or bragged too much about a case he'd won or been beastly to one of the children. 'I didn't mean it.' Becky alone knew he was a softie, and all the more lovable for that.

She'd been right, too, though she wouldn't crow. It had been obvious to her for a long time that Charlie and Kitty were too content with each other's company. But, a little capriciously, now that her deepest fears had been confirmed, she was starting to see the advantages.

'I know it seems bizarre to everyone now. But is it really such a terrible idea?'

She felt Tom shift against her as he prepared to listen.

'The point I'm making is she wouldn't be an unknown quantity. And that could be a real plus, if you think about it. Charlie needs stability.'

He was concentrating now. She could tell from the quietness of his breathing, the butterfly-wing scrape of his eyelashes against her skin as he absorbed the meaning of her words. Both were engaged in a process of readjustment. The ideal wife (daughter of a high court judge?) was fading away and a familiar, far less intimidating person was taking her place, like one picture sliding tentatively over another in a photograph album.

'You heard what he said about the kindness.' Becky paused, thinking she'd been kind to her son, too. 'If he married Kitty . . .' she said and felt Tom's body go into a brief spasm in protest. 'I'm only saying "*if* ",' she hurried on. '*If* by any chance he did end up married to Kitty, then having someone kind and dependable would give him confidence, wouldn't it? You're always saying yourself that if a man's got the right woman behind him, he can do anything.'

He hugged her to him. Of course! He'd met Becky just after securing tenancy in an illustrious set of chambers but, at first, hadn't even registered her because of an obsession with the glamorous blonde sister of a fellow barrister. But Becky had seen him all right. She'd crept into his life like a determined little mouse: laughing at his jokes, sympathizing with his unrequited passion for the blonde, showing a real interest in his work and, all the time, cooking him delicious sustaining meals (for which she even took lessons). In the end she became indispensable. It hadn't been love to begin with – he went into the marriage quite unromantically, just after the blonde had announced her engagement to a banker – but love had come all right. And the funny thing was, Becky became a beauty – in his eyes anyway, which was all that mattered. 'My little humdinger,' he called her in private moments. They met the blonde years later and she seemed to him insipid and self-centred. Thank God he'd shown sense.

'Think about it,' said wise devoted Becky. So he did.

Chapter Twenty-seven

There were several false starts to the conversation.

The first was at breakfast after Charlie had brought in eggs boiled fresh from under the hens sporting inadequate little felt hats some female relation had once made as a Christmas present. Uncle Hector stared at him, fiddled with his napkin, which was tucked into the neck of his shirt like a baby's bib, shook his head, sighed, gave up. When he refolded the napkin and slid it into a silver ring he hissed with exasperation on discovering a blob of vivid yellow on his shirt, after all.

At lunch, he was silent as they ate the braised lamb Charlie had made, though he asked for a second helping. But after the pudding had been served – stewed apples made from wrinkled fruit Charlie had found arranged in an aromatic outhouse – he said abruptly, as if terminating a long internal discussion, 'Nobody's fault.'

Charlie leant forward encouragingly. So he was not to be reprimanded for his surprise announcement of the night before? Why did his great-uncle look so unhappy, then?

But Uncle Hector said nothing further and spent the entire afternoon chopping up logs, which was Partridge's job. It was typical of him to choose to do something unnecessary and even dangerous when stressed.

The village girls had lit the fire at six, as usual, and laid out the sherry.

'*Dutch courage*,' thought Charlie, emptying his glass and covertly pouring another. If Uncle Hector wouldn't talk about it, he would – and delay disclosing that he'd used up a month's housekeeping money in less than a week. His great-uncle seemed curiously guileless about the cost of food, perhaps because he'd never had to involve himself with such matters.

'Poached turbot,' Charlie announced to Merriweather as he arranged a supper tray on his bed.

'He won't like that,' commented the servant, with grim amusement.

The little room felt stuffy and there were crumbs on the sheets, which needed changing. Charlie caught sight of a full chamberpot beneath the bed and wondered, a little guiltily, who would be emptying it.

'Apple pie to follow,' he went on with cheery unconcern, lifting a lid from a second dish, revelling in secret pride. He'd never made pastry before. As far as he could tell, its only flaw was an oddly speckled appearance and he tried to forget about the weevils he'd seen moving around in the flour Merriweather kept in a big earthenware pot.

'Shall I plump up your pillows for you, while I'm here?'

'He thinks the world of his apples,' Merriweather warned with dark presentiment and another wintry smile. But he leant forward so his bedding could be adjusted and Charlie noticed his knobbly spine through the old maroon wool dressing-gown he wore. His thin hair smelt strange, like old lard. At least he had a good appetite, though his back seemed no better.

Uncle Hector enjoyed the turbot, too, and a delicious bottle of Pouilly-Fuissé brought up from the cellar. 'Superb!' he said, looking delighted but mystified. What strange magic caused Charlie of all people to serve up so much more delicious food than his manservant ever had?

Charlie waited until they were back in the drawing-room before diving into the conversation very decisively.

'I know we're first cousins,' he began. 'But it's not illegal.'

'What's that?'

Charlie repeated it and his great-uncle cringed back in his armchair. He'd been prodding the subject all day like someone tapping at a hornet's nest with a stick, but now behaved as if all he wanted was to escape.

'I mean,' Charlie bellowed, fixing Uncle Hector with his earnest brown eyes, 'it seemed, well, not exactly wrong to me at first but . . . we have known each other for ever, we've always been friends. Now, though, I think that makes it okay. Because I know who she is. And that seems to me a very great advantage.'

'What's that?'

Charlie gave his great-uncle a stern look. It was no use trying to take refuge in deafness. He had his hearing-aid in properly – Charlie had just checked and, if necessary, would shout the house down.

Uncle Hector looked very old and ill as he leant back in his chair, the waistband of his trousers pulled half-way up his chest by the hidden scarlet suspenders he always wore. There was a butter stain from the turbot on his tie, which would put him in an even darker mood when noticed.

'She's by far the nicest woman I know,' Charlie concluded triumphantly.

'Oh dear, oh dear!'

Charlie blessed his sense of duty in wading through Uncle Hector's monograph on the family one rainy afternoon in the wasteland between lunch and tea just before Merriweather's back had given out. It had afforded valuable ammunition. In the eighteenth century, Laura St Clair had married her mother's nephew, Theo Culverston. They'd had six children, one of whom had been his great-great-great-uncle.

He began, 'As you know, my great-great-great . . .'

'Yes, yes, yes!' interrupted Uncle Hector a little snappily. 'But it was different then.' He felt for his stick. 'I want to show you something.'

He tottered to his desk between the two big windows and stirred around in a blue and white pot. Then he unlocked a drawer with a small key he'd unearthed and removed a dark red leather photograph album. Scuffed and peeling at the edges, it seemed old rather than well used. He limped over to the sofa and patted the seat beside him. His hands gave off the scent of old rose-petals.

As he opened the book, releasing more faint musty odours, Charlie took in the faded purple ink captions beneath black and white records of a vanished world.

The first elegantly turned scrawl read: 'L. and H., Lavenham, July 1911.' Charlie's grandfather would have been nine years old, his great-uncle seven: solemn little blond boys who bore no resemblance whatsoever to the grizzled old pair of today. They wore pale smocks over loose dark trousers that came half-way down their calves and heavy black boots laced around the ankles.

Uncle Hector turned a page and sighed as he indicated a photograph of a beautiful carefree young man with a little crayon of a moustache. 'Uncle John.'

Charlie knew about this favourite uncle, who'd set off so eagerly to fight for his country and returned in a coffin. Lionel and Hector were fortunate indeed to have been children, at the time. As it was, they'd been caught up in the Second Great War, and one had only just survived.

Uncle Hector turned the page and gave Charlie another poignant meaningful glance. This photograph was a head and shoulders studio portrait of a young girl of about sixteen. Charlie absorbed long hair caught up in a loose chignon, an egg-shaped face with matt pale skin, large dark eyes and thin well-defined lips. She wore a formal high-necked dress with big sleeves, a pair of drop pearl earrings. *Wouldn't kick her out of bed,* he decided.

His great-uncle was waiting for his reaction.

'Lovely,' he offered politely.

'Must have ordered her not to smile . . .' Uncle Hector made his characteristic 'Ha!' sound.

Over the page were more photographs of the same girl – executing a backhand shot at tennis in a decorous knee-length pleated white dress, seated on a veranda in flowery cotton and a straw hat – and beneath was written 'N., Lavenham, 1916.'

'Your sister,' said Charlie. He'd guessed straight away.

'Nancy.' Uncle Hector confirmed, voice clotted with tenderness and regret.

Charlie had only ever before seen one photograph of his great-aunt. It was tucked away in another album at his grand-parents' and she wore a hat so you couldn't see her face clearly. But then, people of that generation didn't seem to keep photographs around – unlike his mother, who had even placed montages of her family in the guest lavatories.

He studied the images more carefully. Women seemed so blank and coy, in those days. In one group shot, the girl stared deadpan at the camera while Lionel and Hector looked tortured by inappropriate mirth. Did people laugh at different things, then? Charlie sensed pandemonium. The photographer pleading with his subjects from under his black cloth? Stern parents hovering in the background?

'She had everything. Oh yes! She was the most beautiful funny creature there ever was.'

'Funny?' Charlie echoed, surprised. But, then, his great-aunt had died so long ago. He knew virtually nothing about her.

'AND CLEVER,' said Uncle Hector immediately, in case Charlie should mistake her for frivolous. 'Nancy had a far better brain than Lionel or me. She could have done anything she put it to. Anything! Oh, she could have been a brilliant advocate, even though there weren't any women at the bar then. Nancy might have changed all that! But she wasn't interested in the law. No, *she* wanted to be a writer. So she won a scholarship to Oxford to read English. Remember, this was just after the Great War! She had everything.' Then his face changed: the pride crumbling away, eroded by sadness.

'Why didn't *you* write about her?' asked Charlie, honestly surprised.

'Write about Nancy?'

'Yes, in your monograph.' After all, he'd devoted half a page about a damning (but unpublished) indictment of Darwin that a Cecil St Clair had made in 1860; and even more to a Rupert St Clair more than a quarter of a century on, who'd battled successfully for a Conservative seat only to be forced to resign because of a marital indiscretion (Uncle Hector had phrased this very tastefully). But all that his monograph revealed about Great-Aunt Nancy was her dates – 1900–1925. She'd never married, which might have been surprising. But, then, by the time she reached marriageable age, there were so few young men left.

Uncle Hector looked very sad and also strangely ashamed. Then he began to crank himself up from the sofa again ('No, no, no!' he protested quite irritably when Charlie offered to help), stumbled to the window on his stick and pulled back the curtains. 'When I say she had everything . . .' His voice tailed away as he stared out into the darkness.

The fire crackled in the grate but the room still felt chilly. Charlie finished off his port. His brain was fuddled from all the alcohol. At the same time, he had the growing conviction that this was to be as real a conversation as the one a few nights earlier when Uncle Hector had confessed to disliking his own father. Intimate discussions were rare in their family. Perhaps something even more significant would emerge. Why else had his great uncle been gearing himself up all day?

'Sometimes, even now, I can't believe she's gone.' Uncle Hector sounded miserably bewildered. 'She was so alive . . .' His voice petered away once more.

'So she just had a heart attack one day, did she?' Charlie prompted very gently, trying to appreciate how hard it must be to relive the heartbreak, even though his great-aunt had died almost half a century before.

Abruptly, Uncle Hector turned round. 'No.'

'No?' echoed Charlie blankly. Then why had this piece of information become family lore? '*Your Great-Aunt Nancy died of a heart attack when she was only twenty-five. It was a great tragedy . . .*' He couldn't even remember when he'd first been told or by whom.

Uncle Hector pulled the curtains to with a harsh rasping sound like a sob. 'If only it *had* been her heart . . .' he said to Charlie's astonishment.

He wobbled back to the sofa, sank down on it, put his head in his hands. Charlie touched him on the shoulder for support and comfort but he didn't seem to notice: he who treasured signs of affection from those he loved.

Charlie waited with a growing sense of unease.

His great-uncle began to speak in stumbling half-finished sentences. 'That lovely innocent brilliant girl . . . And she was so frightened – I could see it in her eyes . . .'

Suddenly Charlie felt utter terror himself. He sensed the power of the darkness outside like a black glove threatening to enfold and stifle the house set on its own in the countryside.

'She didn't know what was happening,' Uncle Hector went on, 'and I believe she felt it coming . . . So determined and unforgiving . . . Lying in wait for her . . . pursuing her . . . Oh, it was the most cruel and wicked thing imaginable . . .'

Charlie's eyes suddenly opened very wide in shock. Incredible, but he believed he'd got it! Nancy had been murdered! This was surely what Uncle Hector was getting at. A savage loony had stalked her: an obsessive. It explained why she'd been airbrushed into obscurity. A murder wouldn't fit into a family like theirs.

'Paranoid schizophrenia,' said Uncle Hector very decisively, as if he'd guessed at Charlie's direction and decided to nip it sharply in the bud. 'From *skhizein* – to split – and *phren* – mind,' he added from sheer force of habit, though well aware Charlie had had a classical education, too.

The medical term seemed inappropriate in that big old-fashioned room with its drifting elusive scents of wax and faded flowers, its grand heirloom furniture and fine worn furnishings. Charlie didn't even know what it meant beyond some fairly extreme form of mental instability.

'So your sister went . . .?'

Uncle Hector nodded with panic-stricken eyes, stopping Charlie before he could spell out the shame even though it would surely make no difference now.

'So how did she . . .?'

A deep, deep sigh. 'Oh, Charlie!'

'Don't talk about it if you'd rather not,' urged Charlie kindly. But he had gone pale.

'We must!' All of a sudden, Uncle Hector had become very stern. Courage and discipline were, after all, the twin planks of his ideology. And, besides, after hours of procrastination, he'd finally come to the point. The family secret was out.

As his great-uncle told the story – stopping every so often as if his whole system needed to take this very gradually – the pieces of the past started to shiver into place for Charlie.

Nancy had never been in this house, of course. It had all happened at Lavenham: that old feather in the cap of the family, long since plucked away. Charlie had once been taken there as a child. 'That was ours,' his father had announced with grim pride as they'd stared at the gloomy intricate edifice like a huge ornate decaying cake iced by a fanatic, the four dried-up fountains, the overgrown gardens and ragged yew hedges. Too fussy to be beautiful, but imposing all right. Charlie remembered being glad they didn't have to live there any more even though his father had behaved as if they'd been robbed. He'd been especially annoyed because the place was about to be turned into a conference centre. He'd snorted with irritation and contempt all the way back to London. Lavenham? Conference centre indeed!

Alcohol and anxiety created a cocktail of unreality. As Charlie listened to his great-uncle, he imagined a third person slipping into the room to listen – the girl in the photograph, very subdued now, slender and shapely in her long white dress, the material rustling softly as she settled in the green chair in the shadows by the fire.

'We accept difference in our family,' said Uncle Hector with a touch of complacency, and Charlie was reminded of some of the relations. There was Claude, of course, and the capricious and foolhardy legal actions that had bankrupted him; and Harriet, who'd spent a lifetime writing mostly unread letters to the family – newsletters, self-introductions to far-flung members, and even (in a bad menopausal patch) the odd poison-pen missive. And there was also Cousin Jamie, a landowner in Scotland, who had erected a large placard in beautiful Gothic script, an invitation as it turned out, beside his massive gates – 'Aliens land here' – before his equally grand neighbours made him take it down.

'Perhaps we admire it in our way,' Uncle Hector ruminated, and appeared oblivious to Charlie's wry expression. (*'Has he forgotten how my father treated me?'*)

However, Nancy had been more different than any family member, before or since, and now Uncle Hector needed to justify her strangeness in the most positive light possible.

'After all,' he went on, 'nobody would achieve anything exceptional if they weren't different. People wouldn't have invented the wheel or composed symphonies or stumbled on the theory of relativity . . . *She* wrote a sonnet when she was eight – AND A JOLLY GOOD ONE IT WAS, TOO! Mmm . . . Ha!'

Nancy might have glanced up through her eyelashes like a sly fawn at that.

'Ah yes, and at thirteen, she wrote a novel,' Uncle Hector continued with a fond smile, exactly as if he'd been prompted. 'It was about vampires: the cleverest wittiest thing you could imagine. And we knew – Lionel and I – that she had us beaten into a cocked hat, that sister of ours. Our parents didn't! They refused to read it. A girl like Nancy writing about vampires! Well, who knows? Maybe they feared for her – even then. We were sent to Eton, of course; and, after that, Cambridge. But she had to fight every step of the way for her education. Oh, indeed!'

It seemed to Charlie that the girl he'd conjured up nodded serenely. That battle was long over.

'I cannot describe to you what fun she was!' Uncle Hector's plump face creased up and his eyes glistened with the memory. 'If I went to a party and wanted to find Nancy, all I had to do was listen for the laughter.'

Charlie thought, '*He could hear then!*' He imagined his great-uncle turning his head (covered with hair in those days) this way and that, like a hunting dog; and Great-Aunt Nancy, sparking away on all cylinders in the dullest of gatherings.

'She saw through people. But she wasn't cruel. She was the kindest human being I've ever known. She'd notice if a person was upset almost before he knew it himself. It was as if she possessed some extra quality denied others. An enchantress.' He repeated the word like a comfort and its lovely syllables settled into the silence like the scent of briefly disturbed old rose-petals.

Uncle Hector attempted to fling his real leg over his false one, as if back in his undamaged youth, and winced with pain and his mood shifted. 'Maybe it was always there – ticking away like the damned mine that tore this off.' He rapped at the hard artificial surface, like someone knocking on the door of a long vacant house.

'For a time,' he went on sadly, 'I was obsessed with finding out as much as I possibly could about the condition. I was haunted, you see, by the fear that I could have done more. I had this idea that if she'd gone in for a calm life – husband, children – that might have stopped it from happening. I thought if she'd been encouraged more in that direction . . .' He sighed. 'She was engaged twice, you know. Good matches, too.'

'What happened?'

'Oh, it was she who ended it both times. Heart-breaker!'

'So she didn't want to get married.'

Uncle Hector shrugged. 'Perhaps she hadn't met the right man yet. Or maybe she sensed she shouldn't marry.'

Charlie sat very still on the sofa. He thought he could feel his head buzzing. Whose decision had it been to keep quiet about this? Had a family conference been called by his great-grandparents? Had they sworn his great-uncle and grandfather, then in their early twenties, to secrecy? It had hardly been Nancy's fault.

'Why did everyone say it was heart?'

Uncle Hector silenced him with a gesture, patted him on the

shoulder as an afterthought. He was steeling himself to describe the end.

'In retrospect,' he said, 'she'd been behaving oddly for weeks ...'

It seemed to Charlie that the shade of Nancy nodded sadly by the fire. It was true. Actually it was quite an understatement.

'That day at lunch ... she was talking about *Satan*!' Uncle Hector made a despairing, miserable face and Charlie believed he could picture it all: the formally set table in the enormous cold dining-room overlooked by family portraits, the dismal food offered round by servants and the desultory obligatory conversation prohibiting religion and politics (and, God forbid, sex!) Nancy, who'd shamed her parents with two broken engagements to eligible men, had been packed home from London like a child, said Uncle Hector, because other people had noticed the odd behaviour, too. There she was – that gifted sensitive girl – striving her hardest to behave normally, he told Charlie indignantly, when all the time the voices in her head were cutting across the decorous chitter-chatter about gardens and social engagements and suchlike. She informed her family with tears in her eyes that she was Satan's child. Her crime was stealing souls, she explained, and she must be punished. They pretended it wasn't happening, at first. They went on talking resolutely about other things. Her mother actually said in her precise way, 'We might all have a game of croquet this afternoon if the weather holds.' Then her father said stiffly, as if he'd reluctantly come to a decision, 'Nancy, go to your room.'

After that, said Uncle Hector, they had continued to behave as if nothing was amiss, though his mother had looked very troubled. But it was he who – once the interminable meal was over – had stolen upstairs to find Nancy. Lionel, their father's favourite, had stayed behind. Lionel was like them, said Uncle Hector, in so far as he was able to see only what he wished.

Nancy was pacing her pretty girlish room: pale mauve, he remembered, with the panelling picked out in white and gauzy hangings round the bed. The old-fashioned setting didn't fit with her brand new London look – the bobbed hair that had so appalled her mother, the pleated tunic dress. She was smoking, of course: one of her clandestine Egyptian cigarettes.

'What's wrong, Sis?'

'Get back!'

But this wasn't addressed to him. His spaniel, Troy, had followed him, as usual, a trembling tan and white shadow.

She loved all animals. (As a child, she'd taken a brief passionate stand against eating meat, but their nanny had made her sit in front of her plate of cold food hour after hour until she recanted.) Now, however, she seemed genuinely terrified.

'It's Troy!' He picked up his pet, who nuzzled his face. 'Just the same dear old fellow as ever was.'

She shook her head violently. Her dark eyes were full of panic, and he could see patches flowering in sympathy under the armpits of her dress and smell the perspiration. But why be afraid of Troy? She knew as well as he that the dog was the gentlest of creatures.

Her room was a mess. It had been tidied only that morning by servants but now there were books strewn all over the floor – one of them, he noticed, Rousseau's *Confessions*, the spine forced, the pages crumpled.

'You've spoilt it,' he said, as he picked it up.

She laughed but the sound was harsh and forced. 'Spoilt,' she repeated as if the word appealed to her, even though this was one of her favourite books.

Hector caught sight of his reflection in her long mirror: a plain and serious young man with bushy hair parted in the middle, a nondescript nose and eyes set too close. No wonder, he thought, that his parents had found it hard to love him. But having Nancy as a sister had made up for all that.

'You have to understand, Charlie, that people looked up to us!'

Charlie stared into his great-uncle's anxious, guilty eyes. '*So?*'

'We had a responsibility to society – our parents *impressed* it on us.'

'*What's changed?*' thought Charlie. He felt sad and weary, strangely old.

'How could they have admitted there was anything wrong with Nancy's mind? Or told people what happened after that? They mustn't be blamed . . .'

Hours later, Charlie lay in bed unable to sleep, listening to the creaking settling noises of the old house round him. A wind was getting up outside and he imagined the multitude of leaves on the cedar shaking and shivering as if the tree knew of its imminent fate. He could feel a rough darn in the linen sheet under the small of his back, through his pyjamas, and smell the starch in the top sheet tucked over the blankets under his chin – but all these sensations were experienced as if from a distance. Once, he switched on the light and drank a tumbler of stale water from the carafe by the bed, staring into space and feeling his mouth against the glass as if it belonged to someone else.

He couldn't get his head round this but he must try.

Nancy had been sent to a mental institution. Uncle Hector

had informed him in a flat determined voice that the family put out a story that she suffered from a weak heart and had been sent to Switzerland for her health.

'I went to see her once . . . A dreadful place, like a prison . . .' Uncle Hector's mouth trembled with distress. 'I was glad, really, that she was incapable of recognizing me.'

The last day Nancy ever spent at Lavenham, she'd butchered his spaniel Troy. It wasn't her fault, Uncle Hector told Charlie with tears in his eyes. She'd been ordered to do it by the voices in her head. They must have gone on and on at her, he said, until she was beside herself with agitation and anguish: 'Fetch a carving knife from the kitchen. Kill the Devil!' over and over and over again. And after the cruel act was committed, she became a silent shuffling young woman who passively allowed herself to be led away.

In the space of a night, Uncle Hector lost his adored sister and his pet. It wasn't so surprising that he could never bear to look at a dog again. In fact, he was lucky, he'd been informed by a specialist. Although the real Nancy had doted on him, if the disembodied voices had commanded her to, then her alter ego might very easily have killed him instead.

'She died in 1925.'

'That's correct, Charlie.'

'But there was nothing wrong with her health, apart from . . . ! You said so.'

'Nancy was murdered.' Uncle Hector looked very stern, as if this was the only way he could confront the tragic, wicked fact; and Charlie's jaw dropped open because, as it turned out, his original guess had been correct. 'She was attacked by a violent patient. She died about six months after leaving Lavenham.' In answer to Charlie's unspoken question, he went on just as stiffly:

'They told people the treatment hadn't worked.' But then, sounding miserably bewildered and ashamed: 'I think my mother came to believe it.'

Silence fell. Charlie had forgotten to feed the fire and it had sunk to a fragile crust of embers and the room was becoming very cold.

'I'm afraid it's out of the question for you to marry Kitty.'

'Sorry?' Charlie had felt his heart jumping inside his ribcage.

Uncle Hector had explained very patiently that the spectre of psychosis, the rogue gene, the invisible threat to the family, had stopped him from marrying at all. The shock of witnessing what happened to his sister had been so extreme, the terror of such a thing recurring was too great. But Lionel had gone ahead, even though Hector had implored him at least to warn Eleanor. ('You must!' he'd have urged, thought Charlie – just as he'd been seen to do nearly half a century later, at the end of his birthday party.) Lionel was lucky in his temperament, said Uncle Hector, somehow managing to sound both wistful and judgemental. It was he who'd spent a lifetime of watching and fearing, wondering if or when the terrifying illness would show up next.

'I'll chance it,' said Charlie with a boldness he did not feel. After all, his grandfather had gone ahead and created a family ... And the decision had been justified, hadn't it? Nothing had happened!

'It's not as simple as that, dear boy,' said Uncle Hector, looking even unhappier. If two St Clair first cousins wed, he explained, then the risk of their children developing the condition could only increase. He was sorry. Such a marriage might have been acceptable in the eighteenth century, but it was quite out of the question now. 'And besides ...' He shook his head, looking down into his lap, didn't finish the sentence.

'*Does he think I might have it?*' thought Charlie. '*Is that another reason he's told me all this?*'

The fear had stopped him in his tracks. Was what had happened to him – a momentary loss of control almost certainly caused by overwork – really so serious? For the rest of the evening, he'd found himself behaving with elaborate care, painfully conscious of getting each gesture and word precisely right. Could a mad person (who'd never really cooked until ten days ago) have produced a delicious three-course dinner? Would a sane person have imagined he saw a long-dead relative crouching in the shadows?

But alone in his bed, still dazed with shock and alcohol, he thought he began to discover a strange new freedom. '*If I am going off my trolley,*' he decided, '*then I'm going to do what I want. And even if I'm not allowed to marry Kitty and have children with her, there's nothing to say we can't have an affair. It was pretty nice the other night, actually.*'

Then Charlie thought sadly and very sanely, '*No, I can't do that to Kitty. I know better than anyone how vulnerable she is and it wouldn't be fair. What I ought to do is end it without hurting her feelings too much or revealing anything.*' For hadn't Uncle Hector impressed on him that the story of Nancy must continue to be kept secret? 'I've entrusted this to you,' he'd said very solemnly and Charlie understood that even his own parents must remain in ignorance of the truth. He could sort of see the point. His father would over-react for sure and then his mother would get in a state, too. The fact was, Great-Aunt Nancy had gone stark staring bonkers and been murdered and nobody had ever said a word. It was a very great deal to take in.

However, the discussion had resulted in one firm resolution, at least. *'I'm abandoning the law. I'd rather do almost anything else. I'm just going to have to face my dad and he'll have to accept it.'*

 Chapter Twenty-eight

If Suki hadn't been so preoccupied, she might have taken the surprise visit of Camilla's housekeeper more seriously. As it was, she was still worrying about Uncle Hector's booming unequivocal telephone call early that morning: 'I WOULD LIKE SIMON TO DINE WITH ME AT THE TRAVELLERS TONIGHT. MAKE SURE HE'S THERE AT SEVEN THIRTY SHARP WILL YOU, DARLING?'

'Mrs Win'low-Carter?'

'Sorry, Philomena. You were saying . . .'

They were sitting in the kitchen and it was even more of a mess than usual, with newspapers and letters strewn all over the table, smears on the wooden surfaces, breakfast still not properly cleared away. Suki felt sufficiently embarrassed and ashamed to tell Philomena a whopping untruth: 'I'm afraid my cleaning lady didn't turn up this week.'

Even Simon had started commenting on the neglected state of the house. But these days, Suki felt as if there was a lump of matter in her head that blocked off all energy and real thought. Most of the time, she just sat passively, hoping for enlightenment so she could at last understand what had happened to her marvellous husband, her perfect marriage.

'*Wish I had a housekeeper!*' She wondered resentfully how it might feel to be a person who never had to scrub a lavatory or wipe the toothpaste marks off a basin or peer under beds for disgusting old yoghurt pots and balls of forgotten underwear.

Sitting at the table, the housekeeper looked very neat and trim in her dark blue two-piece made out of some artificial material, her shiny black hair pinned up in a bun. She wore a red enamel brooch in the shape of a peacock on her left lapel and Suki found herself idly wondering who had given it to her. How old was Philomena? Thirty-five? Forty? Did she have an admirer? Or had the brooch been a present from her family? Did she even have family? Suki knew so little about her. She'd been with Camilla and Anthony for about a year now. They'd always had a high turnover in domestic staff, for some reason.

'Biscuits!' Suki exclaimed with a sudden false smile, as if really concerned to make Philomena feel welcome, and she found four flabby flapjacks in a tin and laid them out on a plate under the black incurious gaze of her sister's servant.

'So?' she went on encouragingly, thinking of all the jobs she should be doing and feeling a little irritated by Philomena, even though she'd only have sat there in a trance otherwise. It was noon. Why wasn't Philomena in the house in Eaton Square, ministering to Camilla?

Camilla was probably only just getting up, she thought – snatching a slightly irritated glance at her watch – and then she'd have the arduous task of deciding what to wear. Suki looked down at her own flowery dress that was at least five years old and none too clean. There was a whole pile of washing that needed doing, dumped on the floor by the machine. Philomena had probably noticed that, too.

After Camilla had had a long soak in one of her exquisite bathrooms, she'd prink and pamper herself at her dressing-table. Then there'd be lunch in an expensive restaurant with similarly idle and rich women and a bit of shopping, or maybe even some grand occasion like Ascot Ladies' Day.

'*I can't remember the last time I went to Ascot! I can't even remember when it is!*' Suki made a sudden involuntary face as she compared their two lives and, sitting opposite, Philomena looked a little taken aback.

'Mrs New'am, she very busy, Mrs Win'low-Carter,' she said, as if replying to an unspoken question.

'Sorry?' said Suki, frowning a little irritably.

'Very busy,' Philomena confirmed with a little smile as if she'd made a joke.

'In what way?' Suki didn't mean it to sound quite so sarcastic. But she couldn't imagine why Philomena had said such a thing.

'She no sleep.'

Suki failed to be struck by the strangeness of this reply. 'As a matter of fact,' she said with a tight smile, 'I can't sleep either.'

Philomena was thinking about all the activity that went on during the night at Eaton Square – the running of baths at dawn and the tramping up and down the stairs and the telephoning. Sometimes it sounded to her, huddled in her basement quarters, as if several people still occupied the main part of the house.

'I come from bed in nightdress,' she informed Suki solemnly. 'I say, "I make cup of tea for you, Madam," but Madam she tell me, "Go away, Philomena."' The housekeeper stared at Suki, her almond-shaped eyes quite blank, as if her employer's rudeness had washed over her.

'*Wish I had someone offering to make me tea in the middle of the night.*' Suki thought of staring up into the darkness, hour after hour, mind churning with anxiety as she listened to Simon snoring serenely beside her. '*How can he sleep so well?*' Did it signify that he was a shallow person, unable to appreciate the enormity of what he had done? After all, he'd expressed no proper contrition. He was carrying on in his usual insouciant well-bred fashion, as if he honestly believed the whole problem would eventually go away.

'*I'm being impolite,*' thought Suki rather guiltily and pulled herself together. 'My sister's been through a bad time,' she said. 'I dare say she's lonely. It's understandable, isn't it?'

It was the most she was prepared to say to Philomena on the subject of Camilla's marriage problems and Max's defection. Besides, servants knew every detail of what went on in a house – which was exactly why, in spite of her grumbles about having to do all the housework, Suki didn't really want one herself.

'*If only she realized the trouble we're in,*' she thought wearily, very thankful that Philomena didn't.

Philomena was thinking that Mrs Winslow-Carter's cleaner should scrub the tiles behind the sink with bleach and wipe down the chrome taps above the sink with lemon juice. That sort of attention to detail made all the difference. But in spite of the mess and dirt, this house had a far warmer atmosphere than her employer's. She liked the traces of family everywhere: the old sweater slung across the end of a radiator, the food-spotted recipe books piled in a corner. And when a stray cat wandered proprietorially through the French windows it occurred to her that nothing ever came into the house in Eaton Square by chance.

She was wishing she could tell Mrs Winslow-Carter what had happened the day before. It was out of the question, of course, because her own behaviour had been so unethical. She was not paid to spy on her employer. Somehow or other, she had to let Mrs Newnham's sister know what was going on without laying herself open to blame.

'Another cup of tea?' Suki inquired, even though Philomena hadn't yet touched the first. It was a polite way of suggesting it was time to go – because it seemed the servant would never get to the point. Perhaps there wasn't one. Philomena's mores were bound to be very different. *'Is it the Philippines she comes from?'* thought Suki, with a little frown. Perhaps Philomena had simply decided it was time for a social call.

However, there were far more important things to think about. Maybe Uncle Hector had finally come up with a solution to their problems. Perhaps that was what the dinner at the Travellers was about. She longed to believe it. She smiled a little painfully and saw Philomena, opposite, look down at her lap as if taken aback and confused.

Madam possessed enormous wardrobes. They were the size of small rooms and packed with beautiful dresses and suits; and there were round boxes for exquisite ornate hats and cotton bags to protect her numerous pairs of handmade shoes. And yet, when she went out for the day now she invariably wore the same clothes – a pair of Mister Max's jeans, one of his hooded tops and scuffed old sneakers (which probably belonged to him, too).

Philomena thought she understood the reason for this. It was a magic spell. Mister Max had gone away so Madam was recreating him in spirit to comfort herself and perhaps entice him back. Poor lonely Madam. In the space of a few weeks she'd lost the master (who'd always been a kindly employer) and Mister Max. No wonder she couldn't sleep.

But it was strange because, before setting off so early on her mysterious expeditions, Madam certainly considered dressing as befitted her wealth and station. When she'd left the house, Philomena would find lovely garments strewn all over the bed in the master bedroom, in among the telephone directories and address books. The clothes would be inside out and crumpled and smelling of perspiration. She'd imagine Madam turning her tall white body with its big feet and hands this way and that in front of the long gilt mirror, as if in search of her true self, too.

'I expect you're kept very busy, aren't you, Philomena?' Suki inquired a little testily.

There was so little to do in the grand house in Eaton Square these days; no meals to cook, because Madam had no appetite, so the stove never even got greasy. The house stayed neat and clean, too, though it looked bare without the usual flowers. There were no visitors to bring in dust.

True, there was tidying up after Madam, who spread chaos

like a whirlwind, pulling towels off the rails in her bathroom, scattering powder all over her dressing-table and covering sheets and sheets of paper with her surprisingly neat handwriting, only to screw them up and throw them in the wastepaper baskets.

She was very fit. Yesterday, Philomena had had to struggle to keep up – she on her short little legs, Madam taking great long strides. Occasionally, Madam showed her profile in Mister Max's black hood and, very fearful of discovery, Philomena would catch glimpses of her scarlet mouth moving. She was well aware that her employer sometimes talked to herself. She'd hear her in the middle of the night holding a passionate, but one-sided conversation as she roamed the house.

Suki said: 'I'm sorry, Philomena. But I do have an awful lot to do today. Was there something in particular you wanted to talk to me about?'

They'd walked all the way from Knightsbridge to Tooting (Philomena knew because she saw a big sign with an arrow after the strange name): past a barracks where soldiers wheeled and marched behind railings, and over the great fast-flowing river; past increasingly run-down houses with peeling paint and under railway bridges and across a great green sweep of common where dogs bounded and fishermen were stationed by muddy ponds.

She'd have liked to stop for a moment and rest on a bench. But Madam never slowed down once or even hesitated, so Philomena could only conclude that the journey was very familiar.

Finally, after more decaying streets, they reached a place of markets that reminded her of home: where cheap dresses were slung on rails and fruits and vegetables were piled in profusion on barrows and men shouted at the crowd as they tried to sell to them. It had been strange for her, seeing her employer in this entirely different setting. It made her less afraid of discovery because, suddenly, there were many people who were as dark-skinned and dark-haired as she. So she stole right up behind Madam to try and discover more.

She seemed to be talking all the time now. But Philomena – who had experienced her employer's remoteness – was shocked to hear how angry she sounded. Trailing in her wake, she couldn't make out the sense of the jabber jabber jabber – only the fury. As if Philomena were Madam herself, she perceived the reactions of the people who approached. Their faces seemed to change as they took in the situation: became first knowing and then shut off, as if they wanted nothing to do with this.

Madam suddenly shouted something with great force and Philomena couldn't even see to whom it was addressed.

They were outside a big greengrocer's stall and the owner (an Indian) said, while continuing deftly to arrange a pile of glossy aubergines, 'You please watch your mouth, lady.'

And another person, not nearly so polite, snarled, 'Get back to the funny farm.'

Philomena had puzzled over this. How could a farm be funny? In her country, they were deadly places. She would have liked to be able to ask Mrs Winslow-Carter. But this was not possible, of course.

It was strange the way she hadn't asked her a single question about Mrs Newnham. She presented a baffling mixture of dreaminess and impatience. You'd think she'd be grateful that her sister's housekeeper had come all the way from Belgravia – and on her day off, too.

Philomena's conscience was clear. While registering her own concern and unhappiness, she'd delivered an explicit warning. Tomorrow, without a word to Madam, she'd pack up her belongings and leave. And the family would be unable to claim that she hadn't behaved like a good and faithful servant.

 Chapter Twenty-nine

Tom knew about police statements, of course – it was part of his job. Even so, he was getting unreasonably irritated by the length of time this one was taking, and also its traditional and sometimes ludicrously unsuitable language. He glanced at his brother-in-law, relieved he was holding up so well. He looked weary – after all, they'd been there for more than two hours now – but he spoke to Detective Inspector Dodd very clearly and even quite authoritatively. *'Like a proper St Clair,'* thought Tom, with a touch of pride overlaying the exasperation and anxiety.

'That's right,' Simon agreed in his familiar self-assured manner, and took a sip of the tea he'd been given, now sadly cold. 'I loaded the cars up and drove them down to the West Country all by myself.' And he actually gave a tiny smile, as if – despite the horror of his present situation – he remained proud of the feat.

The Detective Inspector addressed his notebook. 'I conveyed the said vehicles to the West Country by means of a transporter I had assumed sole charge of, without the aid of an accomplice.'

Tom snorted but, as an afterthought, blew his nose to make it appear harmless. It was as if Becky were there in spirit, reining him in, warning him to keep his cool for Simon's sake.

'And you are . . .?' Detective Inspector Dodd had asked him without great interest.

'Mr Winslow-Carter's brother-in-law, Tom St Clair.' He added, without hesitation, 'Q.C.' And then, from long force of habit, 'That's St Clair – two words – not Sinclair. Shall I spell it for you?' Let this officious policeman know he was dealing with a family who knew what was what – even if it afforded private amusement that they might soon have a jailbird in their midst.

He couldn't act as Simon's lawyer himself, of course, but he'd arranged for a bright spark in a chambers run by a trusted friend to do the job. He could always stick his professional oar in discreetly, from a distance. As he watched the young man absorb the situation very efficiently without displaying the slightest hint of bias, he thought of his son Charlie with both wistfulness and anger.

The evening before, he'd discovered that, instead of making a start on his legal work, Charlie had become the cook at Cedar Manor. Uncle Hector hadn't meant to give this away but they'd just finished dinner. Roast beef with onions and carrots and roast potatoes, he'd informed his nephew proudly, followed by treacle tart with custard. Tom could hear the relish in his voice though, immediately afterwards, he'd gone, 'Ha!' as if to cancel out the information.

COOKING? Tom snorted once more. He'd had a great deal to say to Becky on the subject.

'Sorry,' he said as he pulled out his handkerchief.

Tom's first inkling of the fix his brother-in-law was in had come the previous evening with a summons to dinner at the Travellers. There'd been no advance notice. 'Top priority,' Uncle Hector had warned without going into details: meaning, all other engagements must be cancelled, which, in his case, meant a long-planned and much-looked-forward-to evening at Middle Temple Hall. Family orders, thought Tom. They didn't come often but, when they did, you were obliged to jump to attention.

When he arrived at the club, he found his father and his uncle huddled in armchairs in the library, talking intently over glasses of Scotch as if they'd been there for some time. Tom caught a brief snatch of the conversation before they became aware of him.

'He took it very well, considering,' he heard his uncle boom.

'And you're *quite* sure he won't say anything?'

'Who won't say anything?'

'Ah, Tom!' They both looked unreasonably startled and his father said a little too quickly, and nervously: 'Nobody you know.'

Tom let it go. 'Simon not here?'

'Not yet.'

This hadn't been arranged on purpose. In fact, Tom was always too early and Simon often ran late. So there was just time for Uncle Hector to sketch in the situation, pausing impatiently while the waiter brought another glass of whisky and set it out with the usual ceremony.

Tom was astounded. 'Simon?' he kept repeating. He got

along well enough with his brother-in-law but had always held him in faint contempt. He was so laid back about everything. And why couldn't he have made more of a success of that garage, anyway? But this extraordinary foolhardiness showed there was more to Simon than he'd ever suspected.

He could feel the dropping-jawed goggle-eyed expression still pasted to his face when Simon sauntered in, as dapper and poised as ever. But he pulled himself together and briskly shook his brother-in-law's hand, while trying to hide his real thoughts. (*'He must have been out of his mind to think he could get away with it! What in hell is this going to do to <u>my</u> reputation? <u>And</u> he still looks cool as a cucumber!'*)

'I say, how nice!' said Simon, his brain whirling. He hadn't expected his father-in-law and Tom to be there. All he knew from Suki was that Hector had invited him for dinner in a tone that brooked no argument. For once, he hadn't cherished an invitation to the club, having no doubt what the agenda would be.

'What will you drink?'

Simon appeared to consider for a moment, then smiled most charmingly at the hovering waiter and said in his languid imperious way that gave no hint of what he was really thinking: 'D'you know, I think I'll have a Scotch and soda, too.'

Silence fell. It was if each person was waiting for another to begin. But for all his usual confidence, Tom knew that, this time, he must hold back. It was his elders who'd organized the meeting. They must play it as they chose.

'Nice weather,' said his father gruffly. 'Thinking of spending the weekend fishing.'

'Where?' asked his uncle.

'My own water, of course.' He sounded exasperated. Where else? Unlike Hector, he was lucky enough to have a trout stream running through his garden.

'Thought it was all clogged up with weed,' commented Hector through sheer force of habit.

'Are we ready to eat?' asked Lionel, cutting off the familiar sparring. He wanted to catch the ten o'clock train back to Hampshire, if possible.

After Hector had written down their orders on a pad – according to the tradition of the club – and handed it back to the waiter (who would have made a far quicker and more legible job of it), Simon surprised them all.

'I say, I really have been the most frightful ass, haven't I?' But he raised his eyebrows mockingly and gave a self-deprecating smile as he said it, effectively hiding his terror of his father-in-law, almost as if treating the whole thing as a joke. He now realized Lionel must have been told the full story about the missing cars, even though Suki had assured him that very morning this was impossible. What was more, he could tell from the way Tom was looking at him that he knew about it, too. Had Eleanor been informed, as well? But even as his mind skittered away in panic from this scenario, Simon was almost certain she had not. The family hid things from her.

'We're not here to go into that,' Hector told him a little pompously. He tasted the claret he'd ordered, said a little testily to the wine waiter, 'Yes, yes, that'll do.'

'Well, actually . . .' Tom began after four glasses had been poured and the waiter had departed.

But Hector quelled him with a look.

'We're here to help you – and darling Suki, of course,' he told

Simon very kindly. 'To work out what's best. And we're going to come up with something. That's the whole purpose of this family meeting.'

It was amazing what they came up with over leek and potato soup and roast partridge. One part of Simon could only listen, astonished and faintly amused. But he was aware, of course, that it wasn't only his reputation that was at stake.

'It's a pity we can't pay Fortescue off,' ruminated Tom as he bit into a game chip. He gave his savage smile. 'Get him to hang on to the cars – for ever, if need be – for a price. Make him an offer he can't refuse.' The phrase was familiar, somehow. He frowned as he tried to remember where he'd heard it.

'Unfortunately, it doesn't sound as if he needs the money,' said Lionel, slicing into a piece of bacon while studying it intently through his thick spectacles. It was said in exactly the same jocular way – as if it wasn't really them, two distinguished members of the legal profession, discussing this matter.

'Could we perhaps collect the cars and take them off somewhere?' suggested Hector, who hadn't even heard the last suggestion properly. 'That big place of Jamie's up in Scotland . . . He'd never even notice. Man's blind as a bat.'

Lionel glanced round with the brutal expression that, as usual, signified profound concentration. But it appeared that none of the other diners were listening. 'Those cars have been reported stolen,' he warned. 'The police have the licence numbers. They'll be watching out for them.'

'It's a risk,' admitted Hector, who'd managed to extract the essence of what his brother had said by studying his mouth, shiny with fat.

'Then what?'

'Burn them,' said Hector decisively.

'Cars aren't bodies,' said Tom dismissively. 'Not that bodies are that simple to get rid of, either,' he went on authoritatively.

'What's that?'

Tom shook his head, looking ferocious. He was hardly about to repeat at top volume what he'd just said.

'What sort of person is this friend of yours?' Lionel wanted to know.

'Fortescue?' Simon frowned and caressed his chin as he conjured up his fellow Harrovian. 'Not really a friend . . . Not any more . . . Outdoor man. Excellent oarsman, I remember.' He gave his charming smile. 'Fine cricketer, too.'

'You haven't answered the question,' said Tom, as tersely as if he were in his black robes and horsehair wig.

'Sorry!' Simon smiled again, a little ruefully. 'Perfectly decent sort of fellow. Well, mind you, the sort of background he comes from . . .'

'What in God's name possessed you?'

Hector was craning forward, trying to follow the conversation through his earpiece, which was already fighting a jabber of noise from the other diners. What was Tom saying to Simon now? He'd been afraid of this. Tom was a natural bully. It partly explained why he'd made such a good barrister. But it was true that he had every right to be angry on his own account. It was all the more reason why the three of them had to come up with a solution.

Simon put down his knife and fork with a clatter, even though he'd not finished his partridge, which he adored. He looked quite different, suddenly: terrified and vulnerable. 'I don't know,' he stammered. 'I must have gone crazy to have inflicted this on Suki and the children.' He was almost in tears. 'That's what it was – a moment of complete and utter madness.' He attempted another grin, but this time it was more like a grimace. 'It's very good of you all to be trying to help us. But it's no use. I'm going to have to turn myself in. There's no way I can get away with this. I see it now.'

And he'd been right, thought Tom. Better to stop the thing in its tracks before it involved anyone else. Insurance scams were bound to fail – especially when they involved enormous unwieldy objects like cars. But his uncle had tried to persuade Simon out of it, even then. He'd suggested painstakingly dismantling the cars and depositing the pieces with relatives all over the British Isles, while his father had listened with his stern expression, which meant he was seriously considering it, too. But by that time Simon was adamant, resigned to his fate, and (though still very angry) Tom could only admire his courage.

The police didn't. To them, Simon was just another foolish person who'd really believed he could cheat the system. A toff, to boot. They'd throw the book at him, if necessary. And serve him right.

 Chapter Thirty

Kitty banged the heavy front door and waited for the usual melodious greeting to come floating up from the kitchen in the basement along with the delicious smell of whatever was being cooked. 'Is that you, Kitty?' – even though she was expected. Besides, this visit was special. Her mother had said so, hadn't she?

But she couldn't have heard.

'Ma?' Kitty called and wondered why her mother didn't reply. 'Tell me it's not true,' she'd begged after Charlie's announcement at the party. But by the following morning, Kitty sensed a sea change. 'Family conference on this,' her mother had warned, but there was a cautious smile in her voice as if it had already been decided which way it would go.

'But I'm not ready for Dad to pop open champagne and Ma to bang on about dresses and receptions,' thought Kitty a little petulantly. She felt

so confused – still cross with Charlie for telling the whole family and horribly embarrassed they all knew – and yet tucked away somewhere was a strange serenity as if a major worry had been removed.

It was a good thing Charlie was in the country, really. 'Lots to tell you,' he'd informed her last night, awkwardness in his voice. He hadn't mentioned their engagement. Well, if there weren't servants rustling about in the background, thought Kitty, there'd be Uncle Hector trumpeting away. 'LONG DISTANCE CALLS COST MONEY!' He was always reminding them.

It took her a few moments to absorb the fact that she could smell only the faint cheesy whiff of Phil's sweaty old plimsolls, slung in a heap by the door, and the house seemed very still. She'd never before felt frightened or lonely in that comforting happy place, but now she dropped her bag on the tessellated floor of the hall and ran downstairs to the kitchen.

To her astonishment, she found her mother sitting at the table. She was staring at a vase of roses and twirling her hair thoughtfully round one finger but didn't seem to have noticed that the flowers had lost all their petals, which lay scattered over a heap of newspapers.

'Didn't you hear me, Ma?'

Immediately her mother jumped up and kissed her. 'Darling!'

'That's not breakfast!' exclaimed Kitty, staring in disbelief at the used cups and plates, the crumbs everywhere.

'Is it?' She sounded as if she was still thinking about something entirely different.

'Ma?'

'Oh dear, I'm afraid I just haven't got round to it yet.'

'Aren't we having supper?' asked Kitty, already clearing the table, wiping it down with a cloth and noticing marks that meant it hadn't been properly scrubbed for days. Come to think of it, the whole place was neglected, even filthy. The stove was covered in grease and the sink was piled with dirty saucepans.

'We'll have a celebration,' her mother had promised on the telephone. 'Well, not *celebration* celebration,' she'd qualified – because the stamp of approval had, after all, yet to be given. 'We do need to talk about this.'

'Supper?' her mother echoed now, looking almost frightened. 'What's the time?'

'Half past seven.'

'It can't be! Of course we're having supper!'

She pulled open the fridge and Kitty noticed how extraordinarily empty it was. There weren't even any bottles, and her parents always drank wine. Even though, a moment ago, she'd been dreading any kind of fuss in her honour, she now felt affronted. What was going on, tonight of all nights, in this house where hospitality and abundance had always ruled?

'Oh dear, there's some cold spaghetti . . . Or I suppose I could do something with this mashed potato, only it's a few days old now . . . And there's a bit of fish, but not quite enough . . . I did mean to go shopping . . .'

Kitty said, trying to keep the hurt out of her voice, 'Dad won't be happy.'

'Dad?' Her mother sounded quite extraordinarily indifferent. 'I'll open a tin,' she went on, even though they all knew he disliked tinned food.

So did Kitty but that seemed irrelevant.

*

He'd left. Either that, or he was about to. He'd found someone else, thought Kitty, with a sharp new contempt, like a bad taste in the mouth, for her beloved father. It was the only explanation, she told herself, remembering Aunt Camilla's revelations about Uncle Ant that terrible evening when Max had been here. Aunt Camilla had insisted she stay and listen, too. 'It'll be instructive,' she'd said. But it had been only horrible for Kitty to learn such things about someone she'd always respected and loved.

How different the kitchen had seemed then: the warm and comforting heart of the house. But now the years of happiness that had given the house its special and welcoming flavour appeared meaningless. Her parents had turned out to be as unreliable as everyone else's.

It occurred to Kitty that her mother had looked exhausted for days. She'd been snappy, too. Even Phil had remarked on it. 'Do you think she's having the change of life?' he'd asked his sister in his wobbly new voice, intrigued and also appalled.

'Is Dad going to be here for supper?'

'Who?' Her mother actually said that. And then she piled a heap of pallid sticky spaghetti on to a dish and seemed to be wondering what to do with it next. After a moment, she reached into a cupboard and brought out a packet of almonds. She studied it thoughtfully before tut-tutting sharply under her breath and substituting it for a tin of tomatoes.

'Dad, Ma! Is Dad going to be here?'

At last she had her mother's full attention. 'Of course Dad's going to be here! Why on earth shouldn't he be?' she went on, sounding sincerely astonished. 'See?' Because, at that moment, dead on time, they heard the door bang up above.

Kitty's spirits lifted – so it was all right, after all – and she
waited for her father's familiar cocky chirpy call: 'Anyone ho-
ome?' But it never came. And then she realized that, even
though her mother looked more unkempt than she'd ever
seen her, she wasn't going to brush her hair or put on
lipstick. This time, she wasn't even going to remove her dirty
apron.

'Family conference,' Kitty reminded her with a forced smile,
as if handing over a bouquet kept hidden behind her back till
now. Let Ma plan away for a wedding to her heart's content, so
long as she started behaving like her old self.

'Yes,' she agreed, looking very alarmed, and – to Kitty's
horror – she actually brushed away a tear.

Phil pronounced: 'But it was so-o dumb!' He sounded more
wondering than shocked – as if, given time and chance, he'd
have thought of a far more effective way of cheating the
system – and Kitty felt a deep pity for her father, having to
endure this. But, though he'd taken his customary place at the
head of the table, he seemed strangely absent. It was her mother
who did all the talking. And meanwhile the cold spaghetti lay on
their plates untouched, like a taste of the real poverty that might
be in store.

Phil loathed the minor public school he'd been sent to. It was
a dump and mere: he was always saying so. Recently he'd even
started affecting that he was a socialist and opposed to private
education. But when warned that he might have to be
transferred to the local comprehensive, he became quite
extraordinarily upset.

'It's not fair!'

'Look, darling, it hasn't come to that yet. And maybe it won't.'

'Why did you say so, then?'

'I'm sorry – perhaps I shouldn't have.' Suki cast a despairing glance at Simon, who was being no support whatsoever. 'I just thought I ought to make the point that every one of us will have to make sacrifices.' She paused as if summoning all her strength. 'But if we pull together as a family we'll get through this nightmare.'

'*He* won't!'

'What *do* you mean, Phil?'

'*He* won't have to make sacrifices!'

'Dad's going to have to be braver than anyone,' Suki informed him earnestly, and seemed not to notice her husband's grimace. 'I think we should all remember that.'

But Phil was far too upset for pity. 'Remember when I stole those humbugs,' he countered in his see-saw voice and Kitty saw her father flinch at the word 'stole'.

'What about it?'

'He stopped my pocket money for a month. He said it was for my own good.'

'It was.'

'I was eight, Mum!' Phil was roaring with the unfairness of it all.

'Oh, Phil!'

'He's the humbug! And he's forty-six!'

'Don't you dare talk to your father like that!'

Phil stamped up the basement stairs like an angry elephant and soon afterwards they heard his bedroom door slam thunderously.

'I'll go,' Kitty offered, longing for the chance to escape and guessing that, for all his bravado, Phil would be inconsolable.

But her mother told her, 'Leave him. I'll talk to him later.' She gave a deep, deep sigh, and then her expression changed. There was the flicker of a smile. Suddenly, it seemed, she'd remembered the original purpose of the evening.

'It *was* a bit of a shock at the time,' she said, 'but Dad and I have had a good talk, haven't we?'

'Yes,' Simon agreed dully. Had he noticed her new habit of pronouncing on something and, only as an afterthought, including him?

'Actually, we've rather come round to it now, haven't we?'

He didn't seem able to look at Kitty any more, which she found even more upsetting than learning about the foolishness and dishonesty.

'It's only the idea that's strange. I mean, heavens, you and Charlie grew up together! But there's nothing to say first cousins can't marry and he's a darling, of course. A most welcome son-in-law – besides being a well-known nephew!' Suki warned: 'I'm afraid you're going to have to put up with lots of jokes like that.' She tried to look amused but only appeared strained. 'I know he's had a bit of a blip but he seems perfectly fine now, doesn't he? He'll go back to his chambers and we're sure he'll do splendidly, aren't we?' She paused before adding a little uncertainly, 'Tom and Becky seem happy about it, too.'

Kitty thought, '*So that's me sewn up.*'

She was silent for a few moments and then she asked very quietly, 'What will you do, Ma?'

'Oh, I'm afraid it'll have to be quite small,' her mother told her with another unhappy smile because, for years and years, she'd looked forward to Kitty's wedding and now, just like everything else, it would have to be dictated by their financial situation. 'It'll probably have to be quite soon, in the circumstances, darling – in fact, the sooner the better, probably, unless . . .'

'*Unless we wait till Dad's come out of prison.*'

'I *am* sorry, darling. You know there's nothing we'd like more than to give you the wedding you deserve. But in the circumstances ... You do see, don't you?'

Chapter Thirty-one

When Kitty returned to Chepstow Place, it was only half past nine. But once the engagement and a possible wedding had been discussed, a profound silence had fallen. She sensed her parents' deep embarrassment, like a wound. It wasn't only she and Phil who'd been let down, of course: it was the whole St Clair family.

Always before, leaving them had felt like shutting the door to a party. However fond their farewells, they made it clear they couldn't wait to get back to the fun. It had accentuated her loneliness, caused her to despair of ever finding a similarly happy set-up herself (which might explain why, until now, her choice of men had been so unwise). But this time she was the guest urged to remain for the sake of the hosts. Even her father had gathered up the shreds of his old energy to plead, 'Do stay a bit longer, Kitty darling.'

She imagined the two of them silent and lost now – together and yet apart, the thread of communication severed – and found herself wondering with a new maturity if a straightforward act of infidelity would have had so devastating an effect.

The lights in the flat were all out but, to her surprise, Max was home. He was slumped in an armchair in the wedge of a sitting-room in his black leather jacket, staring into space. Was it pity he was after, in choosing to show himself so aimless and solitary? To her surprise, she found that she couldn't care less. She felt none of the usual apprehension – just simple exasperation that he, who enjoyed so many advantages, did so little to help himself. '*My father might go to prison.*' It hadn't sunk in yet.

'Where's Liza?' she asked without real curiosity, snapping on the light and thinking how pathetic he was to want to sit in the dark.

Max blinked and shaded his eyes. He seemed quite un-interested.

At that exact moment, Liza was feeling upset and guilty.

It was the first time since her father's death that she'd not thought about him as she walked up the street to their house. The realization had stopped her in her tracks, staying her hand on the latch of the iron gate. It was because of her news, she told herself – feeling so triumphant and certain, at last.

Usually, each sight in the street tripped off another memory, as if her father were preparing her for the house, where there was no escaping him. The overgrown bush in the garden of 24 where he'd once teased her that a tiger lurked; the bad piano music pouring haphazardly out of the open windows of 30

('*Not* the Moonlight again!' he'd groan); the yowling cat still shut out of 39 ('That animal will get run over one day,' he'd prophesied). Mrs Murphy behind her twitching nets at 41, opposite, brought him back too, as did the old man leaning on his gate. 'God help either of us if we ever have an affair,' he'd tell Jane in Liza's hearing because it was a joke and would never happen, of course.

'I'm going to bed,' said Kitty abruptly.

To her amazement, she saw Max look startled and even a little hurt, as if he'd been waiting all evening for this opportunity, even though, for weeks now, he'd taken such pains to avoid her.

'What about your hot drink?' he muttered, which was his way of asking her to stay.

But she shook her head. She'd no intention of discussing her relationship with Charlie, which must be what he was after.

However, to her further astonishment, he asked, 'Is something wrong, Kitty?'

She shook her head even more brusquely. It was because, to her horror, she could feel tears pricking at her eyelids.

He went on with an awkward hunch of his shoulders as if it were painful and also awkward for him to utter such kindnesses: 'If you want to talk . . .' His leather jacket creaked in sympathy.

Kitty was really taken aback. There hadn't been time for the family grapevine to crank into action, surely? Could it be that Max, so famously self-centred, had noticed her distress? No, the truth was that he was unused to being ignored – especially by her – and also capricious. But even as she dully acknowledged the reasons behind this surprising behaviour, she found herself sitting down. Her legs were trembling. The evening had been very upsetting. She said, giving in, 'I think there's a bottle of red in the cupboard. And some candles. Let's have candles.'

The old man across the street had observed Liza's hesitation, her pensive attitude as she stood by the gate.

He'd seen her glance up at the front of the house, too. She'd have noticed, of course, that her mother's bedroom curtains were drawn. But the lights were all out, so she probably assumed nobody was at home. He saw her make a disappointed face. He nodded. He seemed to be waiting for something but, then, he always was. You needed patience to stand outside in most weathers, just watching.

Liza felt impelled to share her wonderful news, even with a stranger. 'I'm going to be in an opera,' she called across the street in her high clear voice.

'Eh?' The old man's face was so deeply weather-beaten that it was hard to identify its expressions.

'*Rigoletto.*'

His lips moved as he repeated the unfamiliar word.

'I got the part! It's only in the chorus, but . . . I've made it!' She added kindly: 'It's about a father who loves his daughter a bit too much,' and a tear pricked her eye. '*Rigoletto,*' she repeated, so he could keep hold of the name.

And then, still smiling graciously, hugging her triumph, she pressed the catch on the gate. She was anxious to see her puppy (which Kitty had refused to allow in the flat). The gate groaned as it dragged across the tiled path. It had come off its hinges the week before her father died and it was her doing that it hadn't been fixed. 'Don't!' she'd begged her mother, as if any change was a disloyalty. It was crazy but something in Liza believed that, if they kept everything exactly as it had been, there was still a chance her father might walk back in.

At the sound of the gate, the puppy started barking inside: but the sound was muffled, distant.

When Kitty had finished her story, Max asked, looking a little scared, 'What'll happen to him now?'

Kitty shrugged with an unhappy smile. 'He's owned up to it so there won't be a trial.'

'Why did he do that?' Max sounded astonished.

'He just – realized he wouldn't get away with it. Uncle Tom told Ma he'd done the right thing.' She swallowed, because it was very painful to have to admit such things about her father. 'He's been charged with attempting to obtain money by deception. He'll come up before the Crown Court in about six months. Uncle Tom says he'll probably get at least eighteen months.'

'In prison.'

Kitty nodded tersely.

'What about, you know, his job?' The soft, flickering light glanced off the pure planes of his face and made his dark eyes with their long lashes even more seductive. But Kitty was beyond all that now.

'He'll lose the garage.' She was only repeating what her mother had told them. ('He'll lose the business, of course . . . Won't you?') What had her father thought on hearing his beloved Pudding (who'd always before deferred to him) spell out his future so unequivocally? He'd never get another job, thought Kitty sadly. For who would employ a middle-aged public school ex-con? Poor old Dad. The garage might have been a dreadful worry to him, especially of late, and unsuitable for a man of his background (as her grandmother was always not so subtly inferring) – but at least he'd been his own boss. It was the sum of his achievements, really.

'What about, you know . . .?' Max, who'd been born into great wealth, could not envisage being without money. He didn't need to finish the sentence. He knew Kitty would understand because suddenly, by some magic, they'd been transported back to the ease and happiness of the past. It was as if none of the terrible upsets in their relationship had ever occurred.

'I asked Ma about that.' Kitty made a face. 'She thought I was talking about the wedding.'

Max frowned. 'You mean, you and Charlie?'

'I suppose.' She felt herself flushing and Max glanced at her a little uneasily as if waiting for her to explain that astonishing development to him, too.

Silence fell.

'I don't know . . .' Kitty began. She couldn't go on because, suddenly, she couldn't believe it had happened, here in this very room: Charlie sitting a few yards from where Max was, she leaning over and kissing him while his familiar and much loved face became more and more alien. '*I can't!*' she thought in a panic. But it was too late to back out now. It seemed the whole family had decided a marriage was a good idea.

Maybe the confusion and anxiety were written on her face because Max reminded her gently: 'You were saying about your ma . . .'

Kitty smiled at him gratefully. After another gulp of wine, she went on, 'She's never had a job. Not even the sort of non-job I have.' She gave a self-deprecating smile. 'And now she's forty-three, nearly forty-four actually, and what's she supposed to do? Oh Max, it sounds so self-centred but I never ever want to find myself in that scary situation. And it's all made me think.'

'Grandpa and Grandma,' he began encouragingly. He was really making an effort.

'I suppose ...' The grandparents were not poor. Of course, they'd step in. They'd never see the family destitute; most likely, they'd pay for Phil to finish his education, too. There'd be a price, though, and, in her heart, Kitty knew what. Her parents' marriage would never recover its legendary happiness. How could it? Everyone would know that her father had deceived her mother: endangered what should have been most precious to him. And nobody would allow them to forget it – however much Uncle Hector stressed that her father had acted for the best of all possible reasons, which was family.

'What did Grandma say?'

Kitty looked blank. It hadn't come up in the conversation with her parents. After a moment, she said: 'She'll probably pretend it's not happening at all.'

'Yes,' Max agreed. 'Or she'll say' – his face changed suddenly, became haughty and full of certainty – "It's going to be quite quite all right."'

'Exactly.'

They beamed at each other but straight afterwards Kitty's eyes filled with tears.

Max silently rummaged in a pocket of his jacket and unearthed a handkerchief.

'Thanks, Cuz.' It didn't smell very nice but she wasn't concerned. Was she laughing or crying? It seemed all the same, somehow.

In the candlelight, Max looked distressed but also eager as if he were struggling to offer even more comfort. She remembered the time he'd made her weep by being unkind – here in this room where so much else had happened – and felt pity, though not for herself. Poor damaged Max, who'd learnt to crush down feeling and even invite rejection so he'd never be hurt or disappointed again. As his lifelong friend who remembered him as a tender and open child, she should have understood.

'Kitty . . . I've found this place I can go to.'

'What sort of a place?' she asked very gently, but at the same time experienced an inexplicable chime of dread. It was like hearing the tall clock in the grandparents' hall sound the hours in the loneliness of the night.

His voice was a little hesitant as if he were still feeling his way. 'Like an island?'

'Go on . . .'

'But in my head.'

Kitty kept her expression very neutral. 'Go on . . .'

'Like, not part of here or anywhere? Somewhere I can get away from things? Somewhere I can just be?'

And then Liza came in.

'What are you doing?'

She took in the evidence of intimacy at a glance: the dark room, the candles and the empty bottle of wine. She hadn't been anticipating this.

'Just talking,' said Kitty with a smile, making an effort to include her.

Liza pouted a little. They didn't know, of course, that she'd just received a massive shock. The memory made her chin wobble but she knew she must not share it. If Max had been alone, she'd definitely have stayed quiet – or so she told herself afterwards.

'It's been nice,' said Max to Kitty's very great pleasure.

She shook her head warningly at him, meaning, '*Please don't say what I just told you*' (because she wasn't ready to tell Liza about her father yet), and Liza caught the look (because nothing escaped her) and took it personally.

It was one of those moments she'd relive forever. Being Liza, she'd justify it. She'd tell herself that Max would most likely have found out sooner or later. But then the mature Liza would catch the questions coming in, unbidden, like static on the radio, all beginning, 'What if?' and 'If only . . .'

'Have I got some gossip!' she exclaimed. Rewriting the evening afterwards, she'd have herself quietly going to bed.

It was the way they'd looked – Kitty pretty and relaxed, Max so handsome in the candlelight and patently enjoying her company. For the second time that evening, Liza found herself in the painful role of the outsider bursting in on a room full of secrets.

'I told you my mother was having an affair!'

They were pretty sure she hadn't. But Liza often played games, and it was typical of her to make a grab for their attention the minute she entered the frame. They stared at her, a little taken aback because she was known to be very protective of her mother.

'Well, you'll never ever guess who with!'

She made it sound cheap and sordid, though she understood very well in her heart it was not.

There'd been an odd scent as she'd opened the front door. Sandalwood? And a brief snatch of music from upstairs, too, before it was abruptly cut off: light schmaltzy stuff her family would have disapproved of, lilting violins and suchlike. And frenzied barking from the puppy, who had indeed been locked in the kitchen for some reason and was extremely glad to see Liza.

And then her mother had come running down the stairs.

'What are you doing here?' she asked, very agitated. Her jumper was back to front, Liza noticed, and she had bare feet.

'I live here, Mum!' Liza replied, though she'd been staying at Chepstow Place for more than a week now. She was cuddling the puppy, which had a thread of something white in its mouth, but sounded very accusing.

'Why didn't you phone?'

'What's going on?' For something plainly was.

Then, to Liza's absolute horror, Uncle Ant appeared at the top of the stairs – also seeming as if he'd dressed in a great hurry – and she saw her mother look quite despairing, as if this would be impossible to explain.

Liza had felt her mouth fall open and her eyes widen in disbelief.

Then her mother took her hand and pulled her, resisting like an angry child, into the sitting-room, and her uncle followed on behind, his shirt buttoned unevenly, sockless in his polished black shoes with the laces trailing.

What he said next was almost funny in retrospect. 'This isn't what it seems.'

Liza saw her mother give him a grateful adoring glance and then the misery kicked in.

'Why didn't you tell me?' she'd found herself demanding crossly.

It had been awful when they'd laughed – with tenderness and indulgence, but genuine amusement too.

'How could we?' There'd been another maddening exchange of fond exclusive glances.

'Yes! How could you!' she'd replied, turning the question back on them.

Then they'd looked at each other, seemingly a little perplexed, as if it had all been quite beyond their control.

'It's disgusting!'

'No, Liza,' her mother informed her with great seriousness, 'the only disgusting thing about this is the way people choose to view it.'

'You're family!' she accused Anthony next.

But he'd corrected her. 'Jane and I are not related, as you know.'

'You're married to my aunt.'

'I am,' he agreed gently, 'but I hope that won't last for ever.'

Liza didn't know, of course, that he'd never said this before. Witnessing her mother's shy delighted beam, she simply assumed that there were numerous other important conversations she'd been excluded from.

She hated her mother to be sad because she loved her. Given time, she might even have accepted Anthony who, she could see, made her very happy. She was one step behind her mother but beginning to let her father go, too. After all, she'd seen the evidence of that just a few minutes before.

'And I had something really nice to tell you, too!' she raged.

The immaturity and jealousy should have finished there, when she turned on her heel and left the house, slamming the door behind her.

But Liza was quite out of control: as if some demon were urging her on.

'What have you done?' exclaimed Kitty, horrified. 'Run after him! Quick!'

'Now?' She was very frightened by this time.

'Now!'

But even then, in the street below, Max's car was starting up with a frantic vroom vroom vroom. Before Liza could reach the front door, it had snarled away into the distance.

'I didn't mean . . .' Liza began, tears in her eyes.

'Didn't you?'

'It's all very well . . .' Liza began, trying to justify herself and also seek comfort.

'No, Liza, it's not. You *know* what Max is like! How could you?' Kitty shivered as she remembered how he'd changed in a trice. Even she, who'd experienced the very worst of him, had never seen him look quite like that – sparking cold black hatred, as if he knew for certain now that he'd never be able to trust anyone ever again. She imagined him spewing out bitterness and filth as he roared through the night, just as he'd done that terrible evening when they'd left her parents. 'Fucking bitches, all of them!' Ram the gear lever up into fourth. 'And as for that fucking fucking bastard!'

'We must go after him!' she said.

'Where?'

'We must go after him,' Kitty repeated. But she'd no idea, either, where Max had gone. Could it be that, at long last, he'd decided to confront his father?

'He'll come back,' said Liza with a pout and a shrug. But when Kitty failed to agree, she repeated, like a frightened child, 'He'll come back to us, Kitty. He's got to!'

Chapter Thirty-two

'We stand here in the house of God,' the speaker began. He waited for his audience to absorb this momentous reminder before going on gently, 'but I suspect that many of us are at this moment questioning his existence.'

A burst of rain pattered on to the leaden roof of the chapel like applause while the air grew still darker and the motionless flames of the four candles arranged in an oblong in the chancel seemed to brighten suddenly.

'I must confess, to my sadness, that I didn't know Max very well . . .'

There was a small shriek from somewhere in the church. It came from one of the young people, who were worst affected of all. It was not the admission that did it but the name. It was as heart-rending as the first awful sight of the coffin heaped with white flowers, conveyed very slowly up the aisle by

Anthony and Tom and Charlie and Phil, all ashen-faced. Beautiful Max, now broken and still, lay in that box. The speaker had been right. How could the Almighty have permitted such a thing?

'But –' Max's old drama teacher went on in a calm level voice, as if he'd decided it was best to ignore that involuntary cry of horror '– I'd like to share my memories of him, if I may.' He was a small tubby man, with white hair and glasses. His voice lifted as he described the Max he'd known. A lively boy full of enthusiasm, he said, and a startled hush, broken by occasional sniffles, settled over the chapel.

Several teachers at Max's old school had volunteered their services. It was usual, it seemed, when a young person died. The waste was so terrible and the grief so wild. How could any kind of order be maintained? Only an outsider – preferably stamped with authority – could attempt with gentle perseverance to set the tone for this most miserable of all funerals.

For the family had lost control this time. It was as if all the grief reined in for Henry's funeral had burst out in a roaring torrent. They hadn't mourned that first death as they should have and now they were paying the price. They were dismayed by themselves, and powerless. But, though they didn't know it, they were lucky because the only chance of getting over this terrible blow was to embrace it. They should relive the unfairness and the horror over and over again. Only then was there a chance of the suffering loosening its hold.

Kitty had never seen her family weep before: Hector gasping out noisy sobs as if trapped in a desperate fit of hiccups, her grandmother like an old white statue in the rain. For there could be nothing more tragic than the wasteful and messy death of a young person who'd failed to get his life together.

'Max was a wonderful actor . . .'

Kitty clutched Charlie's hand even tighter and turned to him with an expression of astonishment in her sore eyes. Charlie shook his head very slightly. No, he hadn't known either.

'I remember his splendidly sinister Master of Ceremonies in a production of *Goodbye to Berlin* we did in . . .' – again the drama teacher consulted his notes – '1967 . . .'

Max adorned with a charcoal moustache and wearing a black top hat . . . Max hamming it up with a guttural German accent . . . As the teacher vividly and expertly conjured up his old pupil's performance – a star turn, he said – a chuckle actually erupted in the chapel. It was as painfully involuntary as the shriek that had gone before and it united and soothed the mourners, even as it quite unreasonably shamed them.

The speaker was quietly satisfied as he stepped down. He'd achieved exactly what he'd hoped for.

Anthony thought wearily, 'Another school function I never got to,' and found himself hoping Camilla had been at least. But he doubted this. It was small wonder the teacher's revelations had come as such a surprise. They'd given Max everything, yet nothing.

They should have supported each other in their grief: temporarily shelved all bitterness and shared the same pew and maybe even, on this most significant and awful of days, held hands for comfort. Instead, the warring had escalated and when she'd shrieked down the phone at him that Max's death was entirely his fault, she hadn't even known about Jane. In her anguish, she'd insisted he be seated apart from the St Clairs, on the other side of the chapel, though everyone had tried to reason with her. It was horribly unfair, and an embarrassment, too – for it brought the tension between them into the spotlight. Anthony could feel the puzzlement of his friends, some of whom had scarcely known Max but had come out of kindness to support him.

Besides, there was no need to make him feel guilty.

'*I was absent*,' he told himself. '*For most of Max's childhood I was preoccupied with making money. And that car I gave him on his twenty-first – "that instrument of murder" as Camilla described it – was actually an apology.*' That was the fact of it. And now – in the most awful of ironies – at the very moment of Max's death, the wealth appeared to be fading away. '*I've no energy to fight*,' thought Anthony, shading his exhausted eyes. What had ever been the real point of that obscene pile of money, anyway? Phil was better off than Max had ever been, though he was too young – and presently far too angry – to appreciate it.

Anthony could see Jane's head, small in a black close-fitting hat, on the other side of the chapel, but felt very distanced from her – as if all thought of intimacy must be put on hold for a while. He'd read the knowledge of their secret in Kitty's evasive eyes and pieced together his own horrifying scenario. Liza upset and angry (and thinking only of her own feelings), bursting into the cosy company of cousins – 'You'll never guess what *I* know!'

Anthony knew that for the rest of his life, just like Liza, he'd be tormented by regret. But, as everyone here today was aware, Max had been a notoriously reckless driver. So far as they were concerned, he'd been fired only by the usual impatience as he slammed his foot hard down on the accelerator before the car spun out of control and, with a shriek of steel on steel, a final and terrible bang, concertinaed into a lamp-post on the Embankment.

Anthony tried to concentrate: to absorb each word so he would remember it. But he was back carrying the coffin up the aisle, the inexplicably heavy weight on his shoulder, very conscious of Max lying so still just an inch away from his cheek and thinking, '*When was the last time I carried my son in my arms?*'

Tom got up to read the first lesson – 'In my Father's house are many mansions' – and knew he'd been right to insist because, though he'd volunteered, his father was incapable of performing the task. Tom could identify collapse in the bowed posture, the face set in the grimmest of masks as if it would never again break up into a sweet smile. '*I'm the head of the family now*,' thought Tom, the only son by reason of another accident of fate, an earlier tragedy.

He shivered on his slow way to the lectern, past the ranks of relatives and friends in black. But it was not for Max. It was because, for just one moment, he experienced the heart-stopping terror of picturing his own son shut up in a long and narrow box in this still and musty place, with no chance of doing anything ever again: no opportunity to fail to become a brilliant advocate or break down in despair or even painstakingly and childishly construct matchstick houses.

He caught sight of Charlie – very pale, next to Kitty. He was taking this pitifully hard but, then, a deep gash had opened up in the foursome that had sustained them all for so long. In spite of his shortcomings, and the tensions and rivalries he'd provoked in that group, Max had been a very necessary part of it. Charlie had sobbed wretchedly as he carried his cousin up the aisle.

'*Nothing matters except this,*' thought Tom soberly, '*not success or money. Nothing. If Charlie really doesn't want to go on with the law – as he's just told us – then I shall put the very best face on it I can. I'll say to everyone that he was the most likely pupil to get that tenancy but it didn't suit him and I respected his feelings. And if he really decides to take a catering course – as he's suggested, to my absolute horror – then I shall tell the world that being a chef's a noble profession and I could not be more proud of him.*'

'*It's not so dreadful what's happened to us,*' Suki told herself as she sat dabbing at her eyes with a sodden handkerchief, made more emotional still by the avalanche of sighs and sobs all round her; and she hugged Phil's arm until he frowned and gently shook her off.

She caught the eye of Cousin Sarah across the aisle and found herself staring a little aggressively back.

Her immediate family had been very discreet. Even so, an item (probably leaked by the Met, thought Suki bitterly) had found its way into a gossip column. 'Police have questioned Simon Winslow-Carter about the disappearance of two expensive cars from the garage he runs in South London. Simon's wife, Suki, is a member of the distinguished St Clair family. Her father, Sir Lionel, is a High Court judge; her brother, Thomas, who specializes in criminal law, is one of our busiest QCs.'

Surrounded by tiers of more distant family, Suki imagined curiosity and pity in every glance. '*But we're lucky,*' she reminded herself and knew it to be true. '*Lucky lucky lucky to have our children healthy and safe – and each other, yes. And we'll get through this ordeal as a family. I know it now.*'

Simon would read the second lesson in his beautifully

modulated voice, with its echoes of a more prosperous time – 'Remember thy Creator in the days of thy youth when the evil days come not.' She appreciated that he was an actor in the same secret, accomplished way Max had been. He'd recovered himself now. He would continue to behave as he'd always done – with confidence and ease and even pride – as if he'd only done what a million men might have, in his position.

But if you behaved like an honourable person, thought Suki fiercely (adapting Camilla's guidelines for becoming a beauty), then people would believe it. As for her, she'd found a strength she'd never have believed possible. There was no doubt now which was the strong one and who needed protection.

Lionel sat next to Eleanor and ached with sadness for them both and thought about the extraordinary events of the evening before.

They'd had a better than average dinner at seven thirty as usual (Mrs Percival had been very sympathetic in her fashion) and then they'd played Scrabble, as was their habit, because it seemed to be the only way to endure this horror. And after about half an hour of silent playing, they'd seen the awful coincidence of the words spelt out – 'split' . . . 'pain' . . . 'bones' . . .

Eleanor had gone very pale.

'My dear,' Lionel began, as if the words burst from him.

'I cannot . . .' Eleanor began, shaking her head rapidly as though terrified of what he might say.

'I know,' he murmured soothingly, but looked at her very steadily as if silently urging her to continue.

She seemed to make a great effort before asking pitifully, 'Is this our fault?'

He'd looked around him at the grand but shabby room stuffed with photographs and trophies and other reminders of what had been most important to them in their lives and would remain so.

'No,' he'd said fiercely, 'it is not.'

'Mine, then?' He couldn't believe it was Eleanor who said it: she who'd always appeared so certain of herself. More astonishing still, she was continuing to spell out words though the game had, of course, been abandoned. 'Savage,' she told him rapidly with her knobbly arthritic fingers, her thin old wedding ring embedded in the flesh after almost half a century of wear. 'Bitter . . . Heartbroken.'

'Max was . . .' His voice had tailed away.

She'd looked up sharply. Did he really believe he could tell her something she did not already know? 'Cursed,' she'd spelt out unsteadily.

But he'd shaken his head. 'Not destined to be long in this world,' he'd amended sadly. 'Some souls aren't. And Camilla . . .'

Eleanor had taken a D and two O's and an M and an E – looking at Lionel all the while with the same hesitant terrified expression before he stopped her.

'No,' he went on very firmly, keeping the D but removing the other letters, reassuring his beloved wife, 'Camilla is our daughter.'

Camilla's expensive wide-brimmed black hat with its pretty spotted veil didn't go with the bright red (and not particularly clean) suit she was wearing. Some of the relatives, in uniform dusty black, believed her choice of costume indicated a desire to celebrate Max's life rather than mourn his death. They applauded her courage, they conveyed in meaning looks, even though they themselves wouldn't have reacted like that. But a grieving mother was entitled to behave as she wished and Camilla had always had a mind of her own.

Under her veil, however, Camilla looked surprisingly composed: the sole mourner managing to keep up some sort of a front. The only time she seemed to waver was when her glance lit on Anthony, very white and subdued on the other side of the church. Then, her eyes glittered. But the family forgave her for the venom, too. She'd just lost her precious only child. They surrounded her like a black fence as together they all endured the slow shuffle shuffle shuffle of Max's coffin being carried past, the sight of all the living young people, the sharp pain of the music.

Lionel looked at her with brimming approving eyes as they knelt through the comforting magic jumble of prayers. She was doing magnificently.

Liza huddled close to her mother for comfort.

'*It's all my fault!*' She'd said it over and over again – Liza, whose usual cry was just the opposite.

'Hush!' Jane had comforted her. 'You know how Max was!'

The sadness was, she'd explained, that Max, who might have changed, would remain forever the person who'd died – beautiful but damaged, motiveless and reckless. It was amazing really that he'd survived for so long, she went on, trying to make it better for Liza.

At the same time, she'd thought soberly, '*This has to be the making of her.*'

Liza was too stormy for her own good – too jealous and

ambitious and impetuous. She had to change and it seemed to Jane that she knew it herself.

For the moment, though, she'd reverted to being a child: clinging to security, so frightened and guilty that she'd told nobody what had really happened and (to Jane's great relief) hadn't yet asked her any direct questions either.

It had been Kitty's radical suggestion to play 'Knocking on Heaven's Door' even though the music had bad memories. Max had played it the night he'd sworn at her, driving home from her parents. 'He loved it,' she'd assured the family. She wasn't even sure if this was true but there had to be a personal element at the service, otherwise it would just be the stuff they all wanted at their own funerals. So they'd given in and imported a record player, even though Eleanor had wanted Fauré's *Requiem*. And now it was too much. Of course it was. She saw the family re-read their programmes in disbelief, fresh tears starting with the title.

'Who are they?' Kitty whispered into Charlie's ear as the coffin started its agonizing procession back down the aisle, out of time with the music, like a silent protest by the pall-bearers – because, by then, she'd noticed the strange young people who'd appeared at the back of the chapel. It would have been impossible not to.

He shrugged. He'd no idea either.

'Friends?' she mouthed.

Charlie looked surprised, meaning, '*Did he have friends?*'

Kitty raised her eyebrows in dismay.

'*Besides us,*' he amended with a slight shake of the head, a blink.

'*I* never met any,' she whispered.
'We'll find out.'

At the graveside, silently, like travelling mime artists, they introduced themselves. A pretty blonde in a clinging low-cut dress of vivid yellow velvet kissed a red rose before tossing it into the deep oblong hole the coffin had been lowered into; a young man almost as dark and handsome as Max uncorked a bottle of brandy produced from a pocket and solemnly emptied it after the rose; and another young man, bearded and slender in a pale green waistcoat, produced a flute and pierced the mournful air with reedy quavering notes that seemed to go on for ever.

The St Clairs tolerated all this out of ingrained courtesy, though secretly annoyed and offended by the presump-tuousness. But as they watched and listened, their attitude softened. The fact was, the drama of all this made the terrible business of the interment more bearable. It was because these exotically dressed young strangers were acting as if Max could still receive a kiss or listen to a tuneless dirge composed in his honour or even enjoy a drink. (It had been Courvoisier, Tom couldn't help noticing, though it was all destined to go to waste.)

Afterwards, it was Suki who broke away from the family group and informed the unexpected visitors a little shyly, 'There's tea in the house.'

'Tea?'

'Yes. And sherry.'

'Yeah?'

They acted as if this offer of hospitality was a great surprise. They didn't sound like any of the St Clairs.

'Are you his –?' the girl in yellow began with a wary expression.

'No,' said Suki very definitely, at the same time as noticing that the girl wasn't wearing a bra. She decided it would not be a sensible idea to introduce them to Camilla, so she continued rapidly in a light social way: 'Where have you all come from?'

What she really meant was: 'How did you happen to know Max?' She guessed that, most probably, they'd learnt about the funeral from the notice in *The Times* – though it was not easy to envisage them buying any sort of a newspaper.

'Streatham,' said the girl in yellow. 'Well, Geoff's originally from Brighton and Paul's . . .'

'No fixed address,' said the flute-player with a wink.

'. . . but we've come from, like, London?'

'We missed the turn-off,' said Geoff, the one who'd poured brandy into the grave. 'Been travelling for hours.'

'You must be exhausted,' muttered Suki automatically.

'Cassandra's fault,' said Paul. 'Can't map-read to save her life.'

'Well, it's awfully good of you to have come all this way,' Suki gushed. 'We do appreciate it!'

Once more they looked taken aback, as if she'd spoken in a foreign tongue.

It was lucky the grandparents' house was so spacious. It meant that Camilla could be contained in the enormous square hall, guarded by the buffalo head and the grandfather clock, where refreshments had been laid out, while Anthony could sit quietly in a corner of the drawing-room, where the fire had been lit, in the company of Max's former drama teacher.

'Thank you,' he told him.

'For what?' the teacher asked gently.

Anthony stared miserably at the glowing logs.

Kitty approached with a plate of cucumber sandwiches. She'd come straight from offering them to Camilla. It was like carrying a message – '*Talk to each other, for God's sake!*' – but he shook his head just as Camilla had done.

'I was just telling Max's father what a good lad he was,' the teacher informed Kitty and she found herself sitting down with them, though she hadn't intended to.

Since his ex-communication from the family, Uncle Ant had assumed the persona of a Bluebeard – and they didn't even know about the latest scandal, thought Kitty. Uncle Ant, who'd lost his only child (*and* his money, Kitty had heard one of the relatives whisper) and looked dreadful. All his familiar cheery energy had gone. Kitty couldn't imagine him having an affair with anyone now. But beneath the grief, he seemed exactly the same generous and kindly relative she'd always known. She even felt emboldened to touch his hand in silent sympathy – and was a little taken aback when he imprisoned hers and refused to let it go.

Uncle Hector had recovered himself a little now that the worst bit of the day was over. Also, he'd broken the rule of a lifetime and had a sherry well before the drinks hour. He felt a little foolish and vulnerable, having lost control like that in the chapel, but now he was discussing with Lionel the excellent idea that had come to him.

'A sum of money towards a prize, in his name.'

Lionel focused his attention. 'And what exactly would it be for?'

'What's that?'

Lionel repeated the question, much louder.

'Acting,' Uncle Hector sounded very proud of himself. At last Max had been passionate about something. They'd all heard it, in the chapel.

'Acting,' Lionel repeated ponderously and very doubtfully. He, too, had been delighted to learn that Max had once excelled at drama. But he'd not taken the talent further. And even if he had, he pointed out, there'd never before been an actor in the family. He scowled. 'Wouldn't it be more sensible to make it legal? After all . . .' He and Hector knew each other so well it wasn't even necessary to complete the sentence: '. . . *Max might have gone on to be someone.*'

Death was the end. But it could also create possibilities that might never have existed in life.

Liza told the handsome young man who'd poured brandy into the grave: 'I absolutely have to make it now!'

'Yeah?'

'For his sake,' Liza went on rapidly. She was very overwrought (and unaware that her mother was watching her anxiously from the other side of the hall).

'Good old Max.'

From now on, Liza explained with passion, her whole life would be devoted to success – with each separate triumph every step of the way dedicated to the memory of her cousin. It was the only way to expunge the guilt, though she didn't say this: forget how Max had looked as he'd slammed out of the flat for the last time. For him, she would sacrifice all thoughts of marriage and children. From now on, she announced to the young man, she would live solely for art. But, even as she outlined the ambition, it struck her as narrow, with a vast new emptiness at its heart.

'You shoulda sung to him,' he commented laconically.

Liza looked suddenly alert and anxious. 'Just now, you mean?'

'Yeah!'

'Do you think?' It had not occurred to her. Besides, her mother would have disapproved, for sure.

'Go for it.'

She hesitated. Art demanded a live audience. Besides, it was getting dark and she didn't fancy the idea of going back to the graveyard on her own. She thought of Pa and Max, out there together in the dying light. Her father had once called his nephew a wastrel. And, though he'd never said so, of course she knew Max had considered her father a stuffed shirt.

For the first time in her short life, she was terribly conscious of her own mortality.

'Do it for me, too,' said the young man, picking up a full glass of sherry and grabbing a bunch of sandwiches from a passing plate. He was very handsome.

'Jane.'

'Camilla.'

Jane had been trying to avoid this confrontation and now she waited with fearful dread for what Camilla would say next. She felt that, however much she affected to be unaware of Anthony, her link with him was screaming to be noticed – especially by one so vigilant. At the same time, she ached with sympathy for Camilla, who scared her, but had just watched her only child being buried.

'It seems there was a special girlfriend.' Under the black veil, her eyes looked hot. They seemed to be deliberately avoiding Jane's: searching for Anthony in the distance.

'Sorry?'

'And I never even knew about it.'

'Sorry . . .' This time, Jane said it so faintly that she could scarcely be heard.

Camilla snorted. 'It was outrageous!'

Jane flinched, thinking, '*Any minute now she might smash that glass she's holding just like she smashed Anthony's plates.*' She could feel violence trembling in the air. '*She might even shove it in my face!*'

'That obscene pantomime outside with the rose! Anyway, I don't believe a word of it!'

'Sorry?' asked Jane with a new energy.

'Is that all you can say?' demanded Camilla very irritably. 'Didn't Liza tell you?'

'Liza didn't know,' said Jane very definitely, pulling herself together.

Nobody had known. But now the blonde in the inappropriate and very revealing yellow velvet dress was making sure the important ones did.

Kitty was next.

'You're Kitty, aren't you?' She smiled very charmingly. 'I said to myself "That's Kitty," cos you're just like Max said.'

'Me?' Kitty felt very defensive.

'Lovely eyes?' The girl nodded as if she could only agree.

Kitty felt absurdly pleased, while reflecting, '*He wouldn't say that now.*' She could hardly raise her lids because of the grief. '*I look like a currant bun.*'

By contrast, the blonde appeared very fresh and composed: at ease with the terrible situation as if Max was only in the next room, rather than lifeless in the graveyard.

'He never said, like, about this?' The girl waved a hand

studded with silver rings at the enormous house, the old
inherited furniture, and Mrs Percival bustling in and out with
freshly filled plates.

'Didn't he?' Kitty was unsurprised. Max had always been
secretive.

'I came to your flat once?'

Kitty became instantly alert.

'Chepstow Place?' It seemed she turned every statement into
a question as if uncertain of its reception.

'When?' Kitty asked, looking strangely anxious.

The girl pondered. There was a silver star on her forehead
and glitter round her eyes that caught the light with every
movement. She'd probably pasted it all on especially. 'Like, two
months ago?'

'You didn't stay the whole night,' said Kitty, doing the
opposite to the girl: making a very definite statement because
already she knew the answer.

'He wouldn't let me.' There was no question about that.
She laughed, though, as if it had been unimportant. 'He
picked me up at midnight,' she told Kitty. It was strange the
way he'd arrived without warning in his car. He'd told her he
wanted to take her back to his flat, which he'd never done
before – they'd always met at her place. 'Like he wanted to
prove something?'

She was the one Max had chosen. No wonder she'd striven
to look her best for his funeral.

'Are you all right?' asked Jane in a low voice.

Anthony gave a faint smile as he shook his head. He was
managing, in the circumstances. He said just as softly, 'My
car's outside, waiting to take me back to London. But I want

to have one last look. Will you come with me?'

Jane was about to refuse as gently as possible. It would not be wise, given Anthony's reputation and with all the family there. But nobody was watching them – not even Camilla, who was talking to the girl in yellow. She'd pinned her against a wall. She seemed to be firing question after question at her. And Liza was similarly absorbed in the dark young man. (They'd disappeared a moment ago, but now they were back, Liza flushed and seemingly happier.) So, without another word, Jane followed Anthony.

It was cool and quiet in the graveyard: like entering a room used only for special occasions. They could hear the decorous sound of the funeral party in the distance. On one side of them was the chapel – as dark as the house was glowing, as empty as it was crowded.

In the dim light, they could make out the rest of the freshly turned soil that would be shovelled into Max's grave the following morning by the sexton – and an odd pale triangle shape laid on it very neatly as if on purpose.

Anthony bent closer. 'A cucumber sandwich?' For a moment, he sounded as uncertain as the girl in yellow. Then he understood. Just like the brandy, it symbolized sustenance for the next world.

Jane said: 'You're thinking that he's been taken from you, aren't you? That the family have moved in, just like after Henry's death?'

She saw him look at her, a little scared, before he nodded.

'But you have to know that he'll be properly taken care of here – just as he should be. No one could do it better.'

Anthony let out an involuntary sob, as if he could hardly bear to think of this.

'Listen,' Jane went on very soothingly, as if she hadn't noticed, 'I want to tell you that every Sunday morning there'll be freshly cut flowers for him – white – just as there have always been for Henry. This whole garden will be geared to produce those flowers, week after week, month after month, year after year. There'll be roses and lilies for him in the summer when there's a mass of blooms to choose from, chrysanthemums in the autumn when the garden is dying, hawthorn and witch hazel when it's all empty and bleak and frosty. His grave will never be bare. You can count on that.'

'Thank you,' Anthony muttered.

'And there's no chance of them giving up on him. You have to know that, too. Because of Max, they'll stay here till the end. You see, even if they wanted to sell the house one day, Tom wouldn't allow it. I just heard him say so. Really.'

Anthony made another noise in his throat but she continued steadfastly.

'He'll take care of them, make sure they go on having people to help them even when Mrs Percival and Mr Blackstock have retired. And when they've finally joined Henry and Max, I wouldn't be a bit surprised if Tom doesn't move here himself. You see, the house is different for him now.'

She knew she was right. The past had taken root here in this place that Tom had always until now treated as second best and dispensable. He respected the force of it at last.

'And they're not really against you,' said Jane, who had watched Anthony attend the funeral of his own son like a lonely ghost.

He turned his white face to her in the dusk. 'Aren't they?'

She shook her head. 'They always loved you. You're still the same person.' She paused. 'You might not be a St Clair. But they know what she's like really.'

'I wonder . . .'

'Of course they do!' *They just refused to recognize it*, thought Jane, *because it was too uncomfortable*. Camilla was highly strung, volatile – anything but hysterical and possibly unhinged. They'd listened to her lies because she was blood and it was easier and Anthony had always been different; but with each day that passed, they must surely doubt her more. It was lucky the family was large and eclectic enough for containment. It helped that eccentricity was common in their world. And, besides, hadn't Charlie's wobble demonstrated that unpredictability and fragility could lurk in them all? For as long as they possibly could, they'd continue making excuses for poor Camilla, who'd lost everything now.

'I just wish . . .' Anthony began.

'Me too.' It would be a long time before they could forget what a terrible chain of reaction had been set in motion when they began their love affair.

'I need to think for a bit,' he said gently as if she needed persuading. 'Be on my own for a while.'

'I understand.'

'Really?'

'Of course I do.'

'And then I'd like us to meet,' he went on, as if he'd all of a sudden changed his mind.

'I'll wait,' she told him, even though she suspected in her heart that this might be the end. What sort of relationship – what kind of people – could survive this?

But, in some curious way, she thought, it might not matter.

Their love affair had brought her finally back to life and there would remain a deep gratitude that it had happened.

She saw him glance round carefully and very nervously. Obviously, it would be imprudent to give her a kiss. But he was going to do it anyway.

Chapter Thirty-three

Kitty said with a tremor in her voice, 'For me, he'll always be here.'

'Yes,' Charlie agreed. 'More so than anywhere.'

They could feel Max somewhere out there in the darkness because they couldn't bear to think otherwise. Despite the finality of what they'd witnessed, they waited for him to make an entrance. It was foolish, of course – and they knew this even as they acknowledged that no pain could ever again be so intense – but it seemed strangely possible since learning about the acting. Max was capable of surprise. 'He will come, won't he?' Charlie had asked Kitty in this very place, back in the summer. 'I think so,' she'd said, even though she hadn't believed it at all.

'We'd got back to how we were,' she told Charlie very determinedly, almost certainly not for the last time. He understood that it had to be seen as a comfort rather than a grief that, right at the end, she and Max had reclaimed their old closeness. Nor must any doubt be cast on the genuineness of his behaviour that last evening. He was sorry for everything, said Kitty, although, typically, he'd been unable to say so. This was the Max she'd remember. She was making sure of it.

She'd come back to Cedar Manor for the night at Uncle Hector's invitation; and now that dinner was over and their great-uncle had gone to bed, the two cousins were perched on the haybales in the barn. Still in their funeral clothes, they were absorbed by the night: as invisible, for the moment, as Max had become. They breathed in the familiar sweet and musty smell that had always meant safety and happiness, feeling their ears tingle as unseen bats flitted precisely around them and listening to the occasional mournful hooting of the tawny owl perched on the branches of the old cedar tree.

'He won't be able to do that in two days,' said Charlie.

'No,' she agreed, catching Charlie's drift, like always. He'd told her earlier that, in two days' time, the cedar was to be cut down. Uncle Hector was distraught, couldn't bear even to talk about it. 'But why?' she asked.

'You know what he's like,' said Charlie. Even though the tree stood on its own in a clearing, it would have to come down. It was immaterial that it still looked strong and healthy. The disease was eating at its heart.

'But where will he sit?'

'He'll keep on coming back for a while, he'll be really puzzled to find it gone, he'll probably fly round and round in circles. And then I suppose he'll get used to it and find another place he likes.' For some reason, Charlie started thinking of how Uncle Hector still complained of cramp in the toes of his right leg even though they'd been missing for nearly thirty-five years now.

'Do you think,' asked Kitty, moving on in her fashion, 'that she really was his girlfriend?'

'We'll never know . . .'

'What about the others?'

'They did come to the funeral.'

Paul and Geoff had certainly claimed real friendship with Max. If they were to be believed, he'd met with them nearly every day in the Fox and Goose around the corner (though so far as Kitty and Charlie knew, Max hadn't frequented pubs). Good old Max, they'd said fondly. Lovely chap. Funny as hell. They wouldn't have missed paying their last respects for anything.

They'd spoken about him in a strangely proprietorial way. Max had had plans, said Geoff authoritatively. 'What sort of plans?' Charlie had asked curiously. 'Just – things he wanted to do.' Geoff had frowned a little as he said it, as if Charlie had implied some sort of criticism, and not only of Max. 'He was very talented.'

On leaving, Paul had unapologetically touched Charlie for a loan. Well, it wasn't really, he'd explained, looking Charlie straight in the eye, because Max had borrowed the cash off him. Ten quid. There was no way of proving it, even though Max had always had money. Of course Charlie had paid up.

A set of teaspoons had gone missing, Eleanor murmured when the funeral was over. But, as it transpired, Mrs Percival had never put them out in the first place. However, the point had been made that the surprise visitors – 'Max's funny little friends' – looked the sort of people who might have pocketed the family silver.

*

'You'll have things you want to talk about,' Uncle Hector had pronounced as he set off for bed earlier than usual. He'd looked at Charlie with meaning, pressed his shoulder as if to impart courage.

All through that muted dinner, his eyes had glistened while he watched them, as if witnessing their contentment in each other's company was another sadness on this most distressing of days. Ranks of family had sat at his dining-table through the years: a rolling selection of nephews and nieces and cousins, near and far, followed in time by their children. Despite the regular injections of new blood, he'd seen the family likeness pass through like a trail of sand – with the occasional startling exception such as Max had been. He could see Suki and Tom in these two, who were so special to him: Suki when young and unprotected, Tom with his sensitivity bared. Who could miss children of their own when privileged with company like this?

As he'd watched them chat across the candlelit table, appreciating the flavour if not the full meaning of their conversation, he'd marvelled at how much easier it was to be young these days. Oh, definitely! – despite their complaints about pressure to achieve, pressure to get married. He'd been a success in his business all right and few men were so widely and deeply loved, as Tom had pointed out in his speech at the birthday party. Even so, he felt as if all of his life he'd looked at other people's happiness from behind bars. But, if he was honest, something in him had shrunk away from intimacy, perhaps even been grateful for the excuse not to have been put to the test.

'We should talk,' said Charlie a little nervously.

It felt wonderful to be with Kitty again: all his old affection for her had come rushing back. He was learning to stand up for himself, wasn't he? He'd informed his father he wanted to leave the bar, so who said he couldn't defy Uncle Hector, too? But, even as he contemplated this, Charlie recognized that Uncle Hector was the personification of the family as well as someone he was greatly indebted to.

He and Kitty hadn't even kissed yet and it was a little surprising now that they were alone together in this private and significant place. It was as if each waited for the other to make the first move.

He lay back on the hay for a moment in his black suit as if encouraging Kitty to take the initiative once more and then sat up abruptly, as if chastising himself. They should talk. He'd just said so, hadn't he? But the truth was, he couldn't bear the thought of hurting her.

Kitty said, 'Are you really okay now, Charlie?'

'Oh yes!' he said very definitely. 'It was just a blip. I get this panicky feeling sometimes, a kind of squeezing thing in my head, but it's only when I think about going back to the chambers.'

Kitty sighed as if very relieved. As she saw it, Charlie hadn't felt able to express rebellion and so his body had silently done it for him instead. After a moment, she asked: 'And is your pa really okay about things?'

'Think so. Actually he's been brilliant. Says I can stay here for as long as I like and then we'll talk.' Charlie made a gloomy face in the dark because he wasn't particularly looking forward to more discussions with his father, however understanding and positive he was striving to be. He'd had a change of heart and was now thinking he might like to become a carpenter. He pictured his father fighting back irritation – he hated indecisiveness – saying, 'But I've told everyone you're going to be a chef!'

Kitty thought about her uncle at the funeral: of how kind and supportive he'd been to all the relatives, including Camilla, and how old and frail her grandfather and Uncle Hector had suddenly appeared. Uncle Tom had organized everything, been so unusually thoughtful. '*I might even go to him myself*,' thought Kitty, who'd decided that she, too, needed to rethink her future. She wanted a real career, she'd tell him. And he'd give good practical advice, even if unable to shake off all his old bossiness. 'Let's try and think of your good points,' he'd probably say with a frown. If she felt brave enough, she might even confide a secret but growing ambition to take up the career Charlie had abandoned.

She said abruptly: 'I'm sorry, Charlie, but I can't marry you.'

'Ah!'

'The thing is, I've had time to think now and I've realized it wouldn't be right for either of us.'

'Ah!' said Charlie again and Kitty stopped for a moment, puzzled, because for the first time she couldn't guess what he was thinking. The fact was, she'd expected him to sound far more disappointed.

'The thing is,' said Kitty. 'I'm not sure I want to get married yet. I'm only twenty-three – well, *nearly* twenty-four – and besides . . .'

She felt the hay rustle as he turned towards her in the dark, as if he was listening intently now.

'I think we know each other too well.'

Did Charlie agree or disagree? He was strangely silent.

'When you fall in love,' Kitty went on gently as if still

convinced she needed to approach this very carefully, 'half of the thrill of it's anticipation, isn't it? Because it should be an adventure . . . Wondering what it'd be like to get into someone's soul, wondering what you might find there . . . I mean, it could be bad . . .' Kitty winced, remembering some of the worthless men she'd been out with, 'but I think love should always be about hope.'

'Maybe,' said Charlie slowly.

'But how can you have those feelings when you already know everything about a person?'

'I suppose . . .'

'You and me, Cuz . . . I know exactly how you drink your tea in the mornings – you always leave about two inches, did you know that? And how you arrange your toothbrush after you've done your teeth – upside down in your mug. And what you say when it's time to go to bed – did you know it's always "Think I'll turn in, actually"? Oh Charlie, I'm not making fun of you. I know you could say precisely the same about me.' She laughed. 'It's sort of like we've already been married for years and years, isn't it?' She thought of her parents, who could hold entire conversations while saying almost nothing. 'I mean, it's really nice, in a way, to think of being that close to someone and it always will be. But I can't marry you. And, Charlie, I don't know what you were *doing* telling everyone at the party.'

'I don't know either,' said Charlie. 'A moment of madness?' But she knew he hadn't meant it to sound unkind.

'So you're not . . .?'

'It's fine.'

'Honestly?' Quite unreasonably, she felt a little cheated. She'd have hated to upset him, but even so . . .

'Absolutely honestly,' said Charlie, sounding perfectly content.

Charlie thought, 'That's that, then!' and felt a quite unjustifiable chagrin mixed in with the relief. Kitty hadn't wanted to marry him, after all. Women! Okay, he'd blurted out his suggestion that night just before Max had turned up at Chepstow Place, but it was Kitty who'd got the two of them into bed.

He wouldn't have to explain at all now. He could honour his promise to Uncle Hector. Ironically, as it had turned out, Uncle Hector hadn't even needed to tell him the secret in the first place.

Then the tawny owl hooted despondently in the doomed cedar tree and Charlie was reminded of the sin that had been committed against his long-dead relative. Great-Aunt Nancy was perhaps the most interesting St Clair who'd ever existed and yet, to discourage awkward questions, her photographs were hidden away and her considerable accomplishments not even mentioned. A reader of Uncle Hector's monograph on the family would assume that her brief life was typical of her class and era. Poor brilliant Nancy, whose only crimes had been to lose her mind and then allow herself to be murdered.

Charlie thought a little indignantly, '*If I had gone completely off my rocker, would they be pretending I didn't exist?*' For a moment, he saw himself shut away in an upstairs room in one of the country houses, gathering wrinkles – another dark embarrassment to the family.

But this was almost 1975, for God's sake! They lived in far healthier times, didn't they? He might tell Kitty about Great-Aunt Nancy, anyway. He'd no idea where she was buried – it was another family secret – but it seemed to him that revealing her story at last might feel like laying flowers on her grave.

'Kitty . . .' he began.

'Mmm?'

Uncle Hector had warned with great significance: 'This is between you and me, Charlie.' He'd only shared the confidence, he had explained, because he'd felt obliged to. And now, after that brief unhappy display, it must be put away like an ancient garment re-interred in faded tissue paper. It was for the best. Charlie must surely appreciate that. Best for his beloved long-dead sister, too – though Uncle Hector didn't say this – not to mention the whole pressing weight of the family.

'What, Charlie?' Kitty pursued, and – for the second time that night – had no idea what was really going through her cousin's mind.

But Charlie still hesitated to tell her the truth, even as the tawny owl hooted once more, outside in the blackness.

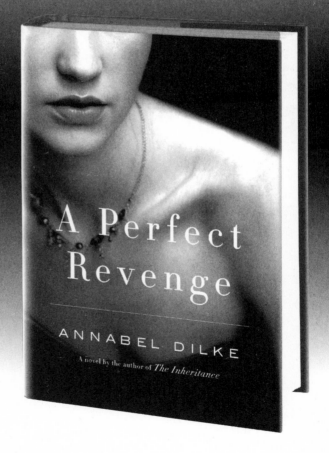